PLEASANT
HELL

John Dolan

Format & Design Copyright © 2005 by
Capricorn Publishing, Inc.
Cover Design by Dasha Mol'

ISBN: 0-9753970-4-4

Published in the United States and Great Britain by
Capricorn Publishing, Inc., in 2005

Capricorn Publishing
www.CapricornPublishing.com

1

My first year here, I used to walk out to the cliffs to visit the coastal fortifications. Stand inside the gun-emplacements firing back at where I came from, little exploding noises out the side of my mouth.

No one else ever seemed to notice them. There wasn't even any graffiti. It amazed me, these things lying there unfilmed. If any coastline in California had been so beautifully sculpted for war, they'd be filming there every day. But here—nothing. For a long time I didn't get it. Now I think I understand: this is "Peace."

Ten miles offshore is the war. Unfilmed too, unnoticed. It's been going on God knows how long, and it doesn't matter to anyone. Out there where the continental shelf drops off to the mid-ocean trench, there's an upwelling of "cold, nutrient-rich" Antarctic water. Every year the squid come to meet it. Squid by the billion. More squid than God could count. They feed, mate and die, in that order. For a few weeks the water is paved with squid, a Sargasso Sea of animate sashimi squirting DNA around in little clouds of egg and sperm. Then, having donated their genetic wills to the general fund, the squid just die. And drift slowly down, falling for days till they settle on the mud, fuzzy with decay, patiently lying still until they can be vacuumed up by the grotesque bottom-feeders of mid-ocean, creatures from Lovecraft's worst nightmares.

This has been going on for—oh, roughly speaking, "forever." And nobody films it. Nobody notices it at all, except for a few

local biologists and the Korean fishing boats. The Koreans show
up on schedule every year, like carnies making their annual scam-
visit to a hick town. They're old pros, Barnums who know exactly
how to attract the squid with banks of light so bright that from
our dank little town it looks there's a Vegas-style strip operating
offshore, just over the horizon.

There isn't. Just grimy rusting Korean squid-boats with banks
of searing megawatt lights hung out on either side, and nets to
haul in the galaxies of dying squid sliding around under the lights,
queuing up to get killed. The squid stoically mate and die; the
Koreans glumly harvest the squid; the birds come and eat the dead
and dying squid; the local science-column devotes a paragraph to
the "fascinating" life cycle of "these remarkable animals"—and
that's it.

Last year I actually did the math and figured out that the *Otago
Daily Times* allots this hecatomb approximately one column-inch
per billion dead squid. And those inches are not exactly high-rent.
After all, the front pages have to be saved for the big stories, like
"Sheep Injured" or "Local Couple Married 2,000 Years." The
Squids' obit is printed on the back page, alongside the letters to
the editor—a morbidly interesting selection usually featuring
something by this loony Creationist who goes by the valorous
pen-name "Canny Scot," and insists on disputing the fossil record
with a hippie expat in our Biology Department. In his latest,
"Canny Scot" asks how we can fail to see the evidence of God's
plan in "the world of Nature all around us."

I say tie him to the light-rigs of one of the squid boats. Facing
down. With his squinty old "canny" eyes tweezed open like the
guy in Clockwork Orange. Keep him out there all night, while the
sullen Koreans try to process the billions of mindless, eager squid
squirting around under the lights, trying to crowd into the nets:
"Duh . . . me first! Me first!" Let him spend the night looking
down into that squirming mass of eager, gelid protoplasm sliding
and flopping around, gleaming in the million-watt lights . . .
animate jelly so thick you could stroll around the boat on it,
bouncing along like kids on those McDonald's PlayZones filled
waist-high with colored ping-pong balls . . . walking on water,
buoyed by several million squid-per-square-foot . . . bouncing over

slurpy tubes all eager to get closer to the nets, avidly fouling the water with milt and eggs, all trying for a ticket into the net.

And the Koreans smoking cheap Russian cigarettes to stay awake, then spitting back in the water—so that some Japanese office worker a year from now can scowl at his mute wifeling, "You made the squid taste like cheap Russian cigarettes again, stupid wife!"

Let "Canny Scot" have a good look at God's plan from the vantage point of a light-pole off the side of this squid-boat. Let him look down into that writhing, pulsing water and see in it God's divine plan for this antipodean Alcatraz. Let him see how much we matter in the grand scheme. Rope him tight to that light-pole and keep him out there facing the water all night, drooling half-frozen ropes of spittle. Let him have a good long look at God's plan.

In fact, let him stay out there, ten yards out the side of the boat, while it steams back to harbor here. A little fresh ocean spray will do him good. Taste God's cold pickled water. Smell God's cheap diesel fumes. Watch God's choppy waves for ten hours, spewing God's fish-and-chips into the chop at intervals. Then when the boat reaches harbor, untie him and let him drop to the smelly concrete dock. Let him commune with the old stains of fish-blood around the gutting table. See if those stinking old stains form a grand pattern in the concrete. Pry his mouth open—knock some of the rime off it—and jam his false teeth back into place, then ask him about God's plan for this place.

I can tell you God's plan for this place very concisely: *God created this place as a critique of me.*

A week ago I found out that they're actually making t-shirts against me. I was minding my own business, walking across campus innocently whispering "It's not my fault, It's not my fault!"—a nice normal day, in other words—when I was grabbed and pulled into a doorway by this little neo-medieval nerd I vaguely recognized from last year's course. I gave him a B-minus, if I remember correctly—which means I probably destroyed his lifelong dream of becoming a doctor. (They need an A in my course or they don't get to go on to the second year of med school.) So I didn't blame him for savoring this opportunity to tell me bad news. I don't blame him, or for that matter any of them; I'd just rather they didn't exist.

He pulls me into this doorway and warns me in a conspiratorial whisper, "Uh-h . . ."—looks around for eaves-droppers—"I thought I'd better warn you: they're making t-shirts against you . . . against English 124!"

English 124 is the compulsory "Communication" course I was imported to teach to 700 unwilling med students from all over the Commonwealth. They hate it. They hate me. They hate the whole package. You can actually calculate the amount of hatred focused on me if you set it up as a story-problem:

If an imported Communications professor teaches 700 students per year, and every one of them hates his guts, how many students will hate his guts after three years?

Yes? You, with your hand raised: how many?

That's right, "2100": *At the end of three years on this rock in a freezing ocean, he will be hated by 2100 students.*

Not counting this year's crop. Include them and I'm inching up toward the 3,000 mark. If (X) equals the amount of hate a single student generates, staring down at me when I teach in the pit of that huge auditorium, then my life equals (X) times 700, times four years.

No matter how little value you assign to (X), you get a pretty substantial figure. It was almost big enough to finish me off, that first year. That one was close. I keep trying to tell myself it's not so bad any more, that they don't really hate it or me so much. But every time I convince myself, another little bomb goes off, another Indian arrow thwacks into the wall two inches from my head. Like this little news item, the voodoo t-shirts directed against me. Rebellion by t-shirt. What next, the Black Spot shoved in my hand by a passing pirate? Two pounds of semtex wired to the ignition of my Subaru?

I started groaning when the little informer told me about the t-shirts. Mistake! His smile got instantly broader and happier when he saw my terror. They can smell fear.

I tried to get details from him: "—Where?—What shirts?—Who?"

He looked very solemn, very self-consciously honorable, and said, "I can't tell you who. Just—in the student hostels. A lot of people . . ."

"Oh God . . ."

He stared up at me solemnly, a little Titus Oates, so proud of having this inside info about The Papist T-Shirt Plot. A hint of his pleasure in giving me the bad news shone in his face. He was enjoying this moment in all kinds of ways: savoring my guilty terror; feeling noble for warning me; and glorying in the notion of himself as secret courier. He thinks he's in some Jacobite conspiracy, whispering secret intelligence to Bonnie Prince Charlie i.e. Bonnie Prince Me.

I know those nerd dreams of valor and intrigue so well! This guy's about five-eight, with cokebottle glasses and buck teeth— but I know that he has superimposed on this ludicrous encounter a scene from some medieval war film, where the rebels whisper secret information in dark doorways before storming the town. I bet he believes with all his heart that he would've done well at Agincourt . . . well, so would I, little fool! Little kinsman . . . But we don't get Agincourt anymore, kid, we get this: this career anxiety, this unlovely terror at the podium, this humming voodoo-death-ray generated by 700 crazed adolescents.

And for that matter, the career-terrors are way harder to endure than Agincourt could've been. Since facing the med students, I've decided that the knights were wimps. The arrow cloud at Agincourt was nothing compared to the voodoo-death-stares every Monday evening!—And not just once but twice, because I have to repeat the 5:00 lecture for another shift of paranoid adolescents at 7:00. Let's see the flower of French chivalry do two Agincourts in one day! And each of my lectures lasts 50 minutes, which adds up to a total of 100 minutes per week being subjected to the arrow-cloud of angry med students' death-stares. Let's see Roland or Richard the Lion-Hearted face that! Then they can talk about how lion-hearted they are.

But in the meantime there was this little snitch to deal with. Couldn't stand there too long with the foot traffic passing between the library and my office building. Too many people drawing a bead on me. I thanked the little nerd-conspirator, detached his hand from my coat, and fled.

I just hoped I wouldn't have to hear anything more about the t-shirts. Not looking for trouble, no way. I'm one of those Jacobite Pretenders who would've been more than happy with a nice estate in Spain. *"No, no . . . the time is not right for our return to England, Don Alfonso—let us wait another year before we overthrow the usurpers! When the weather is warmer, perhaps."*

And I had to get back to the English department . . . just in time to meet the morning mail call. One of those brown envelopes with CONFIDENTIAL, in big red letters. Tottered back to the office, shut the door and opened the thing up before I lost my nerve or puked my guts.

Turns out to be from the Vice-Chancellor. He informs me, on letterhead, that he's forwarding "the enclosed letter of complaint concerning Course ENGL 124." Fingers shaking (Parkinsonism, long story), I detach the enclosed voodoo letter. It's a real charmer:

From: Kwan-Ying Chin
To: Professor John Dolan
Re: English 124 Test

I am a first year student in your English 124 lecture. I am writing to you about the advert analysing test. In that test, I set it twice. You decided to give me a zero for that test because you think that was cheating. But, it was not cheating and it is not fair to give me a zero just because I sat the test twice. The followings are my explanations:

First, it is not cheating. Cheating involves copying other people's work. I did all these tests by myself, how can it be cheating?

Second, I don't even have any advantage of sitting both exams. If I sat 7pm's test only, I could still borrow my friend's test and go through it at 6pm(just before the test). Besides, these two tests are totally different (except that they are both about cars). Since these tests are not relevant at all, how can sitting both tests be cheating? Moreover, students willnot get a zero just because they hand in two assignments or go to two lectures, will they? Then, how can I get a zero just because I sat the tests and these two tests are different?

Third, I did work hard for that test. I wrote many analysing essays and asked the tutors to correct them. I also analysed lots of advertisements by writing out their features. It wouldn't be fair to give me a zero and ignore all my hard work.

Fourth, I am only first year. I do not know that sitting these two tests will violate the system (Besides, this rule would be more reasonable if these two tests were the same.)

At last, if you still think what I did was wrong. I would rather happy to get a detention instead of getting a zero. You should punish me for what I did wrong, but not ignoring my work.

There: multiply that by 700 students and you get my life. "And welcome to it," as the man said.

Of course, the letter neglects to mention the key point that her tutor told her three times, with witnesses present, that she could not under any circumstances take the test at both the 5:00 and 7:00 times. But she's Chinese-Malaysian; she's looking for an angle, because her family has convinced her that she'll let down the whole desperate clan if she doesn't make it to the second year of med school. There are cultural reasons for this, bla bla bla . . .

There were witnesses this time, Thank God. So she gets a zero and that's that. And of course that means saying goodbye to her chance of getting into med school. Goodbye, lifelong dream! Goodbye, hopes of entire desperate Overseas-Chinese family! Another day, another young life ruined! They talk about academics living in an ivory tower. And true, some do: the lucky ones, the first to hatch, the basking babyboomers who ate their younger siblings or exiled them to places like this guano rock in a cold ocean . . . But as for my job, this job—Christ, it's about as ivory-tower as driving a bus in East Oakland.

That last paragraph of her letter, though—that was interesting. What was it? Something about how she would be "rather happy" to accept punishment. Not just "happy" but *rather* happy," would she? "Happy to accept punishment?" Well, well! Let's use our imagination!

But no, no, no time for that stuff, and too scared anyway. So I didn't even waste any time—well, a minute or two—on the range of possible punishments; just wrote out a quick letter saying in padded bureaucratic diction, "No, you get your zero and that's that."

Then one of my tutors came by the office. She was smiling but not very convincingly and her voice was off-tone. I kind of guessed, even before she spilled it, that she had to tell me something. She was being very tactful, very delicate—as if she were about to break the bad news of my own death or something. Not that, turned out, but close: she'd heard about the t-shirts the med students are selling—in fact, she even saw one. And what she wanted to tell me was that, in addition to the anti-English 124 message, the shirts have ". . . a cartoon of [me] . . . which is . . . sort of mean."

I can imagine.

The cartoon made it much, much worse. Let them make fun of my voice, pretensions, anything. But not my body. I paid in advance.

Felt like I was about to throw up. Hands shaking, stomach clenching. These things don't happen! I never knew anybody who was so hated by their students that they actually resorted to wardrobe venues for their malice! This doesn't happen! I should sue them for sheer implausibility!

As always when I get seriously hurt, I relaxed. Once the hatred becomes overt, a weight of nervous tension or hope drops from me. I thanked the loyal tutor and, once she was safely gone, left the office myself, thinking calmly, strategically. Bombing run. Pre-emptive strike. Step one would be seeing the shirt itself. So I walked casually into the university library, looking for the little nerd informer who'd first told me about the shirts. I knew he'd be there. I get this weird sort of hunting sense when I get hurt badly enough. Actually feel a lot more at home. Calm down, get more confident, once the world finally takes off its Dentyne smile and shows its real, crooked-fanged, pus-oozing face.

I could've found the little swine with my eyes closed, just by the sound-tendrils of revenge my body was extending into his fungoid habitat, the swamp-like undergraduate library. And there he was, the little frog, in the swamp where he belonged: sitting at a big study table where anybody could spot him. I pasted a big smile on my face—I'm at my most repulsive when I smile—and went over to him, with the high-blood pressure singing the helicopter music from *Apocalypse Now* in my left ear. Came up behind and sat on the table leaning into him—one hand just accidentally happening to come down right on the book he was reading.

It worked; he blinked, scared. I leaned a little further in, just to see that flinch, and said in a voice several shades too loud for the library, "Hey, I was thinking about those t-shirts." He nodded again. Adam's apple bobbing. I went on, loud, smiling: "Listen, I decided I want one of those t-shirts. The ones you were telling me about? I want one, definitely . . . maybe two, even. Can you—"

He tries to answer and slide his chair away from me at the same time. Both moves suffer as a consequence; his syntax goes to Hell—real B-minus syntax, I note happily—and his leg flies out, having lost traction on the slick linoleum. Maybe you wouldn't have done as well at Agincourt as you think, my little Pacifist-Warfare, fake-battles-with-papier-mache-armor Knightling. He stammers, "Yeah uh OK, right, I can—I—they're—"

"Yes, how much do they cost?"

"Uh they're twunny each."

I write him a check right there, making as much noise as I can. The whole study table is watching. It hurts me too—I'm more scared than any of these people—but I'm a lot older and a lot tougher than they are. And when it comes to social pain . . . well, I was raised in a tough neighborhood: the suburbs of California, toughest neighborhood in the world for the uncool.

So what I'm doing, by sitting on his desk, making a scene which will embarrass both the medieval nerd and myself, is like radiation therapy. I'm bombarding *both* our bodies with radiation—with shame-rays, the most lethal particles—on the theory that his weak and evil cells won't survive the bombardment as well as mine, which have walked out of Ground Zero.

He got his revenge two days later, when he brought me the t-shirt. Pure kryptonite. "100% Kryptonite—Made in China—Cold-water wash only." On the front of the shirt is one of those red circles with a diagonal slash through it. In the middle of the circle is "English 124." Not very imaginative, is it? But then these are science students; not very creative.

I was underwhelmed by the front, but the informer said eagerly, "Look at the back! Look at what's on the back!" Like some little Christmas grinch, eager for me to unwrap his unpresent so he could see my unpleasure.

I turned the shirt over, and there I was. *Behold the man:* a round pumpkin head, completely bald. Jowly, pouting, puffed cheeks. Mouth set in a blank scowl. Eyes half-open, one lid drooping. And over the head the caption, "BLA BLA BLA."

A student came in just after I got the shirt and saw it before I could put it away. Recognized the face on it instantly, and said, "At least they didn't draw you fat."

Ah yes. A look on the bright side.

There really isn't any comeback to diffused group hatred like this. Once the primate troop decides you smell wrong, every ape of them goes to work chipping out hand-axes to use on your skull. All you can do is try to stay out of their way. And that's not so easy either on a little outcrop like this. Over the weekend I made a mistake of that sort and paid for it.

This place changes on Fridays and Saturdays. The same students who are too timid to look you in the eye Monday through Thursday turn into drunken pigs at precisely 4:00 PM Friday. You can actually hear the whooping screams begin as they troop through the campus, pulling off tree branches like chimps displaying dominance. You always find lots of mutilated trees when you walk across campus on a weekend morning.

I normally have enough sense to avoid the main drag, George Street, on the weekend. That's where the rat packs head after their deforestation marches across campus. The big pubs are on George Street, and the weekend mating rituals are held there. It's a quaint primate rite: groups of six same-sex adolescents march together to the pub. A group of six young males, all dead drunk, ritually collides with a complementary group of six young females, also dead drunk. Next the vomiting ceremony, ritual prelude to actual mating. It is traditionally held on the sidewalk outside the pub, and features competitions for volume, distance and accuracy. Couples then pair off for the night with full deniability all round. Sex with that rancid digestive acid mixing on two breaths . . . but they're young, the hormones require little help.

It's the kind of spectacle that even a trained zoologist would want to observe only from the safety of a shark-cage—or better still, the rolled-up windows of a moving car. Not the sort of thing you want to dive right into, like a Jehovah's Witness at an oceanic-whitetip feeding frenzy. But last Saturday I was having a spasm of guilt about the increasing convexity of my belly, and decided I had to start walking again.

The traditional objective of my walks is a statue on the rugby pitch near the ocean, a white stone monument to the locals who died in the Boer War. These people have been duped into dying in every land-grab war the Brits ever started.

Ritual demands that I go up to the statue—which shows a mustachioed trooper in a "bush hat," a cowboy hat with one side pinned up—and touch the "O" on the word "Boer" on the marble plaque before I can turn around and head back.

But last Saturday there was a gaggle of "Bogans"—the local white trash—sitting on the steps of the monument drinking beer. Looking around sniffing for a victim, stubbed snouts testing the air. Pit bulls, albino like their masters, on short leashes at their feet. No way I was going to get to touch the "O" without some verbal harassment at the very least.

This made for an intense internal argument: ritual demanded that I touch the monument no matter what the risk, but the moderates in my cranial parliament reminded us that we were doing this for exercise, and that combat with people half our age was not going to be of much aerobic benefit.

The issue was in doubt when the moderates added a much more powerful argument: they reminded my parliament that I was wearing sweatpants which, now that I'm regaining weight, barely stay up when I'm walking, thanks to the new convexity of my abdomen. It's like trying to put pants on a basketball. So the real fear was not being kicked to death by drunken goons but the much scarier image of my pants falling down while I struggled with the Bogans. The whole town would be retelling that moment till the sun goes nova.

So for once the moderates won: I veered away, touched a tree instead of the monument, and turned for home. Not so much as a shouted insult from the Bogans. Maybe I'd wronged them, poor marooned bastards.

That was a happy moment. The walk hadn't been as hard as it might've, what with the new weight and no practice. And on the way back I walked behind a woman wearing a velvet cape, with a pit bull trotting beside her—a weirdly sweet elf-maiden/street-waif mix. I dreamed a whole long sweet colloquy with her as we walked a few yards apart, back up George Street to the center of town.

Then I became aware of groups passing. Students, mostly. The usual sex-segregated groups hurrying to some beer-node to meet their counterparts for a vomity grope. Most of these grope-groups—as naturalists who study their behavior have called them—ignored me completely. Being ignored, invisible, is a real luxury in this twitchy town, and I savored it as Nature's recompense for being old and ugly, having passed outside their sensor-range at last. But I couldn't quite relax: that t-shirt had just come out, and it *was* Saturday night on George Street.

A half-dozen groups went by without incident. I was near campus—almost home safe. But as I should've known, the fringes of the university are the highest-risk area. You don't have to be Jacques Cousteau to figure out that the sharks roam mostly around their home territory. And their territory is the ring of fetid "student flats" which surround the university: old houses with burned couches on the lawn and a fine scatter of brown glass halfway out into the street.

And sure enough, just when I thought I'd make it back safely, there they were. Dead ahead and coming up fast. Battlestar Medstudent: a group of eight or ten of them, in agitated weekend mode . . . a central clot of six or seven, with dweeb outriders tapping car hoods and whapping parking meters so passers-by would be sure to notice them. And as they got close enough, excited little yips came from the safe center of the group: several voices yelping, "English 124!" and ". . . HIM?" A couple of them tried a chant of, *"He's got no hai-ir!"* but dropped it to chant, *"BLA BLA BLA!"* in allusion to the t-shirt. It was perfect for cowards like these: oblique enough to be deniable. So they shouted it out in a ragged chorus as they trooped past me—some of the braver, or drunker, actually leaning their hydra-heads toward me, forked tongues flashing, from the central polyp of shoulders. Even after they were past me, tromping down the sidewalk, there were hoots of joy and last volleys of *"Bla* bla!" "Bla bla *bla* bla *bla!"* *"Bla bla* bla bla bla!"—prosodic experiments receding down the street.

I walked back to my office whispering letters of resignation to the head of the English Department. "It is with real regret . . ." But I didn't resign. And won't. Even if this whole campus gets plastered with hate-letters to me.

Which is not so far-fetched. Already the Arts building is marked by testimonials to the hatred I have drawn to myself. I should give guided tours. The *Me-Hatred Campus Tours*. Fun—and Educational too! We could begin by filing into the men's toilet downstairs. Last year a major discovery in the archeology of hatred was made there. By me. I went into the stall on the end, like I always do, and WHAM! It got me. A little love note painted on the inside of the stall door:

DOLAN—KISS MY WHITE ASS AND SUCK MY DICK

Written in nice big block print. In typewriter eraser, the stuff we call "whiteout" in the US and they call "twink" here. Must've taken a good five minutes to paint it on the stall-door. And they say craftsmanship is dead! In fact, so diligent was the crafter of this anti-personnel device that, unsatisfied with his first effort, he wrote the word:

PUFTER

above and to the right of my name, then carefully drew an arrow leading from "Pufter" to "Dolan." Of course the conventional spelling would be "poofter," as several of my colleagues pointed out by way of consolation, when I told them about my discovery. I was not consoled. Odd how they always bring race into it, though; why "*white* ass"? And for that matter, why "ass"? They say "arse" here—British spelling. Call in Sherlock Holmes, see what he can make of it. Is "white" a red herring, perhaps? Meant to lead us away from the crazed Hong-Kong med students who might otherwise become prime suspects? And what do you make of that American spelling of "ass," Holmes old man? Would you say it suggests we look for one of these, what d'ye call'em, "Yanks" as our murderer, eh? (Watson's getting dotty . . .)

No, Watson; I'd say it's more like *Murder on the Orient Express:* they ALL did it. How many times do you have to learn that one and only life lesson?

It has always been like this, and it will always be like this. Even where I began, in the true Lothlorien: California in the hippie days. Even there, in the long summer of peace and love—in that unprecedented upwelling of bliss and warmth—somehow, impossibly, it was just like this.

2

Mostly it was verbal, till Gary Flowers just up and punched me in the face by the creek . . . and I just stood there, frozen, shocked. Said nothing, didn't move. He gave me some sort of lecture about keeping my fucking mouth shut, something like that. I didn't move, didn't answer. Every night for years I had to replay that scene before I could sleep; he was kicked to death a thousand times over, night after night. But in the daytime, when it actually happened, it had happened the way it'd happened and that was that. Big flat twentieth-century fact, and served me right.

And Gary Flowers wasn't even very tough; when Kevin Kilker punched me at the Ecology Center, at the recycling bins, he knocked me down with one punch. But then Kevin Kilker was big. He was on the football team. I fell slowly, like Byzantium. So slowly I could even think, as I was falling: *Wow, I've been "knocked down."* As in a film. It didn't hurt, not at the time. Physically. I stayed on the ground while he delivered a lecture, something about learning not to mess with people. That was always the sequence: punch, then lecture. Don't know which I disliked more. The lecture took more time and in the end probably hurt more, all things considered.

Much later, when I took up boxing at UC Berkeley, I was punched by an even stronger guy, the bench-press champion of UCB. That time it was different: it was due to courtesy. I'm a very polite person. He and I were the biggest of the guys who showed up for boxing tryouts at this smelly concrete cubbyhole under the stadium—his weight was all muscle though—so they paired us up, put the gloves and helmets on, and had us spar. I awaited the command to begin. It didn't come. A bell rang, true—and I did vaguely, shyly wonder if that might not be a signal to begin—but that little diffident bell didn't seem like sufficient permission to do anything as saturnalian as defending myself. I was awaiting some more explicit permission.

The bell was permission enough for the bench-press champion. He hauled off and clubbed me with a big roundhouse right. It was very embarrassing. Another social mistake, another faux pas. The bell was the permission, stupid! You missed your cue, stupid! He was right and I was wrong. It wasn't release or violence at all: it was the same old thing, me getting rightly punished for a social mistake. And with people watching!

I just wanted out. Obviously boxing wasn't the missing link between the Dark Ages and the present. It was just like school: I was the center of mocking attention. I hopped around the ring for the required three rounds with little cartoon birdies circling my head.

The lean snake-looking coach was very nice. As he took my gloves off he commended me for keeping "mentally alert" after that punch. He explained about the bell. But by then my armies were in full retreat, the gunners lashing their horses, the infantry throwing away their rifles as they ran. I nodded non-stop, deafened, my half-red face burning, as he unwrapped my useless fists, back in my weight, sagging against the ropes into California, the present tense, daylight. I just wanted to get back inside my big quilted jacket that smelled safe, like me, like a sofa-fort you could wear. And flee.

And in a few minutes I was out, back on the street, a guided missile in a dirty quilted jacket, homing in on the nearest chocolate-chip cookie retailer.

3

I couldn't even claim handicap. It was very important at Berkeley, having a handicap. But I had none. No wheelchair, no white cane. "White male." Though to be fair, there were some whites who could claim trauma, like the white kids whose progressive parents insisted they attend black urban high schools. Those kids would never lose the flinch they'd learned on those playgrounds. But they had a right to their damage, while I had no excuse: it was a bland, indifferent place, Pleasant Hill High School.

A great imagination they had, those suburban planners: "Pleasant Hill High School" was where you went after you graduated from "Pleasant Hill Intermediate School", which was where you went after graduating from "Pleasant Hill Elementary School." But here's the good news: *not one of those schools still exists.* My generation forgot to have babies, so: no Pleasant Hill Elementary . . . no Pleasant Hill Intermediate (the Christians had bought it) . . . and best of all, no *Pleasant Hill High School!* Like the three bears, only this time all the bowls are empty—the little one, the middle one, the big. *Someone's been sleeping in my bed . . .* don't get me started.

None of those schools existed when I was born, and all of them closed within ten years of my graduation. So go ahead: tell me about tradition, values, continuity. Where I come from those things just flat-out don't exist. Be in favor of them if you want, but while you're at it you may as well be in favor of unicorns. Yes: everybody in favor of tradition in California send their donations to me, c/o Save the Unicorns Foundation. I'll see that the unicorns get it.

Everything in California is re-zoned, re-named, resold or repossessed. Even the climate of the place has been adjusted since I was a kid. There are trees everywhere now, Eastern deciduous trees, and they've imported squirrels to run around in the trees and make the place look like Massachusetts, like a prep-school lawn. Somehow they even persuaded ducks, actual L. L. Bean mallards, to swim in the canal.

Didn't use to be that way. When I arrived, a plump squinting toddler, it was baking desert, raw adobe some developer just dropped ranch houses on. It looked like Los Alamos—the "After" shot. With houses added to fool the Russians. No grass, no trees, no interest first 24 months, GI loan. I'm the puffy, wincing child beside the car. I remember that wince. Baby's first wince! It was the sun I was wincing at. I woke to the California sun, and it hit me like hot aluminum. The glare, raw dirt, a house and car . . . all the ingredients dumped on that hard adobe. "Just add water!" Which they did: that was the canal. Then wood and concrete, and lastly some names commemorating what wasn't there: "Sherwood Forest," "Gregory Gardens" . . . "Pleasant Hill."

Pleasant Hill was a zoning commission's invention, a fiscal jigsaw-piece of valley floor, a chunk of three-bedroom houses distinguished for tax reasons from the rest of the valley, which was randomly divided into Walnut Creek, Martinez, Pacheco and Concord, but was really "Roofland." That was what I called it, looking back as our car went over the hill: an inland roof-sea, a Captain-Crunch serving of roofs in a yellow hill-bowl.

Sometimes if I really concentrated when we drove down into Lafayette, I could see a Tolkien landscape imposed for a moment on that valley: cottages "nestling" at the base of the hills, watercolor smoke winding from their chimneys. But it took a lot of effort, and I tended to resent interruptions, sulking in the back seat as sullen and foul-tempered with my parents as I was cowardly and groveling at school. And Middle Earth was so fragile that if anybody so much as opened a window, it was sucked out in a vortex of asphalt and dead straw, windmilling like a gum wrapper around the center divider.

It was a spell I could never master, the magical passage to the forest of Lothlorien—that is to say, access to the hippie goddesses of Pleasant Hill High School. I saw them every day at school, and in their train followed so many blessings—like, for example, *other people*, and, and, and . . . *the other stuff,* the peace-and-love stuff—yes: the willing, even fond caresses of those most glorious, most beautiful . . . Even now my nose and eyes sting when I think of them, lump in my sagging baleen throat just remembering their smiles, O most beautiful, to-be-adored-even-in-the-depths-of-Purgatory goddesses, the twelve-odd hippie girls who graced the ninth grade at Pleasant Hill High School.

I worshipped them—and will maintain till death that *they deserved to be worshipped!* They were the crown of that creation . . . of that time, that place. You weren't there; you don't know. You didn't see Leigh Akers' dark-gold hair float against her black sweater and caress her perfect profile at lunch period.

Or if you *were* there, you were already a jaded, prematurely "mature" Californian, who never worshipped anything in your carefully modulated life!

I worshipped them—and they agreed with me. Called themselves "the Super People." Which they were. Listen to their names! Names date very quickly, I know, but these can never breathe anything but perfect pre-Raphaelite-hair-and-features-plus-orthodonture willow hippie beauty forever: *Leigh Akers. Mayberry Lanning. Laura Muller.*

Do you hear that? How beautiful they were? Ah God—

Best in the mild California winter. That's what I remember. One day especially: "Ecology Day." Mayberry rode to school on her horse that day, for the ecology. It was cool and rainy, so my wincing whale eyes could open fully for once and see them as I still see them, in jackets too big for them, their long straight hair waving in the breeze. Winter in Pleasant Hill is what summer is for cold climates: the nice time. The dead brown hills go green for a couple of months, and with the live oaks darkening in every green crotch of the hills, it becomes easier to superimpose the Tolkien world on every vacant lot. The air has a live green smell, and the pavement smells of rain. Puddles spangle the playground, so that the basketball courts' painted lines link mirror-fragments of cloud.

And the Super People hold court by the teachers' parking lot on a bench painted a civil-service green—green for the winter and ecology and Ireland. And they are laughing, leaning together in their too-big coats. Twenty feet from me. Five steps away.

They would have been fourteen. I too, watching from behind a pole which would hide at least some of me. Looking or trying to look "preoccupied" in the hope they'd inquire about it.

They didn't; and the hardliners won in my head, once I knew I was excluded forever. I made a poster for my bedroom wall, in pseudo-psychedelic letters: MAKE WAR ON LOVE. Your classic nerd's revenge . . . Hell, it's *all* revenge of the nerds! Nietzsche's most basic point is that the entire intellectual history of post-Socratic Western thought is one big revenge of the nerds—by, for and of the nerds!

But of course the nerd doesn't really want revenge. That comes later. At first the nerd simply wants someone to notice him hiding behind the pole over there, by the tetherball court, and become interested in him the way Barbara Feldon gets interested in Maxwell Smart—interested enough to persuade the nerd to drop the sulk and accept the key to Lothlorien.

It was a sort of flirting, an obscure—no, "stupid" is the better word—a very stupid flirting. Hours spent parrying wholly imaginary questions about the ramifications of my private anti-hippie cosmology, when nobody on the planet could possibly have cared less what I thought—except my poor parents.

But I won't speak about them. I promised myself when I started this.

Anyway: the Super People. Right—well, they wouldn't've been impressed with my Talmudic elaborations anyway, because as proper flower children they weren't much on argument. Laura Muller wrote in my yearbook, "Hello. You are too smart. Goodbye." With a peace sign in lieu of signature.

Hello; peace sign; goodbye. Sort of sums it up.

But back then I just couldn't understand why my pose of noble defiance wasn't working. In the movies, the sullen guy who wouldn't join the crowd was always the focus of everyone's attention. Beautiful girls got interested and tried to talk him out of it, like planets revolving around a sullen misunderstood sun.

One little theoretical error! One mistake! And the subject's whole predicate is dust. It would be so easy to fix, too. A little tinkering with the social skills. All I need is one crummy time machine. In the silence here, me and the Antarctic wind, I lie in bed dreaming of going back in time, planting a post-hypnotic suggestion to myself, so that the very first time I hear a particular chronologically keyed phrase, I will awake, fix myself and have the life I never had.

Seriously, I spend hours a day thinking about exactly which phrase I'll use—some combination of words whose first occurrence you could date precisely. For example: "Kent State." I would never have heard those words spoken together until 1970 (or whenever it was there was the massacre at the obscure Midwestern college of that name). I whisper that noun over and over, like a spell. "Kent State." A blood-sealed magic, those four dead hippie students part of the dark spell which sends me back to live it all so differently, awakening to sentience, hygiene, sex, love. All of it—the first time I heard the name "Kent State." I'd be sitting in the hot family-room watching the news when that noun comes on . . . and then, blinking awake, I would instantly do, be, become everything: dress right, exercise, beat the living shit out of Gary Flowers, take up guitar, and go find Leigh Akers . . . like Scrooge on Christmas morning: "The spirits have done it all in one night!"

Or maybe the post-hypnotic suggestion phrase would be "Neil Armstrong"—because I'd be sure to hear that name in 1969 when he walked on the stupid boring moon; his name was all over the place with that bad poem, "One small step for a man . . ." I go back in time and plant "Neil Armstrong" in my head, then when we're on the back patio watching his lame Vietnam moonwalk, I hear his name; blink; freeze—and instantly my mind is flooded with blunt remedial tips:

Remedial Tip #1: Someone has to want you in the first place if you're going to play hard to get, you imbecile! And why don't you wash that filthy quilted jacket while you're at it, slob! And comb your hair if you're going to try to wear it like the hippies do! Right now it looks like a pair of musk-ox horns curling up over the earpieces of your stupid, scotch-taped horn-rims!

Tip #2: This one goes out to any pubescent goddesses who may be reading: Never be nice to nerds if you're a beautiful girl. A lot of girls die that way, and their parents and siblings and anybody else who happens to be in the house . . . and the nerd too, last of all, barrel in the mouth, toe on the trigger, the Beloved half out of bed in her room, beautiful golden hair now streaked with viscous dark, blouse clumsily rebuttoned from one shy necrophiliac fondle; her mom sprawled in the kitchen, stopped in her tracks mid-casserole; and her Dad, head dripping onto the back of the sofa where he first raised his head from the paper, annoyed by the noise of the sliding door being jerked open.

Noblesse oblige . . . sometimes too much—the *noblesse oblige* with which beautiful suburban hippie goddesses patronize nerds.

Leigh Akers.

Their Galadriel—the finest of the Super People. *Leigh Akers.* The most beautiful and the brightest and kindest of the whole pantheon.

Worst of all, she was nice. To me.

Her locker was next to mine. An obvious sign from the gods! And then one day she gave me a picture she'd drawn, a psychedelic cartoon titled "Pie in the Sky over Boise, Idaho." An obvious signal that she wanted me to fall in love with her.

It becomes the stuff of American movies after that. Not the happy ending but the first half hour, where we see the twerp getting shoved around the school hallways and subjected to other varieties of sexual humiliation prior to the arrival of whichever supernatural agency, alien spacecraft or magical weapon has been cast as the happy ending. Except that there weren't any magic weapons in Pleasant Hill that I could find; and if any aliens ever landed there they probably had the sense to leave, if not the decency to obliterate the whole of Roofland on their way home. And I know from experience that there were no magical beings willing to help a nerd with his social problems. Because I tried.

In my quest for Leigh's affections, I called upon the Faerie Host, the *Sidhe*—their real name, an Irish word which is pronounced "she," aptly enough. (The only word of Irish I knew until I learned all that IRA stuff—but that was later.)

I knew about the *Sidhe* from the books on the green shelf. They all had "Irish" or "Ireland" in the title and were bound in green rotting cloth; and they were all about losing. Losing gloriously. Losing and becoming a legend, a song—luminous, adored, dead. And I was desperate, a couple of months shy of my fifteenth birthday, just sane enough to know that the distance between Leigh Akers' affections and me was roughly 12 centuries—the distance between The Dark Ages and Pleasant Hill. Which meant that extra help was required if I was going to press my suit. And my suit badly needed pressing.

So I called upon the *Sidhe*. Summoned them in all solemnity in our backyard. Dusk—my time. A hot day cooling off toward evening. The Sowers's backyard with the shed half-fallen . . . the canal beyond it a white concrete line . . . then the back fences of Ellis Court, a shadowy tan-brown matte of fence, dry grass and shrub which was the undercoat of everything in Pleasant Hill. And above: "the Gloaming"—another word I'd picked up somewhere in the green books. The Gloaming meant, as far as I could tell, when the beige suburban sky for a moment did what skies did in books: expressed something.

In the Gloaming the superimposition of worlds was for a moment tenable. The worlds were merging, and my seething squinting fourteen-year-old body was about to burst into white flame and consume all of the Diablo Valley, turn it into a cauldron of ranch-houses. It's amazing to me even now that it didn't; amazing that that inhuman longing *didn't* Hirosheem and Nagasack the entire Diablo Valley. That I couldn't kill with a glance. Always amazed me when my stare of pure hatred failed to set fire to things or kill people. Loose wire somewhere.

But I could still call upon greater powers. The auguries were there, the whisperings of something vast, immanent, ancient that did not laugh at my medieval seriousness. All the elements of a miracle were present: the low surf of Interstate 5, our patron river-ocean, beyond Putnam Boulevard; and in the East the Bactrian shadow, the two-point shark tooth of Mount Diablo itself, going all the earth-color crayons: umber, sienna. And past the canal the white oven-glare of stadium lights, with occasional wavering tubas oomphing and tiny cheers. It was a Friday night and Pleasant Hill High was playing at home. People I saw in the school corridors— people who got phone calls—were there, having their mysterious, unattainable "fun." Leigh. Maybe Leigh was there too. Would she, a hippie girl, go to a football game? She was somewhere, right now. Somewhere within a square mile of me, a dizzying thought. Summon her . . .

I heard a scratching noise and saw the tip of a white pole behind the fence: Mrs Pratt scraping her pool, a well-known eavesdropping technique of hers. Let her! Let her try telling the cops what she saw at the moment of transcendence, when I burst into flame and walk like Godzilla to collect Leigh, *my hand pushing through the roof of her father's house as through a balsa model of a galleon.* Let Mrs Pratt see my Phoenix Assumption, let her burn like the rest in my hecatomb vindication!

Of course after I'd lifted Leigh from her parents' house and revealed my affection to her, holding her unhurt in my Godzilla hand, I would be consumed in my own flames and die. While she watched, sobbing gently at the great inhuman medieval love which once burst into flame for her here in the Gloaming. No matter how she begged me to stay, I would burn and burn, subsiding to elegant ash. Yes, yes . . . it would be wonderful, my enormous death—a triumph, as in the green books.

In one of those books there was a story: the Irish, in one of their doomed rebellions, were attacking a walled city held by the British conquistadors. They had one cannon, or rather one cannon-barrel; the gun-carriage had been smashed. There was a man there, a big and terribly strong man, who saw that only this cannon could break through the great gate of the city. And saw that the gun-carriage was smashed, and that the cannon-barrel would not work without a powerful frame from which to fire.

You know what happened—if you are a proper man you know. He put the cannon on his back, and held it there, with his great arms clamping it down, fingers locked, head down . . . and he carried the two-ton cannon barrel up to the gate, and told his men to fire it.

The gate was smashed and the Irish poured in and won the day. The man, of course, was ripped to shreds. That beautiful phrase, *"to shreds,"* ". . . every bone in his body broken . . ."—but he was remembered forever.

Yes! My throat swollen with hormonal glory, wings stirring under my shoulder blades, claws sprouting from my fingers, I bow my head toward the surf-noise of the freeway and the purple glow

over Mount Diablo, where lurk the dim figures of the *Sidhe* . . .
They will come! It has to be now, while the two worlds are
overlapping; while the purple-khaki curtain stays aloft in the east;
now, while the Venn diagram of worlds shows rich glowing Area
(A), pure overlap: call upon them now! Offer them your soul, for
Leigh, for Leigh to love you!

But what if you only have a concrete back patio to kneel on?
The hopelessness of it came down out of the Gloaming, pushed
into my chest, bruised my pulsing thorax. If the *Sidhe* were up
there at all, in the gloaming, they were probably hooting at me, a
supernatural version of school, ectoplasmic rubber bands
launched at me from the sky . . .

But maybe that very hopelessness signaled the moment of
Grace? That was how the best stories went: when the hero falls
utterly, something good happens. When the nerd-hero of every
movie is most alone and lost, the doorbell always rings and it's the
beautiful girl. And the same in the green books, and even the story
they told at Mass—Jesus, the ultimate nerd hero, who went from
lowest to highest in three days.

But that Crucifixion never impressed me much, as
martyrdoms went. For two thousand years the whole world has to
apologize for a relatively mild torture-death like that? Here I am
still in my first year of high school and every night the revenge-
brain in my lap thought up much worse than crucifixion. All the
nerve-endings in a human body, and the worst God could inflict
on his son was a couple of nails in the hands and feet? It seemed
like purposely pulling His punches. Nepotism, actually.

I would offer better than that: dentistry without novocaine,
maybe? "For thee! For thee!" ("Thee" sounded better. Though
there was a minor prosody problem, unwanted internal rhyme:
"Leigh/thee." But that could be surmounted . . .) *Give her to me, O
Lords of Dusk!* I will make a secret deal that novocaine will never
work on me again; all my dentistry from now on will be at full
medieval pain level. Give me a penknife, I'll splatter my signature
on any parchment you make appear. For Leigh.

—Her hair a creek of tarnished gold ribboning the black
sweater, the time she opened her locker next to mine. Call that
mere chance? One foot away . . . "One small step for a man . . ."
but several eons from me. From my locker to Leigh's arms, that

was the true crusade. Walking on the moon, what was that—what was the crewcut hick Neil Armstrong, compared to actually being allowed to touch Leigh Akers? For that, let the world end. Any price! I summon thee: *Sidhe*, Balrog, Nazgul; come to me now! Bring Aztec priests with obsidian knives, tear out my heart, do to me the thing I thought up with the vise and one finger every four hours; only give me this one thing! Host of the *Sidhe*, Celtic deities exiled to the Ionosphere, Ticonderoga house-gods, static-ghosts of the Aurora, Attenuations of Dusk, Patrons of the Defeated: *give her to me!*

Now or never—the waves of the freeway lapping at my ears, the stadium happy-kids noise. Now! I opened my arms to the Gloaming, to the *Sidhe*. Kneeling on the concrete, trying to look *through*, not-see, the back yard: our crippled birch tree that had something wrong with it and never got more than five feet high; the cracked concrete—even the ground cracks there in the summer, from the heat, with little clumps of dead yellow grass holding each adobe clump together, you're supposed to water it but our hose wouldn't reach or something—

Unthink it! Look through it to the Gloaming! I knelt in supplication, devoutly not feeling the concrete under my knees; not smelling the dry grass, baked adobe and sweating trees; not hearing Mrs Pratt's pool-pole scraping away. *None* of that world was real . . .

Or if it was, I was doomed. There was a bark chip from the elm tree under my knee, sabotaging the prayer. The elm grew in a dirt triangle in the concrete, preferring to subsist on a few shrivelled leaves rather than give our patio any shade. Only its roots were active, breaking up as much concrete as they could with the limited photosynthetic energy available. Never mind, unsee it!

It was hard to concentrate, kneeling on the patio with that chip under my knee. And what if my mother came along while I was kneeling, arms outspread, on the patio facing the canal?

But what if the pain and the fear of humiliation were the point, as at Mass, where one "offered up" the pain in the knee when kneeling? They would be watching, the *Sidhe*, and would post their scores in the Otherworld, without informing me that I had failed their test. So I stayed kneeling, a tiny pain novitiate in the sky-wide arena. The knights kneeled all night. The Saints and the Samurai and the Sadhu, they all kneeled for their whole lives. This was nothing. Even if I kneel forever I won't be in their league. On the other hand, it hurt. Which proved I was unworthy—can't even stand a few minutes, when everybody who was anybody knelt for centuries!

Then the pulse of hope came back, the hormonal surge—at any price, to die kissing Leigh, to say farewell to her as they led me off to die . . .

The idea of kissing Leigh in a death camp, just before we were both executed, was my first—what would you call it?—my first "erotic fantasy," the first I could entertain respectably, in daylight. As opposed to the coffles of slave-girls, a wholly nocturnal matter. The healthier, love-type death camp fantasy went like this:

. . . *They* (an unspecified "they," vaguely Nazi with some Black-and-Tan influence) *had invaded and conquered Pleasant Hill.* The valley was a bowl of ash, pillars of black smoke from the roofs of Roofland. They had rounded up all the survivors and lined us up to be shot, so that we would fall directly into a mass grave, a bulldozed pit. And Leigh was just ahead of me in line! What luck!

I spent hours working on the seductive speech I would make to her in those romantic moments as we waited our turn to be killed. People ahead of us—jocks, guys who'd made fun of me—would be sobbing or otherwise revealing their weakness. Kevin Kilker, sobbing like a stupid baby . . . Gary Flowers begging the guards not to kill him. Cowards! It was not their world any longer. The Dark Ages were come; the wheel of *my* world had rolled over their balsa/plastic model world! They who thought themselves so suave—lo, they shamed themselves! Cravens, cowering at the thought of death!

Whereas I would be way more relaxed than usual, right at home in that death-line. Luckily, they were taking their time with the mass killings, so the line moved forward pretty slowly, punctuated by bursts from a machine-gun. "An M60, standard-issue heavy machine-gun, tripod mounted—you can tell by the level sound of the bursts." I mention this interesting information to Leigh, just casually. An icebreaker.

Impressed with my nonchalance and specialized military knowledge, she calms down, gazing deeply into my eyes, finally aware of my hidden depths. In the silence between machine-gun bursts, we look into each others' eyes. I speak softly: "Before we die, Leigh . . . I just wanted you to know that I've . . . always loved you, dearest, my beloved, always, with all my heart."

A tear falls from her eyes. Another machine-gun burst prompts us, reminds us of how little time there is to consummate our love. I was a little vague on anatomy, so "consummate" was elided in the narrative; I went for the kiss. I whisper, "May I kiss you?" And she doesn't laugh at all; she smiles and nods. We kiss. She's naked, of course; they would have stripped us so they could make soap from our clothes. And there would be no embarrassment about being naked, because we were going to die right afterwards.

The guards motion us along. The crack of whips. Shouts and sobbing. We shuffle forward a few paces closer to our deaths.

Bliss! And healthy, too: no slave-girls. All love and victimness. I was so proud of having merged with the sensibility of my hippie peers that I would have told the death camp fantasy with pride.

Luckily, there was no one to tell. I had to learn the hard way to stay in the Dark Ages. By trying to carry my pubescent mythos into Pleasant Hill, with predictable results. *Cut to:* the last day of the school year, Pleasant Hill High School. A blank-faced boy with glasses has been asked to carry some papers to the Principal's office—he's popular with teachers, if not students. On his way out of the room he awkwardly slips a folded note onto the desk of a beautiful hippie girl. Thinks he's being very suave, very James Bond.

Of course everybody in the room sees it and the note is quickly grabbed—I like to think Leigh herself had no part in the transfer—and passed to Corey Hass, class clown and designated hitman of the dominant clique. It's a perfect venue for Corey: last day of the year, cookies, red punch in dixie cups, carnival. Mrs Zemke has allowed the students to wander free. They gather at the back of the room, reading the note with an avidity which naturally makes their English teacher very proud.

Corey begins reading the note, falsetto. *Close-up of the note:* we see that it's written in what attempts to be Gothic script. It doesn't look much like Gothic but to be fair, it doesn't look at all like normal writing. Stylized pine trees extend from the first letter of the first word and the last letter of the last word, to enwrap the entire text—an interesting technique combining touches of medieval illuminated manuscript with the graphics of *Yellow Submarine.* It could well be the work of a novice monk who has been ingesting a bit too much ergot-contaminated medieval bread. And reading too much Tolkien.

As we look over the note, we hear Corey's maudlin reading of the pine-wrapped salutation: *"O Dearest Leigh..."*

Hoots from the entire troop; a primate voice howls "Dearest! Dearest!" in something like hysterical ecstasy, until Corey tells him to *Shut up asshole,* and pushes him. Corey goes on:

"O Dearest Leigh—Much have I wished to give to you some testimonial [sic] of my affections, yet I know not how. Willt [sic] thou meet me by the stream ere the sun touches the western pines?"

Pretty sic. One footnote: the "stream" was the concrete-lined drainage ditch that ran by the playground; the "western pines" refers to a line of scrubby Monterey pines planted along the edge of the playground, over by the ditch. But the sun really did touch them, sometimes. That part is accurate.

There is much joy in Mudville after Corey's reading. There has not been such joy since that fat woman teacher's bead necklace broke and all the beads fell through her dress onto the classroom floor while she was trying to make us *feel* a passage from *The Red Pony.*

Best of all, the performance has only begun. The author of the note is due back any minute. The primate troop now splits up for the hunt. Several males go to Leigh's desk and push her out of the room. The rest wait just inside the door.

When I got back I could pretty much guess what had happened. My hand had bumped Leigh's desk and the handoff had not gone as James Bond-ily as I'd imagined it would. The gap between the daylight world—California in June, hot, petrochemical—and the Tolkien world was suddenly clear, because I was falling down it.

I could see the set-up instantly. I was big on military history at that age. Corey had wisely positioned his forces in classic V-shape: four or five guys on each side, verbally enfilading my advance— "John! Hey, your sweetie wantsta see ya, whooo!"—like beaters driving me toward Corey. He had the note. He was waving it.

They folded around me: "Hey man, Leigh got your note! C'mon, man, she really wantsta seeya, Go on . . ." I tried to reach my desk, but Corey was planted in my way. I turned to make for the sink at the back of the room, which by tradition was sanctuary. But not this day. They'd've harried Thomas a Becket right up the high altar if he'd written that note. So I bounced and bumped around the room, herded—a herd of one, as Thoreau might put it—outside, where they had Leigh waiting. They held my arms and stood me in front of her.

She was good about it though; Leigh was a good person.

What it costs me to say that! But it's true. I hate those exceptions! This is how God must've felt when some Mesopotamian scrupuland reminded him he couldn't vaporize whichever Old-Testament city he was mad at, because there were two or three "just men" lodged inside it—a handful inconveniencing everybody, wasting God's time, standing in the way of progress, i.e. annihilation. These damned last-minute Quaker writs against capital punishment! These damned ex-nuns holding some mass-murderer's hand after his 37 appeals have enriched half the lawyers in the state! The "just" ones, the good ones—they're the whole trouble! Like the *Marighelistas* said when they began their campaign to kill selected saintly, charitable rich Brazilians: it is the good, virtuous, kindly *bourgeoises* who are the real problem, who must be most ruthlessly . . . excised. Because they confuse the picture, blur the image. Kill the good ones first!

Anyway . . . what happened? Hard to remember this part. Had my eyes almost closed. I guess I stayed standing there . . . with Leigh. I must have faced her, because I remember her shoes. Sandals, with laces up the ankle. I don't think I managed to look any higher, because that's all I remember. Besides, I already knew what she looked like. She really was very beautiful, and kind too. No rancor at the embarrassment I'd caused her, and that's saying a lot for a fourteen-year-old girl.

She shouldn't have been nice to me in the first place. Never be nice to anyone like me if you're a beautiful girl!

I looked at her sandals and made my mouth move. Mumbled something apologetic about hoping I hadn't embarrassed her. She said something to the effect that it was OK. Her big toe was twitching a little . . . I hoped, for a very long second, that it might have been a message of hidden affection, like the "I'm lying" gestures the American POWs were supposed to be making in their TV messages from Hanoi. But it was simple nervousness. And the POWs were probably just twitching with fear, too—I never believed in making saints of people who break under interrogation.

We completed our conversation. I suppose. I'm not still standing there, so logically it must've ended. I suppose I went back inside, and I guess she did too.

Leigh went on to fall in love with a scrawny hippie, shorter than she was, named "Jacques." How he got to be a "Jacques" I have no idea; he spoke California English with the mean nasal monotone of the born cool. Jacques was the perfect male of the Peace and Love era, nothing but bones and passive meanness, 120 pounds of ice with long hair on top. Add a couple of plastic palm trees and he'd've been the perfect anti-ship weapon: an iceberg with long hair and some song about love playing non-stop to attract ships. That was sex in the era of peace and love: he plays the iceberg—seven-eighths of it underwater, glacially cold and sharp as a steak knife, nothing but the long hair above water—and Leigh plays the *Titanic*.

I saw them together sometimes at lunch period. They sat on the grass, Leigh looking at Jacques and Jacques looking at nothing. The next I heard about Leigh was from some cool people talking admiringly about Jacques in Spanish class. It seems Leigh and Jacques were in his car in the high-school parking lot, and Leigh said, "Jacques I love you so much!" And Jacques—this is what they found so admirable—Jacques said, "Hey, that's your trip." They couldn't get over the coolness of that line.

So just don't ever try to tell me about peace and love, OK? You mellow memoirists of the hippie days. I know better—I sat behind you in Spanish class.

At the time, I didn't even grasp the context in which Leigh must've blurted out "I love you" so uncoolly: post-coital cliché. And he brags about it the next day, gives everybody a good laugh. A good sneer.

And *I* was the monster? That's the really sick, really funny part: there I was, dreaming of the slave markets every night, firing from the lap nine or ten times before I could sleep, convinced that

I was the monster, the sadist, the bad person the cops would take away!—while the normal, cool people like Jacques were leaving floods of pain behind them, smashing pre-Raphaelite faces left and right, a trail of blood with bare footprints and bell-bottom scuff marks . . . peace signs smeared in blood over the walls of Leigh's bedroom . . . the last of the happy hunting grounds for any male who had a cold enough heart—And me wiping my hand on my underwear, abasing myself in shame at my "cruelty"!

Leigh and her family moved to Oregon over the summer. All nice families were trying to flee North to Oregon or Washington, where there were still forests and rain. When we all sulked back to school in the Fall, nobody even bothered to hit me. PHHS couldn't even field a football team any more. It was a hungover era, its anthem James Taylor's acoustic whine about life in rehab. Nobody even cared enough to be mean any more.

I took their indifference as a sign I'd gotten better at hiding, and hid all the more carefully, sneaking around those sunlit beige corridors like Gollum in Moria. I failed half my courses, but got into Berkeley anyway. SAT scores, maybe—or the cool people were just too thrashed to send in their applications.

4

Fall 1975. My first semester at Berkeley. The Fall of Saigon—
and of the hippies. To their utter astonishment, the women
defected. The check came due for the male slaughters of the
sixties—for Woodstock, the stylized rape that passed for sex
among the peace and love people. And the waiter brought it
straight to me.

I graduated from high school too late for Vietnam but just in
time for BART: BART allowed me to commute to Berkeley. And
live at home.

BART: Bay Area Rapid Transit. A light-rail system which was
the technological equivalent of the Vietnam War. BART-NAM.
With subway gremlins standing in for the Viet Cong . . . little red-
star Looney Toon gremlins stealing a weight-bearing girder here,
altering a blueprint there, then snickering in Vietnamese/Gremlin
patois as they watch the test-train get buried under a million tons
of sandstone.

The blueprints were classic con-game stuff: soaring suburban
rail stations, approaches lined with trees as supple and willowy as
models on a catwalk, the stern noble canopy of the station, the
sweep of the aqueduct on which the trains would carry happy
dads to work in the city. BART was supposed to carry lebbenty-
zillion commuters at almost the speed of light. They would never
age, even. Dad would come home younger and cleaner-shaven
than when he'd left, and there would be the whole set-up waiting
unchanged: toothy kids, well-groomed dog and docile loving wife.

They never saw it coming, the docile-wife problem. She was a weight-bearing girder as far as they were concerned—and then she sues for divorce.

Ten years and a trillion dollars behind schedule, *just* in time for my freshman year at Berkeley, BART started running. Sort of: three trains per hour, prop-like aluminum shells, "futuristic" in a dated way like the monorails of old science-fiction films. Inside these chrome bodies were weary ancient engines capable of toiling to San Francisco at about 30 mph unless they broke down, which they invariably did. Then you had time to look at those poor losers zooming home on the freeways—they didn't know what they were missing!—while you stood (there were never any seats) and held onto something, the side of a seat, or just tried to keep your balance. There were no handholds of any kind, because as we had been told for the 15 years we'd been paying it off, no one would need to stand on BART. There would be trains arriving every 30 seconds and taking off at nine-tenths lightspeed. After all, this was not filthy New York, this was no dirty subway. This was the clean zone, the golden time.

When they christened the first shovelful of BART back in 1965, the guest of honor was the president after Kennedy, a Boris-Gudonov regent known as LBJ. I was a child, and we went there to see him. Americans still wanted to revere their presidents, and no President had ever come to Roofland. So we went to the site in the heat, the terrible summer smell of straw baking; people were there, waving Soviet-style placards: "Join us, Comrades! We are building the Future!" For me it was confusing, a clash between vision and smell. I could smell some really bad omens: dust, baking straw. But all around I could see the smiling placards.

Should've believed my nose and run off to someplace nice and cold. Antarctica perhaps. But back then I believed; my parents believed; and so did the half-million neighbors. Most had arrived early in their feckful Protestant way; we, naturally, were late, had to park a mile away and walk down a gauntlet of sun-flashing mirrors and windshields to the even brighter glare of the model-home BART car.

Rohr, the company which made the BART cars, was in the fighter-plane business. Which accounts for the fact that the model car gleamed so bright it hurt our eyes, and for the 2,000% cost overruns and decade-late delivery time, which was standard Defense-Department procedure. Not that any of us knew that. All we saw was that futuristic glint, not the money pouring down through the rails. The car hurt to look at, it was so sharp. A sharp aluminum nose like an F-4 Phantom. It had cost as much as a Phantom, too—and that was without an engine. As the sign by the car said, they would add the engines later. Do you not trust the engineers of the people, Comrade? The main thing was the gleaming Soviet shell. So shiny, Comrade! It would do Mach 3 on the straightaways, intercept oncoming ballistic missiles and still get you to work ten minutes before you left. The shock-wave of its passing would blow all the smoggy evil cars right off the freeways, and the sonic boom would scour every dingy tenement in Oakland. Another sign explained that the train would have "a human operator," though it didn't need one. The Computer would make all the real decisions.

The chrome prop sat on a 100-yard stretch of track—all the track which BART had actually laid. All around were stacks of rusted rails. The rust surprised me; I thought BART wouldn't rust. But I was ashamed of myself for noticing it. They probably *wanted* the tracks to rust before they used them—a kind of tempering, like firewood. It was just another proof of my stupidity that I even noticed! So I erased the rust from my sight, like a good Soviet child.

We wove our diffident way toward the circle of dust and dead grass where LBJ's helicopter would land. A hundred thousand trusting villagers ringed that circle, eager to lend their faith to restoring the Royal magic which had poured out of JFK's broken head. We stood in a circle and waited. And after two hours in the heat, we heard the big drum of the rotor announcing the royal Presence. Helicopters were full of pride back then. "Futuristic," that's what they were. Someday every suburban home would have a helipad, the same grinning dad waving to the kids as he got aboard. He got around, that futuristic dad; he just seemed to go from one conveyance to another.

It was another couple of years before the helicopter lost its magic—before people got tired of seeing jerky footage of them landing in unpronounceable rice paddies, disgorging bewildered cannon fodder from the high schools of America to fall face-first into paddy water that was two parts human shit and one part grenade. But for us, waiting in the heat for the President, the helicopter still meant the future, the royal steed, grace descending on the populace like Pentecost. There was a hum of excited gratitude from the crowd as LBJ's copter hovered overhead, then descended to our level through a column of cyclone.

And then the tornado touched the ground—the hard adobe chips and dry straw—and flung it up, a claymore mine blasting the Rooflanders with supercharged dust, blades of straw that could pierce a flak jacket, and clumps of adobe hard as concrete. The crowd hunched and cowered; parents tried to shield their children; and the helicopter continued its descent, though by the time LBJ walked out only a few combat-trained photographers were still facing him.

The official figures were that a couple dozen people were injured and several more "treated and released." But the lawsuits went on for years. And everyone knew, though as good Soviet citizens they never said it: the dynasty was cursed.

And now, ten years later, just as I was ready to go off to college, BART was finally up and running, just in time to let me commute to Berkeley—just in time for me to live at home.

If BART hadn't opened, I'd've had to move to the dorms. The dorms saved many, many of my kind. They met their kin there, learned to live without the flinch. Most of the tormentors were left behind in the suburbs. The SAT filtered them out of the admission line like substandard tomatoes. They had to stay on the hot, dull side of the hills: Concord, Walnut Creek, Pleasant Hill, there to fill out their days fixing cars. Or selling them. Or gassing them up.

But their cars never got them to Berkeley. Many a Tolkienist learned to walk upright for the first time in the gentle dorms. In fact, I found out much later that one of the student co-ops was named Lothlorien after the Lady Galadriel's sacred elven-wood of Middle Earth. Galadriel would have welcomed me, I know, into her room at Berkeley. Elven goddess with open arms . . . She would have been wearing glasses too, and her perfect face would be hidden behind them, hidden from all but me.

I would've been saved. I know it. I know there would've been someone for me there. There are girl nerds too, and many of them are beautiful, if you look at them by yourself, without relying on their embarrassed suite of gestures to construe them. It wouldn't even have required divine intervention or lottery-level luck. A full 50% of the first-year students at Berkeley were female! One out of two! The odds would actually have been in *favor* of something happening for me! Imagine it—in *favor!*

But thanks to BART, I figured out a way to beat those odds: commute, stay in my stinking airless room in Pleasant Hill.

Solitary confinement. Good behavior but no parole. The simple life: I came home, ate all the food in the house, snarled at my parents to shut up and leave me alone, and lay on my bed. And closed my eyes, and took myself in hand, and found the slave world, and tortured long-haired beautiful blonde girls as many times as I had to, to drain that abscess of what I had once feared was blood and now knew was pus.

Life without events. If another passenger on BART asked me what time it was, that was an event. It had to be, in lieu of any others. That little micro-event, pressed into service in the dead silence, would worry me for days: what did they mean by asking me what time it was?

You can vanish at Berkeley . . . the gray stone and the courtyards, languid Northern California old-money landscape, the dark cypresses, trees of good stock brushing crisply against gray stone. Lighting by Maxfield Parrish. Ishi hid there in the grace of his protectors, the founders, Quakers and communists of good family, scions of the Mayflower fallen in love with Polynesia, benefactors whose three interchangeable Saxon names lived in every imaginable combination on the doorways of the gray stone buildings. The buildings themselves had a tall, stooped, sternly kind posture. Their interiors were public grandeur: high rococo ceilings of the aristocracy, and beneath them carrels and tables in plain gray. Aristocratic socialism in architectural form. Over my head.

I walked around that campus attracting no more attention than a Snickers wrapper. It was miserable, but that went without saying. And it was easily explained, in historical terms. Remember, I was a Soviet child, raised on public lies and no wiser at 18 than at eight. And if, in the year 1975, you were very, very stupid and bookbound and naive—if you never talked to anyone, and believed everything you read in the papers—you just might be dumb enough to think everyone was alone now, because all mating, all men/women business, had officially stopped.

I was dumb enough to believe it. I was *more* than dumb enough! Aztec-level, Mormon-level dumb! So I swallowed all of the lies of the Steinem era and didn't even hiccup.

As far as I could see in my big lecture classes, no one at Berkeley ever . . . well, had "relationships"—that kind of thing. They made a show of not noticing each other. Walked in alone; took notes; left alone. And every Sunday, in the Pink Section of the *Chronicle,* there was another essay on the defection of the docile wife, her conversion to pure anger and determination to be alone.

Like everyone who has no pleasure, I took pride. I was the new norm, walking point for the new way things were—alone. And I'd been living like that even before the essays announced it. My wretched existence was a paradigm.

So stupid! So *stupid!*

Sade started writing in prison, you know. They put him in solitary—no charges, no trial. *Lettre de cachet*—loosely translated, "Until You Rot, Baby!" Sade wrote increasingly crazy begging letters demanding to know the charges. But there were no charges, and they didn't have to tell him anything. So they didn't. His case may simply have been forgotten in the administrative chaos of the Old Regime. The jailers weren't particularly worried. Just checked the peephole and passed his food through the slot. And he passed the time screaming and masturbating and scribbling. And screaming and screaming and screaming. That's where those torture novels started.

They had me in a trickier form of solitary. I was allowed to walk around. And around and around. From the student cafeteria to the library to class, and then back to the library, passing under the elegant ceilings, down echoing corridors to the basement room where periodicals were kept. They had these magazines there: *Armed Forces Journal. Aviation Week & Space Technology. Proceedings of the Institute of Naval Warfare.* What *Penthouse* was to you healthy people—and the sports pages, and the *New Yorker* as well, not to mention, come to think of it, reality, sex with other human beings, even—what all that was to you, the chronicles of each magnificent new weapon's perilous course through the appropriations committee and the inter-service rivalries was to us.

We all come from there, you know. All of us *Waffen-Twerpen*. My loathsome, sluglike soul mates. Tom Clancy. He comes from there. Do you know what it was like for me to read *Patriot Games?* At the time that book came out (1988), I was devoting all my time to Irish Northern Aid, sending all the money I could spare to Sinn Fein—and then Tom Clancy, my fellow Irish-American war-nerd alumnus, comes out with a groveling Brit-sucking novel about Northern Ireland. And makes millions off it, and Harrison Ford plays the lead in the movie. At which point, I read in People magazine, Clancy immediately left his first wife Wanda and their four corpulent kiddies to shack up with a lissome 20-year-old groupie. That's the way to play it.

A cuckold in everything.

But don't imagine that confessing my kinship with Tom Clancy amounts to what you would call "the narrator's self-indictment." In the house of the *Waffen-Twerpen* there are many mansions, and many cousins who have passed each other in the hallways for 20 years without speaking. Clancy is a relative—and a swine. I can see him so clearly, a fat Republican dweeb sliding on a trail of mucus down to the periodical room to drool over the latest copy of *Armed Forces Journal.* I spent many an anxious hour down there, grazing the war mags with his ilk. (We're an ilk, all right.)

I would stroll, oh casually, around the reading area, casually checking what journals my fellow virgins clutched in their baby-fat hands, seeking the rival who had beaten me to the latest hot issue of *AFJ* and *Aviation Week.*

I would find the thief soon enough. There were only three species in that airless basement, and they were easy to tell apart. First, of course, the healthy people, thin and clean. They didn't matter; they were there only to research something, and would head back upstairs to the sunlit and ventilated part of the library as soon as they could. Then there were the wretched foreign students, drooling over a Delhi starlet's exposed ankle or checking for relatives in the latest beheading news from the Emirates. And lastly the rival *Waffen-Twerpen* who had preempted the new *AFJ*. The new issue was supposed to have color pictures of the prototype twin-40-mm "Sgt York" anti-aircraft tank, as well as an AAI ultrahigh-velocity 75 mm rapid fire cannon mounted on a light tank turret and supposedly combining self-defense capacity against aircraft and attack helicopters with the ability to penetrate up to 200mm of conventional tank armor at a 35° angle. That platform made my mouth water. Pix of the rapidfire 75-mm turret!

I had to see it, I needed that magazine. It was all I had to look forward to for the next month. You have no idea. I saw later where you'd been, why I never saw any of you. You had dorm rooms. With watergun fights—that led to sex . . . and stoner sessions—that led to sex . . . and going down to the cafeteria to complain about the food—which led to sex, and kept you thin as well.

While we who had nothing but the pictures of the new weapons distractedly ate entire boxes of Oreos, with a big bottle of coke to wash them down, cookie crumbs floating on the backwash fizz. And got fatter without even tasting what we gulped.

Now the healthy people have taken up military stuff, it's all become easy and fashionable. Now everyone can quiver as half-mile-square chunks of jungle turn into giant Molotov cocktails, and 1,500-lb porpoises of plastique glide like nimble terns into a bunker, mating once and for all. The Gulf Wars brought all that to the ken of the healthy/happy. Who paid nothing. Who never pay. Never kept vigil with us.

Why are they always given *everything*, when they pay for *nothing?* You can order a box set of Iraq target-cam DVDs on Amazon now, in a moment, just enter your card number and hit "Checkout" Pop them in, watch them with a few beers and boom, you, the sexually healthy coolster, have accessed all the secret war porn me and my pudgy, miserable comrades spent years seeking in that airless periodical room. All through the dark civilian seventies we waited kneeling, like Provos denied the Host.

And outside the Periodical Room, we had nothing. Can years go by without anything happening? It's not supposed to be possible . . . but I think so, I think they can. When it rained I spent the hours between classes in the Student Union, another kindly tall room with redwood paneling and soft lighting which made it impossible to read. You could sit in dark squat chairs, popular with the street people, so the room smelled like the Elephant House and hummed with one-person conversations. I drew Viking battles and wondered if you could get lice from a chair.

But that didn't happen; nothing living would touch me. Things happened in the world, newspaper things. The last of the big student demonstrations went echoing down Telegraph Avenue. And the SLA, the "Symbionese Liberation Army,"—Berkeley's first real Communist terrorist group—made a big hit.

Their first move was not too bright; these people were not Baader-Meinhof material; they killed the first black school superintendent Oakland had ever had. With cyanide-tipped bullets. They shot him eleven times, at close range—so the cyanide, though a nice poetic touch, probably wasn't all that necessary. They could've tipped the bullets with Tiger Balm and he'd've been just as dead-dead-deadsky.

That debut had even the local radicals scratching their heads. But the SLA's second number was an instant hit: they grabbed Patty Hearst, daughter of the man who owned the *San Francisco Examiner*, from the Berkeley apartment where she was slumming as a student. Three men in masks bopped her weedy boyfriend on the head with a wine bottle (the Bay Area equivalent of a Glasgow Kiss: the "Chardonnay Slap") and bundled her away. She was cute, too—small, fem, shy-looking. And of course the kidnapping of a young woman is for us the central sexual story.

Her boyfriend was a contemptible man. He was tall and thin and weedy—and his name, unbelievably, was Weed, Stephen Weed. He'd been her teacher at a private school. He was much older than Patty. He showed up at a press conference, with a showy bandage on his head, looking like a forlorn egret—decorative, but useless when the fight came.

I would not have let her be taken so easily. But then I would not have been in her apartment in the first place.

Weed was a regular on the news, repeating his pleas and rehashing his grief, right up to the time Patty sent a tape declaring her allegiance to her captors and calling Weed a tool of the bourgeoisie. That was a good moment. If only I'd known at the time that Patty had been converted by being locked in a closet for weeks, regularly raped by the males and . . . played with . . . by the

dykey females of the entire "Symbionese Liberation Army"—all
fifteen of them—it would have been an even better one.

I read all the background stories about Patty, not so much out
of human interest as desperation for anthropological basics. Like,
how did this boyfriend of hers *become*, as it were, a boyfriend? How
did a "Weed"-mammal come to be in the same apartment as a
"Hearst"-mammal, so that they could mate and be in love and
drive around the country in a hippie van and live on the beach and
run through fields of flowers with that Judy Collins song in the
background and be insanely happy, the very opposite of me?

Most other species had open, fair arrangements, as shown on
the documentaries. Elephant seals, for example, gathered at a sub-
Antarctic island. Those males who aspired to control a harem
simply blubbered up to each other, roaring their fish-breath
challenges, then took turns stabbing their canines into their rival's
blubbery mantle of carbuncled leather. The one who couldn't
endure enough pain to gain the right to mate wriggled away in a
slapstick shimmer of humiliated, gelded fat. The winner was left
sole lord of the harem.

They always used that term, "harem"—as if a troop of Arabian
slave girls awaited the bellowing master on his frozen beach. Of
course it was only seals, but the females *were* sort of attractive,
once you saw how thoroughly they were possessed. Steinem had
clearly gained no beachhead on that frozen shore. The females
were nicely tiny—one-fifth the size of the males—though
technically a little overweight. And beautiful eyes. Well, after all,
that's probably somewhat like how your average Arabian slave girl
looked too; hence "harem." All in all, a simple, sound, honorable
and, above all, *easily understood* system.

Among the ruminants, the male mating contests involved
headbutting or antler-wrestling. Elk were always shown fencing,
one rack of antlers clacking against another, in a meadow beneath
a placemat-perfect landscape of the Rockies. The two males,
expressionless, would jab and twist their kendo racks, eyes forced
to the rocky ground. Completely silent; only the wooden clack of
the antler-racks while the does watched, expressionless. They
knew whose side they were on: they were on the side of the *winner*.
And they are utterly fair, disinterested, in the outcome of the duel.
They awaited the attentions of the winning genes.

Two male elk will continue fighting until they starve to death. (As is proper!) Sometimes two males will lock antlers and get stuck. Eventually (cut to a close-up of two elk skulls, antlers entwined, resting by a mountain lake, flowers poking through the eye-holes), they die locked together, and make a memorial sculpture in bone, a monument to simplicity and honor. Sometimes one will live a little longer than the other and the survivor will continue to wrestle the other's corpse back and forth as if it still stood in the way of his right to mate.

People were like that once. Dying after two months' hunger strike in a British prison, Terence MacSwiney, Lord Mayor of Cork, said, "Victory will go not to those who can *inflict* the most but to those who can *endure* the most." But MacSwiney wasn't from California. Some other criterion operated there. I could never figure it out. Survival of the . . . the what? "The cool," I supposed. But "cool" begs the question: what were its component traits? If only it were as simple as fangs on a freezing shingle beach or horns locked in a mountain plateau. Or swords, or pistols, or battleaxes in a darkened room, or rattlesnakes in cardboard boxes, or cigarette lighters to each other's fingertips, and the first to flinch loses. Anything! Choose your weapons! I was more than willing to maul a rival male—the male elephant seals even *looked* like me!

But you just didn't see that kind of thing at Berkeley. The males at Berkeley never locked horns or traded stabs. They weren't built for it. Thinner, more slippery, more like eels or herons. Like Patty's Weed. They won their mates via some sly system no one had managed to photograph, like the mating of eels. The nature shows informed me that in three centuries of looking, no one had managed to find the eels' mating-ground. That was ominous. I suspected it would turn out to be Berkeley.

Only one thing made my celibacy bearable: the certainty that mating, in our species, was already coming to an end anyway. It was in the papers every Sunday. Women were angry. It was in the movies, those brownish '70s movies about people that always showed Liv Ullman very slowly, earnestly getting sick of her Swede man. And Jill Clayburgh with her American. And Jane Fonda's soldier husband killing himself, to give her room to get to know herself.

And there were also the "well-written" essays—a civics teacher's notion of eloquence—which filled up my schoolbook, the *Norton Anthology*. These essays explained that men and women had to go their separate ways now, because history showed it was all bad, their couplings, and had to be done away with. It was Oppression, like Central America only with gender.

It fit with what I knew about the ideological sequence in Irish nationalism: Parnell leads to Pearse; nationalism leads to separatism. And it fit with Vietnam. Q: how many soldiers did the South Vietnamese Army have? The correct answer was: *none*. There were two million men wearing the uniform of that Army, but none of them were really loyal to it. And if you applied that to gender, it went, How many women are there who actually *like* men—now, in 1976? The correct answer, of course, was: *none*. Which explained a lot. *No wonder I was alone!* Everyone was, or soon would be. The whole condemned edifice was being torn down. As it deserved to be, because in seventeenth-century England it was OK to beat your wife before ten o'clock.

It did seem a little unfair that these people who'd just spent ten years in a non-stop orgy of sex and love had finally had enough and with a hungover grumble rolled over and told everybody it was time to go home. Alone.

But it was the march of history; that was that. My own fault for not having gotten when the getting was good, showing up too late and too shy. Off limits now, boarded up. Go on home.

If you live at home, with parents who are actual Catholics, you'll believe any grim, arbitrary privation. It hadn't occurred to me that there might be a discrepancy between ideology and way of life, because God knows there wasn't in our house. So I believed the essayists of aloneness—actually believed that *they too* lived the ideology they wrote. Took me ten years more to learn that most Americans don't mean a word—I mean literally *not one word*—of what they spout. It's a nice little historical irony: I was the one studying Russian, but they were the real *sovyetskie lyudi* ("Soviet People").

And, to be fair: aloneness had its compensations. For one thing, nobody punched me or laughed at me any more. Nobody could see me at all. I'd sit next to people at lectures or on benches, separate and not nearly equal. Of course I occasionally wanted

someone to see me . . . that one there, walking across Sproul Plaza
with the wind in her pre-Raphaelite hair, the smile the hippies had
from birth, that beaming look of pure unintellection...that one
could, maybe, fall in love with me . . . Was that much to ask?

Yes, said the stern Sunday Feature thought pieces. It's too late for
that. We must all be alone now.

Well, at least we were all in the same boat. That seemed fair.
Like Tacitus' Romans, "They made a desert and called it peace."
Though, being more advanced than Tacitus, they called it "Peace
and Love."

Which is why I took up karate. The world was so peaceful that
I would've walked across the continent to find some way of
hitting back. I joined the UC Berkeley Karate Club. And that, see,
that led to an EPIPHANY, just like in the big literature they had
us read! Joyce and them. A certifiable EPIPHANY.

For all the good it did.

The way my epiphany happened—see, I'd never stayed in
Berkeley in the evening before. But the Karate Club met in the
evenings, so if I wanted to learn to smash people—which I very,
very much did—I had to stay in Berkeley till late. And that's how,
for the first time in many years, I looked around and saw
something that wasn't in the papers. That contradicted everything
in the papers.

It was a Tuesday evening, after karate. Late for me to be
leaving the campus—seven o'clock. I was clomping down the
creekside path to BART, tired and proud after two hours of
miming kicks and punches at the gym. It was Fall semester, still
warm most evenings until the blessed sea fog, like the soft and
comforting hand of Mary in those blue-white Catholic statues,
came across the Golden Gate, passed over Alcatraz and stroked
the genteel oak hills of Berkeley. After a hot day like this one the
sweet sea fog would come across the Bay and steep from the
ground the smell of bay laurel. The laurel trees love water, and
they grew all along the creek beside the path to BART. You
inhaled their promise that soon, soon, life would begin.

The crushed laurel rising to the wall of fog, the lights of San
Francisco, the pride of two hours spent hitting back, the desperate
hope of the Irish books, that all is not lost—all of it at once,
inhaled—

Then I heard something; a girl. Laughing. Oddly enough, she didn't appear to be laughing at me. She was ahead of me on the path. Heading off-campus, toward BART. But the funny thing was that it looked like . . . she was . . . *with* someone. Someone male. And somehow . . . they didn't look like they were just friends. Something about the slow, coy flutter, side to side, in the way they walked, shoulders merged, tilted toward each other. They were weaving from one side of the path to the other like drunk drivers without a car. But it was too patterned to be drunkenness: they would veer left as he leaned against her . . . and she would laugh, the way she had that first time . . . and as they reached her side of the path, when it looked like they would be forced off the path entirely, she would lean against him, and they would veer to the right.

I couldn't escape the conclusion that it was some sort of mating ritual. No matter what the papers said. There just wasn't another plausible interpretation. It had to mean that they were . . . like she was . . . you know, *with* him. In that sense.

I walked closer as quietly as I could. Which was unfortunately not all that quiet. Because I was wearing the same motorcycle boots I'd worn for the last two years. I found their steel toes comforting (and they made me look taller) and besides, I was afraid I might have to talk to a shoe salesman if I tried to get another pair. The biker boots were ill adapted for surveillance: for one thing, the nails had been poking up through the soles for a few months, ripping many small craters in the soles of my feet. These suppurating holes tended to bleed excessively if I walked too fast. And the slick, sticky jam of blood, pus and lymph made my feet slide around dangerously inside the boots, causing me to wobble. And this, combined with the smell of my stain-camouflaged coat and the loud hissing of the once-brown corduroy pants, tended to attract the attention of the surveilled. A symphony, I was. A one-man band. Multimedia. Hard to miss. Clomping like Igor after this sweet clean couple as they wafted down the street among the genteel trees.

But they were far too wrapped up in each other to notice me. They—it was incredible. She—I'll never forget it—she turned, so I could see her profile, and on her face was this look of adoration, total unqualified adoring affection. And after holding that look for one or two paces, she leaned up on her tiptoes and kissed the guy right on the face.

Don't tell me I didn't see it! I saw it. I have the video. In my head. My Kennedy-assassination tape. Proof of a massive conspiracy. Because it was obvious: she was *with* him. Despite what all the angry-woman writers in the Sunday-Feature articles said, despite the alleged historical inevitability of my noble isolation. All that, I realized, was a lie, and not worth one millionth of what some generic male had been given, *RIGHT IN FRONT OF ME*—

All ongoing battles were lost at once: Persian darts pierced my phalanx, again and again. Longstreet's corps broke on the bayonets of the bluecoats. Ludendorff's offensive stalled in the bloody mud of Verdun.

The more it hurt, the drooler I peeped. I had to see every bit of it, a high-level spy plane collecting data: *She leans her head against his shoulder. He puts his arm around her. They veer down the path. He nuzzles her hair, she jumps slightly . . . did he bite her? Do they bite? Is that part of what they do?*

But bite or no bite, there could be no doubt about the main point. She, he, they were together. Couples were not extinct.

And when I accepted this terrible conclusion, it all clicked. A massive conspiracy. Look at the evidence! Look at how the two of them were dressed! All in bright colors and everything—what they call "dressed up"! In class, people at Berkeley dressed *down*—but these two were all dressed *up*; in class, people pretended to be glum as anything, glum as me—but look at these two laughing as if there were an endless supply! They didn't have to pretend to be depressed any longer. They were smiling. *She* was smiling.

She wasn't angry at her companion; she didn't hate him; she didn't blame him for "the past 3000 years of whatever"—she *liked* him. Probably even the other L-verbed him. Saw it when she smiled at him.

I'd forgotten what it looks like when a beautiful young woman flicks on that smile . . . how the world sort of explodes. Secondary explosions were continuing as the great cities inside my head burned out of control. Let it burn. Let it burn. Let it all burn.

I knew where they were going. In the end, after their—what else could you call it?—their "date." To their apartment. One of theirs—hers, maybe his. Same one for both. *Both of them to the same one.*

Think of how a wolf would howl if it was a fat, dough-faced wolf, freckles and glasses, walking along a path trying to stay off the nails in its boots. If it was late. Late evening, late 70s, late everything. Too late. A stunned steer, not a wolf. *Album title: A Stunned Steer Moos the Blues.* A wolf/twerp Rosetta Stone to translate this into chords I could sell. No, no chords, no jokes, no metaphors, no. Just plain no.

But how could they . . . they said all that stuff was *over! So they lied, huh? And you're surprised? I guess that's big news . . . if you're stupid.*

Meanwhile they were getting ahead of me. But what was developing intracranially was more urgent. My parliament files into the High Council Chamber for a solemn summit. Still-drowsy deputies, many still in their nightclothes, mutter in puzzlement, then hush as the front wall opens to reveal a huge viewscreen. Drowsiness gives way to horror, then rage, as they watch this appalling anomaly, this Cuban missile footage: a youthful student couple walking down the Strawberry Creek path, displaying unashamed affection *in clear violation of our treaty with Dusk!* The deputies cry out in bewilderment and rage, cry out for vengeance.

And I, their hound, their loyal *Cu Chullain,* follow the target, the happy couple, imagining a procession of weapons in my empty hands. That's what karate means, you know: "empty hands." And that's why all losers take karate. I filled my empty hands with all the weapons of sacred vengeance; Morningstar mace, falchion, Agincourt arrow-cloud, Thirty-Year pike wall, T-34 overrolling Kursk, Khe Sanh claymore mine, Laotian arclight strike . . .

But my weapons were useless. I was losing ground literally; the two young people were walking faster, getting away from me. They turned off onto Shattuck Avenue where all the restaurants were, the neon zone, outside my range.

As they walked away, leaning into each other like joyful drunks, I stopped on the corner, the gentle hand of the sea fog brushing my face. I looked around me; and whether it was the later hour or that seeing the lovers had somehow broken the blindness-spell upon me, I could suddenly see such couples everywhere. Two more walked by that corner while I stood there drooling like an idiot. "Extinct"? They were about as extinct as sparrows!

All you had to do was walk through Berkeley after 6:00 PM The student community seemed to have some strange Ramadan-like prohibition on displays of affection before sunset. But after that . . . there was a traffic jam of these supposedly extinct couples.

What was strangest was that the rumors of extinction were being published and promoted *by the allegedly extinct species themselves!* The same bright young people who wrote somber thought-pieces about the advent of an Age of Sacred Aloneness, how women were angry and wanted nothing more to do with men, were to be found heading off campus every night in clearly sexual embraces!

Which meant—I worked it out slowly, like an elephant seal doing algebra—which meant, um . . . yeah: that there was only *one* person living the life of anger and aloneness they talked up. Three guesses who it was.

But how did they do it? And I mean . . . *why?* This sort of ideological double-bookkeeping was so far over my head that I couldn't imagine the sort of consciousness it required as habitat. How could a person write propaganda for a life they didn't lead or even *want* to lead? What sort of greedy, indiscriminate mind could come up with a triple-cross like that?

I didn't get it. But so what? *It* got *me.* You don't need a medical degree to die of malaria.

That night, in the cities of my head, we rioted. Stormed the Reichstag where that doomed Parliament of "moderates"—i.e. traitors—met. Crawled out of the sewers and went hunting through the petit-bourgeois districts favored by the "Moderates," hunted down all advocates of "compromise" and "reason," and kicked them to death and set them on fire with kerosene and hanged their greasy smoking corpses from the overpasses.

Then we did a propaganda remake of the key encounter. It went something like this:

Epiphany, Take Two: I walk behind them in better boots. Silent boots. I now have a wasp waist to go with my gorilla shoulders. In silence I step behind them, blood tango, precisely matching their lazy sybaritic pace, then lean forward and draw my razor-knife deftly, courteously, through his smile-tendons, his laugh-windpipe,

his smug carotids . . . and lift him with one hand. (I actually
could've lifted an average man one-handed back then. I may not
have been well but I was terribly strong.)

He is now a very messy package, a broken ketchup bottle, a
hoe-cut hose. He is interrupting our *tete-a-tete* with his crude
gurglings and his red sprays, dangling at arms' length, distracting
my lovely interlocutor. So I toss his spouting carcass casually,
offhandedly, into Strawberry Creek . . . Then turn, a wry smile on
my newly angular face, and say to her, "Sorry for the
inconvenience. Allow me to introduce myself . . ."

It helped, a little. My critics said it was "formulaic," but it kept
me working: lifting more and more in the gym, kicking harder in
the dojo.

And twice a week, after karate, I walked the same path by the
creek, body politely hidden in my horse-blanket quilted coat in
spite of the heat I radiated, keeping my sweat and dirt to myself,
as an unending series of couples passed me, a comedy of surplus
epiphanies, a rain of loving couples like coconuts falling on Curly's
head. And dreamed, on good days, of killing the males and taking
the females. And on bad days dreamed of nothing but getting a
train and clomping home to eat greased sugar, snarl at my parents,
snuffle into bed and find Lapland.

All I could actually do when I walked past the couples was
straight-arm the nearest street sign, make it clang loud and hard,
and hope that they jumped out of their mingling skins. I never
looked back to see, though . . . and I had to stop doing even that,
because I whopped so many street signs that my wrist got hurt.
And I needed both wrists for lifting and karate.

5

Karate. *Empty hand* is right. Hands don't get no emptier. So I joined the Empty-Hand Club. The real scripture: *Make of thine empty hand a club . . . and thy plowshares into fists.* Tuesdays and Thursdays I bore my white fighting outfit up the hill to the old gym, to kneel on the hard wood floor, waiting for Sensei. It was weird to be among people outside of school hours. All around me there were people, off-duty, in their medieval Japanese bathrobes. I prayed that they'd talk to me, and that they wouldn't.

Needn't've worried. The class was run on the lines of an Imperial Japanese military academy *circa* 1939. Minimal chit-chat while waiting for Sensei, who always walked in late, like a pop star. He was Japanese, about five feet tall, perhaps a hundred pounds, and widely believed, by what I overheard in the locker room, to be made of titanium and able to kill with a glance. He ruled from the top of the room, seated on a little platform, and spoke to the multitudes through his lieutenants, two huge white guys. Very rarely he would descend to floor level and do someone the honor of miming their deaths for them, coyly brushing the edge of their windpipes with his open hand or snapping a kneecap backwards with his dainty foot. Those so honored went back to their places with a blush of pride.

I was not often so honored. I didn't perform very well in the *Kata,* the mystic ballet which seemed to be the focus of the club. Real, full-contact sparring was very rare. I did very well at that— an instinct for how to hurt and be hurt—but this was not noticed.

Sensei usually just sat on his throne and watched us perform the mystical kicks and punches which showed our "harmony," or some such impractical tripe.

It bothered me to spend so much time on my knees. Not that I had moral objections—God no! But the Japanese formal kneeling position was extremely uncomfortable for my barrel body. Discomfort leads to heresy: I wanted to see Sensei up against a heavyweight contender, a 230-pound middling heavyweight. Not even the champion; just a very large, very quick black American who had spent his whole life hitting and being hit, rather than dancing this Zen ballet. I had my little doubts. I tended to see Sensei hitting the wall, a dainty Archeopteryx splatter of bones and blood. It was agony there on the hard wooden floor. My ankles were about to break—it was like balancing a refrigerator on a couple of wooden coat-hangers.

Each of us was trying desperately to become a warrior. There was no sense of community, though. What nerds want above all is to get the hell away from anybody who reminds them of themselves. Betray each other in a second. Not a very prepossessing lot, either: they were mostly short, skinny guys—I was a giant in that group—and the high-school flinch still showed itself from time to time, along with its counter-move, the worthy nerd's desperate courage and determination to die rather than be bullied again.

That Tao of flinch and defiance was admirable in the abstract, but kind of disgusting in person, simultaneously manifested on a hundred pallid, small-boned faces. Some of them were extraordinarily graceful, sweeping about in the Kata, but somehow I didn't see them busting up muggers, becoming the stuff of urban or even suburban legend. The longer I had to spend on my knees, listening to a hundred high-strung asthmatics mystically inhaling during our "meditation" sessions, the less I believed. And worst of all, I could smell my mould.

The *gi*, the ceremonial white fighting outfit, was the problem. Those karate sessions got very sweaty. We'd start out doing pushups on our clenched fists. This not only got us in shape, but was incredibly painful. The central notion of Sensei, this refugee from General Tojo's staff, was that pain was good for you. Not inflicting it—which would have been fine—but enduring it, which

I didn't really need organized help with. Sensei, the Church, and the Irish martyrs of our Green Shelf were of one mind about the superiority of enduring pain to inflicting it: why do pushups on your open hands when you could crunch your knuckles on the hardwood floor? Then sit-ups and other exercises, retooled for maximum pain effect.

It got you very sweaty. Two hours of torture ballet under the gaze of Admiral Yamamoto and you were dripping. I was, anyway. I sweat like a pig, and the white fighting tunic was like a used towel by the time we were allowed to get up off our knees and shower. I understood showering but I didn't get what you were supposed to do with the dirty clothes. My mother washed mine, I suppose. I think she did; at any rate they disappeared from the floor of my room, then reappeared, hung on the doorknob of my room like propitiatory gifts left outside the ogre's cave; and when they reappeared they bore a new non-organic smell. Presumably they had been "washed"; but I knew nothing of the actual process. I simply grabbed them and wrenched them onto my body, trying not to notice the implied waistline, before snarling farewell and heading off to BART.

But the *gi* was different. It was secret. I couldn't let my parents know I was taking karate. Not because they wouldn't understand but because they *would*. All too well. People talked about their parents not understanding them; I feared being understood.

Besides, discovery would ruin my secret war plan. An animate weapon was being built inside the tent-like quilted coat. And nobody was going to see it until it was too late for them to do anything about it. So I kept the *gi* zipped up in the ratty Pan Am bag in which I carried my unread textbooks and chewed-up, woad-dripping pens.

After a few weeks of this routine I made a scientific discovery: sweat on white cotton medieval Japanese tunics makes a great medium for the incubation of green smelly mildew. Especially helpful is keeping said tunic zipped up tight in a flight bag. Mould cultivated under these conditions, we have found, shows astonishing growth rates.

At first I was puzzled at these big green spots on the armpits and the back of my fighting tunic. What was going on? Dye from the bag I kept them in? Some weird chemical reaction unknown to science? It was a deep mystery, and painful to contemplate, because the Pan Am bag was a souvenir from a trip to New York when I was a little kid, when we still had money. And now I was dragging it around dripping pen-ink all over it, turning it green, wrecking it. Better get an XL Coke at the student union and not think about it.

After another week, the green spots merged, formed continents, and finally the bag actually began to leak spores. It was their smell which finally told me (and anybody else in the same building or BART-car with me) that the green continents were mould. If you opened up the bag, a whole season of spores rushed out to propagate their kind. The stench was pretty sickening, even to me. It was like opening up a storage shed full of old newspapers. I decided not to do anything about it.

This inaction facilitated the growth of the mould continents. Another week and the bag began to leak spores even when zipped shut—spores so fine that they passed through the sides of the flight bag like diatoms through a salmon-net. They floated out behind me, undaunted, bravely meeting the world.

Heads began to turn, or at least flinch, when I walked by; the old days of invisibility seemed a lost Golden Age. The air of decay followed me like the Reaper all around that sunny campus: *Pepe LePeu meets Charon.* I was the Johnny Appleseed of Berkeley: "Johnny Moldspore." Benefactor of future generations, selflessly spreading a harvest of mildew, a zephyr from the crypt, through the public glades of Berkeley.

It was baffling what to do about it. Short of telling my mother. Well, I wouldn't actually have to *tell* her—I wasn't much on that direct-conversation stuff at home. "Say it with a snarl,"—that was my motto. I could just sort of stomp up and hand the karate outfit to her, in a "Wash this!" kind of way . . . but then she'd know about karate, and understand. And I couldn't have that.

After weeks of intensive speculation, the *gi* had developed distinctive green continents, not unlike the shroud of Turin. Only greener. The sweatspots on my back and under my arms spread their wings, great Amazonian forests. Every day they got bigger, until one night, kneeling before Sensei at the end of karate class, pretending to focus on proper breathing, I became uncomfortably aware of the intensity of the mildew smell radiating from my reeking body, and noted for the first time that no one was within twenty feet of me. It was a big room, but still . . . they were sort of clustered over there on the other side of the hall. I wondered dizzily, for a moment, if it was due to the antibiotic effects of mould: the whole room like an agar slide, with my penicillin mould keeping these organisms at bay. But there was a much simpler hypothesis, much more embarrassing and therefore true. I stank.

No wonder Sensei had sent me down after a few clumsy moves when it was my turn to do the *Kata*. I had probably dishonored the Emperor with my reek. Probably making a faux pas right now by not committing ritual suicide in front of the entire karate class, the whole Empty-Hand Clan.

My face instantly flushed with shame. Shame and stupid, for ever. *You always have, you're so stupid and stupid and stupid, you're so stupid, God get me out, stupid, stupid, stupid—*

I looked around for somebody to share the blame—anybody who might be greener and smellier than me. (The nerd's instinct to deflect the group's anger toward another victim.) Even one other greenie would help . . . but no. None! Not a single one of the other gi's had even a *trace*, a little light lime-green five-o'clock mould-shadow. Green belts, yes; but no green gi's. Pure white. A flock of small people whiter than seagulls, unsullied. And they smelled different from me, too, now that I focused on it, trying to filter out my own Van Allen Belt of aromas. Yes, their smell was—not so organic. More chemical—like when you walk past a laundromat, probably comes from the stuff like "shaving cream" and "cologne" they advertised on TV. "Ban": that was the name of an aerosol deodorant whose commercials I vaguely remembered. But how did people know about those things? Where did they acquire them?

It seemed unfair that they managed not to support even a little mould, to even things out. It should have been more widespread. After all, I didn't invent mould; mould was a fact! Mould occurred naturally. In forests, for example. Part of the balance of nature—breaking down dead trees. How did they override mould growth? They knew something I didn't. Their bodies were non-stick Teflon . . . differentially-permeable membranes: dirt and smell slid off them, yet sexual partners stuck. Once again, the terrible gulf

between their advanced technology and our slipshod peasant
army, the non-fun of being your own third world. It was time to
run away again, time for our conscripts to throw away their
defective rifles and run for the hills. I cowered on my knees,
waiting for the end of the session. *Oh God I swear, I swear if they let
me out of this room, I will run away and never come back, just let me get out,
let them not yell at me in front of everybody* . . . Just give me a head start
down to the locker room and I swear I'll be dressed and out, out
of your way, in ten seconds: run out onto the street, jump in front
of a speeding truck, something quick.

Shame made me sweat harder, kneeling there pretending to
inhale and exhale in tune with the Universe or whatever Shinto
drivel it was we were supposed to be practicing. The heat of my
shame made the spores even friskier; I was ready to choke on the
smell of mould. I looked at the floor to hide the blush I could feel
warming my face. Leigh's sandals were still there. More shame,
endless waves of shame, spores of it blowin' in that wind their
precious Dylan used to talk about—a monsoon of petty
humiliations, tiny harpoons in my whale hide . . . the white whale,
Whale-Eyes, my name for myself, my secret name.

Time went by, presumably, while I knelt there waiting for
Sensei to release us. Everybody was looking at me in disgust. I
could see them through my eyelids as I pretended to focus on my
breathing. We breathed. That's what you're supposed to do when
you panic: breathe deeply. So I breathed.

This is a particular kind of moment which I remember well:
the waiting to run away. Epiphanies in stories and movies
generally cut directly to action; there's a quick cut from, say,
realizing that you're offending everybody else in the room with
your smell, to you running away. But in my experience there's
usually a long time between knowing and being allowed to leave. I
had to kneel there on the parquet floor making a show of deep-
breathing for a long time before I could run to the dressing room,
stuff the *gi* back in its bag and walk down the path to BART.

But I went back to the next class. In the same green *gi*. I
couldn't quit. Sometime, I presumed, they'd have to get past the
mystical dancing-stuff and tell you how to really maim people. So
I kept going. And nobody mentioned the green *gi* or the cloud of
decay which followed me about. They just gave me a corner of the

room all to myself. In this way the spores turned out to be very handy: they actually lessened the social awkwardness I felt. Kept the others at bay. I practiced by myself, even on the two-person drills. "By mutual consent." So I had learned a sort of martial art in spite of myself: a clumsy, peasant form of chemical warfare, which worked on all the wrong people.

There remained the problem of Other People in my classes—as in, keeping them the Hell away from me and my attendant smell. It took a lot of psychic energy to maintain the force-field necessary to keep clean people from coming within spore range, which extended roughly five or six feet around me. Projecting the field was exhausting; the gigawatts needed could have lit a mid-sized prison camp. There was also the problem that it didn't work. Not that I stopped projecting it; I just knew it didn't work. People sat where they were going to sit. I just had to find where they didn't want to sit and hole up there: by the garbage cans, next to the doors that squeaked, by the toilet doors. Those were usually safe.

There was another problem that was worrying me so much I was forced to spend huge amounts of energy not thinking about it. This was the matter of money. I knew, sort of, that when you turned 18 you were supposed to get a job, and from this job you got money . . . but none of the other laws of nature seemed to apply to our three-bedroom, quarter-acre time zone, so maybe that one didn't apply to me either. For the first few months at Berkeley I just snarled the money out of my parents—stomping in while they were standing in the kitchen having their morning tea, snarling "I need five dollars," then stomping out in silence when they handed it over. After a few weeks I refined the process, eliminating the need for speech: I'd just stomp toward the kitchen with my hand out. Because it made me feel bad, somehow, the asking. I knew they were poor, that they subsisted on tea and toast while I sat in my room gorging myself on all we had in the house. . . . But what else could I do? Busy man! Things to do. Laplands to visit. I knew I was a pig, but like everything in that hexed house, my pigginess was stone-set and unchangeable.

Besides, there was a world of hidden nuance in my morning rite of gruff snarl, money-grab and sullen stomp, nuances of

infinite shared grief, apology, shy loyalty and even filial affection.
. . . And if they didn't get those nuances, too fucking bad!

And besides, I paid it back on the long walk to BART. It was a
mile and a half to the BART station. And every step drove the
nails of those boots into the infected sores on my feet. I walked as
on a high wire, trying to keep the worst nails from getting me—a
bizarre high-wire act dancing down the long dusty shoulder of
Geary Boulevard past the convalescent homes, while the cars went
by me. A mile and a half, how many steps was that? That many
steps multiplied by that much pain per step . . . well, I couldn't do
the math, but Hell, it had to be worth at least five dollars. It was
like a tiny cash register, measuring pain/penny ratios. *Ouch*—
another nickel paid back . . . *ow, ow* . . . another two cents . . . and
by the time I got to BART, my feet were bleeding but I was out of
the red. In theory, anyway.

Besides, five dollars wasn't that much. Wasn't anything.
Except they didn't have it to give. And I knew that.

As the wise American proverb says, "Even buzzards
sometimes gag." Cuckoo in a wrens' nest, I had the one trait
disastrous to cuckoos: I felt bad for them, a little. Every time I
walked to BART with their last five dollars in my grubby jacket, I
kept seeing snapshots: the rotted interior of their old cop-surplus
Plymouth; the way they ate their bleak tea and toast standing up in
the kitchen while I pushed a chicken and a box of cookies into my
mouth between lap sessions in my room; the frightened
conversations about bills, hushed when I entered. And the
buzzard gagged at last.

One hot spring night the full weight of their diffident poverty
broke through my normally impermeable self-absorption. That
night I came home in a bad mood even by my standards: slick
with sweat from the long walk; bleeding badly from the boots; and
more than usually stunned and miserable, like a dog in a cage
getting electroshocked every day in the interests of science.
Because something terrible had happened that day: a woman in an
elevator at Berkeley had accused me of following her. Which I
hadn't been; for me, stalking someone would have required as
much self-confidence as asking for a date. In fact, I would've had
trouble distinguishing between the two overtures.

So she was technically wrong. I'd seen her press the seventh floor, and that was where I was going too, so I didn't press any button; I hadn't even looked at her till she accused me. But I knew she was right in the larger sense, about me being this sick thing that needed putting to sleep. I was hoping a truck would hit me on the walk from BART, but none even came close. You had about as much chance of winning a lottery as willing a truck to swerve you out of your misery. I slogged up to our front door, ready to snarl with uncommon meanness at whichever parent opened it.

There was a miserable ritual for entering our house, as there was for everything there. Rather than simply ringing the doorbell (which didn't work—well, it sort of worked; it made a sound like a duck getting garroted), I would straightarm the screen door till it popped open. This too was annoying, because our screen door was totally useless; the screen part had come loose from the frame and the gap was big enough to walk through. But they kept it shut and locked anyway—another pitiful attempt at defense. It enraged me, that pathetic failed perimeter—like the dying rose hedge out front and the falling-down fence around the side yard. So I'd pop the screen door off its clip with extreme prejudice, then try the knob of the wooden door to see if it was unlocked. It was never unlocked. So I'd pound on it until one or the other parent opened it, at which time I would shoulder my smelly raging bulk past him/her and swerve into my room.

But this one hot, miserable night they'd forgotten to lock the wooden door. So when I slam-popped the screen door and tried the wooden door's knob, knowing that it would be locked as always, it wasn't. And I stepped unannounced into the living room—

And that's about as far as I'm going to go with that. I promised myself I'd leave them out of this. Anyway, the point is that from that night I couldn't help knowing how truly impoverished we were. I just couldn't keep straightarming the money off them. Not that I acquired any sort of moral sense, but it was obvious that it would hurt more to go on taking their few dollars than it possibly could to go out and "work."

But there was this problem with "jobs": they tended to involve other people. Talking to them, doing what they told you to, smiling at them, making them feel comfortable, waiting on them at tables in restaurants. I had about as much chance of doing that as of getting parachuted into North Korea and passing for a Commissar. The Californians would spot me for an impostor the first time I tried to smile and say "Hi!" like a native.

That conviction of futility was what persuaded me to try the student job office. Of course I'd never actually *get* a job, but I could say I'd tried. And then go back to my room, my National Geographics, and live off my parents with the gag-reflex placated. A justified buzzard.

6

The Campus Jobsearch office at Berkeley was a bright happy place, painted all white, and full of non-smelly students who looked like they were already hired. By the White House or *Time* magazine or something. The walls were covered with job-description cards but upon examination I found that most of them involved helping handicapped people: that is, wiping the asses of senile quadriplegics and listening to their tape-loop reminiscences of Lindbergh's flight. I couldn't do that. To go from no bodies to oozing, dying bodies would preclude any access, ever, to better bodies. Nubiles.

But the only other jobs they had involved *meeting the public*. And if it came to a choice between wiping those aged asses and facing the public—like waiting tables, the other big favorite at Student Jobsearch—I'd've suppressed my gag reflex and marched right into Quadriplegia, toilet-paper banner fluttering bravely and a song on my lips. Even cleaning bodily fluids off a living, leaking corpse was better than *meeting the public*. There was no way in Hell I was ever going to meet the public—except in battle. Yes, in my moldy gi—"The Green Ghost," a legend in the mean streets of Berkeley—but not to hand them their salads. Besides, they had those hygiene rules you see in men's rooms in those places: they check your fingernails, even.

So for a few days I ballooned around the job office, found nothing, and waffled off again, safe inside my coat, able to say "I tried." But without meaning to, I got better at scanning the listings and began to find jobs which met my requirements: *no skills, no meeting the public—salary extremely negotiable.* The first one I went after was in a warehouse. A company called "Real Panes Inc." The ironic company name was a bad sign, but I liked the sound of that word "warehouse." It sounded like nice simple sweaty work: black-and-white movie factory work. Prove what a good dog I was: work like that horse in *Animal Farm.*

And this place had a promising location: West Oakland, down on 59th Street near the Bay, where white people didn't walk after dark. 59th Street implied *no smile required.*

But first I had to get the employer's phone number, and to do that you had to ask the woman at the desk. I surveilled her via her reflection in the right lens of my glasses—an old James Bond trick I had learned in those long lunch-periods of staring at Leigh Akers in high school. She appeared to be a standard terrifying civil-service fat black woman, with the weary, hostile look such women wore except when chatting with each other. I had to walk around the office a few times before I could bring myself to get in line. Three quick circuits: *it's OK, it's OK, you have the right, you're supposed to, she'll be fine she doesn't care she has her own worries don't make a big deal of it come on come on come on!* And ZOOM into place—quickly, before I could think better of it.

I stood in line, radiating fear-sweat. There was a white guy, blond in fact, in front of me. He was one of the White House Intern student types: he had on a white shirt that was almost luminous. It was absurdly clean, ludicrously clean—even when you looked at it up close it was all precisely the same absolute white, unblemished, as if nothing organic had ever touched it. Where did they keep themselves? How did they get like this? Do they Scotchgard themselves before they leave the house in the morning? His hair was the same impossible Prussian carpet: all facing the same way. Force fields? Hairspray?

Naturally, the black woman saw that he was one of the people you had to be nice to. She gave him what he wanted and when he demanded clarification she clarified, hardly sounding weary, even. Which meant—the well-known Rebound Effect—that she'd take it out on me. I could smell the waft of terror radiating from me again, layers of ancient polyester greased with Paleolithic sweat rubbing against each other, making a humid friction . . . Get out! Flee while you can!

And I was out the door and running down the steps. Heart pounding, throat clenched, polyester hauberk making its *whisk!* Noise. Pacing around on the bootnails, right . . . down . . . ONTO THEM . . . to punish myself for cowardice.

But I went back in. I want you to remember this part of the pattern too: this peasant army has broken and fled the field a thousand times; but it has re-formed a thousand and one. I ran away, but I came back.

And there was no one in line, and the black woman's supervisor asked her something while she was getting the number so she got distracted and didn't even stare or sneer at me. I carried off the spoils—the employer's number—to the student union to reward myself, *good dog!, good horse!,* with a piece of cake and a large (what *they* called "large": 16 oz) coke. To be devoured, *good dog!,* in a nice impregnable corner where nobody can sneak up to you— having ascertained that the bus-girl was cleaning tables at the far end of the Union so she won't come here and disapprovingly wipe the table while I'm sitting at it. So I'm safe, invisible, my heart calming, the chested rabbit no longer trying to wriggle out . . . and even though the only cake they had had white icing at least it made a nice paste with the coke, sweet and gritty and fizzy at once.

That night, when I slammed my least-torn clothes onto the washing machine for my mother to wash, there was a new pride in the gesture. These is *job* clothes!—not that my mother was allowed to know. I was my parents' soldier to the death, as long as they never found it out.

And the next bright sunny morning, I went to work. On the bus, down to San Pablo Ave. where Huey Newton shot his last prostitute. Where every weekend night the cops held light shows, red-white-and-blue car-top lights and the big star-spotlights from the police helicopters. In other words, "a bad neighborhood." And in other words—the real words people meant when they said that: "a *black* neighborhood." (Oddly enough, "bad" rhymes with "black" in American English.) In this neighborhood I felt my shoulders very intensely. That was what they were for: for walking around here not being messed with. Because I could break a man's back with these arms. And the boots too: their solid clump, their steel toes—made to promote orthodonture among my enemies. And the practice in pain they gave me, the nails, taking it, getting tough.

There's a way you walk at that age, somewhat like the way a bored gorilla would walk—plenty of swing to the arms, feeling them heavy and strong as Frankenstein's, all but dragging on the concrete . . . and the same dead eyes he had, like nothing you saw could ever impress you. And the legs—not walking by themselves but being thrown forward, bone-over-bone twist from the muscles of the back and ass, the quads flicking over like a Cro-Mag's *atlatl*. Flapping them out with the power in your back till they land, CLUMP, one, then the other, then beginning again, as many as necessary, each footfall registering on the Richter Scale, an elephant with five trunks.

Of course this was all nonsense: I was in fact a top-heavy shy unarmed white bookworm who had half learned a wholly impractical method of unarmed combat. If nobody killed me for walking down San Pablo Ave in this ill-bred parody of toughness, it was simply because no one took me seriously enough, or had any reason to give themselves the trouble—for which my belated apology and thanks.

Real Panes turned out to be a beautiful big shed whose new-wood walls smelled sweet as a bakery. There was a waffled green fiberglass roof that made the concrete floor seem like a lawn. The whole place was all friendly and bright. It wasn't even plausible to be afraid. I was terrified.

They were very nice, actually; they had the clean timber smell of their warehouse and they all wore simple plaid shirts and Levi's. The manager, a guy with a moustache, explained my new job to me. He spoke to me in English and I translated as quickly as I could. He was saying something to the effect that Real Panes was a stained-glass warehouse, supplying the big crafts markets of the Bay Area with the panes for the millions of colored-glass wind chimes cool people had on their porches. He took me around, showed me to the woman who managed the office, and said, "Let's just get to work!" Then he took off in a truck. The perfect boss!

The job was very simple. There was a long room with plywood bins on each side. In the bins on one side was the warehouse's stock of panes: big two-foot by four-foot chunks of pure color dimpled like big Ryvita biscuits. The bins opposite opened onto the loading dock. All I had to do was take panes from the storage side and move them to the loading-dock side, where buyers picked them up.

Best of all, I could work alone. The woman was in an office at the far end of the room. She could see me—she even waved in a friendly way when I looked over at her, and I waved queasily back: *Hello, unknown person, heh-heh! heh-heh!*—but she wouldn't be a problem once I showed them what a good horse I could be. I would load more glass, faster, than any slave they'd ever had. I would build mountains of glass, take my terror out on these helpless panes!

The first order was for five panes of red. They'd warned me not to try to carry more than one pane at a time. I was disappointed—why all those hours at the gym if not to lift whole sheaves, volumes of stained glass at once?—but I obeyed, taking hold of the top of a single red pane. It weighed very little, really, considering how big it was. Sharp on top like obsidian, but I took a good grip, lifted it up and over, began the walk to the bin. Pictures of myself in a future *Life* Magazine spread: big arms, bland face, carrying this load effortlessly: "John Dolan, Legendary 'Scholar/Worker' of Berkeley at work." They did it for Eric Hoffer and he was stupid. So why wouldn't—

It slipped.

It didn't exactly fall, not right then. But when I tried to jerk the pane back up, it sort of decided to ignore me and went ahead with its slow slip down, like the *Titanic*. And when the keel hit bottom, it broke on the pristine concrete floor—that floor that was cleaner than I was—with the loudest noise I had ever heard. Absolute white-out terror. Now I'd really gone too far. Tried to pass for human. And now look: I've broken their glass. They'll kill me any second now. If only they just do it quickly, not yell at me first. Kill me fast, but please, no yelling.

Shards of pure cathedral red lay all around me. I looked over to the woman's office. She was already out, marching smartly toward me. Maybe not kill me, but beat me, probably, or whip me, or at the very least scream and spit in my face for a while. OK, I was ready. Just sort of hoping it would be something physical. Get it out of the way faster.

But I have to be fair here: California people aren't cruel. Well, not in simple brutish ways anyway. She came out, all right; but she didn't yell at me. She was really nice about it. I found I could translate her sounds if I focused very hard and watched her lips. I could barely hear her over the pounding of my heart and my ragged gasping breath, but I got the gist. She spoke slowly, thank God: she was saying something to the effect that breaking that first pane of glass was a ritual all their rookie workers went through. She gave me a whole speech about it, about how it was "like losing your virginity"—I winced a little there, but it wasn't meant to be personal, and of course I grasped the analogy. She said now that I'd had my first "big break" (humor), I could relax. I nodded, off to a new start. Clean slate. Counselor talk, but meant to help. Amazingly kind, in fact. I will pay them back, be good. Back to work!

One hour later I had broken seven large panes, gashed myself badly four times (not counting the intricate network of small slashes crosshatching my hands) and executed a strikingly original blood painting on the floor. Jackson Pollock Meets the Werewolf. And loses.

The woman in the booth flinched more and smiled less each time I broke another pane. After the fifth one, she stopped even looking. Just pretended not to hear the crashes and my subsequent yelps and apologies. She was hoping that the self-flayed blood-spattered bespectacled refrigerator in human form scrunching in blood around her warehouse floor might go away if she ignored him intently enough.

Blood was everywhere. The footing was getting slick, though the glass shards did provide some traction. Every time I broke another pane I went through the same ritual: screech (discreetly); apologize to the woman in the booth and the world in general; run for the broom; sweep up the shards as quickly as I could, just to show I was trying hard; and return for another pane. Which would then slip out of my increasingly bloodslick, slashed fingers.

I tried to sweep up as much of the blood as I could. But blood doesn't really sweep. That sounds proverbial, but it's literally true.

All sweeping did was take the hot-fudge trails and blobs of blood, and smear them into big fingerpaint strokes all over the concrete floor. My boots made sticky scrunching noises when they went over the almond-crunch mix of blood and tiny shards of glass.

But I stayed. Till Five o'clock that afternoon I was the hardest-working glass-smasher in North Oakland. During the last half-hour, as the clock at last took mercy and rose toward five, I composed and revised my resignation speech, interrupted only by screeching and apologies when another pane shattered. At five the woman came out of her booth, flinching toward me. I could see she had worked up her courage to telling the gargoyle dripping onto her warehouse floor not to bother coming back. So I beat her to it: I quit. "Hi, sorry, no, sorry, I, no, God I'm really really sorry about the floor, I tried to clean it up—no I mean actually I just wanted, I don't actually really think I'm very good at, suitable for—"

She smiled. And nodded vigorously. And smiled. Everything was California again; the sun came out, everything was OK. All I had to do was quit. That made it fine. She said something consoling—I couldn't hear the words, but like a dog, I got the point: she was petting me on the head on my way to the pound, wishing me well in my future career. She wished me all the luck in the world—anywhere but there.

Shaking hands didn't seem like a good idea. Too messy. I settled for a submissive dip of the head and limped out as fast as my bootnails would spur me.

And then the shivering release, back in the coat and the traffic, safely invisible. The balmy wind coming off the Bay, and the reassuringly impersonal traffic hisses. And the bus came quickly to take me out of there. And the driver didn't even mind me getting on. They saw worse every day. The bus was great! So indifferent, tranquil. The bus was soft and warm, with a neutral public smell. And the black adolescent on the seat across from me stared in surprised respect at my bloody hands. And pants. And boots.

I stared out the window, resting my hands, bloody palms up, on the seat ahead of me. I let him look, but I was cool about it: *Yeah, there was four of'em. Knives, yeah. Took'em off'em and used'em on'em. Fuckers asked for it, know what I mean?*

Impressing black people: every white suburban boy's dream. It almost made up for the fact that I had just failed to meet the challenge of a job your average retarded hunchback would've considered underemployment.

7

Back to the student job office, where after a week of skulking I found my dream job. The employer's name was "S.I.D.O.D." and the job description read "Security Guard/Attack-Dog Handler." I liked the sound of that. An attack dog would keep everybody well out of range. And another fringe benefit: they could hardly expect me to show up clean and ready to smile at the public if I was toting an attack dog. In fact, they'd probably want somebody exactly like me. After all, I had proved my skill in keeping people away, and that's what the job was about, right?—Repelling people! My dream: me and another canine vs. the bipeds. I liked those odds.

There were a few complications. The ad said, "Must have own car." I had no car. But my parents did, and could easily be terrorized into letting me use theirs.

The best part was where it said, "Must work evenings and weekends." Off-hours: there'd be nobody there! Perfect! Normal people wouldn't want to work those hours, because one thing I knew about them from watching beer commercials was that they regarded weekends as "party" time. The ad also said you'd have to work 20-hour shifts; people with real lives wouldn't want to do that, I bet! So the odds seemed to be in my favor. But just to make sure, I ripped the notice off the board and clomped up to the counter in a rush, too scared of losing the job to be scared of fronting up to the black lady.

S.I.D.O.D. turned out to be a man's reedy voice on the phone. He wanted me to go to his house for a job interview. It was a terrible prospect—into a stranger's *house!* Theseus never had to do that. Well, he did—but not a California house.

To avoid being late I arrived an hour early. In certifiably washed, non-smelly clothing. I parked my parents' Plymouth out of sight and casually walked up the street to find the man's address. It was this tiny cottage, all white with flowers. A doll house, the kind where you can't sit down without breaking the chair or leaving a stain. I checked the address nine or ten times, then walked around the block for a half hour. No watch. Time was fluctuating wildly; I might be already late, or have 49 minutes to go. I practiced the informal California-English I would soon have to speak "live" and at length, for the first time since high school.

By the time I rang the doorbell my heart was hammering like Thumper. But the door opened before I could get up the nerve to flee. And even in my terror, I could see that the man standing there was not really that scary. A little bearded hobbit of a man. Smiling. When I said my name, he offered me his hand in the cool, quasi-black arm-wrestling handshake. I failed that first test—offered my hand the wrong way—but he didn't seem to hold it against me, invited me in. I tried to act "casual," hissing commands to the body: remember to smile (but only at believable intervals)! And keep the voice modulated . . . *Modulated,* idiot! Watch the volume! And remember to monitor his reactions carefully . . . Act like you can not only hear, but *appreciate,* his vocal fluting . . . try to sound intrigued, convinced . . .

And then we were in, and I couldn't hear anything. Inside! It was the first house other than my parents' I had entered in ten years, and I could see instantly that it was not like our house at all. It was all bright and detergenty and sunny—deafening, all the sun and shininess. It smelled like artificial pine needles, the smell a fake Christmas tree would have if there were whole forests of them. Weirdest of all, there were plants—live, full-size plants—dangling from the ceiling. Suspended by huge fuzzy cables of rope. Not good rope. Handmade, folksy rope, more like a servant-girl's braids . . . big brown ropes, unraveling. Some sort of back-to-nature rope.

We walked through the little house, weaving between plants, and out onto his tiny deck, which was full of more plants—*what's going on with all the plants?*—and sat down. He drank coffee. He offered me some too but I refused, on the off chance that he was a Mormon hypocrite or something—and he asked me questions.

I must have answered correctly, because I got the job. I think it was when I said minimum wage was fine; that had seemed to please him. But the interview was far too stunning to recall in any detail. I never remember what people say to me anyway, because I'm too scared; it's just the tone I try to get. And the pauses, so I can nod at the proper time. All I remember is that his girlfriend, a big strong woman—she could've taken him any day—walked around behind me, pretending to tend some plants but actually looking me over, checking the cleanliness of my neck perhaps. But it didn't matter, it was OK, because I fooled them; I got the job. That was what he was telling me.

We had another embarrassing cool-guy handshake to seal the bargain and took off to have a look at the job site. That meant the two of us had to sit in the tiny cab of his Toyota pickup. I tried to compress myself into minimal volume against the door, making sure that my body did not in any way stain, smear, ooze onto or crumple any part of the man's vehicle. By contrast, he seemed to think it was nothing at all to be driving around with a complete stranger sitting in his car and simultaneously "chatting."

I'd seen people "chatting" in movies; I knew how to "chat." I "chatted." It struck me, as I tried to process his jabber, that he was telling me something that made him nervous. When he talked, his voice . . . there was a tone of bluff in it, and something else under the bluff, like . . . fear—yes: fear and guilt. As if he were leading me into something bad, something scary, and vestigial conscience was causing him a problem.

I turned up my audio processors and tried to translate his talk. I was rusty, but got the gist. He was repeating, "Remember, we don't want you to . . . go out there and . . . you know, be a hero, OK? They don't pay us enough for that. Just really, all it is is, just keep a *presence* . . . That's the important thing: keeping a presence. We don't . . . you know. Get yourself hurt. Nobody's saying, like you've got to . . ."

I understood, suddenly, what he meant: the job was dangerous. Physically dangerous. That was all? God, what a relief! I could almost have laughed, even with him right there in the same car with me!

I answered in my best California-patois: "Yeah, right, it's not like it's going to do any good . . . gettin' shot . . ." I was careful to elide the "—ing" sound at the end of the word "getting."

It worked; he nodded.

Pride, Homeric pride: I have guessed correctly! I am so clever! Like James Bond dressed as a Bedouin, I am speaking the native dialect fluently! I am the greatest of spies!

But there was no time to celebrate. This man never seemed to stop talking at me, and I had to process the new words he was uttering while trying to adapt my responses to the shared-predicate syntax which is how Californians show submission:

He: ". . . because we're not cops, right? Just a . . . Not a . . . you know, big . . . macho thing . . ."

Me: "Right, just . . . 'Presence,' show that we're . . . there, right?"

He: "Yeah, sort of—'Presence.' Right. That's it. Anything else, anything serious, you call the cops."

Me: "Right, yeah, makes sense . . . Absolutely."

He: "Right, right. Great."

Me: "Sure, abso—no probl—"

He: "—lem, right, OK, great."

Not so easy, getting the timing right on those contrapuntal predicates. Pretty fluent in fact, given my lack of practice. But God, what incredible luck! A job where the only risk was getting shot!

After a few more nods and repetitions of the word "Right," he was quiet for a moment, and I could afford to look out at our surroundings.

We were heading into Oakland. Downhill. South, down into the flats of Oakland. In the Bay Area, money rises into the hills; poverty slides onto the flats. The flatter, poorer and grimier it got, the more I relaxed, to the point that, very carefully, I let my leg muscle—the right leg, the one against the door, away from the man—relax and actually rest against the door. And he didn't even notice, let alone get mad! People probably did this all the time, riding in each others' cars, "chatting."

But what an epic struggle it had been, that interrogation in his garden house! I was sweating worse than after two hours of karate, and I knew I'd lie awake for hours that night, looking at the film my brain had taken of this epochal summit meeting between me and one of the Californians. My legs would take days to uncramp. And the cranial recovery would be even slower. It would take weeks, maybe months, to debrief completely.

To him, it was nothing. They did this all the time. I just couldn't imagine that sort of mental toughness. How tough, how brave the happy people are! Where did they learn it?

And yet they had this bizarre fear of physical harm. I'd heard it very clearly when the man spoke about not getting killed. It was bewildering, their mixture of contemptible physical cowardice and awe-inspiring social bravery. I put the question aside and returned to scan mode.

We were heading into the blacker, poorer, scarier part of Oakland. We were going "to meet Max." Max was a dog, apparently, an attack dog. My new partner. As we left the freeway, the hobbit-man stopped "chatting" and got down to business, with a very highly marked change in inflection: "OK, it goes like this: Max has to get to know you, OK? Right? OK . . . We have to show him you're . . . you're OK, you're one of his buds ["buddies"—CA patois], let him know you're OK . . ."

Me: "Right, like I'm the Alpha male . . ."

He: "Huh?"

Me: ". . . Uh . . . Like I'm one of his 'buds,' right?"

He: "Right!"

Me: "Right!"

And then a moment of blessed silence.

We were now far into the cigar-smelling Oakland downtown. Except it was all blown up. It used to be all hof-braus and bars with green neon, bars that smelled like cigars even in the morning, next to hof-braus where bummy men gulped down roast-beef plates served up by tiny sullen Chinese who spent the whole working day scowling behind a steam table, up to their elbows in salted fat. My father had taken me there for some reason when I was eight, and I never forgot the scent: cigars, sweat and beef tallow.

We pulled up by a block of half-demolished wino hotels. There was one building untouched: a white corrugated-iron shed with a row of chain-link cages. A very loud, high, angry squeaking was echoing off the blasted walls. I'd never heard anything like it, but neither the hobbit-man nor the winos shuffling past us seemed to notice it at all. It got louder as we parked by the shed (my employer locking his truck very carefully and checking my door too—an affront that would be registered and remembered).

The squeaking had grown even louder when we slammed the pickup's doors shut. It sounded like a hundred eagle nestlings screaming in chorus. I didn't believe in hallucinations—considering them, like suicide, a luxury for the pampered—but it was weird the way nobody else seemed to hear this shrieking agony.

We went into the shed, then through a dark, dirty, shallow room to a row of cages. First to hit was the huge smell of dog shit. Cheery note 2 self: Body odor will not be a problem here. Neither would wardrobe, probably—very unlikely they had a dress code. My smelly tent-clothes would be right at home. Almost relaxed, I followed the hobbit-man down the row of cages. It turned out that it wasn't baby eagles making that huge squeak—it was dogs. Crazy dogs! Big-teeth dogs! Dogs who wanted very much to kill me and were not shy about expressing their desire!

Each cage seemed to hold one insane dog, though it was hard to be sure. Because the dogs were all in motion, leaping against the wire, foaming at the mouth, and . . . squeaking. Not barking, squeaking. They were all big, scary-looking dogs—German shepherds, mostly—but their only sounds were these featherweight hiccups. I hadn't had a dog since childhood, but still . . . Surely dogs made deeper "barking" noises, rather than this bat-chorus of squeaks?

The hobbit-man stopped in front of a cage near the end of the row. The dog in this cage was waiting for him, wagging her tail. "That's Kenya," he said and put his hand to the wire. Kenya rubbed her cheek against his fingers and licked his hand, looking up as if she thought that this time he would take her away. They seemed to have some sort of history. I could tell; I'd had all that practice surveilling romance in Berkeley. His hand dragged away, teasingly, tapping up the wire, as he walked on. I wondered if his cruiserweight girlfriend back at the garden cottage knew about him and Kenya. Still, he'd walked away from her quite casually. Kenya was still looking after him. When he was out of her range, she looked up at me—once she knew for certain that The Beloved had deserted her again. Not in the same way she looked at him . . . but not measuring the distance between her teeth and my throat, either. "Platonic." As usual.

I was very excited about seeing Max. I followed the man down to the last cage. The rubble started immediately after it. There was even a chunk of broken concrete, with a fresh piss-stream, against the far wall. Then I saw Max.

Max was an unimpressive dog. When you saw him, you didn't think "terror" or "almost-human intelligence," or even "possessed by Satan" in the way you'd expect with an attack dog. He was old, for one thing. An old black German shepherd with a grizzled white jaw, filthy shit-smeared fur, and a big wart like a Concord grape over one eye.

Max didn't even look very alive. His fur was dull taxidermy caked with patties of old shit. He was staring dully up at us, unmoving, except for his tail, which was waving very . . . very . . . slowly. Like his batteries were low. The rest of the dogs kept up their Hell's choir of bat squeaks, but Max was silent, looking at us. This is a zombie dog, I thought. This is a George Romero dog. Which would be OK except he smells bad. *Poetic justice!* said the Catholic party in my cranial parliament: *Poetic justice—for you, O Smelly One, to be chainlinked to this even smellier, even more canine canine. It is the great chain of being, the grand design: unto thee, filthy and solitary, caged and miserable, shall be given this even filthier, more alone . . .*

Ah shut up! I was sick of those Catholics, always ready to make bad worse. As I was trying to shut them up, someone hit me on the left shoulder. I turned to my employer—stunned, betrayed, but ready to fight. To my amazement, he—this innocuous little man!—had his hand raised, getting ready to slap me again. I thought: All they ever *do* is attack me!

He must've seen something of my horror and readying counterstrike, because he raised both hands as if surrendering and said, "No, hey, be cool! It's cool! I'm just showing Max here you're one-a the boys, one-a his buds!"

I tried to switch gears midway through the transformation to berserker-mode. Tried to laugh, just to show how amused and calm I was: "Heh heh! Right, right, absolutely! To show we're 'buds', right!" *I'm calm! I'm relaxed!* . . . With my heart trying to jump out of my throat like a rabbit, very toes flexed.

I offered my shoulder again, and he struck it, over and over, with his open hand, while I smiled as hard as I could. I smiled with all my might! First at my employer, then at Max.—*See, Max?—Friend, Max!—Friend!* . . . Clenching that smile, 400 foot-pounds of pressure on every tendon of my smiling face.

I finally understood the purpose of our visit: he was going to let Max smell me, get to know me. Max can probably smell me anyway, I thought. Even humans can. I wonder if being smelly makes you more attractive to dogs. Do they see smelly bums as having more charisma, a more complex aura, than chemically cleaned office workers? If so, I thought, I'm in. Maybe my smell will be a ticket to fame in the canine world . . . A walking olfactory symphony, a stink-movie, entrancing canine audiences the world over . . .

I had promised myself that no one was going to hit me again and live . . . but it was hard to say if this was "hitting" in that sense. It would have to be determined by the Intracranial Parliament in full setting. Later. Meanwhile, it would have to be endured. Every slap on the shoulder was hitting me in the head— inside my head. Each slap on the shoulder would have to be processed later as a slap in the face . . . but not now. Now was the time to crinkle up the ol' smile, and hope it could fool dogs, if not people. *Hi Max! Nice Max!*

Max remained impassive. "Inscrutable," in fact. I had never seen an inscrutable dog in my life; but now, what with Kenya and then Max, I'd seen two in a couple of minutes. Whatever weird Zen training they gave their attack dogs at S.I.D.O.D. it must lead to inscrutability . . . and weird barking, too. Land of the Inscrutable Squeaking Attack Dogs . . . But it was time to listen to the hominid again; he was making words to me:

Hominid: "C'mon, show him you're his bud! Talk to'im, you gotta talk to'im!"

Me: "Right, of course, OK, of course, sorry! [Clears throat] . . . Hi . . . uh, hi, 'Max!'"

Then with more feeling—really getting into the role: "Hi Max! Hey Max! Hi Max!"—After all, was he not a dog and a brother?

Hobbit-man: "Right, looks good. Let's let you two get acquainted." Takes his keys out of his pocket.

I couldn't tell what was making me shake: the thought of meeting Max or the shock of those blows on the shoulder. For whatever reason, I was sweating a lot. They can smell it, I thought; they can smell blood, I mean fear . . . and if they can smell fear, then every dog in Northern California, every dog this side of San Luis Obispo, must know me intimately already; and as for Max, he must be choking on it, only a foot away from me. He's going to rip my throat out because I smell too much for his sensitive nose, just like High School. Only he won't mean BO, he'll mean that obscene stink of fear, pitched too high for humans to smell.

The hobbit-man stepped half into the cage to clip his leash to Max's collar. Max was used to the procedure, and didn't react. He just kept looking up at me inscrutably.

I was getting pretty tired of all this slapping and inscrutability. But now we'd see: time for the summit meeting between Max the Inscrutable and his new partner.

He led Max out of the cage and up to me, holding very tight to the leash, just above Max's choke-collar. I didn't move. I figured if Max wanted to savage me he would, and it would only be physical, no humiliation involved. Physical I can handle . . . like getting knocked down; doesn't actually hurt . . . And you're not *supposed* to hit back if it's a dog. You're *allowed* to be a coward with dogs. In fact, streety ghetto people are more scared of dogs than suburbanites.

Max surged toward me, leaned into the hand I was offering him, and sniffed it. He didn't seem particularly thrilled, but it was clear that he knew we'd be working together, and had decided that for the good of S.I.D.O.D. he'd be civil with me. Cop-show dialogue, the grizzled veteran's first speech: "Look buddy, if we're gonna ride together we may as well get along, right?"

Then he smelled my pants—a veritable *War and Peace* in olfactory form—a 30-volume set of smells by comparison with the slim novelettes of most Californians' scrubbed trousers—and

gave a polite, perfunctory wag. Pretty exciting reading, those
pants, huh Max? Can you smell how many times these briefs have
been at the slave markets of the ninth century, Max? Let's just
keep that info between ourselves, partner, huh?

But Max wasn't the reading type. He was already straining
toward the exit. He wanted to move. He wanted a walk.

The man showed me how to hold the leash. What you were
supposed to do was keep Max in a "heel" position on your right,
while grasping the leather loop at the end of the leash with your
left hand and keeping the leash tight over Max with your right
hand, so you could haul him up short if he went for someone.
Someone he wasn't supposed to go for, that is.

He went through this procedure some eight or nine times
before he let me take the leash. Then we were off, down the
rubbled block. Max seemed dull at first—the same zombie living-
dead dog he'd seemed in the cage. He was looking for something.
The dog world of smells and grass didn't seem to interest him at
all. He was looking for something, casting left and right. I couldn't
remember what it reminded me of . . . questing, cruising, down
the street, with his sharp nose and dead, dull eyes.

He was pulling me along at a fast walk as we neared the
corner. I was still trying to work out what it was that Max
reminded me of. Then a man came around the corner toward us.
A black man. Max saw him before he saw Max. Max's zombie
torpor vanished. He'd found what he was looking for. The leash
yanked tight, cutting into my hand like a Marlin-fisherman's 100-
pound line. He pulled me—210 pounds—along like an inflatable
doll.

I realized what it was that Max reminded me of. A shark. It
was like taking a shark for a walk, its dead eyes and dull skin all
pointing dead ahead through its needle nose, guiding itself down
the Oakland street, looking for prey.

The black man saw Max coming, jumped instantly off the
sidewalk and headed around behind a parked car. Max made the
turn and was well along toward cornering him when I braced
myself against a wheel and got my shoulders into it. I pulled him
into the air and back to me—an angler lifting this furry marlin out
of the water. Leather fishing line. Max was gasping, excited, alive.
I knew now what his hobby was: Max was a fisher of men.

The choke-collar had pulled very tight in mid-air, and he was choking unconcernedly, intent on the escaping prey. I loosened the choke-collar a little, hands shaking. The black man walked away scowling silently, uninterested in my refrain, "Sorry! Sorry! My fault!" (Quavering suburban nasals belying the dog, the shoulders.)

My employer caught up with me, considerably less casual than before.

He: "Yeah, you gotta watch out for that. Max's real . . . he takes'is job real seriously."

Me: "No, my fault, I should've—"

He: "Whew-yeesh! Well . . . anyway . . . Close one! Whoo!"

Me: "Sorry, sorry—"

He: "Yeah . . . no, yeah, but—"

Me: "Yeah, no, I know . . ."

He: "No, it's, I mean, no, but . . ."

Me: "Yeah, Yeah, I know!"

He: "Whoo! OK, OK . . ."

Having analyzed the incident, we walked Max back, crossing the street twice to avoid pedestrians. I learned that other dogs did not interest Max at all; he passed up the offer of a sniffing session with a black lab with a snub that would've wounded a duchess. Other dogs did not exist for Max. Max was a biped specialist. He wanted to cut those long hominid heron-legs down to size. And after all, one could certainly understand if not condone his views.

As we headed back to the kennel, the chorus of squeaks began again, all the dogs wanting to be seen and heard. I asked the hobbit-man about it; didn't these dogs have kind of a weird bark?

He said, "You know: S.I.D.O.D."

I pretended to understand, nodded.

He made a dramatic pause, then said in somber tones, "You know what it means, right?"

I confessed I didn't.

He stopped walking, a few steps from the kennel. Very seriously, very slowly, he said "S.I.D.O.D." and fished in the pockets of his Levi's. He came up with his keychain and held it up to me. On the keychain was a picture of a slavering, snarling German shepherd with huge fangs. Around the edge of the picture ran the letters *S-I-D-O-D,* in letters of orange flame.

He spelled out the letters again and said, "You know what that means?" He was not being casual any more. I was beginning to be a little scared. This had "cult" written all over it. If they thought I was going to hurt nice animals to placate their stupid Satan, they were in the wrong demographic zone . . . He pointed to the first letter of the acronym: "*S* for 'Silent.'" I nodded, trying to look innocent yet interested, "S" for "Silent"; right . . . no problems so far, moral or intellectual . . . "Uh-huh, right!"

He went on, pointing to the dog-picture, stopping at each letter. *I*—"Invisible." *D*—"Death." *O*—"On." *D*—"Duty." Then he summed it up solemnly: *"Silent Invisible Death on Duty."*

"But why are they silent? Are they . . . trained, not to . . ."

He smiled proudly and knelt down to Max. He grabbed the flap of Max's matted throat. There were small scars at each side of it. "They have their vocal cords removed."

"Oh . . . Huh!" What could I say: "That's nice!"?

He let it loose on his face again, the proud smile. He was looking less and less hobbit-like. More like an orc. Half-orc at least. He boasted, "Lotsa guard dogs just make noise. Lets a robber know they're there, but then you can just avoid'em. Our dogs—no sound. *'Silent . . . Invisible . . .'*"

He seemed to want me to finish it—a magic incantation, part of the dog-meeting ceremony, perhaps. Always ready to oblige, I intoned, *"' . . . Death . . . '"*

His goblin/hobbit face crinkled in happiness: *". . . on Duty."* then he added in his own, cheerier voice, "Right on!"

Yeah, right on. Our hunting mantra. One of the boys, accepted into the club, I marched back with Max, and decanted him into his cage. Max didn't seem to miss us much when we dropped him off. No one, not even the hobbit-man, was very real to Max. The other dogs barked at him as we ran the gauntlet, like the prisoners in D Block making kissy-faces at a new inmate—but Max was not interested in their tepid quadruped quarrels. Max was ready to wait until his next chance to get a biped. Those biped prey-animals were the only creatures who were entirely real for Max.

We drove back to Berkeley, where I was finally able to get away from the hobbit-man and back into my parents' borrowed police-surplus Plymouth. To reward myself for being so brave all day, I went down to Brennan's hof-brau, the only hof-brau left in the Bay Area, and bought some solace in the form of the extra-large turkey-dinner special and three glasses of coke. I sat there, convalescing via consumption of huge quantities of fatty food, and inhaling, along with my food, the equally consoling, slobby smell of dinosaur-sized roast beef and heavy mashed-potato gravy. Also eavesdropping, out of pure habit, on the barflies' talk, knowing they'd never bother me, intent as they were on their harmless talk about baseball. Besides, I didn't have to be afraid of them: they were as fat as me, but weak fat, wobbly unmuscled fat . . . and far more vulnerable, perched on those wobbly bar stools, "letting it all hang out." The fear drained away in big bites of buttery turkey on hard white roll, slurry of mashed potato and big suet gravy to convert it to a smooth paste, then down to the badger's lair, the belly, to make me sleep and not be scared.

I had a job. I was one of the brave now. I went home and slept for eleven hours, with scared, exhausting dreams of smiling human faces pressed right into mine, and friendly voices roaring loud enough to knock down walls.

8

My first shift was to be Saturday afternoon straight through to Sunday evening, a 26-hour shift. Even at minimum wage, that would earn me something well into double figures. A very sharp increase on the zero I'd made previously.

It meant early and intensive bullying of my parents to make sure I got their Plymouth. But *that* I was good at.

So on Saturday afternoon I pulled up to my employer's cottage in the hills. I was ready to handle attack dogs, ready to guard things—and followed his little VW in my parents' lumbering cop-car. We coasted down the hills to Oakland, picked up Max at the Prison of Inscrutable Squeaks, and put him in the back seat of my car, where he spread out over my father's books. He knew the drill.

Then I followed the VW far down into the shadowed neighborhoods under the wing of the Bay Bridge.

The smell of Max in the back seat was overpowering—I winced in a little spasm of guilt at the permanent rescentment I was inflicting on my parents' car. I'd bought Max a little dog treat, a sort of imitation beef-jerky stick. I passed it to him as I drove. But I could see in the rear-view mirror that he wasn't interested. He accepted it slackmouthed, then let it fall to the floor.

I tried patting his greasy, filthy head. He ignored me, staring out of the back window like a celebrity in a limo. Except for the un-celebrity-like stink, which was truly incredible. Open windows were the order of the day, clearly, when Max was in the car. The hand with which I'd patted him was now blackened and reeking. I was not overly scrupulous about hygiene, but Max was well outside even my range.

The Catholic faction in my head, always ready to make bad worse, took the opportunity to hiss, *"See? See? Justice is done to thee yet again! As you—I mean 'thou'—inflicted your—I mean 'thy'—stink and filth on those nice clean karate people, so thou art burdened with this even filthier dog! Justice is done to thee!"*

They were always right, but I still hated them, that faction. And they could never get their archaic pronouns straight. The more they tried to reform me, the more I wanted to eat 10,000 calories of greased sugar, then retire to my room to masturbate, fantasizing about torturing nice docile slave-girls. I was willing to sign a confession of evilness, get burned at the stake, whatever; anything would be better than going on for the rest of my life with their petty mean homilies dissecting every stumbling step I tried to take. I turned on the radio to drown them out.

And got . . . Elton John. It was a very bad time for everything, but especially for music. Even then, anybody with any sense knew, could feel, that Elton John and the Electric Light Orchestra were not going to live on in posterity. And yet, as I write—at this very moment—Elton John is undergoing a "revival"! Why do they hesitate? Launch now! "Let's do Launch!" Soon! Now! Now! When the Russians decommission their arsenal our combined megatonnage will no longer be enough to bring the Great Winter, and we will be trapped in organic life for good, prey animals for whatever snake rules this—

But I digress. I was taking you to the truckyard with me, down through Oakland. We were in the DMZ, crossing to the wrong side of the tracks—or, in California terms, the freeway. Wood-frame houses that looked a thousand years old. The houses were greasy, somehow. They had the look of those WPA pictures of Louisiana in the Depression. People stared. Black people.

This was where the Bay Bridge had its mangrove-swamp roots, where the thick cable and primer-coated steel attached to the span wove their way down into a muddy delta of truckyards, Navy storage depots, old wood-frame houses with black people sitting on the steps and steel-barred liquor stores on every corner. You could smell the mud of low tide, and the smell of frying organ meat—spleen or beefheart—which permeates the bayside districts of Oakland.

Like everyone in Pleasant Hill, I was scared of black people. When I was a child, we had had this notion that we and they would hug and make up and all would be well, nuzzled together under the beneficent wings of the United Nations and backed by a demographically balanced—but still white-dominated, like the crew in *Star Trek*—chorus of children singing "It's A Small World After All."

That idea had gone up in the smoke of a few dozen downtowns. The model now was anger. Progressive types at Berkeley would grovel endlessly to make angry black people like them . . . and they usually ended up shot to death as a result. You had to stay away; they weren't in a mood to hold hands. Everyone knew this—but, like the good Soviets they were, no one at Berkeley ever said so. It was something you had to figure out for yourself, unless you wanted to be dead. You had to get it straight that the harmony model had lapsed and the blacks were now using the anger model.

Everywhere all this holy anger . . . anger at school, anger here. . . . But I believed in this anger, the black kind, in a way I didn't any more in the gender anger at Berkeley. The black anger had guns and wasn't afraid to use them. This anger wasn't from the Sunday Feature section of the paper. This anger showed up in the news section, attached to scowling black faces, with a caption telling the number of dead.

The people we passed on our way to the truckyard had a straightforward predator stare. They looked directly into the cars, especially my car . . . God! I was driving a surplus cop car, complete with little searchlight on the passenger side and a police dog in the back! Oh God, they think I'm a cop! Wait . . . maybe that's good . . ? I couldn't decide.

They looked at me and Max for a long time after we passed them. They had an expert stare you don't find in the suburbs: a quick appraising glance that told you this was one of the more serious ecosystems where you had to be able to judge fast, be ready to dart back into the coral when a shadow passed over the reef.

They didn't seem very impressed with our little procession, cop car or no cop car. If anybody was going to be darting into the car—I mean the coral—it was going to be us. Sobering. The job seemed less like a promise of isolation than another chance to fail—this time publicly, catastrophically. Not that I was so sane as to fear for my own life. As always, I'd have been happy to give my life away to anyone who wanted it. If I'd been an Aztec, I wouldn't have waited for the priests of the Sun-God to gouge my heart out with obsidian knives; I'd've walked around the streets of Tenochtitlan holding it out, still pulsing, asking passersby if they might wish to take it off my hands, please. "No charge! My pleasure! Please! Excellent stew-meat!"

I wasn't afraid of death but public failure. Humiliation. The truckyard would be burnt to the ground on my first shift . . . They'd make me pay it off in weekly installments by working some horrible meet-the-public job, waiting tables in a McDonald's uniform, some job where a convincing smile was one of the conditions of employment . . . Where the assistant manager hides in the toilet stalls to make sure you wash your hands every time you urinate, where there's a 39-step Cheeseburger Protocol you have to know by heart on your first shift . . . Twenty years of waiting tables in a paper cap, eight hours a day of smiling, wearing clean clothes and doing impossibly complex tasks like adding up dinner checks and smiling at strangers . . . And all because I stupidly thought I could do this impossible job, guarding the truckyard from the locals. Oh God, I'd be standing there, looking at the ground in shame, in front of the burning truckyard—disgust on their faces as they stare at me, a tear scooting down my smoke-blackened cheek, backlit by the soaring flames . . . Dim figures, looters from Watts TV footage, running in the flames, carting off the trucks' cargo . . . gunshots and screams . . .

There was always suicide. They couldn't take that away from you. Unless—God, yes they could! Of course they could! They could put you in prison and make you remove your belt and all sharp objects. But they couldn't actually put me in prison—could they?—for letting the truckyard get sacked my first night on the job. God, maybe they could. Of *course* they could . . .

"Sacked"—that word helped me. It made it seem almost heroic to defend the truckyard. Yeah, it would be like the Sack of

Byzantium. The Alamo. The Siege of Limerick. Hopeless but heroic . . . Constantine XI, my favorite Byzantine Emperor, died nobly, fighting on the walls in 1453 when the Turks finally took the City. The Turks' great cannon leveling the walls while terrified Greek women crowded the Hagia Sofia, chanting with their priests for God's intercession and thousands of monks bowed their bearded heads in rhythm, swung their censers . . . But God did not intervene. It wasn't their God's day. God and Allah did a trade: Moorish Spain for Greek Byzantium . . . But the Byzantines died well, taking many a turban with them, that terrible day.

And I would die well too, sword in hand, in the besieged truckyard! Like them. Like Boromir. Like Roland. I would make them pay for every TV they stole! And I would get paid for it—that was a new wrinkle, an updated feature! My parents would get the money—and more too, maybe, as a settlement. And there would be the newspaper tributes, when they find my body, with those of five robbers around it. The forensic specialists would reconstruct my last struggles, awed at what heroism has died—*perished*—here. At the terrible price for which I have sold my life in the line of duty. And with my bare hands, too! A plaque on the truckyard wall . . .

I hit the brakes hard. The VW was turning left and I'd almost hit it. We were almost in the Bay already. It was all fill land, dead flat and smelling of the bay mud. Warehouses, blank walls with spray-painted territorial claims. Very mammalian, those graffiti, I thought: marking one's territory, like a lion's scent-spray. Of course lions don't have handguns . . .

Then we were there. On the right, a little improbable park. Green grass, even. On the left, the truckyard, an entire block occupied by semi trailers parked all the way around in a defensive perimeter. A big chain-link fence topped with barbed wire, all the way around the block. The trucks all had CME written on their sides. That was the company we were contracted to.

The huge Fort Apache gate was wide open. The VW pulled into the yard and parked in front of a little office perched on the loading dock. I followed, trying to imitate his actions exactly. My employer got out and came over to the Plymouth. He grabbed Max by the collar and took him over to the steps leading up to the loading platform. There was a chain there. He hooked Max to the chain. Then we went up to the office, a tiny place that smelled like sweat and coffee. Everything was greasy and tough and scary-smelling, like the car-repair places we always ended up getting robbed by.

I could smell that these were unreconstructed men-type men—the kind in old movies only without the kind interior. Just the gruff exterior and gruffer interior. I was in favor of male archetypes of the medieval model, but not this sort of mean-Dad thing. Too contemporary. Too realistic. I'd seen it in other families in Pleasant Hill; dads of that sort assigned onerous household chores, delivered long hectoring lectures, and gave compulsory ill-tempered training in the mechanical arts punctuated by frequent whippings with a leather belt. I was not altogether comfortable working for that kind of dad, being inside its smell in this office.

Another guy came around the piled-up pallets toward the shack. My employer gave him the arm-wrestling handshake. So did I, wincing in the privacy of my mind, twisting the wince into a credible smile. The hobbit-man introduced us: this was "Matthew," who also worked for S.I.D.O.D. on the long Friday/Saturday shift. My employer asked this "Matthew" to give me a little tour of the truckyard, show me the ropes.

I would have given a lot of blood, maybe even a digit or two, to get out of this unwanted social contact, but there was no way out. I walked down the steps with him, sick with dread. Matthew was "cool," in the precise California sense. Like all cool people, he didn't talk much. In fact, he didn't talk at all until we were out of sight among the trucks. He was a skinny white guy in dark, somber clothes. Black windbreaker, black Levi's. Looked a bit like Al Davis at twenty. He was smoking, with a hard squint.

He stopped, stubbed out his cigarette, and asked, "Done this kinda stuff before?" I said no. He walked on. "S-no big deal," he said. "Few things gotta know how to do. Like this. OK, look—" He took a big T-shaped piece of metal from his back pocket and walked over to a trailer. "OK. When the trucks drop'em off—trailers—gotta secure'em. Ya take this"—the T-shaped bar—"and one a these"—a piece of thick, stiff wire about a foot long—"and stick the wire through this." Meaning a clasp which linked the back door of the trailer with the chassis of the truck. He put the wire through the clasp. "An' tie it up like this." He took the T-shaped tool, slid it alongside the wire, and twisted it, so that the wire was twisted into a knot. "OK . . . means the trailer's secure."

We worked on it. I practiced with the wire and T-bar, hands greasy with fear-sweat. My heart was pounding but at last I got it. He nodded and we walked along. He seemed tired and sharp at the same time.

"Only thing you gotta worry about here, you know . . . 's not that big a job. Have to log the trucks in, look busy when they're around, mostly . . . CME guys . . . but mostly . . . no big deal."

I complimented him on his ability to stay awake on the 20-hour shifts, confessing that I feared it would be difficult at first. He looked at me in a weird way. We walked on for a while. Then he said, "Look, you wanna take a nap here—shit, go for it! . . . I mean . . . I do. Do it all the time. You just don't do it when he"—jerking his head back toward the hobbit-man—"might come by. Or no, yeah . . . even then, just stay near the phone. Not that big a deal . . ."

I was shocked. Such unsoldierly behavior I had never seen. Did the man know nothing of Constantinople?

But at the same time, according to the suburban hierarchy I grew up in and believed implicitly, he outranked me, because he was cool and I was not. So he was dead right or contemptibly wrong, depending on which model I was using. But how did you know which world applied in this truckyard? *Which century* was it in this truckyard?

So much to figure out. Weary, weary already, after five minutes on the job. But I had to go on, nodding at the right moments, trying to pass. He kept looking at me oddly. Finally he said, "Besides, ya wanna stay awake, that's no . . . no problem. That's easy." He smiled. I nodded, utterly bewildered: "Right, right, uh-huh . . ." I had no idea what he was talking about. "You know?" he said. He really seemed to want an answer, but what answer? What the Hell did he mean? I had no idea, and was losing points by the second.

Ten years later I'd've spotted him for a fellow speedfreak in an instant. Would've known he was hinting that he snorted crystal meth to stay up in the long shifts, and was trying to see how I responded so he wouldn't have to worry about me being a snitch. Looking back, everything about him was typical tweek: the tired

voice with a sharp edge; the skinny hard face; the urge to talk vs.
the weariness that limits talk to a few terse, mumbled phrases,
ending in a despairing aposiopesis. Even the clothes, black Levi's
and windbreaker, were a perennial favorite of the crystal meth set.

But when I took the truckyard job, I'd never even tasted
coffee, let alone become familiar with the more exotic
pharmaceuticals. Matthew, reacting to my puzzlement, assumed it
was feigned—I see that now, though I had no idea back then—
and responded by shutting up entirely. It made for a long, long
walk. We went all the way around the truckyard in silence. He
pointed from time to time, named things in single syllables: "gate,"
"hole," "back door"—a record two syllables! But no more
"chatting."

He took us back to the office, where the hobbit-man showed
me how to log trucks in and out. He seemed to have had trouble
teaching it to other employees, because he went through it in a
Sesame Street mnemonic: "When a truck comes *in*, you write its
number down here, in the *"in"* column; when a truck goes *out* . . ."
I thought I could handle that part. It was all the unexpected
human contact I feared. Like: what the hell was Matthew mad
about? He sat on the steps and smoked, turned away from us.
Max, on his chain, looked into the distance. It was a close race
between him and Matthew, who could get more contempt into a
silent back. God, even the *dog* was socially difficult! Even the crazy
miserable stinking *dog* is too cool for me!

God, just to have them gone! I take this job for the isolation,
and I'm nothing but a damn social butterfly, meeting and greeting
like the doorman at a casino or something! Twenty minutes on the
job, and I was already trembling with nervous exhaustion from the
effort of showing the right sort of face and making the right
sounds to these bipeds. I was holding my arms very tight to my
body and keeping my dirty coat on, holding myself so tightly there
was ticklish sweat trickling down the fat-ridges on my sides. And I
would not be able to open the coat and wipe them off with the
shirt until these bipeds left me *alone*.

God, bring on the armed robbers! I thought longingly of
armed robbers: nice straightforward people who weren't going to
chat with you, who just tried to kill you! My kind of people! Get
down to business! Honest quiet folk! God, get these people *out!*

The hobbit-man and Matthew finally left, Matthew in an incredibly ratty little French-looking car. The hobbit-man said on his way out, "Remember: we're not cops, right? Anything serious, you just let the cops deal with it."

"Right, right, absolutely."

"Nothing'll probably happen anyway . . ."

"Sure, right, yeah, probably . . ."

"OK, Catchya later, dude!"

And at long last, he left. I was supposed to lock the gate after them and then let Max loose to patrol on his own. I pushed it shut, the big military fortress gate. I liked closing that gate. My favorite part of the job so far. Like a sideways drawbridge . . . besides, it meant I was alone at last. Except for Max. I went back to the office and let him off the chain. I thought he'd zoom off, a good soldier, out on patrol. But he just flopped down in the same spot. It was weird, this complete lack of morale on the part of our troops. They were like the South Vietnamese army.

I tried, Patton-like, to encourage him: "Go Max! Go patrol! Go look!" He didn't react at all. Didn't even look at me. In fact, he never looked at me, or anyone—not even his chosen victims. Only their legs. "Watch the legs": that was Max's philosophy. Watch those long, scuttering, heron-like biped legs. Never mind what noise their little mouths were making, or what flummery their worm-wriggle ape-hands got up to; just watch their stick-like heron-legs.

Except for his hobby of biting those sweet, vulnerable appendages like a little land-shark, Max was in a world of his own. He'd been in solitary longer than me, even, and he was through pretending.

It wasn't until several months later that I found out how S.I.D.O.D. "trained" its guard dogs. It wasn't very complex: when he needed a new dog, the nice little hobbit-man got German shepherd puppies free from the pound. He'd take the puppy back to the kennel, then he'd pay neighborhood kids a couple of dollars to take broomsticks and hit the puppy, scream at it, throw rocks at it and generally terrorize it. I bet they had no trouble finding volunteers. There's never a shortage of people to do work like that.

But the hobbit-man himself would never hit the puppy. Instead, he always fed the puppy, brought its food to it and even patted it, pretended to some sort of affection for it. And the puppy, locked in a wire cage and terrorized by every other human being it saw, clung to this faked affection with all its heart. It loved him. He, the author and profiteer of all its torment—it loved him. The hobbit-man became the dogs' only link with the rest of the world: the puppy would accept anyone introduced by him as a friend. The dogs divided the world very simply between pack-members and Others. And assumed that all other bipeds were tormentors. Torturers. There to hurt it.

And they were right about that. The unbearable part was that only in making an exception to the rule, positing a "good" man, were they mistaken. And that's why I support nuclear winter.

I understood Max a little better when I learned about his early "training." I started having rescue fantasies—always a mistake. Yeah: I wanted to bring him back to life, the way it happened in movies. Every time I picked him up at the kennel I patted him till the stench and grime got to me. I tried sweet-talking him for hours on long solo shifts; brought him more treats. But patting and sweet-talk—even food—meant nothing to Max. He took the dog-treats I bought him, but lost interest, dropped them on the concrete after a perfunctory chew. He would stare off into the distance while I stroked his greasy head . . . not bothered, but not interested either.

Like the progressive whites sucking up to black people, I was simply too late. Max was not there any more. Max was just a pair of jaws now. Old jaws. Not even "sacred rage." "Rage"! Max had no more rage than a bear trap does. He was just a simple mechanism: a pair of jaws that shut if you were dumb enough to step into them.

There was no one in range as we settled in to our first shift, so Max was quiet, lying down by the office while I looked over the log book. It was pleasant there. Quiet. For once I didn't have to feel guilty about not having fun; this was *work*, and justified in its own right. Every hour I sat there, I would be earning a generous three dollars and ten cents. Before taxes. Just for sitting there! If only someone'd paid me for sitting in my room. Guard that. Be a millionaire already.

It was getting nicely dark—my time. And I was alone and safe. I loved this job.

Then the world exploded. A huge crashing, wrenching metal scream that burst over the office like a tsunami. It blew me right out of the chair. Even Max was upset. He was standing, looking toward the far end of the block where the explosion seemed to come from. I stepped out of the office and listened. No more noise. I started running, ready to repel whatever had breached our walls. I charged toward the far end of the lot. Max came too, optimistic about the chance of finding some game.

Max's expression was just worrying enough that I stopped. Called him to me. I didn't necessarily want Max freelancing on whoever it was. I was also considering the possibility that this was some sort of test, some faked catastrophe they used to test new guards on their first shift. The coincidence was too hard to believe: some kind of nuclear explosion on the premises ten minutes into my first shift. And if it *was* a test, they'd want to know that I had control of my dog. I called Max more and more insistently. He stopped, but he didn't come over. He was thinking about it.

I tried running in the opposite direction, trying to imply through body language that the real fun was *this* way, back toward the guard shed. He bought it and came running along with me. Max was not bright. I managed to grab his collar and clip the leash on him. Then we turned around and charged toward the explosion together.

When we rounded the last trailer, I saw the most amazing scene I'd ever encountered. A huge Buick was snared on the chain-link fence, like a seven-gill shark in a tuna net. Three or four sections of the fence were ripped out and woven around its nose. Its lights were still on, despite the fact that it was upside down. It was steaming, and the steam in the lights was very beautiful, yellow and white and red . . . some luminous predator of the deeps, enmeshed in a net.

Then something popped out of the dusk and started breathing and talking at me. Max went crazy, lunging again, till I stepped back, yanking him with me. He settled for snarling and barking (or rather squeaking). The man stumbled into the headlights and I could see him: a short, middle-aged black man who even at this

distance wafted stale alcohol all over me. I'd never known anyone
who drank—which is to say that my parents never did—but I had
seen lots of movies and knew he was drunk. He acted just like a
drunk in the movies: wobbly and incoherent. He would wobble
toward me until Max lunged, and then he would wobble back and
try explaining himself with grandiose semaphore gestures.

Then something else got up from under the car. It wrenched
itself out through a window: another man. Yelling something.
God, how many were there in there?

He stood up and started coming toward me. Max lunged. The
man stopped. Both men were gesticulating at me like a pair of
mummies, staying just beyond Max-range. (They were drunk, but
they weren't entirely stupid.) Max was pulling my arm out of the
socket in frustration, trying and trying to pursue his vocation,
completely puzzled by his handler's timorous policies. He was
going really crazy, leaping harder and harder. Something about the
drunks' clumsy ambiguous gestures upset him.

Time for a strategic retreat.

I ran back to the office with Max and called the Oakland
Police—their number was written in large print in about forty
different places in the office—and then went back to the crash.
One of the men was sitting down now, talking to himself, while
the other wandered around in the dark, occasionally visible, like a
deep-sea fish in the narrow light of a bathyscaph when he crossed
in front of the headlights. Then lost in the dark again. He was
talking too, orating with great gestures, round and round the car:
light, then gone; light, then gone.

Max was snubbing the two men now. Not even looking at
them. Sour grapes. Just because I wouldn't let him have even one
of them. Or perhaps he really didn't see them any more, once he
grasped that they weren't biteable. What wasn't biteable didn't
really exist for Max. But I didn't trust him; he was one of those
people who are very stupid but very sly, and I didn't trust this
show of disinterest at all. So I ran back to the office yet again,
chained him there and ran back to the accident. For all I knew, the
drunken bit the two black men were doing was just an act . . .

Then it hit me: it was all a set-up, a test!

Of course, of course, you idiot, you stupid fool! Agh, *of course!*
The whole thing—my God!—the whole thing might be an

elaborate test of my guarding skills, set up by the agents of S.I.D.O.D.! The old Trojan horse or in this case Trojan Buick ploy! And I fell for it, just when I needed to make a good impression! The two putative drunks could be pilfering the truck-trailers now—or just standing there, solemnly waiting my unworthy return, scowls of disgust on their secret-agent faces! I ran as fast as my decrepit boots and suppurating feet would let me, a Clydesdale charger clomping into battle.

There were new lights at the crash site and more silhouettes— God, it WAS a test!—but after a second of horror and guilt I realized they were the lights of cop cars, blinking red/blue and white. Mixing very beautifully with the yellow, white and red of the netted deep-sea car. The cops were talking to one of the men, who leaned against an upside-down wheel to mime the car's roll. The other one was still wandering around. The cops didn't seem to care. They weren't even excited. The head cop, a hard old white man, came over and wanted to know who I was. He took my name and address, then asked me what I'd seen. To my shame, I could only say that I'd heard "a big crash." He nodded, unimpressed.

"You see which one was driving?"

I had to admit I had not.

"Which one got outta the driver's side?"

Even this was beyond me. I was deeply ashamed. The cop squinted at me with disgust.

"Ya'ave no idea who was driving?"

"No, I'm sorry, sorry—I always thought I'd be a good witness but I must admit I was somewhat surprised by the noise; you see, oddly enough this is my first shift; but it is embarrassing, my fault, I always thought I'd be a good witness but to my embarrassment—"

"Better calla owners, tell'em'bouta fence."

"Yes, absol— . . . of course, yes—sorry I couldn't be of more—"

But he walked away in the middle of my sixth or seventh apology and went over to talk to the other cops. They were all laughing. You could see from the way they stood that this scene was nothing to them. But it was the most amazing thing I'd ever seen, the only time my life had intersected with something that might be on the news from the big crime cities. The lights, the big shark Buick snarled in the chain-link net, the zombie drunks—it filled me with awe. And to be one of *them* you would have to go through so much that this scene meant nothing to you! The implications were staggering.

I called the hobbit-man in Berkeley, and he too treated the breach as a minor problem. He told me to "keep an extra-special eye" on that corner of the yard. So Max and I, camouflaged in the shadow of a truck trailer, spent that whole night in ambush mode, waiting to charge into the ranks of whatever thieves might exploit the breach in our walls for a raid. My own Byzantium . . . Byzantium in its last days, when the Turks' huge cannon had blasted whole sections of the City's great wall into rubble. Night watch over the ruined wall . . . damp, glaring light and utter dark. We crouched like Faramir: Indo-European guerrillas behind Turkic lines.

The night lasts a long time when you spend it under a truck trailer. It got very cold in a typical Oakland way: heavy dew, almost like rain, condensing on your glasses. But we were good soldiers: we stayed under that trailer till the traffic noise began and the smoggy sun showed itself over the Oakland Hills. And no thieves came.

When Matthew showed up at dusk on Sunday (he too unimpressed by my awestruck account of the crash) I could finally get in the Plymouth and go home. I did fall asleep at the wheel three or four times—well, seven, actually. In one especially memorable case I found myself about a half-second from a retaining wall when a kind commuter's horn from behind woke me. But overall I was relieved at how well it'd gone: I had not been fired!

And had seen a great thing, a veritable event.

But when I next went to the yard, only two days later, the hole was gone, the fence fixed. It was as if nothing had happened.

9

I never did manage to attain the noble boredom which is the mark of the true Californian; but thanks to the truckyard, I got a little more used to frequent events and the presence of other people. Because even on that solitary job there were people everywhere. Most of the ones I had to deal with were truck drivers, men of bizarre arrogance. They would roll into the truckyard, usually at three or four in the morning, from cities all over the country. Clomp into the guard shack with their super-mugs and their cowboy belt-buckles and their talk, talk, talk.

They were all alike: white, armed, and racist. Like, *really* racist. Weirdly intense about it. I'd thought that kind of thing went out with Eisenhower. Because the commentators on TV and in the papers try to pretend that this world is evolving, going forward— which of course it isn't. It goes a little forward and then back, over and over, like a trapdoor spider at the lip of its burrow. The white racists, like the couples in Berkeley, were alive, innumerable, doing quite well for themselves, and had at the very most lowered their profile a little. But not when they were safe inside the truckyard; then it was their turn to strut. And God did they strut.

They swaggered around believing their own publicity to a degree which was alternately comic and disgusting. They would pull up to the yard . . . and I'd trot over to the big fortress gate, open it, log them in, and will them to go away silently after dropping off one or both of their trailers. They hardly ever did. Almost always, they clomped up to the shack. They wanted to talk. To me, since there was no one else. They'd spent two straight days on the road, rehearsing some boastful rant, and I and was the only available audience. (And the majority of them were probably frying on speed, too, as I realize now.)

I'd get sick with fear that they were going to come into the shack, I'd beg any demons listening to name their price for fending these guys off me—but the demons were as unreachable as ever, and those cowboy-boots almost always clomped up, shoved the door open and began woofing at me.

They wanted to talk about themselves—specifically about their greatness. And their toughness. And the sort of weapon they preferred. Something about being in a black neighborhood of Oakland made them prate endlessly about their armaments. I got shown more kinds of handguns and "combat knife" than you'd see at a Kentucky flea market. It was an icebreaker with them, a conversation-opening: "Hi, I'm Gary (or Dwayne or Darrell), I'm tough and smart and a genius of a truck driver, and this is my double-plated snuff-steel Smith and Nigger .57. It'll stop a wetback at 200 yards. 'Specially if it's my yard, har-har!" To which witticisms I invariably offered the tribute of a queasy laugh.

The pedantry of their preferences for this or that particular brand and caliber of handgun easily outdid anything I'd seen in my professors at Berkeley. In fact those professors, in an equally sleazy but much less ingenuous way, seemed to go out of their way to talk about the NBA or baseball or anything which marked them as populists, as if they wanted to live down their arcane knowledge. No such kinks for the truck drivers . . . Ignorant people don't know enough to be shy about their pedantry. Flat-out truck-size egos on parade. CB-style monologues yammered out at me while I smiled grinchily, nodding as necessary . . . Wisdom about guns and trucks, calibers and gearshifts . . . and their favorite topic: elaborate descriptions of what would happen to anybody, especially any person of color, who touched their trucks . . . or their Harleys . . or their wives. In that order.

These monologues were very painful. And not just because enduring them in a stinking shack at four in the morning offered a very plausible preview of Hell. No, what was hardest to bear was that they disproved a big chunk of my ideology. After that terrible epiphany on the way back from Karate, I decided that I was going to believe the opposite of whatever the hippies said; and since the hippies described a world which was dominated by cruel arrogant white men, the truth must be that whites were the losers, the wimps. And it *was* that way—at UC Berkeley. Or at least seemed that way, if you were young and bitter and alone. On-campus white people cowered before blacks; men and women played a tricky game in which if anything the women seemed to have a slight advantage.

But now I had to sit there through the dank, stinking Oakland night listening to the boasts of some coffee-breath imbecile with a buck knife on his belt and a Colt Python in a shoulder holster going on and on about how the world was going to Hell because of this or that non-pale-male group. These Darrells and Dwaynes and Garys were core samples of America outside the tiny anomaly of Berkeley, and they confirmed everything the hippies ever said about the Heartland.

Every single one would recount at length what he "almost" did to some "nigger" who had annoyed him. Like those of all macho liars, the drivers' stories were always about some devastating act of violence they *almost* inflicted on their enemies. "I was just about ready to shoot the bastard . . ." I nodded and nodded and nodded. Four in the bleary morning, and not only did I have to keep my eyes open, but I had to listen to the braggadocio of yet another mean hick whose every word was spoiling the whole nihilist ideology which was my only possession.

The counterparts of the evil white truck drivers were the black robbers who visited our yard from time to time. But to be fair, they were more discreet. At least they had that going for them. They didn't make you listen to them at four in the morning . . . didn't stop by the office after their robberies to strut and brag about their pilfering skills. They came and went quietly, clipping the wire of the fence down at the far end of the yard with bolt cutters, then zipping in to snip the wire knot off a trailer door with bolt cutters and grab whatever happened to be in the trailer.

That was the hitch: they had to pick a trailer at random. Some cargoes were worth the trouble—they'd supposedly lucked into a trailer full of TVs the year before I got there—but most were not. One of the most pleasing sights I saw in my time at the truckyard was a trailer which had been cut open and found to be full of disposable diapers. Boy, were they mad! There were ripped cartons of Pampers all around the truck. Booted in all directions.

But every robbery, whether it was a load of TVs or just Pampers, brought S.I.D.O.D. into lower repute with the truck company. *Sleepy Incompetent Dorks On Duty*. And that covered quadrupedal as well as bipedal employees. Which is to say: Max. As I got to know Max better, I liked him less and less. You wouldn't think such an unprepossessing dog could fall in one's estimation; but Max did, in mine. For a German shepherd he had no sense of duty at all! I took my job very, very seriously, and Max simply did not patrol in what I considered a properly serious manner. Of course I felt differently when I heard about his horrible childhood—horrible childhoods are worth lots of points in California—but for the first few months, I thought he was just a lazy, self-indulgent and (as the Vikings used to say) *un-swordworthy* dog.

For starters he was very deaf, as I demonstrated by experiment (standing behind him and clapping loudly). And although I tried to attribute to him a good sense of smell, I found it wasn't really equal to my own, which—both passive and active, as it were—has always been extremely acute. I could smell people coming long before Max did. Maybe they beat his sense of smell out of him . . . or maybe he just wasn't as scared of the bipeds as I was.

But Max was also *lax*. His behavior on our patrols would have earned summary execution in most armies. He had no fighting spirit at all, no search-and-destroy enthusiasm. I applied to my job everything that my military history books recommended as good sentry technique. Starting, of course, with staggered patrols—staggered in timing, direction and speed. We'd go on a clockwise patrol around the yard at a fast walk, then, after a random interval, say seven or 12 minutes, I'd grab Max and literally drag him on a counterclockwise patrol at a run. Then, after three or five minutes, another counter- clockwise patrol—this time at a slow walk. If the enemy was trying to plot my patrols, they were going to have a damn hard time doing it.

I was hoping to catch some robbers in the act. That was my dream. I could imagine myself being patted on the head by my owners if I did such a heroic thing. So I would sometimes go out on patrol at three or four in the morning—and then, instead of returning to the cozy office, sneak back to an ambush site at the far end of the trailers! Counter-ambush, an old counter-insurgency technique. Max and I would crouch there waiting till dawn. My own Mekong Delta. Instead of elephant grass, truck trailers; instead of muddy water, damp asphalt; instead of tropical insects buzzing, the surf of early traffic on the Bay Bridge . . . and instead of an M-16, Max. There was the rub: Max was not a credible deterrent.

"Stop or my dog will bite!" Not much of a threat in that neighborhood. We feckless guards were probably the only people in a half-mile radius who weren't packing guns. Thank God my little Vietnam techniques worked about as badly in West Oakland as they had in Vietnam If I'd ever been unlucky enough to interrupt a robbery, the scene would have played out as terminal comedy: I come clumping along in my boots, turn a corner and stumble on a group of robbers unloading a trailer. They'd stop for a moment; I'd stop; and after a ritual challenge—something on the lines of "Unclean orcs, unhand those disposable diapers or feel the bite of my blade, if I had one!"—I would have charged their ranks.

They would have had time for a quick game of rock/paper/scissors, to see which one gets the treat of popping this Celtic piñata now advancing toward them at something like 15 seconds per 1000 yards. The lucky winner—"Paper smothers rock! Now *git* out the way an lemme shoot the motherfucker!"

And I would probably have had time to feel just a wee bit foolish—to experience that same old epiphany: THIS IS NOT MIDDLE-EARTH, YOU *IDIOT!*—before a 9mm slug pancaked its way through my diaphragm, making liver pate on its way out through the spinal cord, clipping the nerve-fiber bundle neatly.

Dead if you're lucky; 50 years of quadriplegia if you're not. One of those deals where the dedicated nurse (who falls in love with you in the movie but I bet not in real life) spends three years teaching you how to form words by pointing to letters on a ouija board with a stick attached to your forehead . . . And the first words you spell out, slowly, clumsily, while her proud eyes shine with tears, are K-I-L-L M-E.

In the movie she's "intrigued" by your bitter, lonely stance, and devotes her life to convincing you that yours is worth living. And they do a quadriplegic-sex scene—"frank yet sensitive"

(Cleveland Plain Dealer) and "deeply compassionate" *(Omaha Herald)*—and everybody on the marquee gets a million more for their next movie. But they're not really paralyzed, the stars; and the real thing wouldn't have any quick cuts. Those months in the VA hospital would take actual months, not 90 seconds of montage. And you would mean it, really mean it, when you wrote "Kill me"; and you wouldn't be able to—it would be inadvertent comedy as you tried to hold a razor in your drooly mouth and reach your own carotids.

And the truck thieves laugh about it on their way home, and the guy who shot you gets big street cred for it, and even keeps your glasses as a hunting trophy, putting them on and imitating your death screech whenever he wants a surefire sight-gag; and your parents have to sell their house to pay the hospital bill; and as for your toilet arrangements, let's not even talk about it . . . so yes: all in all, my Mekong-ambush mode was not such a good idea. Some epiphanies cost a great deal, and that one would've cost everything. I had a much safer on-the-job epiphany about guns, though. It was on New Years' Eve.

I volunteered to work the New Year's Eve shift. Nobody else wanted it, and I was more than happy to do it, 'cause it meant my parents wouldn't have to know that I had nowhere to go, no friends and no idea how you'd get from our house to a party. I simply told my parents I was going out and needed the car, allowing them to infer *but not actually claiming* that I had a social obligation. They were shocked, relieved, and impressed, in that order. I snatched the keys with a grunt, clomped out and drove off to get Max.

The lava-flow of taillights ahead of me—all of them were going somewhere where there was a party, with those noisemaker fern-uncurling kazoo things, and twirly things hanging from the ceiling—and mistletoe . . . The magma of red taillights flowing down into Oakland, sparks dispersing to a hundred loud happy houses where people danced and did other sexual prelims in full view. The river of lava those taillights made—how did it disperse so smoothly, each particle of light to the right house?

But I had something to do too, sort of. Me and Max on the town, a party unto ourselves. Whooping it up. Whoop! Whoop!

Just the two of us, like Sinatra and Schopenhauer on shore leave in Manhattan, twin souls cheering in the New Year.

Actually, I did have moments of something like communion with Max. Sometimes in the middle of a long shift I'd be sitting there on the loading dock, staring over at the pitch-black park, muttering too-late comebacks to all the guys who'd beaten me up or the girls who'd trashed my locker right in front of everybody. I'd be whispering and refining these quips until, punctuating one with a nice hard punch, *Wham!* I'd hurt my knuckle on the wall, snap out of it and look around for Max—and find him looking in the same direction, and very clearly thinking the same thing: dreams of biting the world back. Probably thinking of cool bite-lines too: "You not worth eat, stupid two-leg, HA!" . . . Something fairly simple; Max was inarticulate.

So there was communion of a sort. But like most nerd empathy, it was embarrassing for both parties, and I tried to avoid it. Misery doesn't love company all that much, at least not nerd misery. And nerd company.

But I did plan to give Max a special treat for New Years'. I had a pop-top can of ravioli for him. Except for his work teeth—those big yellow canine fangs—Max's teeth weren't all that good any more and he preferred softer, canned food. He was sitting in the back as usual, apparently unaware that this was New Year's Eve. Just doing his best to make the car smell like dog-shit patties, also as usual; and I was leaning out the window, choking and retching from the reek, ditto. When I turned toward the yard, I could see little war parties darting through the neighborhood, gangs of kids going somewhere to burn something down or blow something up in honor of the New Year.

Matthew was waiting by the guard-shack, smoking by his car. *He* had a party to go to. He waved me into the yard and waited by his car, clearly willing to talk before going off to this New Year's party. After a month or so, he'd decided I wasn't a snitch, just kind of slow, and had adopted a tolerant, pedagogical manner with me: "showing me the ropes." We were probably the same calendar age, but he felt—quite rightly—that he was the elder by a decade at least. So he would occasionally pass on to me bits of gnomic wisdom about "life" or "the streets."

As I walked over to say hi to Matthew, I could hear a pattering like rain on the tin roof of the loading dock. I looked up and saw a clear twilight sky, one or two little clouds. I asked Matthew what was making the pattering sound. He stared at me a moment, deciding how to put it in a manner simple enough for me to understand. Whenever Matthew addressed me, he spoke v-e-r-y clearly and veeerrrryyyy slowly, so I'd understand.

He said slowly, clearly, "You know: New . . . Year's . . . Eve."

"Uh . . ?"

"You know: New . . . Year's . . . Eve." . . . in an even louder, slower voice, with exaggerated lip movements to help me follow.

I shrugged, smiling with terrified embarrassment.

Matthew: "New . . . Year's . . . Eve. You know: 'party time'? They're *partying! Partying!*"

I nodded seven or eight times. With absolutely *no . . . idea . . . what . . . he's . . . talking about.* Somebody's "partying" on the loading-dock roof? Did people do that? Christ, maybe they did! Got to say something, sound like I'm conversing.

"Oh! Huh! . . . Really? Wow . . . Um . . . Up there?" I pointed to the tin roof of the loading dock.

Matthew's estimate of my intelligence, never high, fell sharply. He squinted at me, wondering if even I could be that dumb. He decided I could, and tried to explain more simply.

"In town. They're celebrating. In town. There." He pointed toward Oakland, rising on the hills to the east, and mimed someone firing a rifle into the air. "Pow-pow-pow. Ce-le-brating."

And after several seconds of frantic interpretation, I got it. If you fired into the air in the hills, the bullet would fall on the flatland by the Bridge. On our truckyard.

"Wow!" I said, pointing to the roof. "That's bullets? God! That's bullets!"

Matthew nodded wearily, like Henry Higgins on one of his protegee's slower days.

I was awed. That tinny patter—that was *bullets,* pattering like rain on the tin roof. It was the most incredibly great sound I'd ever heard. I was proud to be a part of it. *Real bullets!* I listened proudly to the steel rain. No, not steel—*Lead* rain. And I was soaking in it—a soldier, unafraid!

For the first time, a new year was coming.

That night Max and I walked proudly, slowly, down the Honor Guard of trailers. Solemnly. In martial cadence. Bullets fell onto the trailers, percussion to our march. We reviewed the guard of trailers. Nothing could touch us. Could touch me. *I am becoming. I will become.* As we marched, I whispered one of my most secret and most powerful spells, one I had distilled from the writings of Frantz Fanon: *When the puppet regimes of the Third World are overthrown, it will be discovered that nothing has been accomplished and everything remains to be done.*

It was the happiest prayer in the world.

10

I must have stood differently in the New Year, because I became almost visible at Berkeley. Twice, professors called on me to answer questions—and once this sudden face tried to sell me drugs on Telegraph Avenue! I walked away in terror, of course, and was so upset that it was 15 minutes or so before I could slow down the tape of his mumbled offer sufficiently to figure out what he'd said, and by that time I was a half-mile away. But it was the thought that counted. I was not merely visible, but cool enough to be offered drugs on the street!

And one day, about three months into this new year, the auguries were fulfilled: a thing happened! An event! On BART, where I least expected anything to happen.

After three years of silence, I had taught myself a sort of BART trance which reduced the pain of standing with my suppurating feet pressed against the crucifixion boots in a stuffy crowded train. I would trance out by inhaling the thick recycled air, staring into the sharkskin shoulder ahead of me, pacing my heartbeat to the clacking rails—and fly far, far inside my head, back to the holy battlefields—Byzantium in the last days, the Kursk Salient, pointblank tank duels in the snow—and dream of carnage till the smell of hot straw and the chrome glare of the suburb sun told me we were coming up to Pleasant Hill station.

That was my commute, the first 1,000 times.

But this 1,001-th trip was different: something *happened*. This is what happened: Joanne Whitfield came up and just simply *sat next to me.* She did! Came over to where I was sitting, expressly for the purpose of sitting down next to me, even though there were empty seats elsewhere!

It was Pearl Harbor, but a good Pearl Harbor. I didn't see her coming. She sat down right next to me. I nearly choked.

See, Joanne was one of the Super People from my high school. Not one of the leaders, like Leigh was—but one of them, definitely. And, thus, a demigoddess.

I could see her face, no more than inches from mine. There was no sneer on it, and it didn't run away or flinch. God! We were all but married already! She leaned over the seat and said "Hi, John!" Said my name and everything. From memory. And then she sat down and laughed, actually laughed! In a conspiratorial, non-mocking way. She really was treating me to an uninterrupted display of that long-worshipped, unreckoning, heartbreaking smile of the Super People. My unprotected mind was exposed to several seconds of it . . . a smile/me connection!

She said hi again—in a sort of warm way, more caress than greeting—and asked me where I was going. I told her I was going home. She asked if that meant Pleasant Hill. I nodded. It seemed she was going there too. She told me what she was doing. It turned out she was attending UC Berkeley too, just for a semester, to . . . to . . . I couldn't translate that part, to do some complex administrative thing I was totally incapable of understanding, especially with that hippie-girl smile lasering into my face. I nodded, pretending to understand but actually experiencing extreme hysterical deafness.

We talked. Sort of. Within reason. She would say something, and then I would say something back. Easier said than done. I was decoding, translating and processing information like a prison-camp escapee trying to remember his German irregular verbs, just to try to keep my end of the conversation going over the roaring terror and joy of my own heart pounding. I couldn't actually process the words, of course, but like a dog I could get a sense of what was being said.

I was simultaneously trying to estimate her rank in the hippie-girl aristocracy of Pleasant Hill High. There were very precise ranks among the Super People. There were the truly high elves, Galadriels like Leigh Akers and Mayberry; then second rank goddesses like Laura Muller; then about eight mere demigoddesses like Joanne who derived much of their glory from their alliance with the great powers. They all shared a certain look: they wore their hair very long and straight in the approved Pre-Raphaelite style, and had very straight features. Joanne had that hair, and one of those faces. A sweet, pretty face, not hurt-beautiful like Leigh, but nice small features, waist-length brown hair, an abstracted feminine manner, a goofy giggly laugh. I estimated that Joanne would have ranked eighth or ninth in that pantheon.

In other words: why would anyone of such high lineage be talking to the likes of me? The only other woman who had spoken to me in the last three years (unless you count checkers at Safeway telling me the total) had turned out to be a Moonie trying to pick up new recruits. In fact, the way I'd realized she must be a Moonie was *because* she acted so friendly. She came up and sat beside me on a bench on campus. I actually looked behind me to see who she was smiling at. Nobody there . . . which meant it was me. She smiled and smiled, and she even gave me a plum. Out of her handbag. A nice purple plum. But then she let slip something about "God." I said, "You're a Moonie, aren't you?" And her smile went away very suddenly and she said, "Well only a Moonie would've bothered!" And stomped off.

So was Joanne a Moonie—was *that* why she was sitting next to me? I couldn't see it. Moonies came from places like Kansas. They were poor would-be counterculture people who got picked up at the bus stations by either the Moonies or the pimps. None of the Super People would ever become slaves to a fat-faced Korean Christian like Moon. Maybe they'd fall for an American cult guru with a cool Buddhist spin to his sermons—that I could imagine— but not the Reverend Moon, who looked like a Chinese-American tax attorney, admired Nixon and made people wear ties. Not possible.

All this had to be decided while I "chatted" with Joanne, a marathon chat that lasted the entire journey. I think I must've done a decent job as chatter, because when we got to the Pleasant Hill station, Joanne seemed disposed to remain with me. She even came down the escalator with me—on the very same step. Was she in love with me?

And even at the station our meeting didn't end, because she said her friend Evvie was picking her up and could give me a ride "If you want." If I *want?* I nodded a few dozen times to make it clear that I did. It was warm already, that warm spring when the mustard flowers show their primary-color yellow, splatters of yellow paint atop the grass in every vacant lot that the developers haven't filled in yet. A little breeze, too. It was bizarre how when you got out at Pleasant Hill station with Joanne, the landscape rushed up to meet you like an eager bellhop in some deluxe hotel. When I walked home from BART alone, the landscape was in no mood to flatter me. It had none of these flowers, none of this warm smell. It smelled like exhaust fumes and looked like dry roadside gravel and dead yellow weeds, and sounded like cars laughing at me.

Now, however—the mustard flowers, the sun, the various plant-life type things—it was like they just couldn't do enough for me, like I'd won the lottery. It was smelling very nicely too—or Joanne was, or something was. Everything on parade, everything all smiles! "Spring"—you know, the hero of all those poems, not the raw prelude to heat and glare.

And her friend's car was waiting right there, just as in Joanne's amazing prediction: a big old rootbeer-colored car, very cool in a hippie way; and her friend "Evvie" was at the driver's seat; and we just went over to it and got in—curbside service!—and we were off. I remember thinking how nice it must be to have friends, to "get picked up" at places by people who weren't even relatives. It argued for a very high level of civilization.

And the spring was now fully, hugely, wildly the spring you encountered in English literature. And not just outside, either; the landscape in the car was even more spring-oriented than the outside. It smelled vastly different inside that car; there was—the vocabulary for smells is really inadequate—there was a somewhat cinnamony heated smell inside the car which proved, rather than simply argued for, that same very high, littoral level of social organization. Minoan, matriarchal . . . some "m" word. Look how well they had things set up! Joanne would get off the train, and her friend Evvie would pick her up; and then the landscape would kiss you rapidly through the car's windows; and the conversation would begin, between Evvie and Joanne, Evvie driving and

Joanne beside her, taking Evvie's hand from time to time, as the landscape went by. So sweet, so arranged, so easy, like sliding down a hill instead of trudging up it.

It was all in their favor—all glide, all downhill. The same raw dirt roadside I trudged was an easy swoop for this cinnamon car. Impregnable, botanical, fecund . . . all those things in the poems from the *Norton Anthology*. Who would have believed it: the things iterated in those poems actually existed!

It was not the Cold War where they drove. It was Peace—maybe even Peace & Love—and they had Peace things to do, "fun" things. They were talking about these things, lots of names of other people and references to stuff that was going on in the present tense. Over my head, but impressive. Evvie was nice too, really nice to me, which made it two-for-two! She hardly scared me at all; in fact, she remembered me. Not in a bad way. Evvie was from Pleasant Hill High School too. She had been shuffleboard champion of the eighth grade, a tall, handsome-profiled girl who was distantly associated with the Super People. She qualified for Super-ness as far as I was concerned; I could smell that instantly. She was courteous in that very noble way you get with middle-class Americans of the best sort: she just said hi as if we met every day, and started haranguing Joanne about being late, letting me sit back quietly out of the light for a while. When Evvie finished yelling at her, Joanne used the same goofy spangled smile I'd seen on the train to excuse herself, almost imploring Evvie to forgive her . . . and Evvie went through a sort of grumpy forgiveness . . . and then they talked, in patois far too polished and allusive for me to catch, about things, events—which seemed to happen all the time in their world. Joanne was very excited and childlike when she talked to Evvie, and Evvie was grouchy and sarcastic, treating Joanne like a dense child. Maybe because Evvie was taller.

Joanne wanted to show me to Evvie, she seemed really eager to do that; but Evvie wanted to scold for a while first. Finally she accepted Joanne's apology and Joanne took her hand, thanked her a few times, then went on about this thing she had been trying to do in Berkeley . . . and how snotty Berkeley people were . . . and then she summarized for Evvie's benefit the whole conversation she and I had had on the train, telling Evvie everything I'd said, while I sat there in the back seat, silent but prepared to corroborate Joanne's account if asked, watching Evvie to see if she wanted me to confirm any of the details. But Evvie just told Joanne to "shut up for a second" because Evvie needed directions to my parents' house. I didn't speak too clearly. But I pointed left or right as necessary, and Evvie actually seemed to find my speech problem amusing. She laughed, in a jolly, contemptuous way, as I indicated by gesture that we had reached my parents' house.

I got out, thanking them several times, until Evvie got impatient and drove away. Joanne was still talking as the car roared off; as it zoomed away, she yelled that she might come by my house some time to "have a talk." I nodded several dozen times—but they were gone.

The rootbeer-colored car got smaller as it headed up Belle Avenue to Dorothy Drive, turned and was gone. The event was over for now. My turn to turn, to push through the rose hedge into our yard. It wasn't really a hedge, just a scraggy line of half-dead thornbushes. If anything impeded progress through the hedge, it wasn't the foliage but the spiderwebs. You had to check for crawlers every time you pushed through it. And then you walked to the house over the cracked dead-grass clumps which passed for our "lawn"—always dying, more Sahel than lawn—and then you banged the broken screen door against the real door until a parent looked through the side window, recognized you and undid all the locks so you could push past, grunting "hi", and shove your way to the refrigerator.

Armed with a question-retarding scowl, all the food in the house and a carton of milk to wash it down with, I retired to my room to consider what had happened. I could still smell on my shirt a bit of their car—that Minoan nutmeg warmth, laurelly wool-spiced smell—and I nuzzled my own shoulders to pick up that precious scent and keep it, rub it into my hair. The shirt and its sacred Super People smell were proof that meeting Joanne had not been just a dream. So many images: the car flashing down Geary Boulevard, passing in seconds the dead dirt fields, making broken glass glitter.

I took the scented shirt off and tried to hang it over a chair as an emblem of civilization, a lady's favor—the first in my slow and dismal tournament.

I lay on the bed and tried to think over everything that had happened, remember the nuances, looking for some sign of love-at-first-sight on Joanne's part. She had asked me several questions, and had seemed to hear the answers because later questions built on the information provided by earlier ones. That was promising. It also meant she could actually hear and process speech in real time! Another proof of a higher civilization. Eons of practice, eons ahead of me. "When the puppet regimes of the Third World are overthrown . . ." And they would be! But this rapid processing—was it simply proof of her advanced state, or did it also mean she *liked* me? . . . Maybe not. Maybe a higher civilization could process even insignificant, perfunctory conversations that swiftly.

But Joanne had also *smiled* at me. I counted the smiles: at least ten. The visual record, soundtrack off, was good: two young people were shown talking on a train . . . the long-haired young woman is smiling at the round-faced young man. The audio tapes were scarier . . . It was a while until, fortified by the ingestion of a quart of milk and a package of Safeway thin-sliced ham and some cheese and a loaf of bread, I went over them. I had made several very bad verbal errors, which made for some discreet groaning and hitting myself in the face while I lay there eating.

But when I went over the tape as a whole, there was reason for hope. There was a very clear tape of her saying, as I got out of the car, that she would ". . . see [me] around, have a talk . . . see ya!" I had only to wait.

11

There were two possibilities for seeing Joanne again:

1. To meet her on the train. 2. To be in the house when she came by to "see [me]," as she had indicated she might.

A third possibility—that I might call her—did not occur to me. You imagine as you can, and I could not imagine that. So I waited when at home and prowled while on BART.

BART had no train schedule, the idea being that you should consider yourself damn lucky to get a train at all. So all I could do was go down to the Berkeley station at about the time I'd first met Joanne and walk up and down the platform hoping to run into her again. If I located her, I planned to walk very loudly back and forth in front of her until she noticed me, then act surprised.

Again, the possibility of initiating contact did not occur to me. You see why it was so easy for me to accept the caricatured world of '70s feminism: I was like a grotesque caricature of what they imagined a properly passive man should be . . . though I don't think they anticipated the sort of dreams that monster would dream. (The Countess smiles, a small twitch on the dead face.)

Every evening, Monday to Friday, clomping up and down the BART platform in pain-boots, I hunted through the crowd at the Berkeley station for Joanne. I walked as fast as I could, for as long as I could. Had to: that or explode. It was one of those "Revolutions of Rising Expectations"; the citizens of my head had come awake. They would not go back to their tenements and huts unsatisfied—not this time. They painted a threat on the crumbling walls: *No Joanne, No Peace!*

I had to do something—but all I knew how to do was lift weights, practice karate, eat 8,000 calories a day, and look for her, look for her, pray to find her, please God please, up and down the station platform. Clumping on the bootnails . . . like Long John Silver as an extremely shy young pirate. Up and down, back and forth, on and on, non-stop. Staring down anyone who stared back. The promised world was about to come true—it *must* come true, and now, now, now! No more postponed apocalypse—she must appear NOW! It was in the stories and the movies; it had to come out this way: I had made myself strong and proper; now would come the sweet part, Joanne as the reward given in stories to the protagonist who has sweated, worked, prepared himself for glory. "When the puppet regimes of the Third World are overthrown" And they would be, must be.

I'd get wound up so high, clomping up and down the brightly tiled BART platform, that it was a shock to wake and find that I was in fact a simple human, a mere first-person singular thing. I had thought I was an army, a people, a Golden Horde. But no, there was only the one of me, the me of me, kernel, heart of palm, clumping through the commuters.

Lots of times I'd be slapped awake by a massed groan, to find the commuters looking up at the moving Pac Man headline: TRAIN TO PLEASANT HILL DELAYED 30 MINUTES . . . BART REGRETS ANY INCONVENIENCE . . .

I didn't regret the inconvenience. I was glad of it, because it gave Joanne that much more time to show up. And I would clump off again, scanning for Joanne.

It was three months before I saw her again. And I found her in the simplest way. She was waiting at the platform of another station when my train pulled to a stop. I saw her face go by as we slowed, shining out among the faces of hundreds of strangers. She got into the car behind mine.

A strategic decision was now required. She had not seen me. If we were to meet again I had to perform a series of extremely complex and terrifying actions: get up, turn, walk back through my car and into hers, then initiate a conversation . . . It was a lot to ask of raw peasant troops like mine. The kind of mistake

MacMahon (another defeated Irish émigré) made in the Franco-Prussian War: expecting raw conscripts to execute highly complex marches, *rendezvous* at a precise moment and then execute a coordinated attack. Recipe for debacle.

But if I *didn't* go back and talk to her, I'd sail out of the solar system forever, back into the blank . . . I let fear and longing volley with each other, then used their combined momentum to lunge out of my seat, across several legs, to her car.

She was instantly visible, because she was the only person in that car outlined by a great silvery halo. This made her extremely easy to find—though even more difficult to approach, or even look at.

But I did, somehow, make my legs move until I was standing by her. With the blood roaring in my ears, I went up to her and said "Hi!" And smiled and sat down without even asking. And she seemed to accept this as something one might do every day. And again we talked, and it went fairly well, only a few painful silences; and again we both got off at Pleasant Hill; and again we went down the escalator on the very same step—"our" step, as I liked to call it—and again her friend Evvie was waiting to pick us up; and once again, Evvie made me feel quite at home in the cinnamon-rootbeer car, arguing with Joanne about some burritos while I sat in the back. Joanne pleaded with Evvie, and Evvie laughed, and all of a sudden we were there: the rootbeer car was stopped outside our house.

And again they dropped me off by the scabby roses and I pushed through them into the dead-grass clumps, and into the house, and into my room, and onto my bed, and lay still, trying to process this flood of events which had overtaken me.

Two meetings in three months: I had gotten spoiled. Now I expected Joanne to show up all the time. Every day I looked for her on the platforms of every single BART station; every evening I spent at home in my room, with a set of clean and respectable clothes ready to put on, in case she happened to "drop by"—the very words she'd used in our last meeting. That was it, my little Book of Revelations detailing her promise to return. A Book of Revelations two words long.

But, like the disciples of that other great Promiser, I was disappointed. There was no Joanne, not for months. And the silence of these months was even harder to bear, because the clock was ticking now, and every Joanne-less evening in that stinking, hate-filled bedroom counted against me. I could no longer think of my life as the prelude, the before-time. That day I spoke to her for the first time on BART, the clock had started running.

I was so desperate I began snarling a question at my parents when I pushed past them each evening: "Anybody call?" They always said no, and I cursed myself for letting them see my shame. But I had to know. Shame was not so terrible a prospect as missing the connection, failing to return a call from Joanne and being carried in a doomed ellipse out of the warm heart of the solar system, back into the dark and silence.

Clearly the thing to do was to stay home all the time in case she called; but twice a week I had karate, and I couldn't give that up—what if I met some of my high school tormentors and forgot my karate? Yeah, but what if Joanne came by on one of the evenings I'm at karate? The old guns-vs-butter dilemma. It wasn't just karate, either; most weekends I had to spend at the truckyard, guarding things, earning money, doing my job. It was a terrible thought: that Joanne might call or come by my parents' house while I was marching around Oakland trying to catch intruders. A bad general, bad as the Austro-Hungarians! Fighting on the wrong front at the wrong time!

But work was necessary. It made me feel less damned. And the good part was that while patrolling the truckyard with Max I could make up long and glorious speeches to say to Joanne just in case we ever did meet again. I could go over every sentence of our two conversations on BART and come up with far better responses than those I had generated at the time. And not just better dialogue, either; I also came up with better plot. Like the time on our way out of the Pleasant Hill BART station, these two guys started mouthing off . . . and after politely, suavely asking Joanne to take the bag with my *gi* and books in it, I go up to them, smiling politely, and kick the first one's kneecap till it bends backward like an ostrich's leg, and then treat the second to a nice quick elbow in the face, so that his face fills up, a reddish crater lake, as he lies dead still on the concrete, while the other one disgraces himself with a hysterical shriek of agony, grasping at his backwards ostrich knee . . . and then I dust myself off, smiling mildly to Joanne, take back my bag and say to her in an almost British voice, so calm, so polite, "Sorry about that little interruption . . . no manners, people have no manners at all; you'd think he'd have the decency to shriek a little more quietly . . . Ah! There's Evvie in the car. Shall we go?" Max had to put up with a lot of sudden yanks on his leash as I gave a surprised trailer a good sharp elbow. *Mess with me, trailer . . . you be sorry.* Cowards hit a lot of inanimate objects.

But best of all were the suave post-maiming speeches I practiced saying in that bored British drawl. I polished them endlessly, rehearsed the exact accent: "After all, one might expect the fellow to shriek a bit more quietly, don't you think, Joanne, beloved . . . my love . . . dearest?" And she would laugh in an appreciative way and hold my hand and stuff, and we would walk off hand in hand, while my enemies writhed in agony by the newspaper racks at Pleasant Hill BART. We left the church, newly-wed, and proceeded to the honeymoon limo down an alley of truck trailers in tuxedos, truck trailers making an arch of dress-swords. The groom accompanied by a black German shepherd. The low surf of cars on the Bay Bridge for applause. Condensing dew in the dank Oakland night for thrown rice.

But the truckyard shifts were long, and these rehearsals exhausting; my faith was beginning to waver. It had been months since I'd seen Joanne, and she was passing into the world inside my head, losing her incarnation. The dark between stars . . . I needed to see, to smell her again, to get the samples I needed to reanimate her, freshen her image in my mind. Needed to see the corner of her mouth when she did that smile. Smell the Minoan nutmeg again.

And there were endless work-type distractions in those long nights of patrolling the yard: a truck would pull in and I'd have to activate my face, look at the driver and pretend to listen to his harangue about ethnicity and how it could be solved with a big enough handgun . . . And then the terrible hour, the 4-5 AM time.

It's always worst just before the dawn—that's one cliché which is literally true, as all speedfreaks know. Nights at the truckyard would go well enough until about 2 AM—whispering speeches to Joanne, practicing ways to hurt people . . . Then time would stop, as it did in my bedroom. Staring into the smelly darkness of Oakland: organ-meat, diesel and brine.

Weird things went on in that neighborhood. Sometimes there'd be a very weird animal noise, some cat or dog killing or dying or mating. You could never see much, because the truckyard was so brightly lit that everything beyond it was pure darkness. It may as well have been the Mekong Delta. It sort of was. There was even some kind of guerrilla movement practicing in the little park across the street. It must have been some sort of black organization which for God knows what reason scheduled its drill sessions from midnight till 2 AM. With no lights at all. It always went the same way: somewhere out there in the darkness, a very powerful black male voice would start calling out commands. Then you'd hear a cadenced, roaring response, some sort of chant, from dozens of black male voices. It sounded like an army training over there . . . but you never saw a thing. Not a light, not a hint of a face, just this military noise coming out of the dark, over and over.

The commanding voice would shout something—the soldiers' chorus would shout it back, a huge noise that filled the neighborhood—but you never saw a thing. Just the lights illuminating the trailers, and beyond them literal blackness. I still have no idea what those voices were. If I'd looked across to the park at dawn and found nothing but a pair of speakers and a tape deck, I wouldn't've been surprised. And if the dawn revealed some Black Liberation Army in full battle dress marching in columns to the truckyard, bringing scaling ladders up to the chain-link fence and pouring across to sack the loading dock, that wouldn't've surprised me either.

Would've been kind of neat, actually: Oakland as Constantinople in 1453; me and Max as Constantine XI; the black militants of Oakland as the Turks; the chain-link perimeter fence as the city's walls . . . All in all, a pretty neat idea. Well worth the small price of dying. Unless Joanne was real . . . yes, that was an entirely new factor in the old dreams. If Joanne might someday like me, well . . . then it would be a very different calculation, which would look something like this: If Joanne, then no war. If no Joanne, war. Simple logic—but hard to guess the odds.

And tiring, tiring to think and rethink the old fears, alone with Max in the mudflats all night. By 3 or 4 AM even the voices from the park would go silent, and the concept of Joanne would die inside my mind. There'd be nothing but the delicious idea of sleep, the bliss of floating weightless on a bed. But I never slept on the job. I was a good soldier! I knew the other guards slept right through most of their shifts—but I wanted so much to be someone's soldier. I'd go back by the vending machines and try to read on the pinewood pallets, where I could keep watch on the yard and the office at once. I was trying to memorize a Robert Browning poem. I liked Browning:

> My first thought was, he lied in every word,
> That hoary cripple, with malicious eye askance
> To watch the working of his lie on mine . . .

Groggy and wretched, I would whisper it over and over: "That hoary cripple with malicious . . . with malicious eye . . ." Couldn't remember the rest of the Browning; just those three lines.

It was horribly elemental back there on the pallets, all smells and sleep-lust. The weak Bay breeze sifted through that corner of the dock like a very dirty, slow Mekong, a superterranean stream, the ghost-double of a cave river. Its job was flushing Oakland smells: the burned-tomato smell of the canneries, the rotten egg of the mud flats, the organ-meat smell from the bay flat houses, and the waft of piss from the truckers' toilet where the instant coffee of many an Interstate truck-stop was drained into a single filthy urinal.

A complex and sinister perfume, that whole braid of smells. I knew that this was the real world, the very realest of all and the one most to be feared: the world of lying on a wooden pallet at four in the morning in that smell, trying to be awake, the sacred fire dimming in my head . . . nothing but little tired demons mumbling old, weary plots. I'd half pass out, whispering the Browning to myself: That hoary cripple . . . The working of his lie . . .

It was so bright there, with that fluorescent bar overhead. My first thought was, he lied in every word . . . Like lying on a raft looking up at a tropical sun. Those were slow, slow minimum-

wage minutes—trying to read and smelling whatever the breeze
brought . . . That hoary cripple . . . getting up to check the clock
and find it was only three or seven minutes later than the last time.
(Just to go to bed, just to be allowed to sleep.) Chanting the
Browning so someday at some party I would be able to show off
by saying it with a strange and tragic intonation:

> My first thought was, he lied in every word . . .
> The working of his lie on mine . . .

But there would be a dawn, as always. And that meant
handing over the yard to Matthew, letting him into the yard, and
then talking to him. And the terror of that would get me perked
up—making sure I could remember his name, who he was, what
century this was . . .

The trouble was, the local robbery network in Oakland had
caught on to the fact that as guards, S.I.D.O.D. was L.O.U.S.Y.
Not me, so much—nothing ever got stolen on my shifts—but
Matthew. The first serious, adult robbery happened while
Matthew and Max were snoozing. The robbers hit the office, not
the trailers. CME Trucking didn't like that. They were willing to
accept a certain level of pilfering from the trailers, but they
thought their office—where they, the real grown-ups, worked—
would be sacrosanct. No funny business in there. But the locals
were evidently not as familiar with this code of ethics as CME had
thought; they came in through an open window and stole every
typewriter, along with a very early quasi-computer which had cost
a fortune.

CME Trucking was not happy with us. The hobbit-man called
us together to tell us this. He had clearly attended some sort of
motivational training, because he scolded us in a positive way.
Embarrassing. Even Matthew was embarrassed. "We're going to
have to look into ourselves and draw up that hidden strength!"
Looking at us as we sat on the bright white sofa, under the big
braided ropes of plants. We looked into the floor of his living
room instead. "This is it, guys!" We nodded. I was sick with fear
and embarrassment, but for once I wasn't alone. Matthew was
studying the carpet too.

12

Then it got worse. Max bit his first janitor. Worse yet, there were racial overtones.

The janitors were subcontracted employees like us. They belonged to a tall old black man named Elvin. Elvin was not like the angry black people you saw at Berkeley. Elvin was from an older story, something from Faulkner, some weird deal from "The South." He would roll up in a pickup truck the color of faded Levi's. It was always full of broken brooms and canisters of industrial cleaner. His little sidekick Tomas always rode up in the cab with him, while two or three generic illegal Hispanics hunched in the truck bed. Elvin was the boss—he'd put those Peruvians to work in a sharp choppy tone, pointing them in the right direction and handing them brooms. No dawdling. But he was deferential to us guards. Which was embarrassing. Because it metonymically summoned up that footage from the far, unimaginably old, grotesque South, with white sheriffs unleashing racist German shepherds on peaceful black demonstrators.

Max may have been black, but he seemed to identify with his German shepherd heritage of repression rather than his color; Elvin's tired old truck would roll wearily into the yard like a mule on wheels and Max would instantly go crazy on his chain, making his hoarse squeaks of protest at being prevented from rending the new arrivals, yipping falsetto racist epithets for everybody to hear. The dog straining at its chain, the deferential black men . . . It was like the whole scene was suddenly going to go sepia and turn into

old civil rights-era footage of some unimaginable Hellhole like
Selma, Alabama.

Max wasn't actually racially prejudiced. That's the weird part.
It wasn't fair that it looked like Alabama when Max bit a janitor,
because at heart Max was an absolute egalitarian. He'd've slashed
at the languid, pearly calves of a Rockefeller with the same zombie
lust he showed for the skittering shanks of black janitors or the
stubby thighs of Peruvian illegal immigrants. But, as I suppose a
socialist would point out, there weren't any Rockefellers in the
yard. Your average socialist would probably suggest (in that nasal
drawl they always affect) that the demographics of the yard made
it likely that most of the skin Max would slash would be high in
melanin.

His first leg was, anyway. It belonged to Tomas the midget
sidekick. Tomas would always hop out of the truck and start
ordering the cowed illegals around while Elvin stepped with
elaborate languor from the cab. Elvin managed to compress an
entire duchy in that exit: slow and dignified, to remind us, and
above all his own employees, of his status as boss. Tomas had his
own honorable role in this court as jester and comrade. Only the
Hispanics were wholly without status, changing from week to
week, ordered around and then made the subjects of shared
mockery by Elvin, Tomas and whichever guard was there. We
were all English-speaking Americans together, right? Right. Racial
differences notwithstanding. So notwithstanding that they were
deafening.

It gave me the creeps. I couldn't do my part in the xenophobic
"Si señor" repartee which tradition demanded from the guard on
duty. This deeply offended Elvin and Tomas. In a movie, that loss
would've been compensated by the loyalty and gratitude the
Hispanic extras would come to feel for me—but not in this life.
Wrong movie, kiddo! You're thinking of the kiddie matinee. The
Hispanics acted like scared people do: they said and did only what
they were told. No piñata invitations, beautiful cousins or timely
rescues of the sensitive young white guy who refused to mock
them.

My refusal to play earned me only snubs from Elvin and
Tomas. They started cutting me like a couple of dukes—while
continuing to banter with Matthew. Whenever I was on duty,

Elvin would park his truck exactly one foot further away from the guard-shack. In a marked manner. And Tomas made a point of sweeping fiercely around me without speaking to me or acknowledging me, whisking that broom around my blushing feet like I was a badly placed pillar in motorcycle boots.

All I could do was hide in the shack and pretend to read. The yard had been completely overrun by Elvin and Tomas, who began taunting Max, probably on Elvin's instructions as a typically sly Medici way of destabilizing me. Max was too dumb to notice he was being taunted; as far as he knew, he was just having a run of bad luck, lunging at this little black man who was always just out of reach. With Elvin leaning on his truck and smiling a slight proud smile, his little demon-jester would weave just into the radius of Max's chain, then dart back as Max did his cobra-lunge out to the end of it. Then Elvin and Tomas would share a laugh, and Elvin—Duke Elvin de Medici—would let his haughty eyes flick over to me as I pretended to read in the guard shack with the fear making my heart a taiko drum. It was worse than high school, because now somebody else was getting hurt on my behalf: Max, poor Max—who was really upset at this new game, so hopelessly far over his head. But what were you supposed to do? It wasn't like I could go out there and attack Elvin and Tomas. We hardly knew each other; it would be socially awkward. And besides, they hadn't actually done anything overt. As so often, I lacked a real martial art, one that worked outside of the movies.

Max was in the same position. He knew only one way of dealing with this kind of torment, and it wasn't working. His squeaks got higher and higher, hoarser and hoarser, till he sounded like a bat with a bad cold. I turned away, burying my face in the Browning book so I wouldn't have to watch. That hoary cripple with malicious eye askance . . . But ears can't shut, and I could hear very clearly what was going on. Every few seconds the chain would swoosh out like a slinky, and Max would squeak his rage; then his two tormentors would chuckle.

Then a moment of blessed silence. I looked up cautiously, trying to keep my eyes below their radar. Max was lying down, panting. He'd finally grown tired of the game and had stopped even trying to get at Tomas. Just lay down and moped. So Tomas, good jester that he was, took his act up a notch; he stepped two full paces into Max's range. Max was so worn out from his lunges that he didn't even bark. "Leave that poor ol' dog alone," Elvin told Tomas, loudly enough so that I could hear him, feel his power over events. Tomas, enjoying this display of his master's powers, went off to sweep the dock. I tried to memorize my Browning:

> My first thought was, he lied in every word . . .
> My first thought was, he lied in every word . . .

After a few minutes' silence I risked a cautious peek; and found that Elvin had gone down to the end of the loading dock to harass his illegal-alien workers. Blessed silence; now those poor Peruvians were the prey. But soon the sounds came closer to the shack: tools being loaded back in the truck, Elvin's tone of command and Tomas's croaking tease.

Elvin turned precisely halfway in my direction and called out, "We're leaving now! Heading out!"

This clearly required a response from me. I raised my head, went to the window and waved weakly, whining: "OK! Right! See ya hehhhhh!"

Elvin smiled. Pure Medici scorn in the curve of that smile. The Hispanics were already packed like boxes in the back of the truck, keeping very still and quiet. Tomas, heading for the truck but eager for one last little insult, made an exaggeratedly slow move to Max, stepping just inside his range. Max lay there in despair. Elvin laughed. Tomas took that as his cue. He hammed it up, holding out one leg and pulling up his pantsleg to show Max his calf. Max wasn't even looking. Tomas said, in a stripper's voice, "Come on dog! Here it is!" He turned to share the last laugh with Elvin.

Max was very quick. I hardly saw him move—just heard the slash of the chain as it paid out. Tomas reacted far too slowly. He managed to get turned around, which was lucky for him; but that dangling leg was too slow curving out of the radius of the chain. Max had one good slash at it as Tomas fell out of range, screeching in pain. Elvin, showing the Medicis' usual level of loyalty, stayed well out of range and didn't even help Tomas up. Tomas was up on his own now, hopping around cursing: "Son of a BITCH! Son of a BITCH, Mu-ther . . . Fuck-in' . . . DOG! SHIT! SHIT!" (By the way, I've never understood what people mean in novels and such when they talk about how well and how inventively this or that colorful-type character can curse. I've never heard any swearing which was even slightly inventive. It's just another patronizing belletrist lie.)

Tomas and Elvin were over by the truck, mumbling. Looking at the bite. When suburban dogs bite, everyone asks the magical question, "Did it break the skin?" But this wasn't the suburbs, and Max wasn't some golden retriever irked at the paperboy. Max broke the skin all right. Broke a few more-than-capillaries too, judging by the blood on the concrete and Tomas's shoes.

I went out to commiserate, "Wow sorry wow looks bad call a doctor wow sorry!"

But though I was terrified and convinced that the bite would be blamed on me, I had just enough vestigial decency to appreciate the rough justice Max had inflicted on Tomas's leg.

Besides, Max was a better soldier than Tomas. You could tell by the difference in post-bite conduct: while Tomas hopped around cursing like a baby, Max was the consummate professional. The second he realized that Tomas had stumbled back out of range, he sat down and relaxed. No hard feelings. An old pro. He just sat there panting, a happy expression on his face for the first time since I'd met him. He watched and savored Tomas's pain dance, his undignified caperings, to the full.

13

And I went home to wait for Joanne. I waited for Joanne the way Millennial sects wait on a hilltop, praying to be struck by the divine lightning. The way the great herds of the Serengeti wait for the monsoon, wildebeests pawing at the dusty red earth—that was me.

Farmers of the Sahel, shown looking up at the blank hot sky—me again!

Death Valley in midsummer: your humble servant!

It was, in fact, summer; and the academic year was over, which was a big relief, because it meant that I could wait in the house all day, in case Joanne came by. All day, every day. I holed up in my room in the stinking old-socks heat, with enough National Geographics to weary an entire platoon of masturbators. And waited. And reread the dusty paperbacks that filled the hallway of our house—Agatha Christie mysteries, Goethe's *Selected Works*, and thousands of crumbling, accusing self-help books with titles like *Why You're A Failure*. Anything else that would occupy the hours. Books I'd read ten times already and hadn't even liked the first time. And lay in bed whispering speeches to Joanne, if she ever came back. And mimed the gruesome deaths of my high school tormentors. And wore my arms out trying to hold the National Geographic steady, open to that picture of the Indonesian girl tapping a rubber tree, bending toward the camera with a breast spilling out of her sarong, while a stern-looking overseer watched from the background. Stern-looking . . . stop her

as she tries to pour her yield into the pot—"Wait, girl—why have
you done such a poor job?" Pour her cup out on the ground,
shove it back in her hand and tell her to start again. With a shove.
With a blow of the riding crop he has hidden behind his back . . .
which is why I can't see it in the photo . . . Or simply drag her into
the bush and rip her rags off, do absolutely anything you want,
because she is only a slave, a slave-girl . . . anything you want . . .

And pop! Back to reality, wipe the stuff away, squirm some of
the sweat off my fat back, let my breathing come back to normal,
and settle down again to the daylight world. Where I was no
overseer but a beggar—a failed one.

After months of this odd vigil, Joanne appeared. It was
another day in our house, dark and hot, all the curtains shut tight
and the place besieged by the chiding drone of our neighbors'
lawnmowers, whose Stuka drone reminded us endlessly that we
alone settled for a lawn of straw and cracked adobe, that our trees
were the only ones in the neighborhood which had actually gotten
smaller over the past decade. I was lying in bed with a National
Geographic—browsing for material, as it were—when the
doorbell rang.

I jumped out of bed and was striding to the door in two
seconds, only to find my parents there already: one behind the
door ready to turn the knob, the other looking out through the
curtained window—but discreetly, just a little inch of the curtain
pulled back. We were all somewhat keyed up; the warning bell
going off like that—it was not an everyday occurrence. The
choices were: (A) the paperboy demanding money; or (B) an adult
bill-collector demanding money; or (C) something even worse that
we hadn't thought of.

They motioned me to be quiet, but then indicated by gesture
that it was for me. My heart began to piston—the rabbit leaping in
my chest from hope rather than terror this time—and I was
wearing a t-shirt which had all these weird stains and smells on it,
and old pajama pants, somewhat crustier in the crotch than was
perhaps socially acceptable. I hissed in fury to my parents to
distract our caller while I ran back in my room. Wriggled into my
rhino-sized corduroy pants and a big brown shirt, then back to the
door, now open. Both of my parents were chatting in high voices.
They stood in the little opening to keep the stranger from seeing

inside the house, so I had to shoulder between them to see, standing there . . .

Joanne. In all her glory. In full-body halo. You can't know, you who have had so much, so easily—you can't know what it meant to me to have one of the Super People standing there. Of her own free will.

In my memory Summer begins at that moment. Before, it was just hot; and hot does not equal Summer. Summer was what breathed over me now that Joanne stood on the doorstep to see me! That and that alone made Summer enter my nose and eyes and ears. Sweet fur of torn Levi's fringe, cascade of hair over her dashiki.

All history was for this! The Huns were driven back, the Goth/Roman alliance held at Chalons—just for this intake of breath with Joanne at the door of my parents' house! I am a morningstar mace wheeling in the hand of Charles Martel at Tours—the Hammer of God!

And the smell—the pine trees sweat in the sun, baking a wild turpentine honey which is diffused throughout the upper air for the delectation of those who have visitors. (Not available to the unvisited.) Even though you've lived in that house and sulked around under those trees, killing ants and reading *Life* magazine all your life, you get the honeyed sap wafted to you only when you walk up the path with Joanne. To her car, which is parked right there on the street, for everyone to see. And everything begins at once: the smell of pine honey; the warmth (as opposed to heat) of the air; the sky I never dared look at or inhale before; and the fact that, just as they always claimed, the sky is actually "blue"!

—Everything begins at once! The world admits me, makes a way for us, a nuptial, martial procession through an arbor of flowers, beneath a gallery of swords!

And this sudden inhale of all the summer's upper airs went so well with the smell of Joanne's long hair—it was more than I had ever imagined, a wholly new realm! I realize now—stopping the video at that frame where I first see her standing there in the shadow of our eaves—that her hair was lank and rather oily. But that only proves that I'm a dead old man now, not that she was not beautiful. *"O Emir, it is not that the world is growing dim; it is only that you are dying."* Yes—if I were still alive, Joanne's "lank" and "greasy" hair would bring me to my knees in worship, just as it did then.

I brushed out quickly, past my parents, while Joanne's magic held the way clear. Joanne was being needlessly polite to my parents; as I stood halfway up the path, quivering like a dog waiting for a walk, she wasted time making polite chat with them. And then she turned, and smiled, and walked up to me—and we went up the path together, next to each other! I was close to fainting. The air—I'd never smelled *this* kind of summer before. Usually the Pleasant Hill summer smelled like baking adobe dust and dead yellow straw and car exhaust and lawnwater sizzling on hot concrete.

But now, striding up the path with Joanne, it was like a world-cologne—a wordless immanent Darwinian perfume, perfect for swimming and lying on beaches or picnic-type activities in picnic-places or embracing at length or driving across America together in a hippie Volkswagen van with a guitar—all of the above! And the sky over Pleasant Hill—which I would've sworn was gray in winter and smog beige in summer—was blue as a skiing poster.

Our triumphal procession moved effortlessly up through the thorns and spiders, through the whole web spun around our house, which I had thought unbreachable. The Magic Kiss that breaks the spell (except for the fact that she hadn't kissed me, but how far away could the kissing part be after all this?) Salvation incarnate—in *her* car! A little hippie car, purposely crummy-looking. It was cool to have little ugly cars then. Purposely ugly purple to boot, and unAmerican. That marked it as cool too. A Rolls would not have impressed me nearly as much as this dented $500 Opel Manta.

And we both got in—I waited to be asked, which she seemed to find weird—and then we were off. We were "on our way." The whole street looked different. The Shumways' house across the street was happy for me! Belle Avenue bidding me goodbye!

14

And there were times when Joanne did seem to like me. She even allowed me to play with her body a couple of times. Sitting on the bed in her room with the door shut. She would grab my hands—very rarely, only a few times—and place them on her body. Very few times. One time over the small huts of her breasts. And one time landing them near the Chesapeake intricate tropical fjord between her legs.

Sitting completely still except for my hands, which Joanne guided over her geography. In her parents' weird old house. A farmhouse gone to seed, surrounded by housing tracts but sunk away from them, older and overgrown, hidden in a crotch of shrubs and scraggy trees. You couldn't even see it from the street, thanks to the feral shrubbery.

In the heat, the still air with distant lawnmower drone . . . lawnmower or small plane, same sound . . . Pleasant Hill in the summer. Sitting there in her hot little room.

I think now that it must have been a way of testing her powers. I was the perfect inflatable doll for that kind of experiment: *sort* of like a man, only safer, thanks to my built-in cutoff switch. Someone who, unlike Evvie or her mother, responded to her gestures of affection. Because after eight straight years of Joanne's untiring devotion, Evvie was bored. They'd been married in all but name since they were fourteen years old, and Evvie was a Californian—she wanted some driving room.

So it must have pleased Joanne to see that her powers had not waned. And she wanted to see how far those powers could extend; so she experimented. With sex—but first with a safer variable: food. She would invite me to dinner at her parents' house and cook for me. It was the best food I'd ever had. Made the way her mother'd learned in Missouri: fried chicken that was even better—greasier and spicier—than KFC—another whiff of the unimaginable Old South. Pecan pie. With actual pecans. And southern weather too, the ancient heat of those ominous names: *Selma . . . Mobile . . . Vicksburg.* Not hard aluminum-hot like it was at our house. The heat in Joanne's house was nicer . . . sleepy, fuddled, soft and clothy.

And Joanne would make iced tea, another Southern delicacy I knew only from books, and make me eat a lot, while hardly touching her own plate, and pour me glasses of that iced tea from a big sweaty pitcher. All in the name of science—but I didn't know that then. I thought it meant something personal, my first second-personal in millions of stuck years. Every glass of iced tea reclaimed an acre of desert. And when she was pouring it, she would stand behind me, the arc of her hip once even brushing my shoulder. It was almost too much—all of it happening at once!

And then into her room. Sometimes she'd close the door behind us, sometimes not. I got more hopeful when the door was closed, so I watched carefully for it, like a dog watching to see if its master takes the leash off the hook after grabbing the car keys. Then we'd sit on her bed and look at her photo albums. People's albums are supposed to be boring, but that's just another lie the Beigeocracy tells you, like colorful swearing and redemption. Albums are the most pornographically exciting books this side of *La Nouvelle Justine.* Joanne's—God, even now . . .

They were in two big binders. The first covered childhood: Joanne as a sweetly smiling little girl, posing at the tetherball pole or wrapping her hands around her mother's rhino leg as her mother grimaced, one meaty hand shoving her little daughter's head away from her thigh. Then some pictures of her dead brother in various poses with her mother and father (you could see in the sequence his fatal metamorphosis from clean-cut middle-class boy to altruistic bearded hippie) . . . then school pictures: Joanne in the fourth-grade group picture at Pleasant Hill

Elementary; Joanne as a Girl Scout, ah!—her familiar ditz smile intact in the uniform and the first twin knolls of pubescence on the chest of her tightly tucked beige blouse . . .

These photos in her first album, though very moving, were not culturally alien. My parents had pictures of me which were not so different.

But the second binder! Adolescence. On the cover Joanne had painted a big flower and a peace sign. There was one sequence which took up several pages. It stopped my breath. Joanne, topless, with a parasol, smiling over her shoulder at the camera. The angle changed slightly from first to last, so that more breast was visible as the sequence followed Joanne trailing coyly through someone's garden, head tilted and long straight hair falling over her shoulder.

"Evvie took those. She's a really good photographer . . ."

We kept coming back and back to that sequence, at my request. But there were others which were equally awe-inspiring, if not as exciting. There were "friend"-type shots: Joanne and Evelyn standing on a rock by the sea with some other Super People—the whole gang of them had gone on their own, without their parents, even though they were still in high school. One of Joanne and Evelyn and Mayberry Lanning riding horses in the hills (Mayberry was a legendary hippie-girl Super Person who was so advanced she didn't even come to school after Sophomore year); another of Joanne and Evelyn at Debbie Stack's birthday party, a big gang of people I recognized from high school but had never seen off-campus. All smiling. They could somehow converge in one room at once. But how? Their elusive socio-technological secrets . . .

There were amazing background stories which Joanne supplied with each picture: mescaline casualties, abortions, boating accidents, skiing trips, sleepovers, cop-stoppings, getting-togethers and breaking-ups. I could have swallowed the whole binder, eaten it like a laminated remedial communion host. *So much life!*

And yet—the strangest part—most of it seemed to mean nothing to Joanne. I'd shake my head in awe, whispering "My God!" over and over again at some shot of the Super People on a camping trip, posing on a ridgeline in the Sierras, and Joanne would say, "It wasn't that great; too hot. An' Evvie got poison

oak." She couldn't believe I found all this "boring" detail worth
hearing, and this led her back to my own subtly conveyed story of
my blank, eventless life.

And in trying to tell Joanne the difference between poison oak
and solitary confinement like mine, I learned a trick. I made of the
miseries of solitary confinement both a comic sketch and a
courtship song. This was a lie. It hadn't really been funny or
colorful at all. It was just plain horrible, like being stuck in an
elevator for ten years. But it could be adapted as comic material;
and I wanted very much to amuse, entertain Joanne. And maybe
even get her interested in rescuing me.

It sort of worked: Joanne found exciting my confession that
I'd never touched anyone. "You never . . ? *Ever?* I don't even
mean, you know, actual fucking; but you really never even . . .
fooled around, you know . . . kissed anybody even?"

Headshake for no. Feeling a little guilty because I had kissed
someone once. But it was my Aunt Eileen, on the cheek, and she
was a nun . . . Still, better to suppress that part of the record.

I was praying to all the demons that Joanne's line of
questioning would lead where I thought it was leading: to some
hands-on remedial training.

It did. Sort of. Joanne made it very clear she was only doing
this in case I found somebody—somebody *else,* as she stressed—
who might want me. I'd have to be ready for that day ". . . because
I mean, God, nobody's going to want a klutz with no experience!"

Nod nod nod nod nod! Oooooo, they're taking the leash off
the hook! Wag wag wag wag wag! Drool drool drool, wag wag
wag, nod nod nod!

She shut the door behind me, sat down on the bed and patted
it for me to sit down next to her.

"Here—" She takes my hand. My right hand. Stops,
considering: "Wait—You're right-handed, right?"

"Um, sorry, no, actually . . . left-handed. Sorry . . ."

She drops my right hand and takes my left in hers. Pauses for
a second, considering. "OK, wait . . . How, uh, do you . . . left-
handed . . . OK . . ."

Lesson one: where and how to put my hand. She took my left
hand and guided it over the trailing curtain of the Trapezius, then

the underwater branch collarbone, down to the pleasant hills of her breasts . . .

A first shock, like when you jump into cool water. Feedback override on all sensors, white noise and the heart pounding, then the first valid sensor-reports to survive the EMP. Tactile: the skin not like my dry freckled pelt . . . moist, thinner and warmer, frictionless. And the nipples, the ring of buds like small standing stones around a central megalith—warm Stonehenge . . . I can feel the seismic heart as if it were just under the skin, as if the breastbone were thin, flexible plastic. Like the translucent chicken breasts at Safeway. Joanne takes my obedient hand and takes it on a lap around her breast, circling the nipple like a shark. "See? Like that!" I nod. "OK—slow! Slow!" I nod. She brings the hand downward, down the slinky ribs to the belly, Central Valley, slightly convex and warm. Then I begin to continue, extrapolating from her direction. But this alarms her: "No, no—wait."

Takes my hand and places it on her belly, gliding over the navel and down the warm flank, touching the wingtip of the hip and then down the valley between belly and thigh. To the pubic forest—Lothlorien!—and then she giggles, pushes away: "Wait wait wait! Slow down!"

I stop. Hand freezes in place on the beach-slope of the belly. Everything is humming whiteout; we are at the center of the Sun.

No dungeons now. No Sade, all vanilla: I wanted only to kiss, be held, touch In fact, I didn't seem to require any invented narrative here. No dreams. These tactile/olfactory cues were far more powerful than my night-time narratives. And they operated in the present tense and twentieth century! I knew suddenly a great half-truth: *Stories are body-substitutes for losers.* So that's why the cool people never have anything to say: they have *this*.

You know, you get these *Portrait of the Artist* things where some dedicated literary apprentice decides to abandon the immanent for the imaginary world. I don't get that. They must be insane. Or more likely just lying. You'd have to be stupid, I mean stupid even by my standards, to prefer stories to bodies. I would've burned every book ever printed for the chance to be admitted to a life in the body. Hell, I'd do it now. No, I'm serious; just get me a pitchfork and a five-gallon can of gas, and I'll toss the entire catalogue of Penguin Classics in a mound, and soak'em down with premium unleaded—nothing but the best for the likes of Voltaire, Dickens, Chekhov, all our wise sad witty dead—then take a big Olympic torch from the hands of a fat, puffing science fiction nerd (I wouldn't burn Philip K. Dick or Tolkien—that's different) who's carried it from our anti-Athens, the cookie aisle of the Pleasant Hill Safeway, and fling it onto the pyre. I'll do it on-camera, right now, for nothing. With pleasure.

A body! A life! All my nocturnal stories and anaesthetic books were gone as I leaned forward to kiss Joanne, hands still on her sacred skin. I'd seen it done in films; it seemed the proper thing; and besides (a new sort of idea): I *wanted to*. But it didn't work; she burst out giggling as I attempted to dock lips.

"Sorry—what—? Did I . . . something wrong?"

"It's just . . . *God,* you've got a big head!"

"Sorry! Sorry!"

"It's like the Moon comin' up at ya!"

But the new, fierce vanilla-lust animating my lap was implacable, and I moved to dock again. We touched face to face. What was Neil Armstrong compared to me?

She panics: "No wait, wait—"

She takes my lunar head and pushes it away from her face. But that's OK, that's OK—the taste of her cheek and one curve of her lip's corner will be stored in memory forever, like the cookies under my bed and the sweet grease musk of her lank O never-to-be-renounced hippie-girl hair.

She leans back and laughs. I maintain Asgard arc over the bed, hoping for resumption of these peace talks. The Thaw. The Thaw is coming. That roar in my ears is the ice breaking up.

"OK, that's enough for now."

"One more—practice? For practice?" Leaning toward her—

"No. Git!" (She sometimes borrowed her mother's southern accent in moments of social awkwardness.) "You go sit over there." The floor by the closet.

I went sat over there. But after looking at me for a second, she said, "You know what 'French' means?"

Trick question? Mockery?

"Uh—'of or from France'?"

"French *kiss*. It's when you . . . Here, come up here again."

I materialized on the bed again, moving at the speed of light. She took my hand again and placed it on her shoulder, a static waltz, and positioned my head like a barber—

But at that point—because Dworkin's God-who-hates-women stretches a point to hate me too—there was the sound of a monster giggle in the hallway: Joanne's mother coming.

Her mother matched the house: old and ugly, old and weird. Scary. Joanne said her mother'd been relatively OK until her son David had gotten killed in the Peace Corps. In Africa. Some murky third world death—either a lightning bolt hit him or something else electrical, a short circuit in the wiring of his hut. Or he was murdered. They never found out. A lot of starry-eyed offspring of the suburbs got themselves killed in that Children's Crusade . . . just never came back. Closed coffin and a consul's vague condolences; yearbook picture by the parents' bed; a bewildered, aging couple waking up to that picture every day for the rest of their lives. That was supposedly what sent Joanne's mother really, seriously crazy: the shock of getting her high-minded folk-singing son back from Kennedy's dream as a box of tropical putrescence. Though some of Joanne's stories about her childhood suggested that her mother must have been crazy all along.

It didn't really matter anyway, carbon-dating her mother's madness—not when you were dealing with the *dingbat-an-sich*, The Thing itself slouching down the hallway toward Joanne's room, giggling as she came. You could get a quick sample of Mrs Whitfield's whole craziness in that giggle—the same giggle Joanne had, deepened and amplified by a hundred pounds of fat and a couple of decades of wandering around their Texas-Chainsaw farmhouse free-associating. Joanne's mother was the most instantly repellent person I'd ever met. (This was before I became an academic.)

The sick bit was that Joanne really loved her mother. I mean capital-L *Loved.* A weird same-sex Oedipal thing, strongly related (cause or effect I don't presume to say) to Joanne's orientation. I don't think there is an official Freudian term for it; I doubt that Freud took dykes seriously enough to give that variant a name. He thought the male happy-hunting-grounds would last forever. Ah, the very lice in his beard had tenure! So lush, so lubricious his cleverness—such a winsome blend of pedantry and titillation!

But Freud never had to live in the dissolving world of California. Thought his Vienna would last forever, thought women would writhe on his genteel meat-hook forever, and never bring charges. He's one of them—the disastrous patriarchs, the Shah's officer corps who led us here and left us to our fate, selfishly dying early enough to be spared the debacle they brought about.

Like Marx with his half-smart enthymeme: "The history of the world is a collection of cover-stories for vampire cliques [so far I'm with you]; *Therefore* [here it comes!] . . . *Therefore* the future will be a picnic where everybody shares the fried chicken." *What? Where the fuck did *that* come from? Are you fucking *crazy?* Berdyayev got it right in his parody of "Progressive" thought: "Man is descended from the apes, therefore let us love one another."

Wet dreams with tenure. Every male who lived to adulthood in nineteenth-century Europe was granted tenure, if only of a tiny faculty consisting of his female relatives. It made a certain coral-head lobe of their brains atrophy: Marx falling asleep in the reading room and dreaming up hordes of happy Germans singing at their lathes like the Seven Dwarves. And then he dies in a timely fashion, long before Kolyma and Katyn. They always die early, falling sweetly asleep to their own bedtime stories: ". . . And tomorrow you'll wake up and the tooth fairy will have left the overthrow of the Superego, followed by a dictatorship of the Id, under your pillow! And women will adore your macho lefter jacket!"

. . . And they go to their untroubled rest, leaving me directly in the path of the one and only Central-European mind who matters, who will inherit everything: Countess Elizabeth Bathory.

I met the Countess while browsing in the "B" volume of our encyclopedia set as a child. I had a nose for certain kinds of entries, happened on them by scent in the unlikeliest places. I didn't know what I was looking for in the "B" volume, but I knew I'd find it. Books open for me.

I was eight, Countess Bathory considerably older. But she's very spry. She has hovered over me since, a Nazgul Pentecostal flame. Because I know that history comes harder to you healthy people than to my kind, I will supply a little background. (Or are you one of us—is the name more familiar perhaps than you let people know? Does your encyclopedia set open to "Ba-" as well as "Sl-"?)

For those healthy folk among you, here is your formal introduction to the Countess:

> **Bathori,** or **Bathory,** *the name of a noble Hungarian family that gave a line of voivodes to Transylvania in the 16th and 17th centuries, and one king (Stephen, 1575-86) to Poland. Elizabeth, niece to Stephen Bathory, King of Poland, and wife of the Hungarian Count Nadasdy, caused young girls to be put to death in the dungeon of her castle, that she might renew her own youth by bathing in their warm blood.*
>
> *The details of the monstrous story are probably exaggerated [!], but it at least shows that she was conceived capable of it [?]. When at length, in 1610, inquiry was made into the appalling rumors, it was discovered that this female fiend had caused to be murdered no fewer than 650 maidens. Her accomplices were burnt; but she was shut up for life in her fortress of Csej, where she died in 1614.*

Can you hear the queasy befuddlement in that well-meaning encyclopedist's voice as he tries to tell the story in some way that contains, explains, erases it? First he tells you about the normal, boring male members of the family—irrelevancies, pure past tense. (Even Sade knew that; that's why he had to invent Juliette!) Then the encyclopedist tells, quickly and gingerly, the truth: the hundreds of slave-girls tortured to death. He then starts a second paragraph by saying that what happened didn't actually happen at all ("The details of the monstrous story are probably exaggerated"), and qualifies that by the meaningless psychologizing declaration that she was "capable of" the things he already admitted she did. He then supplies a hard number: 650 girls killed. Huh—I guess it sorta *did* happen after all, didn't it, lying coward pedant fool!

Then he (I use the gendered pronoun advisedly: a "he" wrote that entry) tries to find an ending with something like Justice, so he stammers: "Her accomplices were burnt"—that is, the loyal servants who obeyed their mistress, probably wincing and groaning in terror themselves, were burnt alive for their loyalty, but the Countess herself is . . . subjected to house arrest in a castle. Tough on crime, huh? "No, no! Bad countess, naughty! Put that serving girl down! You've tortured three milkmaids to death already today! You're carrying this to an unseemly extreme! Think of the expense—the amount of fodder consumed by all the girls we've got penned down in the dungeons!"

O yes, think of it. Think of it. Pretty little wrists rubbed raw by the clamps holding them to the ceiling—plenty of whipping room, and no one to interrupt you.

Because of course the Countess was not doing anything as simple and boring as slitting the girls' throats, letting them die quickly, to bathe in their blood. Even you have guessed that much—even *you* know that. That's just Balkan-peasant nonsense, unimaginative serfs.

We want pain, terror and humiliation—not death. Death was just the disposal. She had so many slave-girls to play with that she could afford to throw away the ones who began to bore her, whose whimpers under the lash, and subsequent submissive lickings, no longer got her excited. Death was just throwaway. When she grew bored with their sobs, their entreaties, their desperate promise to do *anything, anything that My Lady desires*—and bored even with the nights when, after giving the little milkmaid she bought last week a nice long whipping, she had the whimpering, terrified girl dragged on a leash to her chambers, gave the little slave-girl a chance to prove her devotion; yes, bored, after a few weeks, the inevitable dissatisfaction with those mild bed pleasures, with even the most submissive and tearful nectarine-girls . . . leading to her wish to see them caper under something more stringent than the whip, to savor the chords of the little milkmaid's scream as the branding iron goes deep into the flesh of her thigh, followed by her touching attempt to crawl forward, chained hand and foot, far enough to kiss and lick Mistress's toes—and the pleasure of giving that teary adolescent face a good hard kick when it comes into range begging for the privilege of licking Mistress's boot-sole . . .

Bathory will come; in a sense she is here already. For many years now she has been the only protagonist of my fantasies. (Did you think *I* was? No, no. God no. Or any other *man*. Always she, only she.)

She is waiting now, immured like Barbarossa in her mountain fortress, technically dead but quite alert. She desires no assistance. She needs none. Her time is coming. She makes no promises. She grins a little, a twitch of the dead flesh or just a trick of the coffin-light . . . seems to grin, something like a grin . . . at my mention of that whimsical Salvation-Army tambourine Klanger, Karl Marx. She has been following the news with complacent indulgence. It amuses her. She savors the thought of Karl Marx . . . *Karl Karl Karl* . . . how amusing a name . . . such a Low German, earnest craftsman's name . . . a carpenter of a manling: a mannikin who makes mannikinen, carving his touchingly unlifelike wooden figures of smiling workmen in clean overalls . . . she has her own critique of Marxism, and she runs her tongue over its high points: the tips of her canines, as she lies there in her lovingly crafted sarcophagus, four stone figures of kneeling, chained slave-girls at the corners.

Her gospel is simple: she promises *nothing*. Except that she will come again. Like it or not. She promises that. She can afford to show herself to me; I am already dead, and her return can't be stopped anyway. It is implicit in the gene-sequence of our syllogisms; the intellectual history of Europe is steeped in it, the whole DNA of history has been reverse-engineered like an East-German grenade to detonate with the return in glory and terror of Countess Bathory: as Freud leads to Dworkin, Dworkin leads to Bathory. It's always led back to her. Freud and Marx and Voltaire and Russell and E. B. White and Erasmus—we have spent five centuries building a Trojan Rabbit, and the brighter secular priests are beginning to realize that the Castle gates are opening, not to accept our half-clever offering but to let Bathory free again. And they are running, heading for the hills.

It's too late. I take some comfort from that. The well-meaning essayists will see her return, experience that Rapture in the flesh, the flesh . . . They will cry to the earth to swallow them up; they will tear their denim garments. But they cannot stop her now. They are only dust, a layer of dust around Bathory's sarcophagus . . . and Bathory's fingers are already beginning to twitch. She will knock that marble lid away like Styrofoam, and Voltaire's dust will be the mote confetti of her emergence.

But not yet. She isn't ready yet. Patience. And I don't want to lose you, do I? We were back in Pleasant Hill ... the mid-70s ... a hot lawnmower afternoon in Joanne's room ... the last time Bathory could have been stopped. The last moment at which her sarcophagus could have been sealed, by Joanne's pedagogical fingers on my body ...

Then we hear her crazy old mother come giggling down the hall toward us ... And Joanne looks up from my tilted head toward the door, suddenly scared. No solidarity from her, because unlike most suburb brats she really did love her Mom. She grabs my hand and throws it away like a spider. And motions me to sit up straight. I whisper an apology and we wait for Mom, Joanne's face stuck in a scared welcoming smile.

And in a second or two, wham!—the door's slammed open, and there's her mom giggling at us: head cocked to one side, balloon body in a huge flowered muumuu. She was beyond fat— she was huge. That southern cooking. She filled the doorway. Head lolling like she'd been hanged. Giggling. It's not easy, making small-talk with a giggling broken-necked zombie in a dirty muumuu. Joanne just smiled desperately and waited for her mother to make the first move.

Mrs Whitfield saw the photo albums open where we'd left them on the bed, and took the chance to insult her adoring daughter: "Put those dumb old pikcher-books away! Why you wanna bother nice ol'John ... *giggle giggle* ... with a buncha old pikchers? ... *giggle giggle* ... You don't wanna see them ol'piksher books do yuh John?"

Eager to please both mother and daughter, I tried to nod yes and shake no at the same time. Joanne tried to change the subject—something about dinner—but Mrs Whitfield wasn't interested in logistics. She giggled and drooled in the doorway for a while, rocking from side to side, as if she were deciding whether to take a bite out of one of us, then finally shuffled off.

On her usual rounds: to squat under a desk and talk to the silverfish, or send letters to Satan at the South Pole ... but more likely she went to her "den" to write. Because Mrs Whitfield had literary aspirations. Of the historical variety. Many times, after barging into Joanne's room, she'd take me off to the den to show me her unfinished masterpiece, a history of Pleasant Hill. She'd stand right next to me, gasping from the bedroom-to-den walk, making me look at photos of ancient Pleasant Hill: Okies standing in front of frame houses much like her own, only with buggies instead of cars. Mean faces, long dresses, bad teeth. Kind of a surprise to me that anybody'd been here before the developers laid it out. It had never occurred to me that *Pleasant Hell* (as the cool kids called it) had a history. Or rather, I took it for granted that it had a very simple, two-stage history: before WW II it was dry grass with cattle grazing on it; and after WW II it was a bunch of three-bedroom ranch houses, pasture for the bipeds who fed San Francisco.

But for Mrs Whitfield, this simple chronicle was full of nuance and meaning. Every Kansas-bred grocer who'd set up shop at the dusty crossroads which was now "downtown Pleasant Hill" was for her a founding father, deserving commemoration. The ground on which Gregory Gardens shopping center stood was holy ground, site of some mean-faced grocer's first enterprise. Every one of the flinty rednecks in those dusty photos had to be chronicled, genealogically traced and pictured in her book. As if this random quadrangle of housing was Plymouth Rock, and every hula hoop dug up in somebody's backyard a piece of the wall of Troy.

Her historical revelations remained unknown, because the publishers were in a conspiracy to keep her out of print, as she told me twenty or thirty times, breathing at me. She was like a UFO freak with her long stories about how the hostility of the local establishment was keeping her muzzled. She showed me letters she'd sent to the editor of the local paper exposing this conspiracy of silence. To no avail, of course—because the newspaper was in on the conspiracy too. Nobody wanted the real blockbuster story of Pleasant Hill's early days to make it into print.

"They jus scared a what I gonna say in it John, jus' plain scared . . ."

I did a lot of nodding and agreeing and deploring—lots of deploring: "Wow . . . Huh . . . that's really awful . . . uh-huh . . . Wow . . . God . . . Weird . . . Wow, that's terrible."

It was hard to guess what reaction I was supposed to have, because Mrs Whitfield kept up the distinctive Whitfield giggle all through her stories of censorship and persecution. "They all jus' jealous, *giggle-giggle* . . . tryna keep it hushed up . . . ain' that awful, doncha think thass awful John? . . . *giggle* . . ."

"Wow, huh . . . that sounds really terrible . . ."

The topic gave out after a while. Then she'd stare at me like a hanged zombie, still chuckling bitterly, and at last slide-shuffle off on her rounds—to chat with the mice or whatever.

Joanne was half embarrassed by her mom's ravings, half grateful that her mom was at least paying some sort of attention to her, even though it was through me. Joanne's mom was happy that her daughter'd finally brought a presentable (that is, male) suitor around the house. And such a good listener too. She liked that. She liked me. Which annoyed her daughter.

Sometimes, after slamming the door open and telling me again of the conspiracy against her, Joanne's mother would drag out her own albums, full of pictures of her family back in the old country: Missouri. Pictures of Mrs Whitfield as a crazy-looking fat girl squinting into the humid Missouri heat which she had somehow managed to import to this house in Pleasant Hill. Then Mrs Whitfield as a crazy-looking fat young woman with one foot on the running-board of a car . . . and finally as a crazy-looking fat bride in a white tent-dress. She pointed to herself holding the bridal bouquet and giggled: "That wuz mah . . . *giggle giggle* . . . wedding dress"

— Ah yes, quite so . . .

"An'thass . . . *giggle giggle* . . . Mister Whitfield, who I wuz gettin' married to."

She giggled louder when she pointed to the fat stoic groom beside her in the photo. She giggled the same way, only with more contempt, when the real thing, her actual half-dead husband, slumped past her on his way to the toilet.

He had to be at home sometimes, though according to Joanne he tried to stay at work as long as he could. Mr. Whitfield worked for Dow Chemical perfecting faster, more lethal biocides. He was a big, sad fat man with an MA in chemical engineering from Harvard, Southern manners much better than those of his wife or daughter, and—now that I think of it—perhaps the most miserable, horrible life in the world. I didn't notice it then—too busy wagging my tail and standing on my hind legs to please his daughter—but Joanne's father lived in Hell. I wonder how many other suburban dads in that era did. A lot, I think. All the ones who weren't jerks, maybe . . . I think they came in two kinds: the domineering, opinionated jerks and the victims. And the quiet, nervous family-man types had nowhere to run. Suburban dads of that generation weren't even supposed to have friends. They were supposed to go straight home from work. And once there, they— the nice ones, the non-jerks—were despised.

Mrs Whitfield would actually follow her punching-bag husband around the house giggling at him and calling him a fool, yelling through the door when he tried to take refuge in the bathroom. And his daughter—who laughed at him and left intimate photos of herself and Evelyn around the kitchen—well, he just tried not to think about her. And his son, whom he'd supposedly liked, was dead for no reason in some crazy hot place in Africa.

He read his Bible for solace. He belonged to a weekly Bible-reading group for middle-aged men who also hated their lives and hoped to find solace in the gibbered promises of Near Eastern goatherds. He carried his talisman, that worn black book, around with him like an impractical little buckler. I even chatted about biblical matters with him as part of my campaign to win the hearts and minds of the Vietnamese people, i.e. Joanne, until I realized that Joanne despised her father so completely that fraternizing with him was counterproductive.

But then the whole Joanne campaign was obviously hopeless, and could end only with my troops scrambling to make that last helicopter taking off from the roof of the embassy in Saigon, or rather "Ho Chi Min City." I sort of knew that from the beginning. That's the weird, or seemingly weird, part: why'd I go on?

This is just another of the fake paradoxes Voltaire & Co. put over on us. Beating one's head against a wall is the norm, not the anomaly—because in Darwin's world, beating your head against a wall can be a valid strategy. A strategy that works one time out of twenty can be a very good strategy in Darwin's world. And we're Darwin's children, not Voltaire's or E. B. White's. After all, America knew about Vietnam, didn't we? We knew we couldn't win. But we didn't get out. We put great effort into not knowing, not believing. And that was the way it happened for me. It took a long series of debacles to make me let go.

15

A week or so after our interrupted sex lesson, Joanne called, all excited, to tell me that she and Evelyn were moving to SF together. They'd found themselves an apartment in the Mission and wanted me to come see it on Saturday. Officially I was glad.

Saturday evening was warm and clear, the setting sun anointing this best of all worlds, late twentieth-century California. Probably the most sought-after reincarnation in the whole Afterlife. There was probably a ten-century waiting-list for virtuous Hindus wanting reincarnation in California in the 70s. I ought to be grateful. There were kids trapped in Malaysia and Irkutsk who were envying me right now. There were cousins of mine in the besieged ghettoes of Belfast and Derry who would've given anything to grow up here. There were cheerful quadriplegics writing symphonies with their toes, there were ebullient legless beggars on the streets of Dhakka, there were girls doing 70 hours a week in Canton sweatshops for two cents an hour and having more fun than I was. It was not only unpleasant, this hermetic misery; it was a mortal sin!

And it *was* magnificent, the, drive to SF that warm evening. Why pretend? The truth is I loved you with all my heart, California, cool Stepmotherland. To be loved perfectly California must be driven. At dusk. As you bank onto the freeway, the Gloaming rises from the horizon and the air cools, skittering in little warm gusts. The freeways of my homeland, so despised by middlebrow fools, are sacred sites, the Angkor of this age. Every

mile of the drive to Joanne's new place was full of portents of
glory. First the ten hot miles from Pleasant Hill to Orinda,
hugging the edge of the hills with Mount Diablo cooling through
all those minor-key colors: umber, sienna, ochre. The glint off
windshields ahead of you as you tilt into the smooth turns, the
easy calibrations of those God-like Interstate designers. The dip
into Orinda and up again into the long, narrowing pass guarding
my and everyone's desire: the inner, fog-cooled star cluster of
Oakland, Berkeley . . . and San Francisco itself.

As you come up out of Orinda into the pass, things get
tight—Thermopylae. To get the freeway through the hills here
they had to blast. You pass between the pillars of Hercules, stone
terraces going back and back.

How many times, from earliest childhood when my parents
taught me about the Greeks, I sat in the back seat as we drove
through here and imagined standing in a shield wall blocking the
invaders' passage through this hot and narrow gate of our
Homeland. Sitting in the back seat poking my finger into my ribs
to simulate multiple arrow-strikes and spearthrusts. Orinda in
flames, death certain, standing firm in a doomed and glorious
defense.

Homeric, those taillight battlescapes. As the traffic slows, the
brakelights make a magma river—and you are one of the
molecules of its flow, waiting with others of your kind in perfect
equality and union for your turn to flow through the tunnel. The
Hot Gates compress traffic from five lanes to two, heating the
brakelight lava, which at last is inhaled by the concrete tunnel,
mid-journey passage through the Tomb World. The radio goes
silent, air is pure petrochemical exhaust, and the light is indoor,
with metal doors leading off the tunnel to many little Hells.

Then the tunnel tilts down to exhale you into Oakland.
Instantly it's fifteen degrees cooler. The air is more blue than
beige. And the smell is finer: no more of the suburbs' dry grass
but seafog caressing old rich trees . . . and as you slide down into
Oakland, the Golden Gate itself marks the furthest west. The
closer you are to that bridge, the richer, the happier, the more thin
and beloved you become. And for two or three seconds, hanging
in the turn where the freeway banks you down out of the tunnel

like an F-4 Phantom, you can see every house in San Francisco across the sheet metal bay, before you dip below radar range to pass through Oakland.

It was strange to ride the roller-coaster onramps toward the Bay Bridge knowing that down below me, in the mud where the bridge guy wires were anchored, was my truck yard. Matthew, or maybe the hobbit-man himself, would be on duty—I was mounting the bridge on my way to a social occasion. That made me one of the cars whose surf-roar meant so much to me when I heard it down there in the yard. I was a molecule in that flow now.

Then, best of all, driving up onto the Bay Bridge. I defy even the most zombie-cool Californian shrug to drive onto the Bay Bridge on a Saturday evening without a surge of joy. It's designed to arouse anticipation. Much better than any ride at any Disneyland. You see the Bridge miles away as soon as you come out of the tunnel, but then the freeway drops down and you must find your way to it through a series of precarious, overcrowded overpasses which teeter like Dr Seuss illustrations done in concrete. This is to test you.

The Seuss causeways bring you to the Bayside mudflats, where you stop behind thousands of cars. This is to remind you. You have to look at the mud, the odd sticks and hippie sculpture decomposing among the reeds, until your lane feeds into the tollbooths. There are a hundred quick joys and griefs as your lane stalls, moves again, is infiltrated by cutters from adjacent lanes, stalls again and at last feeds you up to the booth. Then the tolltaker grabs your change and admits you to the ride. The horizon opens suddenly, a world of lanes released, sprinting like the Oklahoma land rush up onto the span. Your stomach flutters like the Big Dipper at Santa Cruz, only this one is real. The span rises, you flatten, you snake over the top at ten Gs through the Navy's artificial island where they held the world's fair once, then out again onto the second span, the home stretch, the long angelic glide down to San Francisco, the open fingers of the docks reaching to the bridge, sea-fog pouring down the ridges, everything laid out for you. This is to remind you of your goal: Bliss. As cathedrals were designed to remind peasants of Heaven.

But San Francisco is not only a sign but the thing in itself, Heaven as sign of Heaven. Another of those not-really-paradoxes;

because you can be physically in San Francisco without having access to its Bliss. This is the great advance made by the designers of California: there are no guards or prohibitions dividing the bitter ordinary from the higher world. The distinction is metaphysical, not geographical. Anyone can take the freeway into the City—the Bridge is usually jammed: *Many are called.* But only the worthy can find bliss: *Few are chosen.* "Heaven lies all around you," as some hippie said. And he didn't mean it in a nice way, but rather as a grim Calvinist taunt at the uncool. That's the other great advance: Bliss as a moral imperative. With its corollary: failure to have fun as mortal sin. You can stand on a corner in San Francisco by yourself and know that Bliss is all around you, in some fraction of the windows glinting down at you. But you can't break into that Bliss. Or even find it. Bliss is all around you, and you will never attain it.

So, as you come over the last curve down into the City, all the worlds are watching and everything is staked. On this one visit. You're betting something much more precious than your soul: your only hope of a body. If Joanne says no—well, just as San Francisco stands for Heaven, Pleasant Hell stands for itself, an ant lion sneering, "You'll be back!"

My palms were slick on the steering wheel as I banked the Plymouth through the ramp, skimming rooftops and billboards to Folsom Street. From there you must navigate the little streets of ancient frame-houses to the Mission, where the Irish lived once and the Mexicans live now—Catholic peasantry gravitating to the same familiar quarter. Where Joanne and Evelyn live. Their place was on 16th Street, next to a defunct Catholic girls' school. Top floor.

I can still smell that place: diesel fumes drifting up from 16th Street to mix with thick old carpet impregnated with Joanne and Evelyn's very different scent traces, overlaid with ephemeral but powerful cooking smells—especially Joanne's crockpot chicken stew suffusing the whole place by the time Evvie came home at five: punctual, uxorious, gruff.

They had an almost sitcom routine for Evvie's 5 PM return, a ritual which I witnessed many times from a beanbag chair in a safe corner:

Door slams.

Joanne: "Hi darling!"

Evvie: "Uhh."

Joanne: "How was work?"

Evvie: "It sucked! What's for dinner?"

Domestic harmony. It struck me. Forcibly. That they were . . . together.

Not that there hadn't been sufficient clues already. Anybody else would've picked up their couple status after two minutes in Evvie's car. But for me, it was seeing them in the new place that forced me to consider the thesis that: *they're together.*

Maybe it was the way Joanne hugged and kissed Evvie every time she came into a room, saying "I love you Evvie!" to the point that Evelyn used to say, "All right already! You already said that! I'm tired, where's dinner!" Subtle clues, but suggestive. Or maybe it was the way Joanne used to talk to me when we did our weekly burrito evening in the taquerias of the Mission. While I chewed and nodded, she would tell me at great length about the wonderful sex they'd had in the few months before Evvie's olfactory objections made things Platonic ("Evvie said she didn't like the smell.")

Oddly enough, I didn't think of the problem with Joanne as being connected to the gay stuff that was starting to get publicity. I saw the hopelessness of my campaign to win Joanne in terms of National Liberation rhetoric applied to the Steinem thing. At that time, before AIDS, "gay" meant gay men. And unlike the hippies, I never had anything against gay men. They had run a worse gauntlet in high school than I had. I saw what happened to Bob Sylvester when those pigs, the jocks caught up with him for wearing sweaters tied around his neck.

And the gay group which formed at Pleasant Hill High after David Bowie got famous had regularly said hello to me, in defiance of custom. They sat on a safe bench by the backstop with the seagulls and maintained their cohesion despite the occasional apple core tossed in their direction; and when I dodged back there during lunch to get away from the others, they could've made things very hard for me but instead waved and said my name without mockery; and when I did that poetry project in English they were the only ones who liked it. Ken Dyer, who got beaten up on the Senior Lawn for being a faggot, even said so, and when the kids behind him laughed, he told them to fuck off. Right in their face. I never forgot the courage or the kindness or the shared misery. And all the teachers who were decent to me or showed any sign of intelligence were gay, or rumored to be so (because they were decent; because they showed intelligence).

And to the extent that there was a lesbian stereotype, Joanne and Evelyn didn't fit it at all. For one thing, Joanne's hair was, as she put it, down to her ass. Lesbians were quasi-men and wore their hair short; I knew that from British novels. She wasn't like that.

Therefore (I told myself) the struggle to win her affections was not, repeat *not*, hopeless. It couldn't be hopeless. Because she was the only woman who could see me. Nobody had, in almost four years at Berkeley. And if I was beneath notice in Berkeley, the very epicenter of Free Love, what chance would I have out in the bleak working world?

When Joanne saw me and spoke to me on that train, it had to be because she'd known me at Pleasant Hill High. But what odds I'd run into another of the hippie girls from Pleasant Hill on BART? How many times would that happen? How many miracles can one expect? There had never been more than a dozen Super People, and now they were scattered, gone. Joanne was the last chance.

It was like that thing I read about the Blue Whale: a marine biologist said that there were so few of them left in the vastness of the oceans that they might never be able to find each other to mate, and go extinct from sheer social isolation. If Joanne dropped me, I'd be sending out whale-song to an empty ocean. So if the disturbing new theory about her preference for Evelyn was confirmed, I was walking dust.

So, like the US Army's PR officers in Saigon, I collected and disseminated to the Silent Majority in my head a steady stream of hopeful signs. Every one of Joanne's smiles, every burrito invitation, was toted up to prove that more and more hamlets were being pacified, more and more districts coming over to the government, going from hostile red to neutral yellow, and even bright loyal green!

That first Saturday-evening visit to their place was probably my best real chance to start something. The omens were peculiar but good. The first odd thing was that Joanne was alone in the new place. Joanne kept mentioning Evvie's absence, then tailing off glumly. I couldn't see why; it seemed kind of great that Evelyn was gone.

After a quick tour of the apartment (excepting the bedroom, which stayed shut), we walked up to Church Street and joined a long line at this new place called Just Desserts. I'd read about it; San Francisco was very proud of it. Every week there were adoring articles about it in the *Chronicle* Lifestyle section. Its founders, a lanky winemaking couple with the leathery strap-grins of the California rich, were heroes: they were the first to say proudly that their restaurant would serve only desserts—but these desserts would be prepared with the grim pedantry they brought from their vineyard. Even dessert was on the march.

So it was with proper seriousness that we waited in the line, scanning the annotated menu. It was with solemn delectation that we ate our main-course desserts. Joanne let me pay for her. A good sign. On the other hand, she talked unceasingly about Evelyn—a bad sign. Halfway through her Triple Chocolate Decadence, she opened up: Evelyn was out on "a date" . . . only Evvie wouldn't admit it was a date, just dinner with a woman at her work . . . but Joanne said it *was* a date, that Evvie had a crush on this woman . . . and Joanne thought it was really unfair after she spent so long making things perfect in their apartment . . . But Evvie kept saying no, it's not a date . . . but that wasn't true, it was a date . . . don't you think that's unfair?

I did. Yes indeed. But actually, her abandonment might, if the movies could be believed, draw her to me. It seemed to be working that way; we walked back to their apartment like a couple. I counted how many times our shoulders brushed on the way home: three times. An excellent sign.

I knew these shoulder-brushings were not accidents because in those long years at UC Berkeley, constantly pushing in and out of crowded lecture halls, not one woman had ever even come close to touching me. *Yea though I walk through mobs of nubiles I shall feel no touch* . . . Not once did any of them bump into me while hurrying to class, or drop her books at my feet, as happened in films. It was as if I had a reversed magnetic charge; even when one of these bodies in motion was driven toward me by the flow of the crowd, it veered off at the last moment. There were times at Berkeley when I'd actually spot a crowd of students pouring out of some big lecture course and walk into them, just to witness this horrible miracle yet again. And it always worked: they parted before me like a shoal of herring.

There were other clues too, that night: Joanne looked at me, right in the face, at least four times as we went up the stairs together, shoulders touching twice more in the limited space. The sense of rising.

But as soon as she got the apartment door open, she forgot about me and went in calling, "Evvie? Evvie honey, you here? Evvie . . ." But Evelyn wasn't home.

Joanne went over to the bay window. Opened it and leaned out to look. Then sat there, framed in the central panel of the window. In the dusk . . . the gloaming.

She was in profile. A beautiful turn-of-the-century sad profile, like the photos of long-gowned Irish gentrywomen in our green books, Yeats' crushes:

> The light of evening, Lissadell—
> Two girls in silk kimonos, both
> Beautiful, one a gazelle.

Except wait—maybe not *two* girls. Yeats was being dangerously greedy there. Just *one* girl like a gazelle. That would be plenty. I revised the passage:

> *One* girl in silk kimono,
> She a gazelle . . .

Apologized to the shade of Yeats: military necessity.

Joanne said "Shit." Long pause, then, sadly: "I really thought she'd come home."

I nodded: "Yeah . . . s'too bad. Sorry."

"I think this is real unfair. Don't you think this is totally unfair?"

"I guess, yeah kinda . . . yup definitely . . ."

"You know Evvie and I've only been apart two nights since we were fourteen."

"Wow."

"When she had her tonsils out."

"Wow . . . amazing . . . that's too bad . . . tonsils . . ."

Joanne went to the bathroom. A long time.

Buses going by, then their rising diesel fumes—a smell I have always loved and considered an ally. Traffic has its own pathos, unrecognized. Diesel fumes are on the side of the Celts, the mammals, the Army of the Potomac, the Lords of Dusk.

Joanne came out of the bathroom and went, by the sounds, to the kitchen. I stayed where I was. Things banged around the kitchen for perhaps two minutes.

Two minutes is a long time.

Finally she said, "Hey! C'mere!" and I jumped for the kitchen. She'd made herbal tea. I took my cup and sat opposite her at the little formica dining table. I sipped the tea. I must have flinched at the first sip, because she said, "T'sherbal. S'good for ya." I nodded. It tasted like it.

We sat for some time. Sipping the healthy tea to keep my mouth busy.

And then Joanne got up, took my hand, and led me toward their bedroom. The rhythm of this movement was kind of ruined by the fact that I knocked my chair over trying to flow with Joanne's hand; but when I moved to pick it up she said, "Don'worry about it, c'mon," and I followed, to the bedroom itself.

It was a great room, every bit as nice as I'd imagined. Flower-splatter sheets on a big huge waterbed. Posters of colored things, goldfish and plants. And all in the room there was this rubbed skin smell, as if we were already under the covers.

Joanne turned me around and sat me on the bed. Then she got in on the other side. She said, "Take your clothes off."

She watched me take off my clothes. Hers hadn't come off. She looked at me for a while, then said, "Huh—your penis isn't that long but it's really thick."

She produced a tight chuckle and said "Did I tell you how when I was fifteen Tom Rohan said he wanted to give me 'massage lessons' and said you had to be naked to do it? So I said OK and when he was naked I asked him why his penis . . .

erect?—and he said it was always like that when you took your
clothes off? And I believed him?"

We both chuckled, though hers was better than mine.

"His was longer but skinnier."

A long pause.

"He wanted us to have sex too but I said no. It just seemed so
weird, the idea of him, I don't know, just . . ." She giggled in her
mother's way, then sat up in the bed, saying, "I'm gonna call
Evvie. I have to ask her if it's OK. You just stay there."

I wasn't hearing too well, but I caught "stay"; I stayed.

She dialed the bedside phone with a frightened smile on her
face, then said in a soft, submissive tone, "Hi Barbara, it's Joanne.
. . . Hi yeah is she there? Can I talk to'er? Evvie? How's the *date*
going?" A frightened giggle at her own joke, then silence. Joanne's
face got even more frightened and sad. Several times she started
to say, "Wait Evvie—, Wait Evvie please I—" And then, "OK
OK but listen. But wait listen I just wanted to tell you something
OK? John's here an'we were—"

She turned to me and said, "Evvie says hi."

I waved hello, wondering why I hated Evvie for her courtesy.

"And anyway I decided we might, we're gonna have sex—me
an'him, yeah—and I thought . . . I just, I thought you should
know about it, I should ask you about it first? OK? Would it
bother you if I if we . . . did it?"

"OK . . . Bye." Joanne put the phone down. "She said it was
fine with her."

I waited, very still, for some sign that it was time to begin.
Standing naked at attention. Holding point like a good dog . . .
Joanne sat on her side of the bed for a while, then stood and
quickly, with her back turned to me, took off her clothes. Then
turned and tried to lift the covers to get in. She motioned me in,
under the sheets. We were both under the sheets now.

She turned out the light. Then, "You remember what I taught
you about touching and stuff?"

"Yes, absolutely, definitely."

"OK. You can't just rush around . . ."

"Right, right."

But how slow is slow? Not moving at all would be the safe
move: I froze in place.

She said, "C'm'ere." And her hand touched my shoulder to pull me to her. My body jumped to her instantly, more than ready. I was just a passenger now, a spectator, while a hundred-odd million years of mammalhood cut to the head of the line.

I was mainly worried about navigation: where to put the penis, which was very excited and in a hurry to get somewhere, make up for lost time. I bumped heavily around in the general area where the vagina was supposed to be found, too dazed by the envelopment of touch and smell and touch and touch, actual full-body touch. Joanne's skin was everywhere as it had been where I had touched it before: frictionless and warm. Only more so. Everywhere. It was being mapped underwater by my fingers, sculpted by sonar feedback. It was everything bulging and blazing and big in itself, changed from a doctor into an ox. Which made navigation difficult. I knew I had to find safe harbor—that once in, everything would be different; my name would be on the list of living beings, I would outrank Evvie, let alone my virgin self—

As I bumped around that warm coastline Joanne took hold of my penis—"Wow it feels weird . . . it's like it's wood"—and considered it clinically. And met it, pilot boat . . .

The Spanish managed to sail up and down the coast for a hundred years without discovering San Francisco Bay. Poor Catholic losers! Whereas Sir Francis Protestant Drake, who wasn't even looking for a harbor, just sailing up the California coast on a round-the-world voyage, found the Bay without even trying. I was somewhere in between the Spanish and Drake: looking for a hopeless Northwest Passage, winter coming . . . and then breakthrough: the notch, the moorland stream arched with brush. The mammal world: moving without light, moving in confidence by touch and smell alone. The mammal ancestors chorusing encouragement: *This, this, this*—as the penis begins to find its way. I see suddenly why there is an arch of swords at weddings; why fjords are sacred; why most of the iceberg is under water.

We were kissing, up in the Northern Hemisphere above the waist, kissing seriously, not like relatives. Joanne's tongue went into my mouth and I froze for a moment, sure it must have slipped—but she moved it, giggling, and I realized this was design. I moved my tongue into her mouth, mirroring her swirls.

And on the Southern Front, my corps advanced. Joanne slid
sideways and I was there, convex and slotted. You could see—no,
not see but feel, mammals don't need sight—you could feel the
slotting, the design, it was designed for this, Brazil and West
Africa, continental drift reversing, the beginning—and I was
beginning to go inside—not quickly, because Joanne had opened
her knees only a little—but moving along the brink of everything
and in, Byzantium reversed—

Then Joanne yelled, "No! Wait! I don't wanna lose my
virginity!" and pushed me off her. A weak push but sufficient if
you're a good dog. Even a big dog.

She scrambled off, sat up in the bed laughing and said, "I
decided I don't wanna lose my virginity. You know?"

I didn't know.

"My hymen. I don't wanna break my hymen." She was
laughing in a weird way.

This hymen reference was familiar to me from eighteenth-
century novels, *Vie de Marianne*, *Pamela*—the virtue-in-distress
theme popularized by Richardson. The broken hymen as loss of
innocence. Yes. Except, uh, I'd thought that *that* had sort of been
. . . deemphasized in our century. Particularly in California . . .
after the Summer of Love and everything. No? Evidently not.

Joanne kept up the weird laughter, but I could hear at least
one nuance in it now: relief. She talked happily now.

"I wanna stay a virgin. I never had sex actually before. I mean
. . . this kinda sex. *Sex* sex—intercourse. With a guy." She was
giggling normally now, the bad giggle, the one that scared me. "So
I'm still a virgin." *Giggle.* "I like being a virgin."

"Um . . . I thought . . . you an'Evvie . . ."

"Oh yeah. But that's different." *Giggle giggle.* Her mother's
giggle an octave higher.

I waited for clarification.

"You know—doesn't tear it. The hymen. I mean, it makes me
special; I'm the only virgin I know."

"Me . . ?"

She looked puzzled.

"I mean . . . me, you know me."

Still looked at me puzzled.

"Me . . . virgin."

"You're a guy." *Giggle.* "S'different for guys. I'm gonna call Evvie, tell'er we didn't. You should get dressed."

She put on her robe, grabbed the phone and headed for the kitchen, trailing the long purple cord. Then she was chatting on the phone. In the kitchen. Laughing. I could only hear some of it, but that was enough: ". . . wasn't that long but really thick, you know?" Enough to get me dressed quickly and out the door and down the stairs, walking to the Plymouth as fast as the bootnails would let me.

16

Joanne ended up losing her virginity anyway. One year later. But not to me—to a visiting Parisienne named Chantal, who fisted Joanne hard enough to break that hymen and pop Joanne right out of the eighteenth century. I got all the details, Joanne giggling away on that same orange beanbag by that same bay window: "So after we finished there was all this blood on the sheets and I said to her, 'Hey what're you doin'? Now I've lost my virginity!'"

Five people were in their living room at that moment. Joanne, telling this tale; Evelyn, beside her; and two former Super People from Pleasant Hill, Debbie and Deborah, who'd also moved with the times—undergone Lesbianation. And me. We all laughed—me too. Because by that time I was reconciled to things. Officially.

The funny thing is that I could hear that Joanne was genuinely troubled, telling the hymen-breaking story. Because she was a real old-fashioned girl in some ways. So old-fashioned that the eighteenth-century physiological literalization of virginity, as intact hymen, meant a lot. Very femme she was . . . not the dyke stereotype at all, in case that's what you were thinking.

We are, after all, talking about somebody who ended up writing a lesbian Harlequin romance novel, a mythic retelling of her and Evelyn's starcrossed love. She sent me an autographed copy out of the blue, long after I'd stopped speaking to them. I read the damn thing out of vanity: thought my name might be in there, at least in a scene or two—a character role. But there

weren't any male characters at all. Which I think was true for
Joanne from the beginning.

Which raises the question of why she kept me around at all. I
don't have a theory on that, except the theory that no theory is
necessary. Because simple inertia like that is the norm, as far as I
can see. In the world I know about, it's very common to keep
somebody around after your original plan for them has lapsed,
despite the fact that you don't even like them. It's the norm. Why
should it have to explain itself? Let the Humanists explain
themselves! *They're* the anomalies, with their ludicrous major
premise of rationality. Stupid pain on the biggest scale you can
afford to inflict—that's the norm, and always has been. Ask the
Iroquois . . . the Dyaks . . . the Countess. *Je suis partout.*

Not that it was a matter of raw sadism in Joanne's case. Well
. . . some, maybe. A funny kind of sadism I didn't recognize,
because it was so different from my Viking slave-market dreams.
Less historical (Joanne, a pure product of the California public
school system, was innocent of history) and more efficient.
Sadism Lite: portable, updated . . . a sort of toxic playfulness with
a little hook of pain in it, as if by accident. *Just kidding—oh sorry,
was that your eye?*

Like when she spat on me. That was one of the more notable
in a series of Dien Bien Phu's and Tet Offensives, which made it
finally impossible to pretend that I was winning the hearts and
minds.

It was one of my weekend visits. I was a little late, because I'd
elected to take BART—guilt about hogging my parents' car
beginning to catch up with me—and naturally the train decided to
stop halfway across the Bay, leave us waiting in the tunnel beneath
the oozy wormy Bay mud for a half hour. So Joanne was leaning
out the bay window, looking for me. And saw me walking up 16th
Street, and thought it would be kind of funny to see if she could
hit me with a well-aimed loogie. Playing. Playful. She worked up
some spittle in her young and healthy mouth and waited till I was
in her bombsights.

I was striding nervously toward their place, very much aware
that I was late. I was wearing my new suede sportcoat—a suede
Titanic heading up 16th Street to meet its saliva iceberg. The

iceberg leaning out the bay window, giggling in the scary way, the soprano version of her mother's hunting-giggle.

I stopped at the corner, one last rehearsal before that all-important first impression. Remember: be suave! Coat'll help; after all, "suave" has the same root as "suede." Magical folk etymology! Good omen. All the way over on BART I'd been quietly practicing inflections for the word, "Hi." So much depended on that initial meeting at the door of their apartment. Because with Joanne there were definitely good days and bad days. Really bad days.

OK, OK . . . ready. Adjust the suede jacket one more time . . . then I strode right up to their building, bold as a salesman, and pressed the buzzer.

After a while, Joanne's voice came on the intercom to let me in. She sounded happy; she was laughing. Maybe it would be one of the good days! And yet . . . some vestigially sane mammal-instinct part of what passed for my brain was suddenly very frightened, the moment it heard that giggle. Terrified of it.

But why? Officially I was very much in favor of Joanne laughing. My Parliament of Idiots was just about capable of that level of reasoning: "Duuh . . . laughter—good!" But the poor gagged, bound mammal-part, dragged by the head office on an endless round of agonizing, doomstruck fool's errands, must have been desperate to get into the escape pod, hit the "release" button and blast out the back of my skull. It must've been sending out hundreds of job applications for a mammal-steering job in any cranium with an opening; must've sobbed at the lost Darwin chances; must've been non-stop screaming, "Aaaaaaa-ggggg-hhhh, that crazy dyke's *giggling* again! Don't go up those stairs! Didn't you see *Psycho?* Get away! Don't go up there! Aaaaggghhh!"

But that's what it is to be a slave: you learn to ignore that terrified scream the way you ignore a 3 AM car alarm. If you're afraid of everything, it's impossible to know when you really should be scared. So you can't understand the special urgency in the mammal-friend voice when it whines with fear: a friendly she-bear spirit whining a warning in your ear, "Get away! Run!"

This is why cowards rush in where the brave will not go: because we have lived with the car-alarms going off for so long that we just don't know the difference. If that little voice has been

shrieking, "Wolf! Wolf! Wolf-wolf-woooooooolf!" every time the
shadow of a cocker spaniel passes by, then there's not much for it
to say when the real wolves show up. Thus do cowards walk into
the valley of death, unafraid—or at least no more afraid than
when dealing with a barber who wants to make conversation. For
us, great white sharks and talkative barbers are about equally scary.

So into the valley of death rode me; up the stairs of death
walked me. Up the stairs, the hopeful smell of old carpet with a
faint musk of Joanne and Evelyn braided among the useless scents
of old people. Walking the same steps they have walked so many
times. A kind of intimacy, a deerstalker's intimacy, following their
track. Inhale the intimacy, as if we're together already. Up, feeling
the suave of suede, my protector. To their door, on the milky
landing under the skylight.

I pressed the doorbell and instantly Joanne opened the door.
She was smiling. Giggling. Standing in the doorway, not letting me
in, just giggling and looking at me. I laughed along with the joke,
whatever it was.

She didn't move; I couldn't get in. Finally I had to
acknowledge that oddly scary giggle.

"What? What is it?"

Giggle giggle. "You didn't notice?" *Giggle giggle.*

"Notice . . ?"

Giggle giggle—then she pointed. To my shoulder. And there it
was, a little brook of spittle descending from a cirque pool on the
shoulder.

I looked at Joanne. She giggled. Time stopped. The little
stream running down my suede was illuminated, while the rest of
the world went very dim. A barium trace down the suede: you
know what that trace shows. That's why it's luminous.
Terminaluminous.

A long time to process this. To accept the sensory data.

It must've been a good shot. She must've waited, leaning out
the bay window, till I was directly under her, ringing the buzzer.

And now she stood there in the doorway, still giggling.
Watching for my reaction to the glacial melt of spittle down the
suede. I knew right away she'd done it. In some way I probably
knew it in advance. Walking up 16th Street in an endless time
loop: "Ah, time for another epiphany, yet another of the miserable

epiphanies, the one where I get spat on. Literally, that is." Tramp
tramp, up 16th Street for the millionth time, into the valley of
death. You know, after a while you get really tired of the fucking
valley of death and its tape-loop mongoloid epiphanies. Christ,
another omen avalanche. I get it, I get it already!

I knew that by any imaginable set of social rules I was
supposed to be outraged—but I also knew I wouldn't be up to
outrage. Not in the presence of another person and least of all
with Joanne—my Danzig, my one seaport. Outrage was for alone,
in your bedroom, landlocked. There was absolutely no way I could
even fake outrage in front of Joanne. I just couldn't do it.

But some show of outrage was required. That was clear—no
way around it. Being literally *spat on* is hard to spin-doctor, even
for the best public relations firm. It was like the US Command
trying to explain the Tet Offensive . . . Maxwell Smart as
spokesman for the US Command in Saigon: "Would you believe it
was just some very enthusiastic New Year celebrations?"

No. Even I wouldn't believe it. This was hard to dismiss. She
literally, literally *spat on* me. So the Don Knotts clerk who was in
charge of my display-of-outrage office stammered, Adam's apple
bobbing, "W-w-w-we're . . . uh . . . m-m-morally required to, uh
. . . h-h-hit her n-n-now . . ." But Hell, I knew that already. I knew
I was supposed to hit her. Jesus would've backhanded her. Francis
of Assisi would've V-signed her in the eyes. Gandhi would've
given her a good whack of his spindly walking-stick.

I hear you, movie-fuddled reader, asking, "Yeah, why didn't
you? Well you couldn't hit her because that'd be Domestic
Violence [Ha! You people!]. But . . . why didn't you just say, 'Fuck
you!' and leave? Like, why didn't you just wash the karate outfit? I
mean—Jesus! You want me to sympathize with the main
character, but he won't even *try!*"

Right. Because that's how it is. I am the norm. This is the way
it actually happens. People die quietly. That's the historical norm.
It's not like the movies, where people overpower their guards and
escape. They don't even try to escape, even if they know for
certain they're going to be killed. When the Aztec priests came to
take children for sacrifice, the parents bowed their heads and gave
thanks. That's the norm: massacres with the full cooperation and
even approval of the massacred.

But sure, I dream . . . about going back in time . . . suddenly at
the controls of that young and powerful body, standing there at
the door of Joanne's apartment, under the buttermilk foggy light
from the skylight, looking at the spittle running down my suede.
And I stare into Joanne's mean little face, flex my fingers—ah, the
wasted, unused strength of that body! I could have snapped her
neck with one hand . . . But no, it wouldn't be worth it. Why be
angry, if I could be alive in San Francisco in the era of Bliss? No, I
wouldn't waste my chance by hurting Joanne. Instead . . . I slowly,
slowly smile. Ceremoniously take off the suede jacket, carefully
fold it, and place it over her shoulder, spittle side down. Then turn
and leap down the stairs three at a time, radiating enough bodily
joy to set the whole miserable tenement on fire.

Because outside waited California: the world of pleasure.
Before America decided to be Moral again. The pleasures! The
morally imperative pleasures! I would have been free, young,
healthy, loose in California in the 70s, where—as I now realize—
there were still thousands, maybe even tens of thousands, of
women smarter, kinder and more beautiful than Joanne who still
actually *liked* men. Probably no more than half of the female
population had gone lesbian by that time. And if I'd cleaned up a
little, bought some decent clothes, and tried to talk to some of the
straight women around Berkeley—shown a little interest—it's
perfectly possible that one or more could've liked me. A world of
pleasure, sex in some smart beautiful woman's car . . . with a
couple lines of coke on a mirror in the glove compartment . . .
parked in Golden Gate Park with the sea fog rolling in. I can smell
it now as if it had really happened: parked under the eucalyptus
trees near the ocean after a long night of sex and coke and driving
around grinning helplessly at each other, leaning forehead to
forehead in sheer excess of joy. I close my eyes and burrow my
muzzle in her hair . . . and inhale with her scent the other scents of
the park in the morning: the eucalyptus leaf-mulch leaching up
into the cool damp, a faint cologne of car exhaust, a little spice of
diesel from the buses, the faint chord of the ocean—and our
musks and the tobacco-leather scent of the seats . . . and rubbing
my snout in the shoulder of her wool coat as we make out in the
car, I work the smell of this bliss into my head for good, freehold
in perpetuity where it can never be evicted . . .

But I didn't walk away from Joanne. Did what I always did: stood there.

The first wave of intense humiliation is a white-out. Roaring static, hysterical blindness, deafness. When I came out of that first pressure wave, Joanne was leading me into the bathroom. She stood me there—"Just hold still, don't make a big deal about it!"—and got a hand-towel. She licked the towel. I thought *Coals to Newcastle, hair of the dog, saliva vs saliva . . . that's how they fight forest fires, with forest fires . . .* thinking anything but the obvious: she *spat* on me. Well, there's the fact that she's holding my arm, touching me through the same suede; that must count for something, be some kind of good sign—right?

Standing there like cardboard while the cranial factions argue:

Sinn Fein speaks first *Look it's simple: now or never, punch her in the face immediately!*

And the tired answer from the ruling coalition's Fine Gael spokesman: *You know I'm not going to punch her. Just leave me alone. Shut up.*

She toweled the stream of spit on my chest, like currying a horse. And I stood obediently—a good Chestnut-suede horse, like that horse in *Animal Farm*—telling myself the way that horse always did that things are not so bad; after all, she's currying me, brushing my coat; that's a kind of touching. That counts for something . . .

vs She *spat* on me!

Time is very slow in the worst humiliations, because you retreat so far behind your eyes that light takes a long time to arrive, which is how black holes originate. So it was in heavy gravity and slow motion that Joanne brushed a hand-towel over the suede on my chest, and I rocked gently back and forth—in their nice bathroom, with its own little skylight letting in a milky, gentled version of the bright afternoon outside. It was always a nice sunny California day when these things happened. That's what skin cancer is: the biochemical response to that toxic California light.

After a little while, as she toweled me off like a mother cat, my anger faded out like FM in a tunnel. Joanne gaveth and she tooketh away. The suede sportcoat was her doing in the first

place. I hadn't known such things existed, let alone where you got
them.

When she was still living in Pleasant Hill, Joanne used to let
me drive her to garage sales on Sundays in my parents' cop-
surplus Plymouth. Joanne loved these peasant markets. She loved
the things sold there: little physical objects of glass and wood and
plastic. And I loved them through, for and with her. She'd think
out all the logistics: go through the paper circling all the garage
sales listed, then bake some cookies—incredible cookies, palm-
sized M&M cookies from her mother's oven, made for me!—and
put them in aluminum foil. Then she'd call to tell me to pick her
up—and we, the two of us together, would go out looking for the
addresses of these garage sales.

We got lost a lot in the swampy suburbs, the tree-choked
dead-end streets of the housing tracts which comprised the
ancient (twenty-five years old) GI Bill core of Pleasant Hill.
Sherman Oaks, over by Montgomery Ward. Gregory Gardens,
where every street had a girl's name: Glenda Drive, Janet Ave,
Sheila Lane. You could easily get lost in those leafy three-bedroom
bayous, opaque with maples and elms . . . garage after garage with
no sales in them, driving Joanne around, happily lost and chewing
cookies . . . and the weather somehow warm rather than hot, the
same soft and clothy heat Joanne seemed to generate . . . and the
sunlight not as mean either, more glow than glare for once . . . and
sooner or later, wandering among the pickups and tarped boats,
we'd find the address we wanted, 13 Ruth Street or 217 Deborah
Place, and pull up behind the other cars. There would be a blanket
on the driveway, laid with old glass and metal things. And a
woman would be sitting there in a plaid-hatched lawn chair, like a
pudgy out-of-practice Third World peddler.

And Joanne would finger various things—I can't remember
what they were—and haggle with the lady in the chair, and the
haggling would become a chat; and Joanne would thank the
woman, and once we were back in the car Joanne would critique
the prices and quality of the sale items. The two of us debriefing
less than a foot apart on the car seat.

And once we'd run out of garage sales, we'd go to the thrift
stores. Moldy storefronts clerked by wary, well-meaning old ladies.
Joanne would talk to them—she was completely unafraid. Just

"Hi!" and the two of them would be discussing consumer goods and money like they were kin. She liked these old ladies—actually flirted with them. They were like non-biting variants of her mother.

She found the suede coat for me at the scariest of the thrift stores: the St. Vincent de Paul's in Concord, a grim warehouse sitting alone in the middle of a dead-grass field, with a picture of St. Vincent blessing a child over the door. The picture was faded blue-white and peeling, like all Catholic things—the same colors as the statue of the Virgin gowned in spider-webs high in my room. I didn't like the infinitely sad Catholic look of the place—not with Joanne there. I didn't like St. Vincent's posture in the painting, that buzzard lean. It seemed like bad luck to go into this deathly Catholic place with Joanne. Joanne was supposed to be the cure to that saintly eagerness for doom. Reversed polarity or something. But she stepped in and I followed.

You passed beneath St Vincent's picture into darkness and a perfume of mothballs, dust, colognes of the dead, and moldy paperbacks. That was the real essence of Catholicism, that funereal scent. If Joanne hadn't been with me, I'd've run right out. But I followed her, and she moved through it without hurt; and I knew then that with her leading, I could inhale the deathly, ancient air without harm. Safe out of that whole range of smell and color for good.

Proud and happy in armed passivity, I clomped behind her in my broken jackboots, the bodyguard. I loved being her bodyguard, staring down strangers, making our slow way down rows of dead people's shirts and pants. Now and then she'd dart in like a reef wrasse, take a shirt off the rack and hold it against my chest, and I was proud to stand soldierly still, Alsatian still, with only the smallest lean into her hands betraying my canine love.

She found the suede sportcoat by the front counter, just as we were leaving. It was expensive by St. Vincent standards—$20—and Joanne went back and forth for a long time on whether I should buy it. She had me try it on, turn around in it, walk in it, before she decided it looked good on me. And it did—the woman behind the counter said so too. She thought we were "together," and said, "Whoo! You got yourself a big one, honey!" Joanne wasn't happy at that remark. Grimaced and indicated that I should just buy the coat and go. And once we were back in the car she called the St Vincent lady an "old bat." And the ride home was a quiet one.

But the coat remained, prize and proof. It had a warm color, like the names of those crayons and paints which operated on Mount Diablo in the Gloaming: "burnt umber," "raw sienna." Which proved it was effectual. And it was soft, like a shorn rabbit; and fit over my shoulders which almost nothing did; and I wore it to Berkeley three times and all three times people on the street looked at me as other than an obstacle to navigation.

And now she'd spat on it. How did that add up? A negative plus a positive . . . couldn't do the math. Not then, after the fact, standing there in their bathroom being toweled, my feeble anger running like peasant conscripts. Surrender. Joanne giveth and she taketh away . . . dust to spittle, spittle on dust. Can't complain.

After toweling the stain, Joanne made me sit down in the living room and gave me the treat she'd made me: her famous zucchini bread. We were sitting there in their patchouli-velvet living room, quietly munching away, when Evelyn came home. Joanne ran to hug Evvie, then asked how her day had been. Evelyn said, "It sucked," disengaged herself, and plopped down onto the beanbag chair opposite me. Joanne went to get Evvie a slice of the zucchini bread.

Evelyn stared at me for a second, smiled fondly, chuckled and said, "So how're you?"

I have to say here: Evelyn was a good person. I really liked her, despite frequent daydreams in which she got run over by a truck, leaving me with the pleasant chore of consoling Joanne.

I said I was fine thank you. Evelyn was looking at the suede coat sharply. She was always very observant—she was one of those people who actually enjoyed what is called "real life" and would stick with it even if they had a choice. She pointed at the stain and said, "Spilled something, huh?" just as Joanne came back with her zucchini bread.

Handing Evelyn her slice, Joanne giggled nervously and said, "It was an accident."

All I could think to do was nod. But Evelyn wasn't going to settle for that. Evelyn liked details. She asked, "What kind of accident—a pigeon get you?"

Joanne said, giggling, "I just wanted to see if I could hit him from the window . . ." I smile as placatingly as I can manage—because *Please God*, more than anything else in the world, I don't want to be defended from Joanne by Evelyn. I don't even know exactly why not—just that more than anything else in the world, I don't want that.

But Evelyn was implacable: "'Hit'im'? What're you talking about—hit'im with *what?*"

Joanne giggles some more, like her mom used to. She's scared; you can see it. And that scares me. If Evelyn punishes Joanne, Joanne will take it out on me. So I smile and shake my head pleadingly at Evelyn, hoping she'll drop the subject.

But she won't; she grabs Joanne by the wrist and says louder, "Hit'im with *what?*"

Joanne makes what she hopes is a comic mime of someone spitting, then giggles, looking desperately at Evelyn's face for permission to laugh, assurance that Evvie will accept that she was just kidding, just kidding, just a joke.

Instead Evelyn gets very angry very quickly. She says to Joanne, "Did you . . ? God damn it! You *spit* on'im?" Evelyn turns to me and says "Stay here!" and, gripping Joanne by the arm, drags her into their bedroom. And slams the door behind her.

I stayed. Humming to myself so as not to hear what was going on in the bedroom, trying to distract myself with the question of whether the past tense should be "*spit* on" or "*spat* on." Chattering at high speed, shrill and false.

There was a painting on the wall—one of Joanne's from Pleasant Hill High's art class. It was a very brown painting. Showing a woman with her hand out like a stop sign, standing next to a lion. There are these four silhouettes coming toward her over what are apparently sand dunes. Or pleasant hills. This painting used to hang in Joanne's bedroom at her parents' house. Joanne had shown it to me there, made me guess what it meant. I guessed it was an ecology/conservation allegory—the woman was protecting this endangered-species lion from some hunters. Wrong. It turned out that the woman was meant to represent Joanne, and the four silhouettes were typical sleazy horny men who were trying to get her sexual attention. And the hand out meant, "Stop!"

You'd think I'd've caught on, wouldn't you? But that's only because we've both seen too many movies. In real life, people never wise up.

I sat there humming to myself, trying hard not to hear, while Evelyn's voice rose higher and louder. Then there was the sound of a slap. And then Joanne crying.

Now I was really scared. The cops would come; the world would end.

The crying was followed by Evelyn's voice yelling again. Then there was a much longer silence. I tried not to think about it, not to hear or see anything . . . Sgt Shultz in suede, a Californian Sgt Shultz: "I see *noz-zink,* dude! I'm tellin' you man, I hear *noz-zink!*"

They came out of the bedroom, finally. Joanne apologized to me sullenly. Evelyn had obviously ordered her to. Joanne had been crying. And her cheek was still Kirillian red from the slap, branded with Evelyn's palm print.

What happened after that? It all goes white for me here. I think Evelyn took over, made small talk. I was deaf-blind for the rest of the evening, but I know I didn't go home right then. I'm sure we went somewhere, because I remember Evvie going back into the bedroom for her purse, and Joanne looking at me with hatred.

After that night, I had the sense to stay away from them for a while. Which meant I was back in solitary. Lying in bed rereading whichever paperback came to hand when I felt around in the humus of orangepeel and chickenbone and newspapers on the floor by my bed. I chose by feel: anything that felt like a book, that had a spine, whether it turned out to be Agatha Christie or *A History of Medieval Persia,* I didn't care. And for later, the trip to Lapland, I had under the bed my old friend, the Fall 1969 *J C Penney's Catalogue,* with soft, domestic versions of the archetypes of beauty from the time of Peace and Love, when time in the body had stopped for me. Sometimes the lingerie models were shown kneeling before other models. I knew they were only kneeling because it allowed the photographer to show all of the nylons in a small space; but there was another way of construing that pose. Bathory's way. Didn't they tell me at Berkeley that the reader was responsible for the text, a second author? I rewrote many a nylon ad, unsmiled them, moved them to the Countess' castle, outside NATO.

And volunteered for long shifts at the truckyard, just to be out of that sarcophagus room. This meant borrowing my parents' Plymouth for 30-hour slots, leaving them without a car for entire weekends; but that was a sacrifice I was prepared to make.

17

The truckyard was a kind of antidote. Just the succession of ghostly sensory experiences you could expect in the course of a long night patrolling without sleep. You'd begin on a Friday evening by driving into Oakland to pick up Max from his Transylvanian kennel. The Kennel of Squeaks remained for me a holy and terrifying place. Everything about it was serious and un-mellow. The drive in from Pleasant Hill took about half an hour, but the real distance covered seemed much greater. Even the freeway picked up speed and seriousness as you entered Oakland, where the black people lived.

They were stronger than white people. They still killed. They counted. When I first started to get strong, after a few months at the gym, I was shocked to see that I was lifting more than most of the black men there. I didn't think that was possible. Everyone knew they were stronger. And angry. You could see it in the cougar expression on the people who looked you over when you got off the freeway, took to those dreaded "surface streets" and had to stop at a light to be considered as prey by the locals.

The kennel was at the blown-up heart of the black city. When the hobbit-man first took me there to meet Max, there'd been a couple of buildings still standing in the block. But sometime after I took the job they blew up even those, so that the kennel stood alone in a full block of broken concrete. It was untouched, as if it had some special dispensation from the god of destruction who ruled that neighborhood. A note from Shiva telling *to whom it may concern* that this kennel of mutilated, torture-trained German shepherds was sacred to him and not to be desecrated. There wasn't even any graffiti. That place had protection.

There was never anybody there. Somebody must have fed the dogs, and even hosed down their stinking cages every month or so. But you never saw anyone when you went to pick up your dog. There was only the sequence of scent and noise, a kind of nihilist protocol.

The dogs' chorus of strangled yaps—at some point I'd come to like it and even need to hear it. It had a kind of beauty, as if all the massacred wolves of Europe were calling across Space-time, cursing this late, diminished world. Far attenuated vengeance called down on the sunny folk. The yaps were an antidote to pigs like Voltaire and E. B. White, whose inexpressibly vile *Style Manual* they were making me learn at Berkeley. The more time I spent drifting around Berkeley like an overweight dead leaf or shuffling over to SF to grovel before Joanne, the more comfort I found in those yaps. I got into the habit of standing there at the kennel door for a while, wincing at the stench but taking heart at the far chorus, the Dire Wolves of old calling across time that the sunny era would end, this exile would end. That promise harmonized with the Russian proverbs I was trying to memorize at the time. Like the chill slogan of the Nihilists of People's Will, who killed Aleksandr II: "The worse, the better." Or the peasant proverb: "One who's been flogged is worth two who haven't." The dogs were saying the same thing. Roughly.

That didn't mean they were glad to see me. God no—they'd've been happy to rip me into a meat puzzle if they could've gotten out of their cages. Even Max would've taken a few bites with pleasure, once the others started.

Which made the entry to the kennel a big moment. There were two doors. The outer one was dented metal, with the marks of a pickaxe or something, maybe bullets, around the keyhole. That door admitted you to a stinking foyer about two feet deep, with one metal chair and old copies of car magazines lying in the corners. The magazines were kind of neat—there were girls in bikinis sprawled over the hoods of Camaros, really dumb looking, slavish and wholly possessed girls, much more exciting than the contemptuous lesbian stares of the expensive posers in *Playboy*. I wanted to take one of the magazines home to my room, but didn't; I thought they'd trace me, arrest me for theft and perversionism, subject me to a humiliating public trial and take me down to the basement for "nine grams in the back of the head," as my Russians used to put it. So I arrived at a small protocol: I was allowed to look at one of the car magazines for ten seconds—time enough for a quick drool with the yapping for soundtrack—and then had to shut it, put it back *exactly* where I found it, opened to *exactly* the same greasy page, and go on through the inner door.

This door was flimsier, fake-wood paneling peeling back at the bottom corners and grimed around the knob. Opening this door was the moment of truth, because beyond it was the double row of cages, and if any of your colleagues had forgotten to lock a cage, you'd get a toothy welcome. And of course there wouldn't be any barking to warn you. Just one of Max's quiet comrades jumping at your throat.

There was no way to tell. And not much reason to be confident, because by this time I'd managed to figure out that my colleagues in the attack-dog biz weren't exactly *SpetsNaz* quality soldiers.

The smell of that kennel extended downwind in a huge ellipse like fallout from an H-bomb, but you didn't feel the full blast of stench 'til you opened the inner door. My first experience of the dry retch. ("Now I are one," as the t-shirts say.) I had to snorkel in on a held breath when I dived through that door. Then, breathing shallowly, walk down the row to get Max.

Miss America—it was always a little like that, because as you started down the long aisle each dog tried to attract the judge's attention. Not by smiling—well, smiling of a sort: it certainly involved showing a lot of teeth. The minute you came through that door the intensity of the squeaking would increase: not louder but creepier. And the nearest dogs would start slamming against the wire, launching themselves at you as if they could go through the wire in diced pieces, Tom-and-Jerry style, then reassemble on this side to rend you.

Some of them were incredible. The very first cage on the left was a burnt-looking female who'd slam into the wire, then slash her canines across it, scattering foam and making the fencing clang like a bike tire with a card in its spokes. There was something of the go-go dancer in her routine, a delayed charge of something not all ferocity. Two cages down from her was a black male who would lie in wait till you were right in front of his cage, then launch himself into the wire at full speed—hard enough to bounce off almost to the back of the cage. Each dog had some carefully developed routine; never saw anything like it again till Bangkok.

Max's cage was the very last one. He shouldn't have won that competition, but he was the one I had to pick. The other dogs were not the graceful losers you saw on Miss America pageants.

By the time I reached Max's cage my knees would be a little jellied. I wasn't scared but my body was. Knees and hands—it took a while to get his leash out.

Max was always ready to go. Not happy, not unhappy. A body at rest, plus my momentum, equaled his body in motion: it was all dead orbits to him. Kenya, the weirdly beautiful female whose cage was next to his, was much happier to see me. I always hoped I'd get to know her. She was a nice dog, and to be a nice dog in that place meant . . . I can't think about it. I always liked her, but we never really met outside the kennel, and she will have died in lonely, stinking misery decades ago.

Anyway. We'd exit, me as MC and Max as Miss America —a real dark horse candidate, escorted through a truly painful chorus of abuse from the gauntlet of the unchosen. Out into the light of Oakland. The smell lessened once you were through the inner door, and seemed to all but disappear once you were outside the kennel. The outdoor air was so clean and odorless it seemed absurd that people talked about "smog"—what smog? The organic is always worse.

I'd drag Max over to the car, avoiding the few bums who were too dumb to get out of his path and open the trunk. Max would hop in. Matthew had thought I was crazy for letting Max, whose fur was mostly matted shit, sit in the back seat of our car. He showed me how to put him in the trunk. It was fine with Max. He'd spent a lot of time in trunks, obviously; he jumped in mine with neither more nor less alacrity than he would have shown leaping into a limo or a meat grinder.

Then to the yard. Friday evenings, the yard was crowded with daytime people. I didn't like that, driving into a yard full of truck-company guys, because around other people my job somehow became a shameful one.

Max was arthritic, stepping out of the trunk. Slowing down. He'd become very old. He'd looked pretty old when I met him, but now his muzzle was almost pure white, and his eyebrows too, making the big Concord grape tumor over his eye stand out even more.

Unbelievably, Max's life had gotten worse. The one thing that was good in his life—hunting bipeds—had been taken away from him, thanks to this new rule that he had to be on-leash or chained up at all times, even when the yard was empty. The hobbit-man had had some trouble after Max bit Tomas. The janitors had lodged some sort of formal complaint with the trucking company. I tried telling the hobbit-man that Tomas had taunted Max, but he said that that "wasn't the issue."

So now Max had to stay chained up, far away from all the scurrying legs of the Friday-evening truckworkers. Me too; I had to find a place to hide till they left, behind a pillar or something. A nasty high school feel the place had, all that rat-pack laughing and running around, till they drifted home.

As they went, the yard became more beautiful, each departing employee an improvement. The sun would go down over the big Picasso horses which were actually cranes for lifting containers at the Port of Oakland. When the last truck-company man left, I could shut the Fort-Apache gate, leaving the world to darkness and to me. Me and Max.

First patrol through the yard. Anybody in that whole square block who wasn't me was a thief, who you didn't have to be polite to. We were Sinn Fein: "Just us."

Once you knew it was just us, you could breathe deep. Have the air for dinner, a feast of scents: organ-meat, sewage and salt. The occasional pop of a shooting, the surf sound of the Bay Bridge—and over all of it the sweet smog cascading down from the cars on the bridge, people who were *going out for the evening.*

But once it got true dark, the chance passed. No levitation. So I'd get hungry and scrounge around the floor and the seats of my parents' car for quarters and dimes to feed the candy machine. Digging into the pile of books, success paperbacks with pencilled annotations so terrible to me that I yelped and threw them at the

back window. There was never much change in the litter of
paperbacks and Langendorf crumbs; my parents didn't have coins
to throw around. But I could usually scavenge enough for a candy
bar.

Then came the choosing of the bar, a solemn Versailles rite.
My cranial Parliament had long discussions on the merits of the
various nominees displayed on the front of the machine. There
were violent changes of fashion in our procurements: for a whole
month I ate only Caravelles, a now-extinct bar which had a
caramel center coated with chocolate—but the key, the best part,
was the little rice crispies in the chocolate. They provided the
trademark crunch. Since then, of course, the same combination of
ingredients has been revived under many names, but never as
sweetly blended as they were in those Caravelles, spiced with the
damp and the bakery smell of the wooden pallets piled behind the
vending machine. The name had power too: not just a pun on
"caramel," but a summoning of the Armada.

Then fashionable opinion would withdraw into a Tory
aestheticism, and for a dozen shifts in a row I'd get nothing but
Heath Toffee—the Harris Tweed of candy bars. They were small,
a discreet brown wrapper containing just two flat lozenges of
chocolate-coated toffee; but they had a blank pride not found in
the younger bars. And you could scrape the chocolate off the
toffee brick with your front teeth before you cracked down on the
brownstone slabs inside. Sweet headstones of paleo-butter. And a
shard of toffee would invariably lodge in your molars, providing a
brief flashback hours later when it floated free onto your taste
buds.

But of course Heath was a reactionary taste. There was a
hungry-class lobby too, which wanted something more filling.
Never mind the nuances, give us calories. Especially on the nights
when I hadn't had the foresight to empty my parents' refrigerator
before grabbing their car. Then it was time for the biggest, crudest
bars, not excluding the gross Snickers, candy bar of fools. And
other, even lesser brands. The kind for people who like baseball.
The kind with peanuts. When American candy-bar makers target
the base of the demographic pyramid they always go with peanuts,
corn syrup, and quantity. There must be studies showing that the
rabble will eat anything which combines these things. On some

particularly hungry nights I even resorted to Baby Ruths, lowest
taste of all, peanut glop for atavistic Eastern Seaboard scum.

The sugar quickened mind and step. While it lasted, our war
faction wrote the speeches. Joanne crying at my bedside while I
coughed up blood, having fallen in battle, the bodies of six truck
thieves scattered about me. I would gaze up at her, my life's blood
flowing out onto the sheets like the painting of Wolfe at Quebec,
and whisper "O Faithless One!" Medieval diction at last; I figured
that on your deathbed you were entitled to speak the dialect of
Middle Earth without shame.

I'd sit up in the swivel chair of the guard shack and make a
strange sort of love to myself: stroke my own cheek, whispering as
a hypothetical lover would, "I love you . . . My love . . ." Is that
how it would feel? Does your own hand feel like someone else's
hand? It couldn't, not exactly, because you were getting neural
feedback from the touching hand as well as the touched face.
Reality would be one-sided: all receiving.

Then the self-caresses degenerated into Gollum's soliloquy:
"Precioussss . . . Preciousssss . . . We love you, we loves you for
ever O my Preeciousss, yeessss . . ." (Gollum was Irish, of course:
real name Smeagol, clearly Celtic.) And then even the Gollum
voice would lose heart and there was only a babble of mindless
stances sinking into quicksand, with Gollum's best line the last
echo: "We hates them, my Precious . . . we hates them *for ever*!"
What made it so good, somehow, was the way he split "forever"
into two emphatic words.

From time to time there would be relief from noises outside
my head. Most notably the noise of the Black Liberation Army
which held its invisible drills in the little park across from the
truckyard. At least fifty men, by the sound of it. Roaring in unison,
like a basic-training platoon—but always invisible, part of the
interstellar void beyond the glare of the lights.

I no longer had faith in them someday invading the truckyard.
That stuff never happens. The dam never breaks, the floodwaters
always recede, the comet always misses Earth, and no matter how
many Wintrist pamphlets I print they'll never have the guts to
detonate the nukes. The Beigeocracy won't allow such things.

All that happens is little horrible things that don't mean
anything, just feel bad without even registering on seismographs. I

was as invisible to the Black Army as they were to me. Separate but equal universes. Nothing was going to happen.

Except the nightlong progress to complete exhaustion. With several little tortures and falls to give it incident. Stations of the Cross. Around midnight, as the blood sugar dipped, *I falls the first time.* The violent debates between factions in my head turned to warm glue, a parliament of zombies. The procurement debate over candy bars dribbled on and on mindlessly, though I tried to hum pop songs to drown them out. Out-shouting "Buttercup Baby" or "Spirit in the Sky" would come Edmund Burke defending the Divine Right of Heath Toffee Bars; then Burke would be roared into silence by Jim Larkin stumping the Dublin docks for the plain truth of Caravelle. They went on and on, time on the cross, infinite. Like driving across Nevada. The white light from the yard's fluorescent lights pushed in on my eyes; their hum hurt and there was nothing beyond. Not even "darkness"; just nothing. After midnight I understood what the physicists meant when they said that nothing, not even empty space, existed beyond the edge of our universe.

I'd try lying down on the palettes behind the candy machine, but the lights ground into my eyes. And those palettes were haunted. Around two or three in the morning the ghost-scent river of Oakland would begin to flow over me: an incommunicable malevolence which was greater than the sum of its component smells—piss, tideflat, organ-meat and burned tomatoes from the cannery. It slipped in from the Bay like Casper, a few feet off the ground. Insinuated itself, complete negation, like zigzag cartoon smoke. Once it was on you, hope was gone. I feared it far more than any robbers, but couldn't give warning. No one would believe me if I tried to tell them—I didn't even have the nouns. "Memo to CME Trucking: There's an ectoplasmic aboveground river of smells which always comes into your truckyard from the west around 2 AM and means us harm."

But its whisperings scared me enough that I'd get off the palettes, give up trying to sleep, and check out the truck company offices. Partly in the hope someone might have left food around. On nights when I couldn't find any change, I had resort to the box of sugar cubes next to their coffee machine. True, the cubes tended to melt into Elmer's glue on your tongue and down your throat, but they were something to put in your mouth. Finishing off the box of cubes, I'd check the pay phone for forgotten dimes (there were never any) and shuffle back to the guard shack to try to sleep with my head on the counter (I never could).

By 3:00 AM the fine speakers, the Irish rebelrousers, had all faded into senility; *I falls the second time.* Now it was Joanne who stood in Parliament to tell me how justly she despised me. And after her, every one of the rejected candy bars—even the contemptible Baby Ruth, an illiterate jock—made speeches denouncing my cruelty, speeches as powerful as Robert Emmet's. All were wildly cheered. I couldn't even win my own fantasies.

All I could do to drown out the sequence of denunciations was let the clomp and pain of my boots drown out the speakers. Max and I would keep patrolling just to get away from Joanne's gloating in my head. Because it was easier to walk on the bootnails than listen to the endless, querulous factions doing a millionth post-mortem on our great defeats.

Then—O *Third Spirit, I fear you most of all*—the last, most terrible, incommunicable stage of the nightly decline: the true music of the spheres. *I falls the third time.* The debates lost word and became boulder rumbles, faucet dribbles. And even these terrible burbles blurred as they went through the feedback loop, played slower and louder till they were vibration, not sound. Seismic noises, arguments by ice floe. Creaks, squeaks, rumbles— the soundtrack of Bedlam.

How boulders chat. How dirt chitters. Sarcasm of hills. You were not supposed to be awake to hear this thing. I knew this. I knew it was bad luck being able to hear it. It was no hallucination; it was always there, under us, under the sidewalks and streets all day every day; but it was very, very bad luck to be awake to hear it. That was why nobody wanted this shift. You might as well have been guarding a reactor core. Your hair would fall out and your teeth and you'd die young, because you'd heard the malevolent churning too many times. Its only enemy was sleep—God yes, sleep!—and all that mattered was finding a soft horizontal surface to lie down on. The higher mental functions seemed directly related to bipedalism and both traits seemed like a disastrous evolutionary mistake. It meant you had a brain and stood up like an aerial so you heard the world transmitting its true song, pure gibbered malevolence. Therefore . . . mongoloid cognition moving slowly . . . obviously . . . devolved logic . . . *ob* . . . *veee* . . . *us-ly* . . . the solution was to become horizontal again, to give up this arrogant erect spine and rest at length, sleep as deeply as a Stegosaurus lovingly bedded in the shale of Montana. It didn't have to hear the churning. It was home.

God yeah, to be that litter of valuable bones! Safe, happily fossilized . . . a treasured find for some alien archeologist sifting the rubble of what had been Earth. A part of some specific stratum, united with the others of my time at last, verifiably placed within *our* time, no matter what the people at PHHS said. Being pampered by archeologists: dusted off and treated to plaster-of-Paris poultices, then lifted offworld, gently as a sleeping child, to their finest museum to be admired by millions . . . alien parents shushing their children, piles of flowers laid softly by my stony bed each day . . . sleep sleep sleep.

One night there was something crying out there—a horrible nagging cry: "Mmmmyaaaahhhhnnnn . . ." It might have been words or just a noise. Those categories got shaky after you'd been forced to listen to the boulders churning. This was all too much like them, anyway—a tiny soprano version: "Mmmmyaaaahhhhnnnn . . ."

It seemed to have no location. I went out of the shack a few times to find where it was coming from, but it perversely shut up, then yelled quietly again the moment I was in the shack. "Mmmmyaaaahhhhnnnn . . ."

Max didn't react to it at all—just lay there. It was a bad timeloop night at the yard: a single dull horrible sequence repeating like an Interstate landscape across Iowa. The failed attempt to doze, the crying noise, "Mmmmyaaaahhhhnnnn . . ."

After about a year, it began to get light. The light seemed to wake up the Thing; the cries got more frequent. I went out, cursing it for hanging on, and heard it again, right beside me. Not a loud crying far off, as I'd thought, but a very weak crying right by the shack. "Mmmmyaaaahhhhnnnn . . ."

That time it made a mistake: cried out when I was out in the yard. I could hear that it was coming from this dumpster alongside the shack. I dragged back the lid, looked in and half-gagged from the stink wafting up from a white liquid washing around in the bottom of the dumpster. The smell was like solvent with rotten meat stewing in it.

Nothing but floating garbage . . . except—there. This one dark lump: something alive. A dog, a . . . a puppy. Round head—Rottweiler or Pitbull. Something like that. It was lying in the toxic milk, but the front paws were clinging to a tilted Styrofoam raft. Its eyes were shut tight, but now and then it would scream very quietly: "Mmmmyaaaahhhhn . . ."

So now I was supposed to rescue it. *Unhh* . . . But (A) the toxic milk; (B) a whole night of listening to the boulders of Bedlam; and (C) I didn't like it. And (D) the toxic milk. And (E) I don't want to; (F) Shut up and leave me alone. Like the nice Victorian British Christians during the Irish Famine, when a whole people was extirpated right next door without a penny's help or a word of compassion from those good, good people—because (A through Z) *We don't like them.*

Maybe if the stupid puppy hadn't gone to radio silence every time I went out to look for it. Or if it hadn't been for the toxic milk. Or if it was earlier in the shift. If any of the above, then yes naturally of course I'd've rescued it. But God, I couldn't even open the lid of that dumpster without retching. And it was lying in that stuff.

I went back to the shack to consult with Max. If he showed any sign of caring I'd think it over. I brought him down to the dumpster. The puppy obliged, for once—screamed two or three times while Max was standing there. Max either didn't hear or didn't care. I kept yanking his leash after each scream, to provoke some reaction. Nothing. Eyes like black marbles. "Puppy! Dog, Max!" He wouldn't even look up when I yanked the leash. I was just landscape to him, and the puppy's screams just dim industrial noise. Even the yanking meant nothing to him; it was as if his chain had been tugged by the wind.

And the thing was . . . the stupid puppy wasn't even cute, the way a puppy in distress was supposed to be. It was actually kind of irritating. And sleep, sleep.

I took Max patrolling in the damp, bleary sunrise just so I could get away from the little screams and think what to do. I guess . . . yeah . . . I could just put it in the Plymouth's trunk, and then, yeah I guess I could take it to the Oakland SPCA. Or the

Oakland Pound. I didn't know where those places were, but they must exist . . . and probably they'd be in the phone book. It was hard to imagine driving to those places, where I didn't know anyone and would have to ask total strangers for help, but OK, yeah, it was theoretically possible. Yeah yeah yeah, OK.

I'd have to climb into that dumpster to get the puppy, though. Put my feet in that milk. Well, I could do that.—But then I'd have to go to these places, the SPCA or the pound, and talk to clean-type people and ask them to take the puppy off my hands—ask *them* to do something for *me*. And I was wearing—

I looked down to see what I was wearing. Oh yeah: the nylon quilted coat that my classmates had burned a hole in Metal Shop. It had been orange originally; but now, five years later, it seemed to have become more of a grimy umber . . . or sienna, smeared khaki . . . something in the "earthy" range of crayon. And had grimed off-white polyester quilting spilling out like fake snow from the hole they made with the soldering iron. Not, probably, the right thing to wear to the SPCA to ask a favor from clean people.

Proceeding southward from the jacket, I appeared to be wearing those green plaid pants my mother got me a couple or so years back. The waist was too small but if you wore them eight inches too low, they'd still button. What was worrying, now that I looked at them in the quiet dawn light, was the fact that the thighs of the pants were a different, darker color than the rest—also due, apparently, to accumulated grime.

And then, in the far south, the pain-boots. I found them illustrious in a Robert E. Lee's Army-of-Northern-Virginia-circa-1865 way, but they were noisy to walk in, and kind of slick with sweat and pus and blood and so on: not suitable for a tense, snotty, antiseptic place like the Oakland SPCA probably was. Also, in the process of looking down at myself, I noted that I had a distinct aroma. So I couldn't go to the SPCA because, like people said in movies, I had nothing to wear.

Yeah but the puppy constituted a moral imperative. Overrode all concerns of vanity. Must be done. Supposedly.

As Max and I clumped around the circuit I came up with a compromise: I'd try to feed the puppy . . . see if it could eat. If it could, it was viable and I had to give it some grudging Victorian charity; if it couldn't, then it was clearly a goner and thus off my hands. Let it die; Darwin will know his own. Darwin is a Calvinist, right? A Brit. Nothing I can do about it. Feed it and wash my hands of it.

The only food in the place was candy bars from the machine. Not exactly Alpo but better than nothing, still a valid test. So when we got back to the shack I ransacked the Plymouth for quarters, making the paperbacks fly—broken-backed second-hand copies of *Double Your Word-Power* and *Six Weeks to Riches* flung around like dirt-clods. God how I hated even touching them! They smelled like failure itself—yellowed cellophane trailing from their covers, big lies next to pictures of dead salesmen smiling with false teeth. There's nothing more painful than a cop-surplus Plymouth full of mildewed self-help books. Shove E. B. White's nose into the crotch of that back seat, then see if he still loves humanity. Make Voltaire find a needle, or a nickel, in that haystack . . .

It was torment rooting among them, remembering all that had happened to us in bright cheery California—because none of it would even register in the stats. What had happened to us had never happened as far as any record would show. My father, whose light pencil annotations filled those worthless books—I have never met anyone more brilliant than my father, and he lived and died in fear and in Dostoevskyan poverty which cannot have happened when and where it happened— lovely sunny California.

When he volunteered after Pearl Harbor, he was given the usual battery of intelligence tests. On the basis of his scores, he was given another set of tests . . . and another, and another; and on the basis of those tests he was taken from his unit and flown to a top-secret base in Hawaii, learning intensive Japanese and the mathematics of cryptography. The guys in that unit formed the Asian Languages faculties of every major American university. But my father went home to Jersey City and tried to learn to be a glad-hander. And for all his pitiful effort to memorize these damned, filthy salesmanship books, he could never learn that. So he lived in terror of every knock at the door.

Now, thanks to the zombie pup, my nose was shoved into those damned paperbacks again—twice in one shift! And the puppy was to blame, hurting me with these unbearable family

smells, the ones I strove most urgently to avoid ever, ever thinking
about.

At last, rooting among the moldy paperbacks like the bookpig
I am, I found a quarter and two sandy sticky dimes. Enough to
buy a candy bar. Stupid puppy better be grateful.

Once I had the money I had to have a new debate: which bar
would a half-dead puppy prefer? Something chewy, not too hard.
Not a Heath Toffee—even the Tories granted that. Caravelle?
Too arcane. Milky Way? It was big and soft—tastes like sugared
caulking, but half-dead puppies can't be choosers. I got a Milky
Way and took it to the dumpster. The puppy was screaming every
thirty or forty seconds. There was still no inflection to the
screams, no volume. "Mmmyyyaaannnhhh." Irritating. It could at
least try to be convincing.

I leaned over the dumpster and said "Hey" to the puppy but it
didn't seem to answer, just kept up its uninflected screaming. I
called again and again, whistled, but there was no response.

Max was asleep up on the dock, not reacting either.

I opened the Milky Way and pinched off a chocolate-caramel
corner, threw it toward the puppy. It fell into the toxic milk. The
puppy screamed again. "Mmmyaaannnhh."

I tore off another chaw. This one hit the puppy on the head
but bounced into the milk. Tried again and bounced a chaw right
where I wanted it, on the Styrofoam, two inches from the puppy's
muzzle. But it didn't react.

"Hey—eat it!"

Still no reaction.

The smell of the toxic milk was making me sick. I went back
to the shack. By the criterion I'd set, the puppy wasn't viable and I
didn't have to help it. But it resumed screaming as soon as I sat
down. "Mmmyyaaanhhh."

Now that I knew how close at hand the screams were, they
were much harder to take. Wilberforce—who didn't say a damn
word about the two million dead in the Irish Famine—had the gall
to stand up in my cranial parliament and say we had to help this
puppy even if it wasn't viable. For *is it not a dog and a brother?*

Yes, it's a dog and a brother, OK. But I'm tired. It's gonna die
anyway. It stinks. And to paraphrase that other and better
Abolitionist orator, Sojourner Truth: *Ain't I a dog and a brother?*

Nobody never lifts me *out of no toxic milk and throws* me *no Milky Ways!
And ain't a dog and a brother?*

And hungry too. The *Milky Way* was smelling pretty good.
About three-quarters of it left. It didn't really taste like caulking.
Well maybe a little . . . but *good* caulking. And besides, besides . . .
I'd offered it to the puppy; he or she (my Berkeley training in
avoiding gendered pronouns operating even in this semi-comatose
state) didn't want it. Just going to waste . . . Why shouldn't I eat it?

O no no no, assuredly not! Said Wilberforce the Scrupuland in my
head. *O no no no.* Every faction in there agreed: it just wouldn't be
right.

Ate it in three bites. Executive action. Checks and balances are
for the happy people. My people are starving. Fat, yes—but
starving nonetheless. Another non-paradox of the sort common
in this bland Purgatory: starving and fat.

But eating food meant for the dying was undeniably a mortal
sin. This gave the Milky Way a weird infernal aftertaste, as if the
chocolate were sprinkled with Habanero salsa. Not unpleasant.

I sat there knowing I was damned. But I had been anyway—
so it wasn't too bad. Can't kill the dead; can't damn the damned.
And the Milky Way woke me up a little. You can't be damned
more than once. *Yes you can.* No you can't shut up.

The sugar high went away and it was just the truckyard on a
bleary Saturday dawn. Tentative nausea from the candy bar. The
puppy was still screaming a couple times per minute.
"Mmmyyaaannnhhh." Same old stuff: hugely horrible yet
little/stupid.

Time went by in the usual manner: by the second, slowly,
without quick cuts.

Matthew showed up.

I showed him the logbook and mentioned the puppy, babbling
while he smoked: "It's weird I don't know where it came from just
heard it I thought it was out there somewhere but I realized it was
coming from the dumpster don't know what to do about it
thought I should take it to the pound but I don't know—"

A twitchy smile stitched into Matthew's face: "Uh-huh uh-huh
so . . . So you want me to take care of it?"

Matthew was different. Looking at him when he wasn't
looking, I could see his body sort of nodding back and forth as if

he heard music somewhere. And he was sweaty. Not as remote as usual. And that twitchy grin kept appearing on his face. Probably laughing at me. I hastened to disavow what I'd just said:

"Well no not necessarily I thought well no I guess—"

He shook his head six or seven times and said with the same twitchy smile: "I'll take care of it, I'll take care of it, I'll take care of it."

"Ah OK great that's great—not sure how sick it is, actually—"

"S'OK, I'll take care of it."

"OK great well see you later bye."

Matthew had already turned away, humming and nodding. By the time I drove off, he was yanking a two-by-four out of a pile of broken palettes. But whatever happened after that wasn't my fault.

I was on for Saturday night. This gave me eight hours to get some sleep and get back to the truckyard. I drove out to Pleasant Hill, snarled the ritual question "Anybody call?" to my parents, grunted at their ritual "No," and flopped in bed. No Lapland: just seven hours' literal sleep.

Then up again and back to the truckyard, with the Plymouth's gas gauge hovering at the red "E" mark all the way. It spent its whole life at or below that mark. I don't think I saw a car with a gas needle above half a tank till I was thirty. The Eskimos with their alleged ability to make fine distinctions in snow types had nothing on us with that gauge; we knew when it was merely Empty, or dangerously-less-than-empty, or way-below-empty, better-find-some-quarters-and-put-in-a-gallon-or-so. It's funny that it never occurred to me to use some of my wages to put gas into the Plymouth, but it didn't. I just accepted that "E" as part of our fate. A luck gauge. Accurately showing a completely empty tank which somehow still managed to carry us. Our cars always had loyalty, like a starving crofter family's last gaunt horse.

And as usual it took me to the truckyard uncomplainingly. Matthew was waiting for me, leaning on his little car. He wasn't the same jolly fierce Matthew of the morning. He slumped against the car, and wasn't in the mood to hang around. The minute I drove up to the shack, he got into his car and putted away with just a nod in my direction.

I locked the gate after him, then came back and listened for the puppy. Nothing. I looked in the dumpster. Where the puppy had been there was a pile of junk, pieces of Styrofoam packing and cardboard boxes making a cairn. The two-by-four was tossed in a corner. No proof of anything.

Still, the shack felt unwholesome. I wanted to go patrolling. Max probably hadn't even had a walk since Matthew arrived; Matthew didn't much bother with patrolling. I checked the logbook—nobody was listed as being around. And with the gate shut, I could take Max patrolling off-leash. Give him a little air, a little freedom. A good deed to make up for . . . for any unnamed bad deed I might be accused—without proof—of having committed against another canine in the recent past. I unleashed Max and we set out on our first patrol of Saturday evening. The Changing of the Guard, highlight of my week.

18

It was usually a great first clomp, with the trailers saluting our passage and the sun glinting off the rich people's houses high on the hills like camera-flashes from tourists at Buckingham Palace. Didn't feel as great this time, but Max was happy—well, as close to happy as Max got. He seemed almost alive as we swept down the rows, carrying his head low like a knife.

I was cheering up too, already in the middle of my first deathbed speech to Joanne, when I saw something at the end of the yard. A person . . . someone . . . in a white t-shirt. He seemed to be sweeping. I couldn't believe it for a second—sweeping the truckyard? With a broom? It would've taken one of those bulldozer-sized street-sweeping juggernauts hours to do the whole yard, and somebody was doing it with a broom? And on a Saturday evening? It was beyond stupid, beyond improbable. It was downright mythical—that Greek guy, begins with an "A", the one with the stables.

And—instant rush of terror and blame—*with Max off-leash!*

Which he wasn't supposed to be, under the hobbit-man's new rules. Ever.

Max couldn't see the sweeper yet. Max was legally blind. But he was trotting toward that end of the yard. I tried calling him away, like that time the drunks hit the fence, by pretending that there was something eminently enjoyable back by the shack: "C'mon Max! Here Max!", clumping away to enliven the performance.

He looked at me. He was thinking it over. Vacuum tubes were glowing faintly in that ancient Central European brainwerke. Duct-tape was smoking as old wires hummed. Dusty archives were being searched for a dimly remembered precedent. He had some vague sense that this had happened before. And that it had ended badly for him. With the withholding of prey. He looked after me nearsightedly, thought about it—and headed on, toward the sweeper.

I screamed out, "Max! Max! Come!"—holding a hand out from me as if it contained a treat—but he went on, away from me, not even having to think about it. Food never did mean much to Max.

Then he heard the pushbroom scraping on asphalt. His ears went up. He saw the distant biped's arms and legs moving. Down periscope. He charged.

The question was: was I going to run away right now—get in the car and go, maybe to Mexico or Algeria—or watch to see Max in action? My legs were undecided and wobbly. Max was charging slowly, but he was going to intercept the sweeper very soon. Slow radar blips converging in my mind. When they met, the world would end.

I yelled out a sort of apologetic warning yap. The sweeper turned and saw the dog coming.

By the time Max reached him, the sweeper had his broom out and fended off the first bite. Even clumping toward him in terror, some part of my mind spared him a particle of admiration: it was a last stand, very Byzantine—1453 AD, the Seljuk at the gates. He did well. He had the fence at his back, and Max was not especially quick or strong. The sweeper managed to block him with the broom, until Max dipped his shoulder and got beneath his guard. Then the dust flew, and there was a swirl around the sweeper's legs. Then a yell. And then, just as I clomped into the scene, Max trotted off and sat contentedly, satisfied with the traditional one bite.

I was apologizing, out of breath, when I arrived. The sweeper was watching Max, not sure the war was really over. When I ran up and grabbed Max, he looked down at his leg. There was a tear in the pants-leg, and he pulled up the cuff to show the modest gash Max had made in his calf. Broke the skin.

He was a very small man, Mestizo. He didn't say anything. Just fingered the rip in his pants sadly. He seemed much more worried about the rip in his pants than the one in his skin.

I grabbed Max and clipped him to the leash. He didn't resist arrest. He was already going dead again, his moment of fulfillment over.

As I worked I apologized seven or eight times to the sweeper. But he wasn't listening. Talking to him was like speaking to Max. He was one of Elvin's illegal Peruvian serfs. Non-English-speaking. Maybe not even Spanish-speaking. Quechua. Inca. Matthew had explained to me that Elvin preferred to hire Peruvians. Thought they worked harder and cost less than illegal Mexicans. Were even more terrified, more helpless.

After a few seconds of silent grieving over his torn pantsleg, he turned away from my babbled apologies and went back to sweeping. It was over as far as he was concerned. He and Max were agreed on this—some code of the oppressed or something. I apologized a few more times—no reaction—and led Max back to the shack.

It's when you're alone again that you can relax enough to feel the full terror. My God. *Max bit another minority.* My Max. My Selma Alabama police dog. My Auschwitz German shepherd. My shift, my fault. An innocent sweeper, who had—evidently—a right to be here. Of course he had a right to be here; would Max have bitten him otherwise? If he'd been a thief, Max would've ignored him.

I checked the logbook. Matthew hadn't signed anyone in. So technically it wasn't my fault. The yard was supposed to be empty! I thought about calling Matthew and yelling at him. I knew I had the right. And I knew I wouldn't—not in a million years. Me yelling at someone other than my parents? The world would end before that happened.

So it was my problem. But what if the Peruvian didn't tell anybody? No way he was legal, and no way he spoke English. What could he do?

Rabies—he could get a highly-publicized case of rabies. Of course: Max had rabies. Whatever unseen ghouls ran that kennel in the ruins of Oakland weren't likely to've given the dogs their shots . . .

So the janitor will now start foaming at the mouth right there in the yard. And his heirs will be flown in from Lima to sue me for every penny I haven't got. I'll be cross-examined by some radical cool-guy lawyer from Berkeley till I break down and they repossess my kidneys and corneas to pay the punitive damages. Auction off my arms and legs to arthritic millionaires. That typical alliance of the radical-cool, ostensibly acting on behalf of the excluded, which Californians do so well. With an expendable white loser—i.e. me—as everybody's villain-of-choice, like when they need ethnically neutral muggers on cop shows.

I could see it now . . . Stanford Law hippies hugging cornea-recipient heiresses in joy at my "Guilty" verdict for the TV cameras, and both dancing around the courtroom—the heiress nimble on her new ex-Dolan leg—to the sound of an Andean flute band stocked by the cousins of the late janitor. And next day his cousins, pockets stuffed with punitive-damage cash, will carry his coffin, still dripping rabies foam, to the cemetery to the sound of Simon and Garfunkel's ripped-off Andean whimsy: *"I'd rather be a plaintiff than a snail . . . I'd rather be a plaintiff than a white loser security guard defendant . . ."*

God, who wouldn't? I'd rather be dead than the defendant in that trial, the pig with the apple in his mouth who makes the centerpiece of the feast . . . the loser white pig served up for sacrifice in place of the really bigger, whiter pigs, who are somehow never brought to book.

What's the incubation period for rabies? I think a week, from those Pasteur stories about wolf-bitten goatherds.

So about one week from now, the Peruvian will pause while sweeping the yard and start vibrating like a motel bed while the broom slips out of his hand, then pass out, pissing himself like epileptics do, and start speaking in tongues through foamy lips. I know which tongues, too: how do you say *"Punitive damages, exemplary damages, plus forcible organ donations, by defendant the said Dolan . . ."* in Quechua?

And Elvin, his Medici boss, will kneel over the Peruvian's vibrating, foaming body, and smile at me with dollar signs in his eyes. *Ka-ching*! One rabid janitor plus three radical lawyers equals five million dollars—with one organ-donor Dolan left over. Elvin was smooth; I could see him crying in the witness box over the death of his serf, and then laughing it up with Tomas and Matthew afterwards, Tomas getting half of West Oakland in stitches with his limbo-style imitation of a Peruvian having a rabies fit.

So what do I do, *what do I do God*—Just run? Get in the Plymouth and go—like those Beatnik poets, like some phony existentialist in a novel? How do you get to Mexico? South, I guess . . . via LA. Or just run back home, hole up in Pleasant Hill? My room didn't seem so bad all of a sudden . . . a haven of peace, *ackshully*. Go back to it and never come out! That was the mistake in the first place, thinking I could step from that bubble without fatal complications! Nobody every got bitten there, I never did anything actually indictable there . . . My Lapland visits never *broke the skin*, that crucial threshold . . .

But the hobbit-man knew my parents' address; he'd just send the cops for me. And that would be even more embarrassing: every house on Belle Avenue watching joyfully, all those tidy-lawn people who already disapproved of us standing in their doorways, comfy in their bathrobes, Sunday papers in hand, tittering as the block's scraggly-hedge pariah house yields its defective son to repossession by the state. The ritual procession from the house, a jacket over my head to baffle the news cameras, as two proud deputies ham it up waving "Hi Mom!"—their moment of glory as they lead me to the car, red lights strobing my parents' broken faces as marshals shove my head down into the back seat of the squad car . . .

My parents . . . they'd just flat-out die.

And I'd be transferred into a career as Punk of D Block, being interracially raped a hundred times a day: "We got us a educated bitch! Hey bitch, say sumthin Latinate and polysyllabic while I'm fuckin' you!"

So all things considered, it seemed worthwhile to be concerned with the Peruvian's health. You don't have to be a Christian or something; it was downright practical.

If only he could just be scooped up in a copter and returned to Peru. I doubt they do lawsuits in Peru. Put him on a plane to Lima, so the foaming wouldn't start till he was making his way to his ancestral cardboard shack in the barrio . . . stumbling over the burning bone-dry lavafield desert of coastal Peru when he begins

howling and yapping, biting and spasming. They probably collect
ten corpses indistinguishable from this janitor every day among
the heaps of burning garbage in the slums there. Probably use
them for fertilizer. He'd die peacefully on the side of some
stinking hot road, unnoticed and calm. Safe and alone. Sounds
pretty good, ackshully. Maybe I could join him—some two-for-
one ticket to Lima, and borrow some infected spittle from him on
the plane: "Pardoname, señor, do you mind if I lick that airline
coffee cup of yours? Muchas gracias . . ." Enjoy a few days as the
albino werewolf of Peru, biting bus-tires, fighting with other stray
dogs—then slink off, foaming and ranting, to a quiet wind-cave
on the desert coast to wait for some nice archeologists to mistake
me for a valuable aboriginal skeleton, pamper me in a museum
case. A nice dream but not realistic. What I needed was a way to
make sure the Peruvian didn't get rabies. But a quiet way,
something that wouldn't get me arrested. It occurred to me that
money would work. As it did with Joanne. The reason she tolerated
my presence was that I picked up the check, right? The reason
waitresses brought us burritos at those taquerias in the Mission
was money, right? So if I pick up the check for this, the
Peruvian—like Joanne—will allow me to continue living.

It happened to be a moneyed weekend. I'd forgotten to bring
any change for the candy machine, but I did have three twenties in
my pocket. If he took money he'd be quiet. That was a familiar
transaction in the cop shows about corrupt cities. Well this was a
corrupt city, right? It looked like one anyway, all old and grimy like
the places on TV; so why shouldn't it work here?

I took the three twenties down to the Peruvian. He was about
ten yards further along, sweeping the dust from the inside to the
outside of the chain-link fence, the wind instantly blowing it back.

He wasn't limping or anything. Everything seemed fine—
maybe he'd forget the whole thing?

But my plan had too much panicked momentum to alter. I
went up, forcing a smile, wondering if I could recall any high
school Spanish—

Hola, Isabel! Como estas?

Muy bien! y tu?

Bla bla bla, something about what's for lunch; then:

. . . *A mi no me gustan las albondigas.*

"I don't like meatballs myself." For some reason that was the topic of the first Spanish dialogue they ever made us learn. It didn't seem like a good icebreaker here, though—it was at once too topical and not topical enough. *"Pero el Perro, lo gustan las albondigas mucho . . . demasiado . . . ha-ha-ha! øEntonces, nosotros somos amigos, no?"* No, not the kind of kidding-around to attempt with a gashed Peruvian serf. I settled for Californian, took a deep breath and went out to see him, fast, before I lost my nerve:

"Hi, hey, hi . . . um, are you, you know, 'OK'?"

His face was completely blank. Peasant opacity.

"You OK? Did it break the skin? The bite—the dog?" I pointed toward the shack, where Max was dozing.

"El perro? No?"

No reaction.

I was panicking hard, couldn't form sentences, decided to cut to the punchline, the money. Pushed the three twenties at him, saying, "Here, here's some money, OK? So you can go to a doctor, and please I'd prefer it if you were to keep fairly quiet about the whole incident OK? Just think you know it'd be better if we kept it out of the courts OK?"

He looked at the money and took it warily, as if there might be a mouse trap or joke buzzer under the bills.

That sealed the transaction as far as I was concerned, and I walked away quickly, babbling: "Great thanks thank you OK well hope you're OK thanks bye!"

I looked back once, and he was still standing there with the money in his hand.

Sixty dollars . . . It was a week's wages, but without Joanne it wasn't clear what money was for anyway. So that was OK. He'd taken it. Now he'd be quiet. The universal language.

After great fear a sweaty feeling comes. The poor body . . . it thinks we're still in the African rift valley. So it gets all steamed up, gets the boilers of the heart going like some old steam engine, the lungs pushing oxygen into that flame like a double bellows, and the skin radiating heat. There's no way to tell the poor old body that the terrors you face involve litigation rather than running away from a troop of baboons or bashing a baby antelope over the head with a rock. Those were the days, body! No such luck, kid!

You're stuck in an ancient design, and you can't reprogram it. That's why it's so easy to get fat: the body still thinks it's in Oulduvai Gorge, waiting for Leakey to discover it. It thinks the danger is starvation; cardiovascular disease is a negligible risk by comparison. You should live so long! That's the body's curmudgeonly commentary on cardiovascular disease. You won't get it till you're thirty, and odds are you're a hyena's lunch long before you get the thirty antelope-tallow candles on your stone cake! First get away from those hyenas, fool! Then you can worry about cardiovascular disease!

There's no way you can pat your poor deluded DNA on the head and sweet-talk it into accepting that there's plenty of food now, that it needs to shed fat. It's a peasant, a dim beetlebrow hoarder, the body: it knows what it knows, and that's that. Senile. An old granddad mumbling through its gums that the starving days might come back any time, so grab that Milky Way before the cave lions get it. It's an old mammal design, and it's going to do things its way unto death, like a hedgehog strolling across a freeway. The hedgehog knows one thing—a stupid, suicidal one.

So I sat there in the shack sweating out the terror, carpet-bombing my own heart with adrenals, bringing the cardiologist several years closer. Then Elvin showed up to collect his broom serf. That was the moment of real fear.

You can be a connoisseur of anything. Fear. Fear is more than life. Fear is everything. "Ode to Fear"—why didn't Keats write that? What's a miserable Limey hedge-bird or some lame Wedgwood urn compared to fear itself?

Ode to Fear: O Fear, my Master—Oldest element in the universe, Neurotransmitter of the Big Bang, DNA of DNA—double, triple, quad-, quintuple helix, O mighty Fear!

Fear is the one substance which must be measured in those irrational numbers football coaches talk about: 110%, 200%, 1,000%. 100% is the baseline, the resting metabolism of my terror. At my calmest and happiest moment—sound asleep—I am 100% afraid. It goes up from there.

I thought I was scared when Elvin showed up to collect his Inca. Ha! That was paradise compared to the moment when I saw him speaking to the Peruvian! And even that was a piece of low-fat poundcake, no more than 200% or 300% fear, compared to the succeeding moment, when I saw the Peruvian bend down and show his bitten leg to Elvin. And all those terror tableaux were a *Happy Days* rerun, a sappy Elton John ditty, compared to the moment when Elvin stopped on his way out of the yard to point over to Max and ask the Peruvian something, then nod and drive out of the yard. That was fear at its boiling point, 1,000° Centigrade, the temperature of the sun—or me in hygiene class at Pleasant Hill High.

O to be a nuclear device . . . ("Ode to Nuclear Winter," the b-side of my "Ode to Fear" hit single): O to detonate and take all of them with me . . . to be gone, to be *gone*, to combust with extreme prejudice. Everything from the Bay Bridge to the Mormon Tabernacle glinting there, another fake Oz on the Oakland hills—this whole cozy Jacuzzi in which I'm dying so politely, all of it all of it just WHOOOSH in a single fear-trigger Hiroshima. I know I have megatons in me. C'mon, Coach, ya gotta lemme detonate! The "untapped potential" my sophomore-year counselor kept attributing to me. He was right, kindly little bearded man, but he thought it was in the form of better grades. No, my potential is in detonation. I know I'm nuclear tipped, made of an element too dense for California. Why can't I combust? Must be some minor defect, some disconnected wire somewhere—and all my megatonnage goes to waste. One crummy short circuit, cheap Soviet wiring . . . my trigger must've been assembled on a Monday; some drunken fool of an electrician at the secret factory outside Sverdlovsk was hung over when he soldered my detonator, mixed up the green and red wires . . . leaving me unable to impose my sun-hot avenging molecules on the Beigeist hegemony, dooming me to a long life of torment in this happy-dappy, wappy-slappy sunshine, *in this millionth year of the wicked peace* . . .

With nothing to do but watch Elvin's pickup leave the yard, my Peruvian being debriefed as they go. All I can do is wait for the predetermined trouble. A long wait. That's why this isn't a movie: real time is agonizingly slow, Greenwich Dentist's Office time. I had thirty hours left in my shift at the truckyard—the rest of Saturday night and all of Sunday, right up to 6 AM Monday, when I could finally dump Max in the trunk and leave. I patrolled non-stop through most of those thirty hours, because I didn't want to answer the phone in the shack. Or meet anyone. Cops, for example, coming to take me away for infecting an innocent Inca with rabies. A second Pizarro, me.

And they'd be right. That was always the strange part about the Beigeocrats who have presided over my protracted demise: they are always truly, genuinely *right*. And I wrong. I know vaguely that Nietzsche must thus have been right—that I must've accepted a bad major premise somewhere between Socrates and the New Testament—but I can't calm down long enough to track the wiring back to find the fault and fix it. Too much going on with the Matterhorn ride up front, the Sensorium.

19

It made for a long shift, waiting for the cops to come and get me. Thirty hours of trying to nap on the palettes, sugar-cube raids, ectoplasmic river, brown-out . . . the usual sequence. And then the drive home on Monday morning. The problem came very close to resolving itself halfway back to Pleasant Hill: I woke up at the wheel and found myself heading for a retaining wall. I was one second, one swerve, away from being declared innocent by reason of death. Pay my debt to society in advance.

So naturally it didn't happen. Things don't happen, not in this dimension. Am I not myself a thing that almost happened, a herald from the universe of things that almost happen? Yeah— they sent me to tell you we're getting seriously pissed off with you hogging the Indicative mode.

In other words: I made it home; I slept; I awaited the cops. Now the phone was a gamble; it might be Joanne—the one voice which could punch through the crust—or it might be the police asking me to come downtown to answer some questions ". . . and bring a toothbrush."

I tried to love my room, my safe, no-felony room . . . but that was a debacle. One glance was enough to demonstrate that seeing my room was a horrible idea, let alone attempting to love it. At Berkeley they were fond of paradoxes, the kind where prisoners end up loving their cells, not wanting to be freed. Another lie. I hated my cell, and there was no asterisk or "but" to it, no twist. There was never any twist! They lied to me about . . . well, everything, actually—but particularly the twists. If there's anyone like me, like I was when I was young, reading this, listen: there are no twists!

Two soundless days later, I drove to the truckyard for the night shift. Matt and the hobbit-man were waiting by the shack when I pulled into the yard. The hobbit-man looked serious; Matt and Max were looking away. The hobbit-man jumped me almost before I could get out of the car, speaking in quick Californian. It was hard to understand. He was asking me about "Luis."

Luis? Oh God, oh God: the Peruvian, the bitten Peruvian!

This was the big one. This one broke the skin. This was the kind of thing that ends your life, lands you in a literal prison. But there wasn't even time to imagine the horrors ahead, because I had to listen and answer the hobbit-man in real time. He was using my name at every sentence, "John, John, John!" to slap me awake. I read his lips, straining through the feedback roar.

"John, listen, did you were you there when, you know, when Luis was when Max—"

Nod.

"You were there? Why . .?" He stops and shakes his head, then goes on, trying to be composed:

"Well first of all, the trucking company is also interested that's just the start, Jeez . . . I, and I think we'd better call them—John I just don't . . . I want you to help me understand what you were thinking what did you hope to were you trying to do?" Shakes his head, goes on:

"So John you saw Max actually . .?"

Nod.

"And you didn't think to call me?"

"I thought . . . I could . . . take care of it quietly, pay for it myself."

"*Quietly?*"

"To . . . keep it quiet, avoid publicity."

"John, do you realize what could've happened here? I mean it could still happen . . ."

Nod.

"Then why . . . Jeez! OK, one thing I don't get here is how Max could . . . was Max on-leash?"

"No."

"Max was off-leash?"

"Yes."

"Max was off-leash?"

Here is where the dialogue is supposed to intersect the bookworld, where people always come clean: Matt will now explain that he failed to note the janitor's presence in the log, leading me to believe the yard was empty. A little respite, take a few breaths, as I wait for Matt to step forward. But no word from Matt, and the hobbit-man repeats his question angrily:

"Was Max off-leash or not?"

"Yes."

"Shit!" First time I'd heard him swear. "Shit! . . . Major lawsuit, you realize this could be major?"

Nod.

"But John, what I don't get—why was he off-leash with someone in the yard?"

How could Matt want a clearer cue than that? Every script I know calls for him to step up. I even lift my eyes a little from the floor to see him. He's smoking, looking away. The hobbit-man is staring at me. I have to speak:

"My fault."

"Yeah it *was* your fault."

The Protestant males are male, they believe in taking responsibility. I saw them lots of times beating their kids with belts.

"Shit. OK, what about the money: did you give Luis money? He says you gave him money."

"Yes."

The hobbit-man throws his hands up so fast I flinch back. The feedback roar is overwhelming between my ears. He's gyrating in place, making moaning noises.

"John, Jesus, Jesus! Do you understand—I mean there are issues here, CME is potentially liable—"

"I'm sorry, I'm sorry. I'm sorry."

He snorts. "Did you know we've lost the contract."

"I'm sorry."

The Yakuza cut off a finger when they fail their masters. A pleasure. I'd do it right here on the counter. A flogging, anything but this.

"John, I'm sure you thought you were . . . acting . . . in an intelligent way . . ." He gives up, sighs.

"Sorry."

"I know you're sorry."

In my head I am packing quickly, getting ready to leave. I knew this would happen. Their world is their world and I should never have been given a driving license for it.

"How much money did you give Luis?"

"Sixty. Dollars."

Matt reacts for the first time, with a snort. The hobbit-man shakes his head.

"John, I wish . . . Jeez. I really wish you'd called me."

Nod.

"Well, now we've lost the contract. CME called me last night."

"I'm—" But I'm not allowed to apologize any more, so I switch to a nod. It would be nice to vomit now. Not appropriate though. Nice to saw my own head off.

The hobbit-man shakes his head and sighs. I wish he'd hit me. Seconds go by: one thousand one, one thousand two . . . After a while, he takes a card out of his shirt pocket and gives it to me. "Mr Sluder at CME wants to speak with you tomorrow. You better call him early tomorrow."

The card has "URGENT" written on it with three exclamation marks. But Mr Sluder isn't actually in the room; the hobbit-man is. I will accept a hundred Mr Sluder tomorrows for an end to this hobbit-man today. But it doesn't quick-cut, it never does. It slows down and draws out. The hobbit-man sits down, looking at me earnestly.

"Ya gotta think in these situations."

Nod.

"I'm not saying you're a total asshole to've done it. I understand where you thought you could . . ."

Now he's trying to be nice. Worst of all. Take one of my fingers, flog the skin off my back.

The him-being-nice part went on a long time, but I was in whiteout for most of it. It ended with the hobbit-man patting me on the shoulder. I really would've preferred the Yakuza option, but this shoulder slap was apparently a kind of ritual with him. He had used it to show Max I was OK when I began, and now it served as absolution and discharge. I had ruined his poor livelihood and he was patting me on the shoulder. They will always be beyond me. Not just beyond: *above*. They're not different from me, they're *better*.

We walked silently down to the yard. Then he got in his little car and drove out of the yard. Matt took a moment longer to get ready to go. I was wondering if he would confess his guilt to me alone—it happened that way in some movies—but he didn't even say goodbye before driving off.

20

It was still my shift, my last one. Me and Max. I patrolled three times around the yard on my own, moaning and coming down hard on the bootnails with each step, trying to erase what had just happened. On the third lap, feeling better for the pain in my feet, I started whispering, "Not my fault, not my fault," and then yelling it. West Oakland didn't seem to mind. The warehouses seemed amused, if anything. Parodic echoes.

Three laps was enough; I was slipping on stuff oozing onto my bootsoles, sliding like a drunk. Max lay where he'd been chained, on the loading dock, looking at nothing. I tried blaming him—he was arguably beneath me in the SIDOD hierarchy—but Max was not something you could blame. And as I looked at him, I remembered what Matt said once: SIDOD was the only guard service still using Max. The Kennel of Squeaks owned him; we just rented him. Because he was their cheapest dog. None of their other clients wanted him. He was too old, deaf, unpredictable. Now Max had lost his only job. It was hard to imagine that whatever evil spirits ran that kennel would keep Max around for sentimental reasons. They'd shoot him. Or something cheaper: crush his skull with a sledgehammer.

I went up to him there. "Max! Hi Max!" Little clucking noises—not that they'd ever worked on him before. He lifted his head and looked away. "Hi Max!" I patted his greasy head.

The sun was low now, bouncing glint upon glint off the houses on the hills. Me and Max sat there while I stroked his grimy shit-smeared head. Like cuddling a tire iron. The only other thing I could think of was food. I rooted through the mouldy paperbacks in the Plymouth again, and found enough dimes for a Snickers. Max would want a Snickers. I brought it to him, clucking while I held a piece to his nose. He gave it a perfunctory shark-bite, from the side, and let it fall out of his mouth. I tried again but this time he didn't even open his mouth.

My last night and longest. The shock of that interrogation by the hobbit-man had me dreaming awake. I kept seeing the grand old glass doors of buildings at UC Berkeley, holding them open as a crowd poured out, looking for a break in the flow.

Trucks pulled up to the yard and had to be logged in; truckers, more than usual, used me to talk at, gulping coffee fast so as to get on with their unchanging orations about handgun solutions to the problem of there being non-white people. Max barked at them exactly as he did every other night, with his maimed throat, little yips that sounded almost puppy-like. The Snickers sat next to him untouched.

Dawn was early. Brown air is beautiful at sunrise, but full of accusations. Why are you awake to see it? Why do you go around trying to love stupid overpasses and suburban asphalt and these smoggy dawns? You wouldn't see those things, wouldn't notice them, if you existed. You think people in the dorms at Berkeley go around trying to fall in love with smoggy West-Oakland dawns? They have people, actual sexual partners, to look at. These dawns come with a little cigarette-package warning: IF YOU ARE WATCHING THIS, YOU DO NOT EXIST.

It was full daylight when the shift ended and we, Max and I, could go. I let Max ride in the back seat this time, sitting on the success paperbacks. The Kennel of Squeaks was quiet as we pulled up. I took Max in, led him down the gauntlet of dogs. A few barked; the rest just stared us down the corridor to Max's cage. He went in as dully as ever, lay down in the corner next to one of his petrified shits. This was our parting. It seemed to call for some commemoration. I said, "Bye Max!" He didn't react. It was kind of a relief. No melting, accusing glances from the cage.

Even so, false plotlines imposed themselves on me. Disney plots. The little girl who saves the wounded seal, the boy who befriends an orphaned cougar, the lonely spinster brought back to life by a quirky, perky, one-winged owl. I could buy Max from the kennel, get someone interested in his cause . . . But that was all nonsense. Max's plot had no turns. He'd be happier where he was going. It didn't seem like such a bad option. Actually, yeah: I could just kneel next to him when they brought that hammer down the row of cages: "Hi! Mind bashing my brains out as well? Thanks!"

That way I wouldn't have to face what was coming. The trucking company or the Peruvian's lawyers. And because I lived at home, my parents would be liable. They'd have to sell the house to pay the damages. They would be evicted, thrown out on the roads like the miserable Celtic dispossessed in those old sketches from the Famine: gaunt families trudging through the rain with an old cart, a dying horse.

I had brought that brutal fate on us in late twentieth-century California, the most benign landscape in all history. My God, what odds that this Marmeladov ruin could be visited upon a highly-educated middleclass white suburb family in the boom years of California?

I seemed to be making a little moaning noise all the way home, and it was tempting to think that with one little veer the car would obediently ram an overpass support and bring the case against us to an early halt. But it's too flattering really, killing yourself—like *you* could do that, pretend you're that major.

21

Off the freeway, I slowed to Pleasant Hill, the gray-brown-tan-matte unfocused undercolor. It was hard to see Pleasant Hill; far as I knew, nobody ever had. It was never on the news, there were no stories there, just these houses and trees and the lawnmower buzz. I had to focus on it now, though. I had to try to love it, the way Carrie wants to love her house after the prom, because everything else was pig blood poured all over her in front of the others. Love it or leave. Love this! Love the hot straw sun. Love the Latners' dusty pyracantha hedges that make the waxwings drunk. Love that bunch of mailboxes by Isabella Lane. Love the dry grass clump left when they roto-tilled around those mailboxes. Love the gravel the Leonards put in front of their picket fence for their cars. I stopped the Plymouth dead in the middle of the street and tried with all my heart to love the Leonards' gravel. And love the blots of motor oil on the gravel. Love the fifth piece of gravel you count: one two three four *five: a halftrack-shaped blue-gray two-inch piece of gravel.* I love you little rock in front of Leonards who always paid me on time when I delivered the paper there. No response. Unrequited.

I drove on slowly, trying to see and love. But it was so hard to see anything. There were cars. A lot of cars, obviously. Yeah . . . cars. Different colors. I love you cars . . . the sun ricocheting off them hurts, but that's all right, I love you. What else? Trees. Trees should be more lovable, and generally I was pro-tree, but the trees of Pleasant Hill were not lovable. They looked like everything: a

sick mix of too many shapes and greens from almost yellow to
almost black, lime to cypress. The eucalyptuses were the biggest,
but they just looked like giant pond weeds. The poplars were
yellowy, pointy, and the walnuts didn't go with it somehow, and
they all sweated hot sap. The trees just splurged around like
organic neon, blurring the place even more.

It was so hard to see Pleasant Hill, let alone love it. I stopped
the Plymouth once more on Dorothy, beside the last vacant lot in
the neighborhood. In winter grass grew there, green grass; when I
was a kid there had even been tree frogs piping in the spring,
cattails growing in the gutter and redwing blackbirds skirling in the
cattails. But the birds and cattails were long gone. Even the grass
was gone. It was hard summer now, the grass had browned and
then been mown to adobe dust for fire safety, and the field had a
FOR SALE sign with the bend sinister SOLD nailed on it.

Then right onto Belle Avenue, our very street, coasting quiet
down to our house, the scraggly crook of dying rose hedge at the
corner. Looking toward it, trying to look, with love. Like Carrie
coming home, out of alternatives since her prom went bad: *I am
still your soldier!* Because no one else will have me.

I parked in front of our house, sat there watching as it
cowered behind the dying hedge, as fragile as a Japanese paper
bungalow awaiting the Enola Gay. Just sat in the Plymouth,
rocking to wave after wave of guilt and terror, and at last walked
slowly to the door. Pounded on it almost lovingly, and grunted to
my parents to take a message if anybody called me in an almost
gentle tone.

And lay there for a week, reviewing in awed bewilderment the
absolute failure of every single attempt to escape from this little
room. And the door didn't even lock!

Sade lived like this, with nothing but a miserable cell and his
Lapland torture dreams; but they had to put him in prison to
reduce him to it. How can it be that I am chained to this bed
without chains? No soldiers, no roadblocks, no internal passports
. . . yet I can't move from this swaybacked mattress. Can only wait
for the sheriff to come to our door.

Every time the phone rang I lost a few weeks of life. When I
snuck out to the kitchen after my parents were asleep, there were
messages from the trucking company, some from Sluder and

some with new names. For the first few days I shredded them and put them carefully at the bottom of the garbage bag, where nobody could see them by accident. But after a week, throwing them away didn't seem radical enough, so I heated the stove ring, lit the notes on it and ran with the sheaf of burning paper out into the back yard. Burnt offerings; couldn't hurt. Crossed myself as the pink notepages smoked and went out on the concrete.

And maybe it worked, because after maybe ten days of messages, there was a day when no one called. I began leaving my room more often, moving cautiously around the house after midnight.

But they were only changing tactics. One of those sarcophagus afternoons, I heard the strangled-duck noise of our crippled doorbell. I jumped to the bedroom door, holding it shut, listening: a loud male voice was talking to my mother. The male voice was casually arrogant, a kind of bored sneer. Cop voice. This man also jingled with metal. Cops jingle with metal. So they've come for me. Highest SAT scores on Block D at San Quentin. Orange coveralls. Homosexual rape. Repossession of corneas. Confiscation of family home. Death of parents by shame. Here we go.

I was waiting for the jingling tread to come down the hall for me, but instead the front door closed, the voice was gone. My mother's careful footsteps came down the hallway instead. She slipped a big legal envelope under the door, right between my feet. It was stamped "REGISTERED" and addressed to me. I didn't find out what was in it, because I hid it unopened in the dusty toy graveyard in the back of my closet. I put it in the deadest, most hopelessly inert article there: the Tolkien bedsheet/cape I'd worn to the Renaissance Pleasure Faire. It was supposed to work something like magical fumigation: steeping in my room's deathly air, thrown into the tomb dust of that closet, perhaps the envelope would lose its force.

Over the next two weeks, four similar letters were delivered. Well, I assume the letters were similar; the envelopes were, anyway. All I could do was deposit them, unopened, under the cape.

And to my great surprise, the spell worked. Or something did. The truck company stopped calling, and no more letters arrived.

Maybe they decided it wasn't worth going after somebody with no assets. It all just faded weirdly away. Proving that the only magic stronger than my jinx was my event-suppressing aura. If I had been walking under the bomb at Hiroshima, it would have fallen in the weeds with a dull clunk. And stayed there unnoticed, rusting beside my throwing knife.

22

My theory was that the accelerated decay of my feet was the big penance that warded off the truck company. My feet were not in the best of condition. High School PE had made me take some care of them—I got beaten up a couple of times to teach me to change socks more often—but no one at Berkeley ever got near enough to care, and my parents knew better than to try to advise me. So my feet deteriorated into a podiatrist's Verdun: a bloody landscape of craters and pus, especially in a horseshoe shape around the edge of the heels where the big nails from the boot heels had long since pushed through—U-shaped battlefields, just like "Bloody Angle," the cornfield where the fighting was heaviest at Spotsylvania when the Army of the Potomac (fine soldiers poorly commanded) charged time after time, over their comrades' corpses, into the very center of Lee's lines.

But the boots would not remain at an ideal level of pain and decay. They kept getting worse and worse. The nails got longer in the tooth as the heels wore down, and eventually my feet got infected. The first sores appeared on the upper surface of the foot, the smooth river-rock slope up to the ankle. One day a place on that part of the foot got all red and itchy. So I scratched it—and the skin ripped right off. Without pain, almost as if it had a dotted line and "Detach Here" written on it. And the itching stopped as soon as the skin was removed.

And next morning, just like Christmas, there was a smooth scab over the skinned area, like the skin on custard. I could feel

how taut the custard-skin was. I decided to see what was inside,
and squeezed. A smooth custard-yellow pus flowed out. A lot.
More pus than I'd ever collected in a single site. It felt good,
squeezing out the pus. It was oddly like my nocturnal visits to
Lapland: misery localized and literalized as a viscous fluid to be
control-released.

And like Lapland, the scab turned out to be a renewable
resource. Next morning it yielded another flow of pus. And on the
third day, another place on my foot started to itch—and there too
the skin came off easily, and raised overnight a fertile scab.

Suddenly I was a gardener. The morning drain was the high
point of those hot, empty days. I'd wake up happy because I knew
that for once I had something to do. Sitting on my bed, I would
gently envelop a scab, forcing the pus inside toward the weakest
seam, then firmly squeeze it out. Then let it lie on the skin to
savor, biting my lip with pleasure . . . and then slowly, slowly
spread the sweet custard butter over the foot, savoring the sweet
little pain of the deflated scab and the thought that every drop of
pus—so much of it, when it was spread like icing over my foot!—
comprised millions of dead white blood cells, fallen in my defense.
A Gettysburg in every scab! They loved me so—they died for me,
my doomed Union soldiers, veterans of the Army of the Potomac
who had faced the invader and died with honor. There were
microscopic Fredericksburgs every hour inside the dome of every
single scab. (After all, it was sore feet that brought Lee's barefoot
army limping into Gettysburg.) There in the micro world, white
corpuscles were fighting for me—me alone, *Sinn Fein*. They
fought well. Died well.

But the invaders were spreading. By the fifth day, scabs had
mushroomed over both feet. They were the enemy, invaders . . .
but I liked them too, the scabs, the Army of Northern Virginia,
Lee's haggard supermen—every scraggy redneck of them worth a
dozen of Europe's finest grenadiers!

And the progress of scabs coming to the skin surface was a
beauty in itself, the slow rise of new burnt-umber and raw-sienna
scab domes on the white foot—a new map of Middle Earth,
brown hilly scab islands surrounded by red fringing reefs.

First thing every morning I would trace the new, tender,
blushing coastlines, every bay and outrigger atoll. It was

something to look forward to. I could accept the hot metallic sunrise arcing into my bedroom and the no-calls from Joanne and the prospect of imprisonment over that rabid Max-bitten Inca because my feet were waiting every morning to do their little striptease, bring me breakfast in bed, like a kiss must be like.

Forbidden love. My parents couldn't know, because it would hurt them—and everyone else couldn't know because I knew that somehow or other the new sores would turn out to be my fault. Some trumped-up hygiene violation. I hadn't been used as Exhibit A in my high school's sessions on personal cleanliness for nothing. I knew all about their nineteenth-century science that connected dirt to disease.

So no one could know. But the scabs were hard to hide. Not that I went around baring my feet at people, even on the hottest days. But walking in the painboots was much more complicated now, because all the techniques developed over the last four years were designed to keep the soles of my feet from landing solidly on the bootnails, and the sores were on the upper surfaces. The inside of the biker boots was uncured leather, rough as Velcro, and when I tried to tiptoe along, staying off the bootnails, I'd end up pulling the scabs off the tops of my feet. Which (A) disrupted the night's harvest, (B) wasted good pus, and (C) was extremely painful. And (D) must have looked kind of weird, too—like a drunk walking an imaginary high-wire while a DT-spawned elephant stepped on his feet.

At least the timing was lucky: with school out for the summer, I wasn't doing any long walks. In fact, most of my walks were from the bedroom to the kitchen or the toilet and back. But even in those brief sallies something must have shown, because one parent dared to inquire whether there was anything wrong with my feet. A few minutes' screaming discouraged further questions, but there was still the odd late-night trip to Safeway: firewalking the long aisles with a box of cookies, two quart bottles of coke and a rotisserie chicken in its silver-lined NASA bag . . . teetering to the checkout right under the guns of a checker who was probably a fellow graduate of Pleasant Hill High. Not that I looked up to see, but I recognized her laugh.

I got better at scabwalking, but the scabs got better at spreading. They seemed to be gaining, moving up through the isthmus of my ankles like killer bees, and would soon be threatening the Gulf Coast of Texas, then the Continental 48 torso itself.

And they didn't offer a diversion for the middle of the days. The morning's foot ritual over, it was back to the *National Geographics,* the *J. C. Penney's* lingerie section, and whatever broken-back paperback my hand happened to snag, feeling around beside the bed. Poirot. *The Story of Archeology,* with those alluring cross-sections of skeletons sleeping happily in their strata. Bertie and Jeeves.

And the heat. It was poison, that inland heat. It would hit the roof at dawn, and spend an hour or so bringing the roof tar to a boil. Then it would press down through the beams of the ceiling. You could smell each stage: first the faint whiff of tar, then the smell of timber baking, then the heat descending implacably toward me, molecule by molecule being billiarded faster and meaner to sweat me through another day in solitary.

There was nowhere else to go. The backyard was a jumble of guilty wreckage: the bike they got me that I never rode, the electric guitar they got me that I never practiced. Tall dead straw was growing up through them, through the spokes of the bike and the seat of the swing. I couldn't go out into that yard without the Nuremberg Trials starting up again. Somewhere back there in the dry grass there was even a throwing knife I'd bought once, hoping to discover a knack for killing. But it turned out like the rest: the first time I threw it, it vanished and was never seen again. I looked for it for two hours, moaning quiet curses and coughing in the hot straw dust, but it was gone from this world, rusting in some parallel dimension of the inanimate marooned.

And the rest of the house was uninhabitable, haunted by parents. And Belle Avenue led nowhere but to other Belle Avenues, Dorothy Drives, Janet Courts, Sara Lanes, houses and houses. So I had to clamber back onto the bed, a fetid raft on a mud ocean.

They go on and on about Robinson Crusoe. Crusoe had it easy! He had a *reason.* He didn't have to be *ashamed* of not having any friends. In fact, the minute somebody else shows up the two of them form this sickening little inter-ethnic buddy system. Like that girl in the book they made us read in high school—*I Never*

Promised You A Rose Garden. Christ, I hated her! The minute she comes down with a mild case of the blues they take her out of school and make her the center of institutional attention, pampered by the whole staff of an idyllic asylum! Just because she could do drama-club stuff like cutting her wrists! If you've got enough initiative to show off like that, you don't need any help!

Well . . . what about the sores? Would the sores maybe . . . get me pampered like that somewhere? No. Whoever saw them would just get mad at the hygiene violation and give me health brochures like my counselor did in high school. Holding his little arm out as far as it could go over the desk, as if I'd contaminate him across that Formica Mediterranean.

So the sore-garden had to stay private, the days to be sweated out in real-time. The middles were bad, all sweat and despair. "Despair"? What sort of Keatsy nonsense is that, that big romantic word? "Despair" is for people who matter. I had something much smellier and duller than that.

Finally, in the late afternoon, reading a Wodehouse novel for the twentieth or thirtieth time, wiping the sweat off my neck with the grimy pillowcase, I could fade to black and sleep through the worst of the heat. But you always wake up again, and there are still hours and hours of daylight to prove that you should be out there having fun and aren't—the only mortal sin in the Church of the Pleasant Hill.

Forty days and forty nights . . . forty thieves, some cave . . . That part was true enough . . .

And then Joanne called.

23

I could hardly walk to the phone. I hadn't realized how serious the new scabbing was until I tried to jam the boots on and run to the phone at full speed. My best was a bad hobble, and my parents saw it. But Joanne was still on the line when I got to the phone.

She had the same bright girlish phone voice. It was some sort of Southern legacy, Missouri fish-fry manners. And it always worked. Artificial resuscitation. She asked a lot of polite questions about what I was doing, and I tried to think up some answers, wondering what was going to come of all this. Finally she said she wanted me to see her again. "We miss you! I wanna hear all about what's happening with you!"

"O . . . K . . ." That damned "we" of hers—her shifting pronoun, singular/plural alternation of the first person, always worried me. But she had used first-person singular "I" in connection with the verb "to want." It was a chance anyway.

She said we should meet at the SF Zoo Saturday afternoon, then go over to SF State where their friends Debbie and Deborah went. It sounded good to me, especially the Zoo part: the Zoo was a sacred site for me. But when we hung up, it was time to run the gauntlet: crossing that long, long living room without limping. Because there were teacups rattling in there, which meant parents waiting in my path. Think of the hospitals at Gettysburg, long lines of Union soldiers waiting patiently to have their legs sawn off without anesthetic.

Foot up . . . foot down. A hard march across the living room, then limping quickly to the bed to remove the boots. They were slick with pus and blood. It was kind of impressive actually: I was entering the world-class pain league. Which must be why Joanne called! The way Sherman stares at the camera like Hell's own viceroy, and Grant stares with the same burnt flatness—and the piles of discarded legs behind the field hospitals of Gettysburg, all those single shoes to be buried in unhallowed ground. Pain magic: the only kind that works. Has to work, must work.

I woke early on Saturday morning: one second of calm, then I remembered what day it was. A big day, bigger than the SAT. My ticket out of here, my audition with Joanne. The first step was making those feet functional. They had to last through a long stroll around the Zoo. I couldn't show a limp, because Joanne would want to know why. Well maybe she wouldn't; but that would be depressing too. More so, even. Better if she doesn't notice the feet at all.

So I stripped the scabs from the sores, drained them with quick efficiency, not pausing to savor their yields, and stole an old towel from the bathroom—towels absorb moisture, right? This much I knew about the physics of hygiene. So a towel would be best for soaking up unwanted pus and lymph. Took it back to my room to tear it into strips. But the ripping was very noisy. Our inner walls were just pseudo-wood partitions. You could hear your parents coughing or worrying at the other end of the house. So I turned on my crummy little radio to make noise. It was one of the sweet little bubblegum songs Joanne liked: "Afternoon Delight." Fake-country, post-hippie, happy, sappy tune, all tee-heeing about sex.

> Gonna grab my baby gonna hold her tight
> Gonna grab some afternoon delight

Gendered pronouns were no problem for Joanne in that song; no wonder she liked it . . . but my concern was volume, not content. The chorus was loudest, that part about grabbing your baby. So I tried to do my ripping during the chorus. The song ended before I was finished, but I sang the tune loudly for a minute more, disguising the noise of tearing cloth. "Gonna grab my baby"—rip—"Gonna hold'er tight" . . . When there were enough strips, I started winding them around my foot. They were actually very illustrious; it looked pretty neat, because you could see the sores soaking through the winding-sheet almost instantly. And it felt good, grim and poor, like the retreat from Moscow. Russian soldiers wear footcloths, not socks. I was lots of neat things at once: a Mummy, death walking, and a soldier in Rennenkampf's army too. His men, good peasant soldiery of the Tsar, had to walk to their own massacre at Tannenberg with bleeding feet, through hot sunny weather. I read it in Solzhenitsyn, and he was in prison too.

I held my breath to jam the boots on over the towel-strips. Yowza . . . a big sunny painburst. Not unpleasant, just painful. A tight fit, watertight. Pus-tight. Ought to make it possible to walk without sliding around too much.

Then I had to find appropriate Joanne-wooing apparel. Somehow I could not make myself wear the suede coat again. Not with that spit-stain on the shoulder. Or the dashiki Joanne found for me at that garage sale in Pacheco . . . or any of the stuff we bought together.

But the worst omen was that I couldn't wash. In Calvinism, despair comes when the reprobate can no longer pray; in my world, it came when I looked at the shower and knew I couldn't turn that tap and stand in the water.

I knew what this hygiene paralysis meant. It meant that I was damned. The way Johnson explained it when some brittle wit asked him what he meant by that quaint word: "'Damned,' Sir, 'damned'! *Sent to Hell and punished everlastingly!*"

But you have to try. (So you can say you did.) So I tried the Pavlovian approach: turned on the shower, scaring some spiders who'd webbed the tub . . . but couldn't take my clothes off. Couldn't get in. Like the last 100 yards to the top of Everest, that shower. Couldn't do it.

And when I turned to the mirror again and toweled my face to shave, I couldn't shave either. I had lost my faith. All cleanliness and hope had simply become untrue. I felt this in my thighs and the sides of my throat. They said no. *No clean, no nice. No.* They repeated gloatingly, *Damned, sir, damned. Sent to Hell and punished everlastingly.*

There it was in the mirror, that face "like the moon comin' up at ya," as Joanne had put it. Expecting me to shave it, save it, act like I was its show-biz agent. Anything was better than looking at that face, so I ran the shower again, hand in the flow. Our shower had lost its head long ago, so it was a single stream of water, more like a hose. It splattered hard against my hand, slowly warming up. The spiders were frantic from the water shrapnel, trying to climb the sides of the tub. It was useless. I turned the shower off.

I just could not.

I turned around and looked at the bathroom, like I hadn't seen it before. It shone in this light of damnation the way dull rocks fluoresce in ultraviolet: little figurines on the shelf over the toilet: a ceramic harp with enameled shamrocks outlined in dust; a ceramic nymph with her arms raised in supplication to the yellow ceiling, draped with dusty spiderwebs. Things made to be broken. The poster of Ireland on the bathroom door: a pitiful donkey cart driven by a hunched old man passing a ruined castle. How had anyone ever seen anything but genocide and shame in it?

You know the scene where Carrie comes home from the prom covered in blood, wanting to be loyal now to her house— and then the house tries to kill her too? What's outside only wants to laugh at you, and what's inside is Tut's tomb.

Naturally the happy ending, Carrie's telekinetic revenge on her classmates, is totally fake. The good parts of American movies are always lies. The bad part is always true—the twerp's apartment before the starlet arrives, Carrie home from the prom in tears to embrace her house. Which then implodes, taking her with it, straight down to hell.

I had to wash though. And I couldn't. I sat on the toilet for a while. Then, suddenly, it was time to go. Somehow a half hour had slipped by while I tried to make myself get washed. But I couldn't go to San Francisco unwashed—not after so many showerless summer weeks in my room. Maybe we had some of those odor things from the commercials. I opened the medicine cabinet, looking for something that fights smells. One of those spray cans they advertised on TV, anti . . . odor . . . dandruff. All that.

There were no spray cans in there, just my parents' medications, in little brown bottles. Ancient q-tip boxes. Ten-year-old packets of Alka-Seltzer. Medical tape. Rusting razor blades. Nothing promising. Except this squat blue jar. "Vick's Vap-O-Rub." Colds and flu. You put it on your . . . chest? . . . according to the directions. Why chest? Medieval medicine—how could any effectual medication be absorbed through the pecs and breastbone? Besides, my chest wasn't the problem. Didn't smell. But what else was there? Joanne and Evelyn and I were going to be in the Plymouth together. And it was a hot day. My reek would fill the available volume. Needed something.

I unlidded it, sniffed. And gagged. It had a good strong smell of its own. Eucalyptus. A whitish goo. Clearly, if you put this stuff on, your smell would be disguised; a bloodhound would mistake you for a visiting Australian tree and lead the posse right by you. Which was better than going as I was. Because wooing made me sweat. It was hard work, wooing.

Yanked my shirt off, scooped up a handful of the goo and applied it to my left armpit. "Generously," as it said to do in the instructions. Then the right (bad-luck majority side) even more generously. Then I tenderly folded my arms to see how the goo fit. It was a little squeezy, a little gluey, and there was an awkward squishing sound. But it held in place, and I certainly smelled different. I wriggled carefully back into the shirt, let it slide into position under the arms without smearing the goo too much.

Then a last wince at the thing in the mirror. Not its face—that would be suicide—but shoulder high. Its beige-covered torso looked OK, if you like barrels . . . it looked human. No visible staining from the Vick's. Looked OK. Wouldn't vomit if you saw it in the street.

Then the boots. Much easier: simple physical pain. Two good yanks and I was shod. Then with a surly grunt to any parents in the vicinity and a quick key-grab, I was out the door, in the Plymouth, on the road.

The sores on my feet kept yelping every time I had to hit the brakes or accelerator. And by the time I got to the tunnel, the Vicks Vap-O-Rub seemed to be liquefying a little, melting down my sides. It was a good thing we were going to the Zoo, where there was plenty of real eucalyptus; they'd think that spicy tang was coming from the trees when it would actually be the smell-camouflaged me. And the waft of animal dung would explain my vestigial reek.

24

All the pain drained away as I crossed the Bay Bridge. That Asgard descent into the docks. Sacred. All of San Francisco is sacred. But the most sacred precincts are on the far west of the city, by the ocean. Where they put the Zoo. San Francisco faces inland; most of the people and offices live leaning toward the Bay, the milder side of the hills. The Ocean side is gray, quiet, still. Long ago some uncommonly decent Founding Fathers decreed that there would be Golden Gate Park, a long green rectangle leading from the middle of the city to the ocean. And that, where the Park reached the Ocean, there would be a complex of cool gray stone temples to the Animals. The most sacred site in the world.

There were three temples: the Zoo for land animals; the Museum of Natural History with dioramas of stuffed animals; and Steinhardt Aquarium for water creatures. The Museum and the Aquarium lay together in a grove hidden in the depths of the Park, where the gray of the sky and the green black of the cypresses merged: twinned gray stone temples facing each other across a big parking lot with a bandstand and knobbly, pigeoned Chinese trees.

My cathedrals. It was no contest. From the first time my parents let me out of our finned Kennedy car into that blessedly cool gray sky, those somber trees around gray stone, I believed. The Catholic stuff—going to Mass at Christ the King every week, going to Catechism—was only duty. The animal temples of Golden Gate Park, they were the True Faith.

We used to drive out there to escape the worst of the summer heat. No matter how miserably Okie hot it got in Pleasant Hill, we could drive to the Aquarium and find the same well-born cool gray weather. It was the 60s then, and all the way across Golden Gate Park we would pass hippie couples lying together on the grass. The road through the Park was winding and slow like a Disneyland ride. There was time to ingest every embracing pair from the back seat. The sights on the Disneyland boatride— crocodiles, pirates, ghosts and hippos—were mechanical; but these lovers were genuine organic wildlife. My parents were embarrassed and angry with them, but I, hunched scowling in the back, very much wanted to grow into that habitat.

The girls all seemed to be willowy and blonde like that picture of Ophelia underwater in a creek. Iggy Pop sings from that era, "All the pretty girls really look the same"; but he meant it as a jibe—the aestheticism of the satiated—while I, peeking over the back-seat window as we wove through the glades of bliss, noted the sameness of the hippie girls with awe. Because they looked the same the way Kentucky-Derby winners look the same. Alike in splendor.

Which meant that when my turn came . . .

With that promise lingering like a scent, our Chevy would turn into the parking lot between the two great temples. The joy of stepping from our car into the gray stone air, across the square to the most sacred of the three temples: Steinhardt Aquarium.

How can I tell you about the Aquarium? You call me "negative," and I know what you mean—my advocacy of Nuclear Winter—but I always feel like it's *you* who don't believe in anything, who insist on everything being small and mean and smog-beige. Those Raymond Carver stories you made me read at Berkeley—that's what I think of as the enemy of life, those anthologized proofs that the world is ugly, tinny-tiny, bored, beneath contempt. So how can I lead coolsters like you into Steinhardt?

Open your heart!

Imagine driving out of the hot straw of the suburbs into the Lothlorien couples, the first sight of the Ocean, gray water meeting gray fog; then the temples to the animals, and the promise that you'd grow into one of the guys those hippie girls publicly cherished. I was unworthy, but so were those guys; the hippie girls had no real male counterparts, no equal consorts. If it could be unequal for those guys, why not for me in my turn?

It was in the air. Faith as molecules in the sea fog, not a notion, blessing you the instant you stepped from the car to walk to the Aquarium across a Berlin-wide stone plaza.

In the center of this plaza was a huge sculpture in black granite of two Killer Whales twined in the Tao, with water pouring down their black stone flanks—just as people pour buckets over real Killer Whales to keep them wet and cool when a pod beaches.

It made them alive, because there was no difference between water on black stone and water waxing over real Killer Whales' black-Corvette sides—a continuous magical rescue, keeping the Whales wet and cool, the way all the Temple Complex stayed wet and cool and grey even when the rest of California was baking dust. It generated coolness and grayness and Ophelias, a forcefield.

You had to stand at the orca-fountain for a while. There was always a brush of wind from the ocean teasing a little veil of fountain water over your face. Then you had to put your fingers in the water to let the wriggling, fizzy-cold water sniff you, shake hands. You had to say a little prayer then, thanks and wish at once: the hippie girls under the cypresses, the sea fog, the animals be safe and not go extinct. Amen.

Then into the very Aquarium. The doors were heavy bronze, greened and wrenching. When they closed behind you, you were in a different air, mossy-warm, dark and echoing.

The lobby had a hole in its center like a huge backyard goldfish pond. Vines snaked down into the hole. Warm water poppled down the vines and people crowded around the railing. You could slip in between two tall adults to see at the bottom a second set of gods, opposite and equal to the Tao orcas: the crocodiles.

The pit was full of them—more than you could see at first, because they were completely still. Big ones with chipped-fingernail scales, yellow and black like Indian corn. Long heads, all jaw and peg-teeth. Pouched little smirking eyes. The big ones kept to the water. Littler ones lay on flat rocks in the pool. All their clans: the black broad-nosed alligators like recaps on the interstate, the long-nosed harmless caimans, and the real killers: the perfect yellow triangle heads of the Nile crocs.

Not one moved.

Here and there, winking on their yellow, black, brown scales, were red-gold circles—pennies. People threw pennies on them. For what kind of luck? An enemy's death maybe? Dimes and quarters here and there too. For bigger luck. Worse things to happen to your enemies. Cursing whole states . . . Plural curses.

You could stay at the railing till you were parent-pulled away, but the crocodiles wouldn't move. They were waiting for *you* to make a move. Suppose somebody came up behind you and picked you up . . . decided he needed bigger luck from the crocodile gods than even a dime or a quarter could give. And lifted you up over his head, said a fast prayer and threw you in. Would they move fast? Fight over you? Maybe they'd stay very still till you moved. Then—KUSHK!—you'd be clamped in those jumper-cable jaws.

At this point you had to press your chest hard against the railing, simulating the way those buck peg-teeth would close on you. The railing wasn't very high. In a sense, looking into the pool with the railing crunching into your breastbone, you were already down there. Had been for a long time. You could smell the warm algae, the steamy plants. The Crocs felt the coins on their backs and considered whether to grant their believers' requests. They were in no hurry; gravity was in their favor. You'd come down to them sooner or later.

The progress from orca fountain to croc pit was a liturgy in itself. The orcas blessed you; the crocodiles warned. The nave of my ribs braced between two equal and opposite pantheons, a quadrant in the magic carbon circle: blue arrows linking man in a Celtic cross to rain, photosynthesis, cloud.

After paying your respects to the two altars, you could turn to the dark passage leading to the tanks. The only light came from the tanks. I can still recite their exact order: arrowfish, San Francisco Bay habitat, tide pool, leopard sharks . . .

But my aquarium pilgrimages ceased when I became the preferred punchline for dweeb jokes at Pleasant Hill High. Lost my faith. They say that's what happened to the tribes of the Northeast, the Penobscot and Algonquin, the first to go extinct: as they sickened and died of new European viruses, they blamed their totem animals for withdrawing magical protection and started killing as many as they could in revenge—selling the hides to the Europeans only as an afterthought. Kill your magical friends and sell their hides to the virus which is wiping you out. So they winked out simultaneously, the tribes and their totems, blaming each other, enriching the real contagion.

For years I'd been snubbing the Aquarium, the museums, the Zoo—the entire temple complex of Golden Gate Park—because my totem animals had abandoned me. Besides, the Steinem articles said that the Ophelias who had wandered the Park were as extinct as the mammoth, the Irish elk, the megatherium. Long lines of Ophelias at a tent re-education camp deep in Golden Gate Park, standing in line under dyke sergeants' eyes, waiting to be shorn by Army barbers. Shorn ex-Ophelias exiting in combat/lover pairs.

You always know it's too late, you always know, but you always hope you're wrong. I hoped so, driving into SF. Till I saw from the bridge that all of the City lay under the same inland sun. There was not one strand of sea fog waiting on the ridgelines. You might as well have been in Pleasant Hill, or Texas. And the Seuss-ramps which used to toboggan our Plymouth down into the Haight were jammed, so I couldn't zoom down them with the remembered multi-G pulls and drifts. I was just this person in a car waiting behind other cars to get across a hot city.

And when the ramps finally let me down into what had been the Haight, all that wonderful squalor—the squalor of the Elven who were too busy with Bliss to worry about lawns or housepaint—was gone, and in its place was the "neighborhood restoration" the *Chronicle* burbled about, making those tall, rickety Victorians sit up straight, where once they had leaned into each other like hippie couples in the Park. They were all on sale, plastered with real-estate signs.

And the couples—there *were* no couples! The wide grassy traffic islands were empty. No one lay there. And there was a DMV Office at the heart of the Ophelias' country, the corner of Haight and Masonic. I'd never seen it before—yet it was an old building, crumbling stucco. So it must've been hidden through all the Age of Ophelias. And now the DMV had pruned the green-black foliage back to reveal it, their concealed bunker unmasking itself in smug triumph.

DMV and real estate: the real California winning out. Hence the weather, the inland heat, their camp-follower. But maybe the decay still hadn't reached the animal temples, further into the sacred zone protected by the Ocean . . . maybe it had only overrun the Haight, and a bit of the magic still held in an Ophelia Gaeltacht further inside the Park—a fallback perimeter protecting the Aquarium and the other temples. So at Stanyan, where the Haight gave way to the Park proper, I slowed down, looked for any sign of Ophelias, their waterfall manes . . .

There were lots of people clogging the glades, but they were all wrong. Everything about them. Here and there I caught a flash of blonde, but not the right kind. This was a new variety bred on TV: the waitressy, never-even-went-to-college thatch of that stupid Farrah Fawcett-Majors from *Charlie's Angels*. Who you were supposed to put on your wall, the poster with her half-breast winking at you from her disco suit, and think was beautiful. Married to the dumb hick actor who played the *Six Million Dollar Man*. They were a perfect couple: he was a grown-up version of every jock who punched me by the recycling bins, and she was the Platonic form of every teased-hair Pleasant Hill High girl who ever threw a half-full can of Coors at me from her boyfriend's Camaro.

And these wrong Farrah blondes were all the blonde there was. The Pre-Raphaelites were extinct. No, no—keep hoping; maybe somewhere in the depths of the Park the Ophelias survived, creeping out only at night—one of those remnants who have the sense to stay out of sight. But clearly they had not survived in the glades I could see from my car. They were gone from that habitat forever, like the Celts, the grizzly, the timber wolf, pushed away from the roads decade by decade, evaporating blobs of green on the maps.

And if the Ophelias were gone, what would have happened to the Aquarium? Probably torn down. Made into a yogurt stand. A disco. And it would be my fault for deserting the Tao orcas, the only gods who ever loved or tried to help me.

I drove through the Park wincing, waiting for the smoking ruins of the Aquarium to appear. Probably around this next turn—

But the next turn brought me to the ocean. The Park was over and the Aquarium was just gone. Vanished. They disappeared it.

Relief—and then shame at that relief. But it was better this way. Better not to see it. Forget it. I couldn't have helped anyway. Not my fault.

And the Zoo might endure—it had never been as delicately poised against the rest of California as the late Aquarium. It might compromise with Disco, collaborate with the Farrah Fawcetts and the Lee Majors, and manage to last a little longer.

And sure enough, there it was: the great Zoo gate of pumice blocks and wrought iron.

The first step from the Plymouth reminded me that my feet were a mass of suppurating sores. I'd forgotten. A good clean pain, though. Wake-up call. People without significance were passing by in family groups. So that was a lie too—that they'd stopped having families. No matter what the *Chronicle* said about everybody living alone, they were clearly having children again, starting the mating sequence in secret. But all wrongly, in wrong bright clothes and wrong hot sun and wrong chirpy voices.

There were hordes of them, even children with balloons, feeding into the Zoo entrance. Exaggeratedly family-like, these families. Related to the treacherous hair styles I'd seen driving through the Park. And the inland weather coming over San Francisco. *A cuckold in everything*—even the weather.

"Boo!" That was Joanne's voice, sneaking up behind me while I squinted vengefully at the balloon-clutching kids. I turned around, but Joanne wasn't there. Just two women, strangers. Blinking from the sun, I first recognized Joanne by her giggle, then Evelyn incognito in big sunglasses. They were disguised as new-style people. Joanne's face—her hair. It was wrong. It didn't waterfall any more in the streaming Ophelia fashion. It had been warped up into a frizz of some kind. Not exactly the Farrah-Fawcett way, but almost as bad. It didn't stand for love or Middle Earth anymore. Now it stood for the inland conquerors, hot weather and real estate. Maybe because it looked burnt, sun-frazzled. It was *meant* to look artificial. It announced its artifice, and with it the retreat from Middle Earth. *Yay real estate,* it said. *Go Arizona,* it said.

They had bought new everything. It was all wrong. They were both wearing down vests—in this heat!—like flak jackets. And they were both taller. I looked suspiciously at their feet. Not for nothing had I stuck to biker boots, with their two-inch heels, all this time. I was a Heightist from way back, knew all the tricks.

"Frye boots." Evelyn had seen me checking their footwear. "Pretty cool, huh?" Her foot pirouetted for me. I nodded. These were pastel boots. Palomino-color leather and wooden heels. They made my boots very black and ancient, pikes against cannon.

Evelyn was now taller than me. *Which means we have to fight,* I thought—then realized that was dumb. It was still true, but it was dumb, and so had to be consigned to that huge warehouse for dumb, true, best-forgotten things.

Evelyn touched a lock of Joanne's frizz. "So whaddya think?"

Joanne stood still for the answer. Evelyn had moved between me and Joanne, and there was a kind of protective warning in her question.

"It looks . . . neat, actually . . . Curly."

"It's supposed to be wavy."

"Wavy, yeah. It does. How did they, how did you decide?"

"I just got tired of that hair falling around."

Nod, nod. Evelyn took over. "You just get here?"

"Yeah . . . a second or so . . . Wow you . . . neat . . . you both look all, I dunno . . ."

Evelyn laughed. "Same ol' us."

But it wasn't. And it wasn't just the clothes. Something in their posture, the angle toward each other . . . it was a degree or so closer. Maybe there are Othellos in other people's worlds, but in mine the jealous are always proved right. You always know.

But you try not to. Told myself, "It's just the clothes" as Evelyn shepherded us through the turnstile into the old Zoo odors, pachyderm dung and those pink-popcorn bricks they sell nowhere else.

I walked ahead, scouting for old friends in the cages. Because there was something about the new-look Joanne and Evelyn I didn't want to see. I would always forget what it was, then force myself to look back and remember: oh yeah. Joanne's hair. But it wasn't just that. The two of them were walking together. *Together-together*. Evelyn didn't have the old impatience any more. She and Joanne were in step. You always know; Othello is always right.

All I could do was not look back. I needed something to get their attention, and looked around for some totem animals to betray to their infidel gaze. I had already somehow colluded in the disappearance of the Aquarium; betraying this lesser temple, the Zoo, would make me no more damned than I was already. You can't be any more damned than you already are. *Yes you can.*

Maybe if I cough up enough secret lore, they'll, she'll be interested . . . There: the Tasmanian Devil cage! Stumbling back to the two of them chirping, "Here, look, you have to see this!" and dragged them to the cage. "The Tasmanian devil!" They didn't believe me at first, thought Bugs's antipodean antagonist existed only in cartoons, but I urged them over to its cage. There, among the small carnivores: its name on the wire as proof. The cage contained one small doghouse. Nothing else. And no visible devil. There were two earnest Chinese boys eight or nine years old waiting for a glimpse of it.

I pointed at the two boys happily. I had to tell Joanne and Evelyn about my childhood relationship with the devil: how I had waited, just as these kids were, outside this same cage for the devil to appear, but never seen any devil. I couldn't seem to stop jabbering, trying to keep their attention:

"They say it's nocturnal and that's why it never appears but actually that really can't actually be the only reason because most mammal carnivores are predominantly nocturnal—that's one of our biggest advantages, actually, being able to hunt at night—but you still see lots of other carnivores moving around in daytime, but not the devil, it's weird—"

"How do you know there's even anything in there?" Evelyn asked, laughing.

The Chinese boys looked up at her blandly, but I knew what was behind that polite stare: outrage. An unbeliever! I wanted to be on the two kids' side but they didn't understand, they hadn't kissed Joanne; I wanted to call time-out and step out of chronology for a moment, tell them, "I know they sound like heretics but you have to understand I need the smaller one, I need her, and the big one, it's true I want her dead but she's a good person actually but she just likes real life, never cared about sharks or Tolkien, you just have to ignore it . . ."

To Evelyn I said, "Yeah hah maybe they don't, just the same sign and they put food in the cage and take it away at night when nobody's watching—"

The two boys turned the bland stare on me. But I couldn't stop now. Military necessity:

"Maybe it's one of those species that had to be invented, back-formation like the linguists say, only genetic in this case, reverse engineering something like the devil in those cartoons . . ."

Silence.

"God but some of those cartoons are actually really really great. I think Mel Blanc is a severely underestimated artist . . . underrated figure . . . You know the one where the devil gets married? Bugs puts an ad in the paper, 'Seeking matrimony,' and in about two seconds a plane lands from Tasmania with a female devil in a bride dress, all white, and they get married . . ."

A longish pause for laughter. None forthcoming.

". . . But the best, the one where you see all the wildlife of the forest fleeing, elephants and deer, even the turtle, then Bugs is left just nonchalantly chewing a carrot and the Devil comes up behind him . . ."

My head is half turned to Joanne and Evelyn and I can see their hands entwined, discreetly, hidden by the unzipped down vests, and their face-planes bank into a turn toward each other. Officially I'm facing the cage, engrossed in my story—but I can see them all right. I could see them if my eyes were gouged out. So I go on:

". . . And then, I forget how, Bugs manages to—he tricks the devil into digging his own grave . . ."

The two boys leave in disgust. I agree with them completely. Kill me! Go get the Zoo's elephant gun and kill me! But I go on jabbering to Evelyn:

". . . Yeah . . . yeah, but somehow, just when Bugs buries him, Bugs all suave, all satisfied, dusts off his hands and throws away the shovel, and zhoop! the devil is right there in front of him and this is the best part, it's weirdly sort of moving, the devil just stands there, there's still a clod or so of dirt on his shoulder and just looks at Bugs—*My voice is not obeying properly somehow, I can barely finish the narration*—and he, the Devil, he says, 'Why for you bury me inna cold cold ground?'"

I turn to Joanne and Evelyn the better to display my ability to mimic the devil's deep, hoarse growl: It's important, this line.

"'Why for you bury me inna cold cold ground?'"

"God, isn't that a great line? 'Why for you bury me—'"

Evelyn broke in: "So what is this thing, really—since it doesn't look like we're gonna see one?"

"Oh! Actually the Tasmanian devil is a marsupial carnivore, the only marsupial carnivore left in the world! It's a really sad story, Tasmania . . . there was another, this really great carnivore there, much bigger. The so-called Tasmanian wolf—though it wasn't a wolf at all! A marsupial, the only large marsupial carnivore in the world—beautiful huge powerful jaws and a striped back— remember what the Flintstones' car-top looked like? Like that, those stripes. They shot them. God . . ."

Evelyn: "Wait, who shot who?"

"The colonists, the miserable British, as usual!"

"Shot the wolves or whatever?"

"Yeah. Just to make . . . just for their stupid sheep. Killed the last one only about 40 years ago. There's this picture of this pig-faced farmer posing with his rifle and the carcass of what was probably the last Tasmanian wolf—"

Joanne is tugging Evelyn's arm to move on, but Evelyn seems somewhat interested, so I go on:

"If you had a time machine you could go back and blast, I'd volunteer in a second, kill all the stupid British bastards—killing the last great marsupial carnivore for some lousy sheep! God, just show up with a sniper-scope M-16 and blast every miserable settler who ever even tried to touch'em—"

Evelyn said, "But these Devil things. They're still around, right?"

"Oh yeah, they're doing OK."

"Just not around *here*! So whadda they look like?"

"Oh. Small, black—I've only seen pictures. Small . . . black . . . big teeth. Not a dangerous animal supposedly, though they have freakishly strong jaws. That's probably the origin of the cartoon devil—you know, chews through trees and rocks—"

"Why'd they call it a devil?"

"Oh, that. Well . . . I don't know, Victorians, British . . . They
hated anything that wasn't a sheep. A Protestant sheep, for that
matter. Killed everything they could. Just like Ireland, you know—
the Famine . . . But apparently the devil was too small, nocturnal,
shy to get rid of. God, they killed—not just the wolf, they killed
the Tasmanians. People. All of them. It's a really depressing
story—"

Joanne and Evelyn laugh. Puzzled, I go on:

". . . The Tasmanians are one of the few races in history
known to have made something like a conscious decision to die.
Them and the Carib that I know of. And the Old Believers.
Though there it was a sect, not an ethnic—"

Evelyn: "Hold it, go back to the, the Tasmanians—what'd they
do?"

"Oh yeah sorry yeah, yeah . . . It's really an incredibly sad
story—"

Another laugh. But I can't stop now:

". . . They'd been alone on Tasmania for thousands of years,
they weren't even in contact with the mainland Aborigines. The
first British settlers decided they weren't human and they were
bored so they started hunting them. For *sport*. Supposedly one of
the few cases in which hunting humans for sport was common.
They'd compare kills, keep souvenirs, body parts."

"Huh. Eeew . . ."

"Yeah, and when there were a few left, the Tasmanians, the
last few, started to just step off cliffs when they saw the British
coming. Whole families, just whoosh! Over the cliff. Holding
hands . . ."

The cliff dream was very powerful. It always distracted me. It
took an effort to see that Joanne and Evelyn had walked away
from the devil's cage and were standing in front of a moated
enclosure. I followed them over; I had to finish:

". . . And then the rest, the remainder, they just decided to
stop breeding. No children. Just decided not to exist. Leave the
world. Like they'd finally decided it was unfit. Think if they'd had
nuclear weapons!" I turned to the crowds and brushed my hand
across, erasing them in a vast superheated wind: "Just . . . Whoo-
ooosh!"

"Have you seen this chimp?" Evelyn was pointing him out to me. In the enclosure: a big grey-bearded chimp swinging on a truck tire. I'd heard about him.

"Oh yeah! Isn't this the one that supposedly throws shit at people?"

"Yeah!" Evelyn said. "He's famous."

We waited for some action. The chimp was rocking his truck tire, staring at us over the moat. Nasty little face: grizzled beard on huge sullen lips. All head and arms, tiny legs, hairy dick and balls, big raw rump which he showed us from time to time. He was looking us over as he rocked. You could see his reasoning: he wants to throw shit at us, but he's learned over the years that it only delights us; so does he deny himself the pleasure of doing it in order to deny us the pleasure of having it done to us? So far he was holding out. He wasn't going to give us the satisfaction.

He was putting on a sex show now, standing on his truck tire and swinging his hips, his hairy dick and balls. The crowd around the fence loved it. A guy in a 49ers windbreaker did a wolf whistle for the benefit of his girlfriend. The chimp was rocking the tire harder from side to side.

"God, the poor guy! I wonder how long he's been in there," Joanne said.

"Too long." Evelyn's view. She sniffed the breeze. "Do you smell sort of a hospital smell?"

"Uh yes rather eucalyptus-y, right?" My preemptive strike. She'd've got it anyway; Evelyn was sharp.

"Yeah that's it."

"Yes I noticed it too, perhaps it's the season for them to bloom . . ."

"I guess. Smells like a hospital."

"Urgh yeah. God um yeah no yeah this chimp's depressing let's go OK?" I wanted Evelyn's cop-like nose to get off the subject of eucalyptus smells. Her suspicion was already making the Vick's Vap-O-Rub in my armpits all nervous, and it was starting to melt.

"It's horrible to do that to something that intelligent." Joanne's contribution.

"Yeah um we should go . . ."

Actually the stupid chimp wasn't depressing at all. That stupid chimp was a celebrity. Probably had his own postcard in the Gift Shop. I envied him his celebrity, envied it bitterly; and to the extent I could sympathize with his captivity, it only made me hate him more. Misery may love company, but it hates resemblance.

I was bombing with Joanne, I could tell. I needed to show her something more Byzantine, more noble. More extinct. I remembered suddenly: The musk oxen. My very saddest totem. Utterest hush, deepest grief. I would bring Joanne to them. When Joanne saw I had a totem as heart-rending as that, she would fall in love with me instantly, remedially.

"Hey actually I know what we should see; they're really neat, have you seen musk oxen before?"

Both laugh. Evelyn: "Not that I can remember."

"Oh, you'd remember. Let's go, you should definitely see them. Here, they're over here at the edge . . ."

Evelyn saw the elephant-shaped snack bar and headed for it. "You guys go see'em. I'm starving."

Joanne went over to Evelyn and they talked for a while. Their foreheads were touching. Joanne came away happy. She smiled up to me, remembering my existence all of a sudden, and we headed for the musk oxen. Somehow the deep grief of the musk oxen had come already. Here, now, where I was, like Hell in that play.

We came to the wooden platform overlooking their pasture. They were grazing—five adults, three calves. An alike and quiet family of foreshortened weightlifters, patient browsers of lichen with tap-dance agile hooves, huge in the chest and shoulders, short-legged, top-heavy, with solemn eyes and horns melting down the head and then curling up in a hook like the greased curls of hick suitors.

They were loyal to the glaciers, could live only near the ice, and retreated with it when the world warmed and waned, falling back on the most remote tundra, where a handful, mantled in great capes of fur, still leaned into the wind.

Every other animal that wore such fur—the Mammoths—most beloved of all!—the Woolly Rhinoceros, the Giant Sloth—had vanished from the world 10,000 years ago. Killed by us, mean little stick figures with stick spears swarming in as the glaciers retreated.

But the musk oxen survived by retreating to permafrost tundra, frozen scrag so barren that no bipeds found it worthwhile to follow. Until the endlessly curious, rifle-bearing whites found them.

And then Darwin played one of his meanest jokes—and that's saying something—on them, turning a successful defensive strategy against wolves, the only predators they'd had to face, into group suicide. When wolves approached, the herd would form up in a shield wall, a circle with the adults facing outward, horns low to rip and gouge, and the calves safe in the center. The wolves would probe, feint, make false retreats, hoping to draw some defenders to follow and leave an opening in the wall. But the musk oxen held formation, only charging forward a pace or two, then stepping back quickly into place. The same tactic that worked for most of the day for Harold, at Hastings—till his troops broke ranks to pursue.

The musk oxen never broke ranks. Their shield wall was firmer than the Saxons'. But Darwin has a sense of humor like Stalin's. He wants to hurt you, think up new ways. He's heard all the sob stories: even the Precambrians, animate jello, blubbered a kind of case for themselves when they got the bad news; the dinosaurs hired every attorney in creation . . . He's sick of it. He doesn't even wait for you to finish; just presses a button and the trapdoor opens. He squints at the memo *re: musk ox*, chuckles, and writes a quick order: *The shield ring that saved them from the wolves will make them the very easiest of prey.*

And the plan unfolds in a few years. At first all seems good to the herd, because the wolves have vanished. Untroubled all through calving, the herd is bigger than it has ever been. The smell of *twelve* sucking ten-week calves is bliss, riches, power and love to every grazing cape in a hundred square miles of spongy spring permafrost.

Then three bipeds walk toward the herd and stop. The herd assumes a defensive circle. Even the youngest calves take their places in the center like veterans. There has not been a bad soldier born of this herd for 50,000 years. The instructions for this exercise are in their minds from long before birth, and they are all born armed and ready. Kin far too close for "love"; these are something much greater: bondlings of the helix, scent-cousins from birth, grown of the same taste milk.

They are ready, as they've been ready for a thousand wolf raids before. No needless shuffling in the line. They breathe in time, steam banners swirling away in the wind.

The three bipeds don't split up and try to flank the herd as wolves would, but form a loose clump, barking at each other. One of them has a single long horn, and now levels it at the biggest bull in the herd, as in a mating challenge.

But the biped does not charge. The horn attacks the ears of everyone in the herd. And before the herd can huff their comfort at this horror, there is strategic complication: the biggest bull in the herd is no longer standing up, is down. And loudly smelling of hot blood. Steam is now coming not from his nose but his forehead.

The herd is now pure balanced unease, exhaling and scenting uncertainty.

A different biped points its horn. The smell of hot springs is blossoming in the eddies around its tip, and little hoof noises click inside it . . . and it has again bloomed with the sulfur hotspring thunder eddies. Cousin brushes lovingly its scent against cousin, fur cape to fur cape, horn to horn. But another of the bulls is lying down, smelling bloody.

The herd brushes against itself, testing the tightness of the shieldwall. The circle is less. But holding. Cousin brushes cousin and gives and takes smell embrace: *we are still this kin, this circle, this only us.* Side touches side; more profound than love.

The tactic which sustained this herd for 50,000 years is now the subject of laughter by three clerks from the Danish Greenland Company, stumbling drunk and laughing at the falling dominos, brown slabs of fur and hot breath. "Stupid as sheep."

After an hour there are there are only three adults left. They disperse quietly to form a triangle around the calves. There are no calves; all the calves have already been killed; but these are good soldiers, loyal cousins. They will protect the calves, though the calves are all dead.

One of the drunken Danes feels a witty impulse, and feints an attack on the three standing musk oxen. It sallies out to him, a disciplined short charge and quick return to the line. The other

biped raises the horn, now stinking of sulfur and hot stones. One
of the three shaggy boulders falls to its knees and rolls on its side.
And another.

One left. Where is the line? Where to form up in a phalanx of
one? A tactical override tells this last cow to charge, take
aggressive action. She charges, further than the usual sally, ten
paces toward the bipeds. Who scatter, laughing. They have
another idea: their lengths bend and come up with two mouths of
snow, which they jam into the long horn. They raise the horn
again and the packed snow is suddenly exploding on the last cow's
muzzle. She shakes it off and waits another attack. They pass the
bottle. Wit has slackened, the clerks want to finish it and head
back to the tent. The horn is up again, the sound attacks her and
takes away her legs. Falling on her cousins' bodies, she stops
expelling her banner breaths at the long blurs.

That was how the last musk ox herd in Greenland died.
Standing with Joanne at the platform, I made a few attempts to
tell it to her. But something didn't translate. My voice wouldn't
work, my throat hurt. Everything was blurry, and I couldn't talk.
Somehow the Greenland story was for internal consumption only,
because I suddenly noticed that Joanne was gone.

I found her and Evelyn sharing a soft ice-cream cone on a
bench. For all Joanne's sorrow over the chimp, she was laughing
now.

They feel no loyalty to their moods; I had noticed it before.
The opposite of one of my proverbs: "To get over anything is a
sin."

Joanne and Evelyn, especially Joanne, had had enough Zoo.
They were in harmony today, and said in stereo that it was time to
go see Debbie and Deborah. The Greenland story kept echoing,
along with something else I didn't want to remember, one of
those catastrophes you'll have plenty of time to deal with later.

Nothing to do but limp along to the parking lot, the suddenly
harmonious Joanne and Evelyn leaning together. The Plymouth
exhaled superheated dashboard when we opened the doors. A
terrible breath of melted plastic coughed out at us, then the slower
mildew reek of the hundreds of self-help paperbacks in the back
seat. *Be Glad You're Neurotic, Think Your Way to Riches, 90 Days to
Popularity* . . . All winter those books lay back there, spilling out of

ancient brown Safeway bags and apple boxes, soaking up
condensation, then spending it all on mould-growth when the
greenhouse heat of summer hit the car.

Joanne and Evelyn bucked like horses and backed out of the
car when the hot mildew hit them. Then, after mumbling
something to each other, they slid together into the front seat. It
made sense for them both to get in front, because the back seat
wasn't really ideal, what with Max having lain his shit-patted fur
there, and all the moldy paperbacks. And naturally you'd want to
leave the driver some room, which explained why it was so
decidedly the two of them in the right half of the front seat, with
me getting the whole left half.

To give them room I held my arms tight like trussed chicken
wings, which made the Vick's Vap-O-Rub melt even faster. It had
been slightly runny already, little streaks of it down my torso,
about the same viscosity as the syrups at IHOP. But the hot,
enclosed and socially awkward Plymouth made the eucalyptus
molecules zap out like popcorn.

Joanne noticed it first. "Pew! Smells like shit in here!"

Evelyn: "Smells more like a vet's office. What do you guys
keep in here?"

"Uh . . . books, for the most part."

"I don't think it's books."

"Well, uh, there is that dog I work with, Max . . . He's not that
clean."

The nerd will always find another, even more benighted nerd
to blame. And it worked; they agreed that it must be that gross
dog; and I relaxed. Sorry, Max. Military necessity. As the Russians
said when executing a comrade, "You today, me tomorrow."

Evelyn navigated and I drove through the silent quarter of San
Francisco, where all the crematoria and mausoleums were. We
swerved around a foggy lake, parked on Brotherhood Way, and
headed for the big pink dorm where Debbie and Deborah lived.

25

The dorms. You Raymond Carver types can't claim there are no good things in the world, because there are: the IRA (till they bought the Beige and quit); leopard seals; John Paul Jones saying "I have not yet begun to fight"; the fossa, which hunts lemurs through the trees of Madagascar . . . but the best thing of all is the dorms.

You who got to live in the dorms . . . why don't you ever give thanks? God, you ought to *worship* them, make a pilgrimage each year, burn incense in their foyers and scrub their walls with the hems of your garments. But you won't even offer simple thanks! You who cornered all the bliss are slyly committed to pretending there is no bliss, like Kulak hoarders pretending to be penniless.

You even write ungrateful Carver-like short stories set in the dorms. You're still playing the cruel game I saw you play that post-karate evening at Berkeley: first you want to inhale all the happiness, then steal the sighs of the miserable, corner that market as well.

Well, I'll say it if you won't: the dorms were bliss. With my first glimpse of the SF State dorm, I saw what I had missed. Walking toward it beside Joanne and Evelyn—they quarreling about who bought the bus pass last month—I saw. I knew.

There were dormies—wonderful name!—coming and going along the grease-bush alley to the door. Bliss in their voices, on their faces. Proud and free—though many were clearly Nerdic in face and posture. To be a nineteen-year-old ex-nerd granted sexual

250 JOHN DOLAN

citizenship by the dorms . . . Heaven could not equal it. And I
don't mean the dumb Sunday-School harpfest of the Christians,
Huck Finn's nightmare; even the Muslim heaven: houris and
nectarines; or Valhalla: endless feasting and brawl . . . Even *those*
Heavens were only poor flea-bitten camel-raiders or hung-over
Nordic thugs tossing in their scabies sleep and dreaming—dimly,
faintly—of the dorms of late twentieth-century California. Bliss, in
every face, unconscious of its bliss.

You could see in each dormie's face that neither the ingrown
grief of home nor the terror of high school touched them now.
They seemed not to know that they were in Heaven. They walked
on the ground—but the ground was higher on their side of the
path. *That's better than being tall*, I thought. Not knowing that you're
in Heaven—that's part of the Heavenliness: "This is just what
happens now that I'm in college."

And when we went into the dorm (through glass doors
cheerily plastered with left-fascist, volleyball and ride-wanted
posters) there was the same Valhalla's kitchen's chaos, people our
age bouncing off the walls, yelling without fear at each other—
with flirtation, with joy, running along the ceiling, pots and pans
clamoring like the happy hammers of Hell, steam and the smell of
wonderful communal spaghetti that everybody could complain
about and still love, that was actually I bet really delicious. All the
good things about an army and none of the bad ones. Above all:
nobody was hunter or hunted here. They change, somehow, in the
summer between the last year of high school and the first year at
university. It's *check your thumbscrews at the city limits* somehow.
People who once specialized in mean sneers and snotty laughter
become busy in a sexual world of their own and cut it out, and
their victims too find themselves regarded as human and begin
standing upright, like a Darwin posturepedic sequence. And begin
to consider the possibility of pleasure. Dickinson's poem in
reverse, played out from high school to dorm: The heart asks first
the courtesy to die . . . and then relief from pain . . . and then . . .
pleasure. Unfolding in the greenhouse-dorm, the heart whispers to
itself, hardly believing, *Pleasure.*

Even the design of this dorm made for accelerated evolution
toward kindness. Because it was vertical. Deb and Deborah's
room was on the seventh floor. We had to get into an elevator to

reach it. Just the three of us. The verticality, I realized, is why they bloom. You can't act like high-school PE on a seventh floor. The pigs who used to shove me around in PE would bleed from the nose and ears if they tried to rule a seventh floor.

We stopped rising and the doors opened gently on the warm hallway of the seventh floor. Carpeted, you could have slept in that carpet like a big hammock. It was too bad we had to find one particular room—which thought woke me up. I'd been so stunned by the dorm that I'd forgotten the hard part: I was about to meet two people with the frightening appellation Deborah. One a "Debbie" and one a "Deborah." God, don't get them confused. Remember to talk. Remember to smile. Remember not to sweat. *God, that Vick's! They'll smell it, they'll kill you; run, get out, run—*

But there was no time to run away, because we were there, Evelyn had knocked and the door was opening. I'd had my chance! There must've been stairs somewhere between the elevator and this door—fire regulations!—and I could've just run down them, Vick's and all.

That's what infatuation gets you, my distracting crush on the dorm. I could've broken free to the stairs somehow if I'd been thinking clearly. No way two girls could've stopped me. Or two NFL middle linebackers for that matter. I'd've made it. That was the image of happiness for the terrible .7 seconds remaining before I was inside the Deborahs' room: running full speed down cool dark stairs, free to smell like Vap-O-Rub if I wanted to. Zoom out to the car, go to a hof-brau and inhale 4,000 calories in two minutes, sedation by cholesterol.

Too late now. In we went. The room was tiny, full of people. Two of them. One of the Debs was standing at the door ushering us in. The other was sitting on one of the twin beds. The one at the door was barefoot, the one on the bed wore kiddie slippers with bears. That was as high as I looked.

There was barely room for the two beds and a little desk between them. Evelyn just plopped onto one of the beds, and Joanne sat more gingerly on the other—the one which already had a Deb on it. The other Deb closed the door, blocking any escape attempts, and playfully shoved Evelyn further down her bed before flopping onto it herself. That made two persons per bed. And me, the proverbial fifth. Two beds by five people . . . The math wasn't working out, and there was no time. There was an oxygen problem, as in there wasn't any.

Evelyn said, "C'mon John, siddown somewhere!"

All four people on the beds began moving in contrary directions, leaving less room than before. I was faced with two choices: jump out the window or commandeer the desk chair. I lunged for the chair. The Deborah closer to me flinched back.

Evelyn laughed, "Don't worry, he's always like that."

I sat down. The chair groaned.

The next minutes were devoted to distributing myself evenly in the chair, keeping it from groaning again, and checking that I was exactly equidistant from all the other occupants of the room. The room smelled fluffy like walking past a laundromat. There were dolls around the beds, little dogs and other animals. In fact, there were many little endearment talismans, photos of people on the corkboard. And on the desk itself a picture of Debbie and Deborah holding hands by the ocean. I looked at the picture discreetly for a while and told myself I was being paranoid. In many cultures it's normal for friends to hold hands. *Yeah, but we're not Eskimos.*

Then Joanne wanted to display me, and there were other things to worry about. She pointed to me and said, "He's at Berkeley."

Sarcastic murmurs of awe. I chuckled as the ritual demanded. SF State was several rungs down the ladder from Berkeley.

"He's learnin' Russian. Say something in Russian."

"Uh . . . sorry . . . Sorry, can't think of anything."

"C'mon, say something. Say, 'I can't think of anything to say.'"

Evelyn interjected "He doesn't have to say anything if he doesn't want to!"

But that was the worst, being defended against Joanne by Evelyn, so I blurted out my most secret and sacred Russian phrase: *"Chyém khúzhe, Tyém lútshe!"*

Regretted it instantly, knew that all magical power was now gone for good from the words, and that my gods would not forgive me for speaking this most solemn oath in front of unbelievers just to suck up. The four blood-soaked words were still hanging in the fluffy air of that little room like black-powder smoke.

Evelyn said, "Sounds like somebody sneezed. What's it mean?"

"'The worse, the better.' It was the motto of *Narodnaya Volya*, a terrorist organization of the late nineteenth century."

Pause. Looking at the floor, I knew the four of them were looking at me. I had to go on:

"They were pretty good; they managed to kill the Tsar himself—Alexander II. It was really well set up: the first attempt failed, but then when the Tsar was standing around with his officers, a second guy, a terrorist, came up and threw a bomb right at his feet, like in a western: 'Dance, boy, dance!'"

I chuckled. To light the kindling, get a general conflagration of amusement started.

"Yeah but the funniest part was after that, after the Tsar got it—there were police telling people to move on, and supposedly I don't know if it actually happened but supposedly this one cop stood on a barrel and started announcing, 'Please move along; everyone who was supposed to be killed has been killed!' Isn't that fantastic?"

A very quiet room, this room.

"Of course I don't know if that's true, it sounds sort of like a Russian joke . . ."

Absolute dead crushing utter silence.

"'Narodnaya Volya' is a neat name too, you have to admit. It means 'The People's Will.' Or 'The Will of the People.' Something really beautiful in that kind of arrogance, like the Inquisition motto 'Error has no rights'—isn't that sort of magnificent? You have to admit . . ."

Time for an amendment:

"Magnificent in a horrible way, I mean."

Evelyn said, "Uh-huh" and laughed forgivingly, with no seconders.

My time in the spotlight was making me very frightened, which was making me sweat, which was turning the Vick's from goo to steam. Though I was crushing my arms against my torso (I had bruises for a week afterward), the smell was still emitting. I could already smell it spieling around me and snaking out to the others. Whereupon they would have me killed. I had to keep talking:

"There's a story about Bakunin, not that he actually belonged to the People's Will, but supposedly he stopped his carriage when he saw some men burning down a house and got out and helped set it on fire—without even asking whose house it was or why they were burning it. You know, that same attitude: 'The worse, the better'; burn it all down. John Donne, same thing: 'But no, it must be burnt . . .'"

A long silence, several eons or so. Eventually talk began again, among the two couples. Joanne was asking the other Deborah a question: "So how'd you guys finally . . . get together?" She finished up the question with a little laugh.

There was no answer, but there was a sort of rustling sound. I glanced up quickly through my eyelashes to find that Deborah's hand had stretched across the little desk to take Debbie's. They were smiling at each other. No no. This cannot be true. Because then it would all be true and I would be dead, it's too improbable and paranoid, just paranoia, to be true. On the other hand, Othello is always right, and what's worst is true, so it is.

Evelyn laughed. "Just like that, huh?"

Evelyn was the only one to laugh. Debbie and Deborah were still holding hands over the little desk, with Joanne looking on indulgently. It was true, it was all true, the very most I feared. Extinction.

Evelyn said, "So why not put the beds together then? Might make the room bigger."

Deborah said "They're built in." And they were. They were wooden boxes nailed to each side of the room. Not that that would stop anything.

Deborah went on: "It just seemed so natural. I don't think I ever really liked it before, with men? I mean after we got together I just thought, God why was I wasting my time all that time? It just seemed natural."

Joanne: "Yeah! Natural."

Debbie said, "Yeah, all that time I was fucking, you know, any guy I could, trying to make it seem like . . ."

Alien Deborah: "Yeah trying to make it feel right . . ."

Joanne: "You were in denial."

Debbie: "Yeah completely."

I always heard that word as the name of a town. Denayo, a farmer's market in the Central Valley. It always seemed like a decent place, where you could go if you didn't want to evolve yet.

Deborah: "I just think women understand women better. Men don't, aren't . . ."

Joanne: ". . . Sensitivity."

Both Deborahs: "Yeah."

Evelyn, laughing: "Sorry John. It's not his day! First we couldn't see the Tasmanian devil—" She turned to the Deborahs, trying to change the subject, "Did we tell you about the Zoo?"

Joanne, earnestly pointing to me: "Not *him*; I told'im before he isn't like other men. It's like he's not one at all."

A compliment. I had Joanne's word on that.

Obviously the Deborahs also took it as a compliment to me—because their silence eloquently implied that I didn't deserve it. I seemed like a man to them, and they weren't happy about Joanne and Evelyn letting one of the Neanderthals into their bower. The funny part was, I didn't mind their reaction at all. A caveman—if only I really was one! Bash! And I'm out of there, free and easy, courtship by club, commuter tartare for dinner . . .

By the way, the Debs changed their spots again. In the Reagan years, when everyone decided that big incomes and nuclear families were cute again, both Deborahs married—married *men*, I mean—and had one child each. Good Californians are Lamarckian, not Darwinian. They can become anything, re-splice their goddamn slippery double helixes, and truly believe that they're reinventing themselves from deep, sincere, uniquely personal impulses. Which they get out of the Sunday supplements.

In fact, now that dykes are solid astraddle the middle of the road, I bet both Debs have begun sneaking up to the attics of their Berkeley houses, digging through boxes for those old lavender overalls. And two husbands and two high-strung daycare brats will soon be living in interesting times.

I was sitting in that creaky chair in their cute little bower, doing some rapid social-science calculations. My sample of nubile females now consisted of Joanne and Evelyn and the two Debs. So defections to Lesbos were running, let's see . . . 100%. I knew that anyway, but it was different, it was worse, when the empirical proof came in. I dealt with that proof, like an anvil dropped to me from a couple of flights up, and was lost to the conversation. Until one of the Debs, the one with the high preacherly voice, said very loudly and dramatically:

"God, what's that smell . . ."

Joanne: "Yeah. I smell it too."

Evelyn: "Kind of a hospital smell."

Joanne: "Cloves or something."

Deborah: "It wasn't here *before*." Meaning: before you brought that ape into our bower.

I did kind of stand out. *Who's wrong with this picture?*

So why didn't I just run? I could've smacked that door off its hinges with one straightarm. Same dull answer nobody wants to hear: because people don't. Ever see pictures of prisoners waiting to be shot? They stand where they're told, even work up a sweat digging their own graves.

All I could do was stare at the floor and count the seconds—sometimes this encouraged time to pass: *One thousand one, one thousand two*—and press down onto the boot nails, paying in advance.

But as I stared down at my boots—God, God! My left foot was leaking onto their nice clean fluffy carpet. Seepage from the sores—the usual red-gold mix of blood and pus. It had flowed down the boot heel onto the curls of the beige carpet. They can arrest you for that. Destroying university property. And the Deb with the mean voice would yell; and the world would end, the world would end. I twisted my foot to cover the stain and stared hard into the floor in sheer terror, the blood roar blocking out all conversation.

After a while, I began to hope nobody had seen the drip. At any rate they weren't talking about smells anymore. They were talking about M*A*S*H*. Deborah wanted to go downstairs to watch it in the TV room. Joanne was anti-TV, and Deborah was defending M*A*S*H*, saying how radical it was that a Hollywood sitcom could make an anti-war statement. Evelyn was quoting some of the funnier lines from the last episode, and Debbie was supporting Deb, or vice versa, by trying to tie Evelyn's quotes to the larger point about the anti-war message.

It was fine with me. Anything to get out of that room alive. I was all for going down to watch it, despite the fact that I hated

M*A*S*H* bitterly. And still do. Even now I would advise Alan Alda not to vacation on this island where I am marooned.

M*A*S*H* seemed designed in every detail to mock everything I loved. All the stupid characters on *M*A*S*H** had pointedly, exaggeratedly Irish names. Hot Lips Houlihan. Radar O'Riley. Major Burns. Only the two cool sarcastic surgeons had Anglo names. Bravery was a joke, love for fools; only bored lust and pro-peace wisecracks were sacred.

My uncle Jerome—Dr Jerome Dolan—had just arrived in Korea as a 24-year-old army surgeon when the Chinese overran his unit. In the middle of the Korean winter, under constant attack, he shepherded his platoon through Chinese lines. He fainted the moment they were safely back inside US lines, and was found to be suffering from advanced double pneumonia. They thought he was going to die for a while, but he survived: a small, kindly, brilliant man who refused to tell war stories even when pressed by his nephews. *M*A*S*H** seemed like a strangely elaborate and wholly gratuitous way of insulting him, our whole family, and every book I liked.

But if going on and on about the wonderfulness of Alan Alda got them off the subject of bad smells and kept their eyes off the stain on the floor by my boot, I'd go along . . . betray my uncle and my world as they willed, nod and chuckle and simper—I'd hum the *M*A*S*H* theme song if they wanted. The one that played at the beginning of each episode, while they showed faked-up airlift copters flying through the hills of Malibu.

The pro-*M*A*S*H** Deb—she was "Deborah" as opposed to "Debbie," I think—was a born preacher. She wouldn't shut up about how brave *M*A*S*H** was. How it could really change "ordinary people's ideas" about war and patriotism. She seemed to be referring to others when she said "ordinary people."

"It could've stopped the bombing sooner probably if it'd been running when Nixon was still there. You know the episode with the wounded Viet Cong where they fix his arm up and treat him like a human being . .?"

Viet Cong? I didn't believe it at first. She thought *M*A*S*H** was about *Vietnam?*

Shame turns to hatred, recklessly lifting my eyes to look at her. A mean little face, glinty. Sharp. Tight little correct body. Not ugly, not beautiful. The widespread Lamarckian flex-weasel design, highly adaptive for California.

To parachute her into North Korea. Yeah: with a *Vietnamese* phrasebook. Let a few months of interrogation by the North Korean secret police show her about common humanity. Oh yes! For example: *All human beings have nerve clusters in the same parts of their body.* And all human interrogators know this. And come prepared . . . Kim Il Sung himself sitting in on some of the interrogation sessions, chuckling at the common humanity of her social-democratic screams, making a few wisecracks to Countess Bathory, his consultant in such procedures . . .

But it wasn't much comfort. Never was. It was for the Countess to savor, not me. I was just the loser, sitting there and taking it, storing up grief-in-advance that would be converted metabolically to fat and bile.

It went on and on, the panel discussion on M*A*S*H. The flex-weasel Deborah was just hitting her stride. Joanne was pleased; Joanne liked virtue too. And Debbie—the other one— was interpolating little coos of approval as Deborah preached. I tried to calm down, screening intracranial highlights of B-52 strikes igniting a ten-mile stripe of jungle like God striking a match on green Velcro . . .

Luckily Evelyn was bored: "OK OK, let's go watch it then; it's gonna be over before we get there."

The Debs shook themselves out of homiletic mode and I could stand, open the door and zoom. Always an eager first out of a room. Making use of those opposable thumbs. And cantered downstairs, pleading exercise, while they took the elevator.

Seven flights on the boot nails erased the debt. But around the fourth flight, the other thing—the one I couldn't think of—welled up again, squeezing my eyes and bruising something in my throat. Something about extinction, the musk oxen but not exactly, the Tasmanians and the cliff dream, only here. Neither the pain of the nails nor the terror of more socializing with the Debs could push it back down completely. It echoed on the government metal of the stairs as I limped down them, some case proved, a big red X.

The dorm's TV lounge was a huge relief after the Debs' bower. It was big and loose, slobby and welcoming. Many cubic feet of air in which any smells could disperse themselves. Random ratty couches and plastic chairs more or less facing a TV. There were two dormant male students slouched in them. And best of all, there was a chair, a solid-looking one, far away from all the others. I grabbed it and relished its embrace. Safe. I could even risk watching the TV.

Something big seemed to be on. There was a subtitle "KPIX Special Report" at the bottom of the screen. A reporter was crouching behind a car, saying, "At this point we don't know—" and then he cringed down further and the camera ducked too, because there were a lot of popping noises. They were fake-sounding, which meant it was real guns. A battle! A real battle, preempting *M*A*S*H*!

Evelyn turned to one of the watchers: "Do you know what's going on?"

The white kid just said, "Patty Hearst."

The other guy, Asian and therefore better bred, amplified: "The SLA . . . they got the SLA surrounded in this house . . ." He waited till the wobbling camera poked up from behind a car to show a small frame house. "There! That one."

Everyone was quiet, getting a sense of where the battle was, how the camera stood. The announcer was gibbering in what sounded like fear. The camera kept swooning this way or that, but finally found the nerve to fix on the house under attack. The windows were all blown out, and little puffs of dust and woodchips were flying as shotgun blasts claymored the walls. You couldn't see anybody inside.

The nervous camera panned away to cover the cops, who were behind their cars across the street. They weren't very good troops, these cops. It was shocking: they barely poked their heads up to fire. Several of them seemed frozen behind their cars, ostensibly talking on the radio.

The four of them—the Debs, Joanne and Evelyn—were quiet at first. Then the Debs took each others' hands. That in itself meant nothing, in many cultures . . . I was waiting for similar moves from Joanne and Evelyn. That was the thing in my throat and it announced itself now in lurid grief: all that I had lied about, denied, not seen, flooding in. Extinction. No rotation of my head, fixed on the TV, was needed to see how Joanne and Evelyn leaned a bit, now a bit more, toward each other. Two millimeters, then another, perfect NASA measurement through the eyes in the back of my head.

The flabby car-cops were reinforced with a SWAT team in black. These new troops seemed better-trained, though hardly Prussian. They moved together, but cautiously, terrified of taking even a few casualties—typical American infantry, always hoping to avoid direct assault. Wincing and ducking, they began to flank the house. More popping sounds, and the camera took a dive to show you a joggled close-up of the gutter.

Deborah-the-preacher said solemnly, "This is terrible."

She and Debbie were sitting on a small sofa, a loveseat. Hand in hand, their faces doing Deep Concern. They were the sort of people who have so long ago liquidated any real emotional response that they really think they're sad when they hear about a bus crash in Bangladesh. They were determined to watch M*A*S*H* after all—to superimpose it on this battle. They themselves would be Alan Alda, disdaining battle, sipping martinis in his tent and wisecracking about the horrors of war.

The horrors of peace . . . Nobody ever talks about that.

Deborah said, "Did they even try *talking*, just *talking* them out?"

Debbie, beside her: "Yeah, might be a good idea, Jesus . . ."

The Asian guy said, "Uh, I dunno, I just got here."

Joanne: "They wouldn't do that, they wanna show off their *guns*."

The Debs: "Yeah."

The camera, which was clearly a chicken, had poked its head up again to show cops bundling black women and children out of the surrounding houses. Then it moved across to the announcer, who had decided to do the remainder of his commentary from a crouch, behind a squad car. He began to reiterate all the things "we" didn't know so far, starting with the fact that we didn't know if Patty was inside the house.

Deborah said, "God, I can't believe this."

The camera went back to the little house. The whole surface shivered with energy, bullets hatcheting through timber and paint. It was magical, the way this ratty frame house in some nowhere suburb of LA, even further from the world than the subdivisions of Pleasant Hill, had become a glorious battle site. Those housing tracts in LA were the most terrifying places I had ever seen. The brown horizon was unbroken by any landmark. Only roof after shingle roof, droning lawnmowers, stale air. But this house—look at it!—was vibrating with fame now. That was why the cameras had come to it. It lived for the first time as the bullets stitched it.

The SLA would be even more famous after this battle. Every one of them had already had his or her picture on the front page of the *Chronicle*. I knew all their names and their motley Berkeley faces, sullen suburb kids who found a genuine black con, Donald DeFreeze, at San Quentin, ballasted their gang with him and some Mao quotes, and made it work. They were *wanted* everywhere, more famous than any band. The first one to be identified in the *Chron* was typical: Nancy Ling, a mean-looking white woman with dark hair. She got her BA from Berkeley, didn't know where else to go, worked at a juice stand, hung around Berkeley getting old and mean and angry . . . But she found this gang to belong to, and now she was famous. People went to look at the juice stand where she used to work. They'd point to it and talk and gesture to each other. There was the dying part, of course—even troops as bad as these cops could presumably blast a single house hard enough to kill everybody in it.

Any good thing involved dying though. Went without saying. Anybody of any distinction is dead—the green shelf, the Irish martyrs; all those people were dead. And better for it. And now this Nancy Ling and her gang were in focus, in that house getting sandblasted by buckshot—ah the glory, the luck!

Deborah broke in: "I can't believe this."

Without turning my head from the TV I see that the Debs are now hugging, consoling each other. That hardly even hurts, though. They are not the point. They are a *case* in point, a point on the historical graph which proves my non-existence, a mere corroboration, a datum; but they are not *the* point. *The* point is sitting on the other couch; *the* point is the very slowly declining distance between the left shoulder of Joanne Whitfield and the right shoulder of Evelyn Baker. Somehow this one will be final. If their heads touch, I do not exist.

Without moving my head at all I can see perfectly well the slow merging of those shoulders on the ratty couch. Joanne's smaller shoulder wants to lean into Evelyn's. Even I understand it.

It's inevitable. The whole gravity of history, the fall of the Patriarchs, and the way ratty couches . . . the physics of ratty couches . . . the way they push two bodies together . . . all of that . . . just all proves it. Two bodies on a ratty couch will tend to lean into each other. That physics, plus the history of national liberation rhetoric applied to gender issues, equals this. And it's all, the whole galactic inertia of it and stuff, is drawing shoulder A toward shoulder B. It has to be. Accepted. You're standing under Niagara; accept it.

That's all right, though, because . . . Yeah: Bathory . . . Bathory will come and this point will be under ten fathoms of blood. Long after my death, but certain. So ha ha. And besides, this has always been Tasmania, I'm already extinct. But my eyes, my throat, are not consoled.

So what do I do? Other than convict myself of treason, nothing. No, wait: study harder in Russian class. That's the only recourse I can imagine against the terrible ultraviolet eyes-in-the-back-of-my-head Vision image of Joanne and Evelyn falling into singularity: study Russian.

Because the Russians suppressed, forbade and froze so much that they ARE the tundra! They still, it still is ice there and all the megafauna, like for example men, are not extinct, just a little chilled. And so maybe they—men and women—at least I think they do . . . I read somewhere that because Russia lost so many men in the war, that men are still "worshipped" there—that's not my word, it was in the article! Confirmed by the fact that they still find mammoths almost intact in the Siberian ice, their meat still fresh . . . that proves it!

They're watching the TV, distracted . . . but I can't flee yet. Because for once the television is speaking for me. God, does this beat M*A*S*H! The Eastern Front comes to the suburbs! Little pops, camera swoops . . . now smoke from the windows of the house. The announcer suggests the occupants will soon have to surrender. *Or die.* He doesn't mention that choice—dying. It doesn't occur to him because he has sex and is clean and in the world. But it will definitely occur to the SLA people in the house. Is that Nancy Ling gonna go back to her juice stand, stay alive just so she can go back to the Hell of the Nameless? The SLA people have been dubbed, like knights, and they aren't going to give that up. Doesn't this TV guy know that? Does he really think everybody is like him, all attached to mere existence?

He knows damn well only fame matters! That's why he keeps harping on how "we" aren't sure who's in the house. What he really means is they're not sure whether Patty Hearst, "Comrade Tania" as she renamed herself, is in there. They're worried about her because she's famous squared: first she was a Hearst, and now she's a hostage. She's swimming in fame, the lucky brat.

My skull-surround radar images the continuing merger of Joanne and Evelyn's shoulders: one more millimeter. They are almost a merged singular now. My head has not moved an inch from the TV.

Deborah: "I mean . . . God, I just can't believe it."

Debbie the backup singer: "Yeah."

The announcer: "Unfortunately we still don't know, as I've said, whether . . . whether one of the people in the house is indeed Patricia Hearst, now calling herself 'Tania' . . ." It upsets him that Tania might be frying in there. Fried Tania.

'Fried Tania' . . . That phrase gave me an idea for a witty remark. I had never thought up a witty remark before, encountering them only in British novels. But here was something which seemed witty, like a line in a play. Better yet, if it worked, it could hurt the Debs. Every time some famous revolutionary was incarcerated, the walls around Berkeley were sprayed with "Free ___" signs (e.g. "Free Huey" for Huey Newton). If "Tania" were caught, "Free Tania!" signs would be spray-painted all over Berkeley. But if she were in the house? There lay the whimsy: because this would require a very different but phonetically similar verb: 'Fry', as in 'Fry Tania!'

If that wasn't wit, what was? And it would hurt the Debs, and any other unnamed two-woman couples who might be sitting on a couch in that room.

I decided to say it before I got too scared to try. I blurted, "Fry Tania!" and laughed. Then tried another, more elaborate version, in a hippie drawl:

"Right *on*, man! *Fry Tania!*"

No one else seemed to see the wittiness of it. The room got very quiet, as if someone had turned off the television. And—and I knew this would happen, as it happened—my witty remark melted the last ice between the shoulder of Joanne and the shoulder of Evelyn. Their shoulders came together, and then—as I could see without turning my head from the TV or dropping the grin I had adopted when making my witty remark—Joanne's new-fluffed head leaned into Evelyn's new-mown head; and Joanne's smaller hand found Evelyn's larger one (Evelyn taller than me in her new boots), and they were at rest, in a stable configuration, with Joanne's head on Evelyn's shoulder, fluffed hair merging. Where it belonged. Where it always had been. Burn all diplomatic files. Report all consolations to counter-intelligence. Catch a copter from the roof. Face facts Shut up and . . . shut up.

Even my stinking room at home seemed not so bad compared to sitting there in the silence after "Fry Tania!" fell flat and Joanne merged with Evelyn. But still, no quick cuts: it was ten long silent minutes before I stood up, turned to the sofas and said to the one containing Joanne and Evelyn, "OK, guess I better head home, get back . . ."

It was warm and sunny as I drove home. All I could do was lean out the window of the old Plymouth to yell "Fry Tania!" at the wealthy dell of Orinda.

<u>END</u>

Books by John Dolan, so far . . .

Slave (poems) *Occident Press, 1988*

Writing Well, Speaking Clearly *University of Otago Press, 1994*

Stuck Up (poems) *University of Auckland Press, 1995*

Poetic Occasion from Milton to Wordsworth *Palgrave Press, 2000*

People with Real Lives Don't Need Landscapes (poems) *University of Auckland Press, 2003*

Pleasant Hell (novel) *Capricorn Publishing, 2005*

*Wanna read notorious stuff, unique stuff,
alternative stuff or simply the best stuff..?
Then check our site regularly for new
publications which you will not find from any
other book publisher. Guaranteed!*

Capricorn Publishing

www.CapricornPublishing.com

!!! Other Classic Titles !!!

Printed in the United States
97072LV00003B/178/A